A BLOCKBUSTER NOVEL

**NOW THE YEAR'S MAJOR
ADVENTURE-SUSPENSE DRAMA**

AVALANCHE EXPRESS

"THROBBING WITH ENERGY."
—*ALA Booklist*

"CLEAN, FAST, HARD-DRIVING . . .
WILL KEEP READERS IN SUSPENSE
UNTIL THE LAST WORD, AND MAKE
THEM WISH FOR MORE."
—*Publishers Weekly*

AVALANCHE EXPRESS

"VASTLY ENTERTAINING. . . . THE
STORY, LIKE THE TRAIN, HURTLES
ALONG SUSPENSEFULLY."
—*Detroit News*

"GUNG-HO CLOAK-AND-DOGMA . . .
EPISODIC, EXTROVERTED FUN!"
—*Kirkus Reviews*

AVALANCHE EXPRESS

AVALANCHE EXPRESS

Colin Forbes

FAWCETT CREST • NEW YORK

AVALANCHE EXPRESS

THIS BOOK CONTAINS THE COMPLETE TEXT OF
THE ORIGINAL HARDCOVER EDITION

Published by Fawcett Crest Books, a unit of CBS Publica-
tions, the Consumer Publishing Division of CBS Inc., by
arrangement with Elsevier-Dutton Publishing Company, Inc.

ISBN: 0-449-24252-8

Printed in the United States of America

10   9   8   7   6   5   4   3   2   1

1

The Sparta Ring

1

Basel and Zürich, Switzerland

It was Wednesday—dangerous Wednesday—and as always the first Wednesday in the month. It was Wednesday, December 1, a bitter cold day with the snow deep in the streets of the ancient Swiss city that throughout history has been the center of so much intrigue.

VAGONE—LETTI.

MOSKWA—MINSK—BREST—WARSZAWA—BERLIN—
FRANKFURT—HEIDELBERG—BASEL.

The destination plate on the side of the single sleeping car on Gleis 1—Track 1—conjured up a romantic and dangerous journey. Standing by itself in Basel Hauptbahnhof, its passengers recently disembarked, it had a lonely and alien look, almost a sinister touch when you read the destination plate. For the sleeping car this was the end of the line. Each week this single sleeping car, constantly unlinked and attached to different trains, made its way from the heart of the Communist empire to the center of Western Europe.

It had left Moscow at four in the afternoon of Monday, November 29—the day the Soviet Politburo had met to assess the vast military maneuvers conducted personally by Marshal Gregori Prachko. It had arrived at Basel Hauptbahnhof at 9:20 A.M. The time was now 9:45 A.M. The staff had left the sleeping car, which stood empty on its deserted track. Outside the nearby station restaurant were two men in dark hats and overcoats, taking no apparent interest in the sleeping car. The smaller, more heavily built man smoked a French cigarette while he tried not to show his distaste for the unfamiliar tobacco.

"No action yet," he murmured in German.

"Patience, Gustav," his taller, slimmer companion replied. "Waiting is our profession."

Inside the restaurant at a table close to the door an English girl checked her watch as she sipped a cup of coffee she didn't want. She had already paid her bill and was ready to leave at any moment. Everything about Elsa Lang was unattractive. She wore a shabby, military-style raincoat, and a large, floppy hat concealed most of her dark, stringy hair. A large pair of ugly horn-rimmed glasses hid most of her face. Her shoes were worn and scuffed at the toes; her suitcase was scratched and a dismal gray color. She went on sipping her coffee until her watch registered 10 A.M. Then she moved as the second hand reached the vertical.

Picking up the suitcase, she shuffled out of the restaurant, walking past the two men in dark coats and hats. The younger, heavily built man glanced at her and then away. She walked slowly, round-shouldered as though her case was heavy, peering nearsightedly about her. Gustav, who had lit a second Gauloise—he had a compulsion to smoke even strange tobacco when under tension —gestured toward her back.

"What a mousy-looking cow," he sneered to his companion.

"Keep your eyes where they should be," Walther Fischer snapped in a whisper.

At least, that was the name shown on the passport he carried in his pocket, the passport carefully fabricated in the forgery section housed in the basement of KGB headquarters in Dzerzhinsky Square, Moscow. Fischer was beginning to worry. The station was filling up with passengers to catch the Transalpin Basel–Vienna Express and other trains. The two men moved forward to try and keep the sleeping car under observation while Elsa Lang paused amid the swirling crowd as though bewildered.

At the same moment a short, plump man in a white steward's jacket appeared from the direction of the station exit and under cover of the crowd walked rapidly to the rear entrance of the sleeping car from Russia. He walked purposefully, as though he had every right to be there, and disappeared inside. Fischer, the taller of the two men, craned his head over the crowd and saw what had happened.

"Someone's gone aboard," he whispered. "Dressed like a steward." He grabbed his companion, who had started to move forward, by the arm. "Not yet. Wait for him to get off. We shall have to do something about that white jacket. . . ." He took off his dark coat, folded it over his arm, waited.

Inside the sleeping car the white-jacketed steward worked quickly, moving straight to the third compartment. Once inside, he closed the door, opened up the corner washbasin, and thrust his right arm deep inside the large waste-disposal channel that emptied the basin. The cassette was fixed to the side with waterproof tape and he swore under his breath as he wrestled to tug it loose. At any moment a Swiss rail guard might come aboard and normally the cassette came away more easily. Taking a firm grip, he wrenched hard and it was in his hand. He stripped the relics of the tape off the cassette and shoved them in his pocket.

Outside in the station more and more passengers were filling up the entrance hall as the steward emerged and walked quickly toward the exit. Fischer and Gustav moved at the same moment, shouldering passengers out of their way. The steward brushed past Elsa Lang, who was caught up in the turmoil of hurrying passengers, and continued toward the exit as the two men caught up with him. At that moment the crowd thinned out suddenly, leaving only one man, of medium height with a droopy mustache, who stood leaning against a wall absorbed in his newspaper. Fischer pressed a 9 mm. Luger pistol hard into the steward's back under cover of his folded overcoat.

"Run for it and you're dead. Now, move over here. . . ."

They eased the steward into an empty part of the hall to the right of the exit. "Put on this coat," Fischer ordered as he slipped the Luger back into his jacket pocket. As the pale-faced steward obeyed, Fischer kept glancing toward the man with the droopy mustache and glasses, who was still apparently absorbed in his newspaper. "Now, get into that Mercedes by the curb," Fischer ordered. "Rear seat. . . ." They went out into the snow; after the rush of passengers the street was almost deserted except for an unmarked laundry truck parked a few yards ahead of the Mercedes.

In the rear seat of the car Gustav ran expert, searching hands over the steward while Fischer climbed in behind the wheel of the rented car and twisted around in his seat. "I can't find a damned thing except this," Gustav reported. He showed a handful of waterproof tape, all twisted and torn.

"Search him again—and be quick about it. We're going to miss the express. . . ." Under cover of the seat back Fischer wrapped a woolen scarf around the barrel of the Luger. It would help to muffle the shot when he killed the steward. The traveling rug in the back draped over the body should delay its discovery, and the car had been rented in Mannheim, Germany. That was where the Swiss police would make their first inquiries, and while they were pursuing them Fischer and his companion would have reached Vienna aboard the Transalpin.

In the station hall Matt Leroy, the droopy-mustached American dressed in English clothes, was walking slowly past the exit, idly smacking his folded newspaper against his trouser leg. The driver behind the wheel of the unmarked laundry truck saw the signal in his rearview mirror, spoke briefly to his companion beside him, got out, and walked back with a roll of clean towels in his hand. Leaning inside the front window of the Mercedes, he spoke quietly in German as Fischer jerked around to face him.

"Get out of the car and step inside the back of that truck."

Fischer stared at the end of the roll of towels the laundryman was holding, stared at the gun barrel just inside the roll. "And I'll take that first if I may. . . ." With his left hand the man in overalls scooped up the Luger from Fischer's lap and slipped it into his pocket. Gustav, in the rear seat, was looking at another gun concealed inside a screwed-up towel held by the second man in overalls who had jerked open the rear door. The steward had already relieved him of his automatic.

From inside the station hall Matt Leroy watched the four men enter the rear of the laundry truck, watched the doors close as the steward climbed in behind the wheel and started the engine. Only when the van was on the move did he run inside the station and then slow to a quick walk as he saw the big clock, which registered 10:08 A.M. Two minutes before the Transalpin departed for Zürich nonstop.

Inside the rear of the laundry truck Fischer asked his question to distract his captors' attention as he felt the vehicle moving. "What did he collect? And how did he lose it . . ." He was still speaking when he tried to knee the nearest man in overalls in the groin. The laundryman jerked away from the blow, swung his pistol barrel in an arc that connected with Fischer's skull. "Very stupid." He nodded once and smiled at Gustav. The second laundryman crashed his own pistol down on the back of Gustav's head. Each blow had been lethal; both men were dead on the floor of the swaying van.

Soon after daylight on the following day a Swiss policeman, patrolling the shores of the river near the thundering roar of the Rhine Falls below Schaffhausen, observed a large cabin trunk that had become jammed between two massive boulders as the swollen river frothed and tumbled past it. Four hours were needed to bring a police boat equipped with a lifting crane and grapple into position below the falls. Another hour was needed to claw the trunk out of the caldron of boiling water. Ashore, when they opened the trunk, they found the naked bodies of two men crammed inside, and there were no means of identification. Both men had died from a heavy blow to the skull.

When Matt Leroy walked slowly past the exit whipping his folded newspaper against his leg as a signal to the driver of the unmarked laundry truck, Elsa Lang was boarding first-class car 43 of the Transalpin Basel–Vienna Express, due to depart at 10:10 A.M. The corridor was deserted as she slipped inside a washroom and locked the door. She then moved very swiftly, taking off the shabby raincoat, her scuffed shoes, and her horn-rimmed glasses and floppy hat. A moment later she had detached her black wig, exposing fair hair, which she quickly combed.

Perching her dull gray suitcase on the toilet lid, she unzipped the outer cover to reveal an expensive pigskin case beneath. Opening the case, she took out a pair of Gucci shoes, slipped into them, and took out a matching Gucci handbag and a sable coat, which she put on. The detachable outer case cover she packed quickly under expensive lingerie, together with the wig, hat, raincoat, and discarded shoes. Locking the case, she used her makeup kit and studied herself briefly in the mirror. The horn-rimmed glasses went inside the Gucci handbag. The Elsa Lang who emerged from the washroom was unrecognizable from the dowdy girl who had entered it only minutes earlier.

Not only had the change of clothes altered her entire appearance; as she moved along the corridor to her reserved seat she was slimmer, taller, for she walked without a slouch, and her way of moving—which so identifies a man or woman—had also changed. She walked with a brisk, springy step, reached the empty compartment, and went inside. To keep the compartment to herself she took off the sable, spread it out on another seat, and perched the Gucci case on a third. Sitting down, she crossed her slim, elegant legs and checked her watch: 10:08 A.M. The express was due to depart in two minutes for Zürich on its long journey to Vienna. Opening her handbag—where the cassette the steward had slipped to her was concealed

11

in a zippered compartment—she took out an ivory cigarette holder, inserted a cigarette, lit it, and took a deep, long drag.

"Christ," she said to herself, "butterflies in my stomach again. Will I never get over the tension at moments like this?"

Then she remembered what Harry Wargrave had once told her. "When you lose the tension you get out of this business—you need that to keep the reflexes razor-sharp. . . ." The recollection was some comfort as she forced herself to relax, to sit back in her seat and feel her pulse rate returning to normal.

It was even of more comfort when she saw Matt Leroy walk past her window on the platform to board the car higher up. God, she thought, he left it late this time; I wonder why? The express started moving, gliding out from under the huge vault of the Hauptbahnhof into the falling snow as it headed east on the fast one-hour lap to Zürich.

The Swiss ticket collector arrived a few minutes later as the express was speeding through Switzerland. He took his time about examining her ticket; he was a man who appreciated feminine beauty. And this one is a beauty, he was thinking as he clipped the ticket and glanced at her again. Level gray eyes looked back at him with the hint of a mischievous smile. The bone structure of her face was striking; a well-shaped nose, a full but firm-lipped mouth, and a jaw that suggested character and determination.

"A pleasant journey, madame," he said in careful English. He shrugged as he looked out of the window. "In spite of the weather. . . ." He left the compartment. An observant Swiss, Elsa Lang thought as she put the round-trip ticket back inside her purse. ". . . madame." He had noticed her wedding ring, although the truth was she was still very much single at twenty-eight. Another detail Harry Wargrave had insisted on. "Married women attract just a shade less attention than a single girl traveling alone."

Outside in the corridor the inspector was checking the round-trip ticket of the American, Matt Leroy, who stood leaning against the passenger rail smoking a cigarette. "I asked for a smoker reservation," he remarked casually. "And they gave me this," he lied. He gestured to the empty nonsmoking compartment behind, where his holdall bag lay on a seat. From Leroy's accent the inspector assumed he was dealing with an Englishman: an accent Leroy had perfected during his two years attached to the American Embassy in Grosvenor Square as security officer. Also, the American wore a camel's-hair coat purchased in Savile Row.

"Plenty of room in smoking compartments," the inspector suggested as he clipped the ticket.

"Doesn't matter," Leroy assured him. "It's not far to Zürich."

He had actually booked the nonsmoking seat to place him close to Elsa Lang. As the inspector moved along the train Leroy checked his watch and touched his droopy mustache. It was always a tight schedule and once again he was hoping to God the express would reach Zürich on time. And the fact that, like Elsa, he was traveling on a round-trip ticket he would never use was just a further detail insisted on by the Englishman Harry Wargrave. "It gives the impression you're going back to Basel," he had pointed out. "Just in case the wrong person is close to you. . . ."

At 11:12 A.M. promptly the express pulled into Zürich Hauptbahnhof. Elsa Lang was already standing with her case at the end of the coach ready to get off quickly. Hurrying through the ticket barrier, she carried her own case to the cab rank that faces the Hotel Schweizerhof across the street and stepped inside the first waiting cab. Only when she was inside did she give the instruction to the driver in a low, soft voice.

"Zürich Airport. And I'm late for my flight. . . ."

Following her off the train, Matt Leroy had taken a different route. Sprinting along the wide side hall past the baggage counter he had the keys of the Citroën in his hand as he reached the car parked at the end of the station. The ignition sparked at the first touch—the car had been left for him only a few minutes earlier—and he drove around to the front of the Hauptbahnhof in time to see Elsa's cab leaving. She was peering out of the window so he could spot her. At a discreet distance he followed her to the airport, ten miles outside the city.

Leroy, thirty-four years old, had a deceptive studious appearance, but there was a steely alertness in his manner as he peered ahead through his silver-rimmed glasses to keep Elsa's cab in sight. Frequently he glanced in his rearview mirror to make sure no vehicle was tailing them. His task, reinforced by the backup team at Basel who had disposed of the steward's interceptors, was to see that Elsa Lang reached Zürich Airport safely. And as on their previous monthly trips it was with a feeling of relief that he saw her cab pull up in front of the airport building, saw her step out of the cab with her Gucci suitcase and hurry inside the building. Leaving the Citroën outside, he followed her in.

It was with a further feeling of relief that, inside the reception hall, he saw a tall, dark-haired Englishman standing by a bookstall apparently studying the paperbacks. Leroy sighed, his task once more completed. Harry Wargrave was taking over.

At thirty-seven Harry Charles Frederick Wargrave had lived three lifetimes compared to the average man of his age. He was six feet tall, slim and easy in his movements, and his eyebrows were as dark as his dense thatch of hair, eyebrows often raised slightly as he regarded people with a quizzical stare. His nose was long, his cheekbones prominent, his mouth wide with a hint of humor at the corners. Everything about him as he stood waiting by the bookstall wearing a military-style raincoat suggested a casual, easy approach to life, an "I don't give a damn" manner. More than one person had lived to regret this assessment. Some had died.

At nineteen Wargrave had gained his wings as a Navy pilot—at that time the youngest pilot in the British Navy. He held a separate certificate for flying choppers. He had driven motor torpedo boats and sometimes described himself as a "mechanical nut. I see something new with an engine and I have to learn to drive or fly the thing. . . ."

Transferred later to naval intelligence with the rank of commander, he had been attached to the British Embassy in Washington to help track down spies inside the States who were passing to Soviet Russia technical secrets Britain had shared with America. But all of this had only been a beginning. Fluent in French, German, Italian, and Serbo-Croat, he had later still been seconded to the British Secret Service—still the best in the world despite certain novel writers' attempts to portray it as a club of professional idiots.

After service in various parts of Western Europe—a period when he came to know well all the top security and counterintelligence chiefs—Wargrave was dispatched to the Balkans. Based in Athens, he engaged in activities that were still shrouded in mystery. "The biggest killing ground in the world," he once called the Balkans. "If a man can survive there he can survive anywhere. . . ." At thirty-six he had retired and emigrated to Canada, where, on the investment advice of millionaire industrialist William Riverton, he had multiplied his small capital by ten. On retiring he had explained his philosophy in typical pithy fashion.

"Like a racing driver, in this profession you get out before you're forty or you're dead. . . ."

Now he stood by the bookstall at Zürich Airport, well aware that Elsa Lang was checking in for her flight, that the receptionist had already placed her case on the conveyor belt that would carry it to the waiting aircraft —although he had not once looked in her direction. He checked his watch: 11:37. A very tight schedule, but once again Elsa, bless her, had made it. And Wargrave had always insisted the schedule must be very tight. In an earlier argument with Matt Leroy he had overruled the American's apparently quite reasonable objections.

"There's no goddamn margin for error," Leroy had protested. "We have the minimum time to grab the cassette off the sleeping car. Elsa has only minutes to catch the Transalpin express. The express has to arrive

15

on schedule at Zürich to give her any chance to reach the airport in time to catch her flight. . . ."

"Precisely," Wargrave had agreed laconically.

"That's all you have to say, for God's sake?"

"The faster the fox moves, the less chance the hounds have of picking up its scent, Matt." Wargrave had grinned sardonically. "A tight schedule makes it tricky for us—but even more tricky for the enemy. Ever watch a falcon dive on its prey? It swoops like lightning, then it's up and away. We're that falcon. . . ."

Wargrave was on the verge of moving away from the bookstall to join Elsa's flight—time was running damned short now—when he was aware that Matt Leroy was standing next to him as the American picked up a Harold Robbins novel. Nothing in Wargrave's easy stance hinted at the tightening of his nerves. Leroy had strict instructions to approach him only in an emergency. Over the public address system they were already making the last call for Swissair Flight 160.

Leroy bought the paperback and then laid it on top of some magazines while he took his time over pocketing his wallet. Wargrave called the girl back and bought a copy of the same novel. He didn't pick it up as she laid the paperback alongside Leroy's copy. Paying for it, he waited until the girl moved to serve another customer, picked up Leroy's copy, and then began running for the final departure gate Elsa had already passed through.

In the first-class section aboard the Swiss DC-10 aircraft Wargrave chose a seat on the opposite side of the aisle and one row behind Elsa Lang. She sat staring out of the window with her long legs crossed, a symphony in nylon he thought agreeably as he fastened his seat belt. And that was another little detail he had instructed her in when they had first started this monthly routine a year earlier.

"On the plane always sit with your legs crossed. . . ."

"Really?" she had inquired ironically. "Is it likely that I'll lose my official virginity thirty thousand feet up over the Atlantic?"

"I have to confess my opportunites would be limited,"

he had assured her. "But if anyone catches me watching you, the sight of your legs will be all the innocent explanation they'll need."

"Or maybe you're simply exploiting your duties for overt sexual purposes?"

Not for the first time in dealing with Elsa Lang, Wargrave had been lost for a reply. He was thinking about this as he studied her legs and then the other passengers while the machine built up throbbing power and then began taxiing toward the main runway. Which is the wrong priority, he reminded himself: the other passengers first, then Elsa's legs. And once in the air he must pay a call to the washroom to extract and read the message Matt Leroy would have slipped inside his paperback.

Outside the airport building, cosily parked in the Citroën with the heater going full blast, Leroy smoked a cigarette, waiting for the plane to take off. It had stopped snowing but the sky was low and heavy with swollen overcast, the threat of more snow to come, and it was only December. Already the long-range forecasters were beginning to mutter about the most bitter winter in Europe for many years being on the way. And that after the hottest and most prolonged summer in living memory when drought had smitten Western Europe and even in southern England temperatures had soared into the nineties. "That's what they call compensation, I guess," Matt told himself. Looking up, he saw the plane.

The DC-10 climbed rapidly, spinning out a dirt trail behind it. Then it was gone, swallowed up in the dense overcast. But Swissair flight 160 was not bound for the United States or Britain, as might have seemed normal if the operation had been carried out three years earlier. Instead, its destination was Montreal, Canada.

2

Montreal and Washington

On the tenth floor of the Baton Rouge Building in Montreal the elevator doors opened at 3:30 P.M. local time and Elsa Lang stepped out, followed by Wargrave carrying her case. It was still Wednesday, December 1. Glancing both ways along the corridor, Elsa walked briskly to a door that carried a plate bearing the legend *Riverton Corp., Inc.* Opening it, she faced a girl receptionist behind a huge slab desk. It was Wargrave who spoke.

"We're expected. . . ." He spoke with an American accent, he did not take the cigar out of his mouth as he spoke, and he wore dark glasses. "Mrs. Perkins and Clyde Wilson. Mr. Riverton expects us. . . ."

Elsa Lang was wearing her dark wig and horn-rimmed glasses, which she had put on while Wargrave drove her in the rental car from the airport. The receptionist didn't give her a second look as she spoke into the intercom and then told them to go in. Elsa led the way through the familiar door and Wargrave carefully closed it behind them as a compact, poker-faced man rose from behind a desk much smaller than the receptionist's.

"Glad to see you back."

That was all William Riverton, the legendary Canadian millionaire industrialist, said as he walked with a slow, deliberate tread to unlock a door at the side of his office. Seventy-three years old, Riverton had controlled one of the most secret counterespionage organizations in the Western Hemisphere during the Second World War. Even now there was a magnetism about this extraordinary man, a suggestion of enormous willpower in his impassive face and slow-moving eyes. Wargrave watched the old warrior with something close to affection as the Canadian unlocked the heavy door and stood aside to let them enter.

The large room beyond the door was windowless, illuminated by overhead fluorescent tubes. On one wall a series of clocks showed the time in different parts of the world—Zürich time, Bucharest time, Moscow time. . . . The atmosphere was overheated.

"Sit down, you must be tired. How did it go? Coffee?"

The voice was American, the speaker a fifty-five-year-old, well-built man of medium height with thinning gray-white hair, a finely-shaped forehead, and a welcoming smile that radiated assurance and good humor. Only the eyes were searching, as though seeking signs of strain, any hint of trouble. Julian Haller embraced and hugged Elsa, helped her off with her raincoat, grinned as she took off the wig and glasses.

"That's an improvement," he commented.

"Thanks, Julian." Elsa gave him her warmest smile. "And coffee would be heaven—I'm jet-lagged out of my mind."

"Timed it perfectly, didn't I?" Julian Haller grinned as he poured coffee from the pot, then added cream just the way she liked it. "There's a large scotch for you, Harry, on the side table," he went on. "Ed phoned in your arrival from the airport." As he handed her the cup he glanced across the room where Wargrave was inserting the cassette he had extracted from Elsa's handbag into a tape recorder. "Why the hurry?" he asked quietly.

"A wee spot of bother at Basel," Wargrave replied. "It looks as though someone is breathing down Angelo's neck—two men with guns grabbed Neckermann after he had passed the cassette to Elsa."

Elsa twisted around in her chair. "You never tell me anything," she accused. "You had plenty of time to tell me on the way here in the car. . . ."

"You were tired. I thought it could wait." Wargrave continued reporting to Haller, who lit a cigarette. The

American's smile had vanished as he listened to the Englishman with intense concentration. "Leroy did well—very well," Wargrave commented. "He spotted what was happening and his backup people rescued Neckermann."

"And the two men who grabbed him?"

"At the bottom of the Rhine would be my guess," Wargrave said lightly. He went on talking quickly as he saw Elsa wince. "I'm going to play the cassette from our unknown Russian friend, Angelo. Ready?"

There was a sudden feeling of tension inside the room as the cassette spools revolved, as the familiar voice began speaking clearly in English, a hoarse, whispering voice obviously disguised, speaking to them from Moscow, over four thousand miles away—a voice they now knew could belong only to a senior member of the Soviet Politburo.

The voice of the man they knew only by the code name of Angelo had finished speaking. There was an appalled hush inside the room. It was the most terrifying signal Angelo had ever sent. Elsa, normally so outwardly calm and relaxed, sat tense and rigid, the burning cigarette between her fingers momentarily forgotten. Haller sat motionless behind his desk, his head turned slightly to one side. Wargrave, the coolest of the trio, removed the cassette and looked at Haller.

"So, the next move is?"

"You'd better catch the first plane to Washington. I'll warn Bruno you're on the way. . . ."

Opening a desk in his drawer, the American checked flight times, checked the clock on the wall that showed Montreal time. "If you move very fast indeed, Harry . . ."

"I'm on my way."

Haller unlocked the door leading to Riverton's office with his own key and Wargrave put on his dark glasses as he hurried out. He gave a little two-finger salute to the Canadian industrialist, who nodded without speaking. Sixty seconds later, Wargrave was behind the wheel of his rental car.

Driving just within the speed limit, he reached the

airport in time to board the next flight for Washington. As the plane took off and disappeared inside another heavy overcast, Wargrave relaxed in his seat, but he was careful not to close his eyes in case he fell asleep. He had the cassette inside his breast pocket and the jet lag of the Zürich-to-Montreal flight was hitting him. For the next few hours he was going to have to forget about sleep. Harry Wargrave was on his way to see Bruno—the code name for Joseph Moynihan, President of the United States.

At Dulles Airport, James Ryder, a large, paunchy American, went through the usual routine. Wearing dark glasses and a vicuña coat, which suggested a person of some importance, he stood with a suitcase in his hand watching the arrival board, which showed the Montreal flight had just landed. Mingling with passengers from the flight, he strolled toward the airport exit and waited while passengers boarded the airport bus. He went on waiting while others took cabs, looking impatiently at his watch as though annoyed at the late arrival of his own vehicle.

Ten minutes later a blue Cadillac pulled in by the curb. Ryder stood quite still while a tall man dressed in chauffeur's uniform climbed out from behind the wheel, walked around, and opened the rear door. Ryder climbed inside without a word of thanks and settled himself in the back as the chauffeur returned behind the wheel.

"O.K., let's go. Make it snappy," Ryder ordered and began reading a magazine he had taken from his pocket.

Through the heavy traffic of early evening they drove to the White House, and during the whole journey no word was exchanged between the two men. Arriving at the White House, both men showed the Secret Service operative the special passes signed by Joseph Moynihan himself. There were no further formalities; they were immediately escorted to an anteroom that led directly to the Oval Office. And as instructed, the Secret Service man left them alone in the room, locking the door on the outside.

Ryder sat down in a chair and pulled the magazine from his pocket as Harry Wargrave removed his peaked cap, straightened his uniform jacket, and knocked on the door leading to the Oval office. Not even the chief of the Secret Service detachment that guarded the President was aware that it was the chauffeur who was the important visitor.

On leaving the aircraft at Dulles Airport, Wargrave had gone straight to a room set aside for his use, a room to which he held the only key. Inside he had quickly changed into the chauffeur's uniform waiting for him. Then he had hurried to where the Cadillac was parked and had driven it around to where Ryder was waiting for him. Ryder was a "blind"—he had no idea who Wargrave was and he assumed the Englishman was a Canadian. A member of the presidential Secret Service entourage, Ryder carried out the orders given to him personally by the President without question—and without informing his own chief of what he did. President Moynihan himself opened the door in response to Wargrave's knock, ushered him inside, and closed the door.

"Some kind of emergency, Harry?" Moynihan asked crisply.

"In our opinion, yes, Mr. President."

Wargrave walked to the desk where the tape recorder was waiting and inserted the cassette. Joseph Moynihan, six foot one and informally dressed in shirt sleeves, went back behind his desk and poured a large scotch. He pushed the glass over toward Wargrave. Moynihan was an impressive figure, and not only because of his height and build.

Round-faced, he had quick-moving blue eyes and he was rarely still for more than a few minutes. Radiating vitality, his expression was constantly changing when he spoke and his manner was blunt and direct. At forty-one he was the youngest man to occupy the White House this century; he was also the most anti-Communist President since the Russian Revolution. Perching his buttocks on the edge of the desk he listened with folded arms as the man they had code-named Angelo began speaking.

"Angelo reporting . . . a major emergency faces Western Europe . . . Marshal Prachko has just completed the most massive military rehearsal for the invasion of Germany, France, Holland, and Belgium. . . . The plan assumes Soviet tanks will enter Hamburg thirty minutes from Z hour . . . within forty-eight hours three major bridgeheads will have been established across the Rhine. One hundred and sixty Soviet divisions will be deployed . . . including one hundred fully mechanized, fifty tank, ten airborne. . . . Advance armored elements will reach the Channel ports seven days from Z hour. . . . Operation Thunderstrike was carried out between Kazakhstan and the Ukrainian border over distances that precisely reproduced those the Red Army would cross in Western Europe. . . ."

Angelo went on to describe in terrifying detail how Operation Thunderstrike had been conducted. Taking a transparent map of Western Europe, the Soviet High Command had superimposed it over an equivalent area of western Russia. The river Volga had become the Rhine. Signposts —unreadable to American spy satellites orbiting three hundred miles over the area—had been erected reading *Paris, 30 km., Hamburg, 45 km., Calais, 80 km.,* pointing toward the Russian city that was the equivalent distance.

One Soviet army group had represented the NATO opposing force. The main attacking Red Army groups, outnumbering NATO by three to one or more—as they did in reality—had been commanded by Marshal Prachko himself. So overwhelming had been the onslaught, so swift its speed of movement, it was assumed the American President would feel it pointless to launch a retaliatory nuclear strike.

As the cassette came to the end, Angelo's final words were spoken in a deep and forceful voice. "It is vital immediately to make a huge demonstration of American power to deter Marshal Prachko and his supporters, who are on the verge of achieving a majority in the Politburo. . . ."

Briefly there was the same hush inside the Oval Office as had descended on the room in the Baton Rouge Building in Montreal when the tape had ended. But only briefly; as Wargrave switched off the machine Moynihan stood up

23

from the desk where he had stayed perched throughout the recording.

"I think we can term this a major emergency," Moynihan commented. "Reports from satellites that have come in confirm major military maneuvers have taken place in the area Angelo specifies. They couldn't tell us what he has told us, of course. And then there's the laser problem —scientists here and in Moscow reckon they're on the verge of a breakthrough."

"A breakthrough to where?"

"Someday, maybe very soon, laser beams projected over long distances will be able to divert missile guidance systems—which means any missile fired will fall back on the original launch point. Result One? End of the nuclear deterrent. Result Two? The Soviets will feel free to use their ground forces in Europe without fear of nuclear retaliation. . . ."

"So what's the answer?" Wargrave inquired.

"This." Moynihan pressed a button on his intercom. "Ed, call an immediate meeting of the National Security Council. One hour from now. I don't care where the hell people are. Get them here. . . ."

Inwardly Wargrave sighed with relief—relief that it was Joseph Moynihan who was sitting in the White House. How many previous Presidents would have taken a decision so quickly, would have acted with such determination? As though to confirm his unspoken thoughts, the President hitched up his slacks and spoke tersely.

"That meeting is just the formality. I've already decided what action must be taken. And Sparta has done a great job. I say that to you personally, Harry." He held out his hand and shook Wargrave's. He had a strong grip. "And you can pass on the same message to Julian Haller. . . ."

The enormous power of Moynihan's reaction became apparent to Wargrave twenty-four hours later back in Montreal. By night, three U.S. airborne divisions with all their equipment emplaned at Fort Worth, Texas, aboard a vast fleet of Lockheed C-5A transport planes. At the White House, Moynihan sat up all night in his shirt sleeves phoning the Chancellor of West Germany, the Prime Minister of Great Britain, the President of France, and the NATO commander in Brussels. And all the time the giant transport planes were taking off, heading east across the Atlantic for the European mainland. Flight schedules were timed for maximum psychological impact—to raise the morale of Europe.

At nine o'clock in the morning—at the height of the rush hour—Londoners hurrying to work were startled to hear a thunderous roar in the sky above them. Looking up they saw the endless stream of U.S. aircraft flying just below cloud level, a vast sky train of planes that came on and on. Less than sixty minutes later the same immense air cavalcade passed over Brussels and within a further hour the airborne force had landed in West Germany. To ram the point home, Moynihan made a brief television broadcast beamed worldwide by satellite, a broadcast made in his typical direct language.

"Let no one make any mistake—the American defense frontier lies along the West German border where it adjoins the Soviet prisoner states. As to what has just landed in the Federal Republic, well, there's plenty more where that came from. . . ."

"Sparta has done a great job. . . ."

President Moynihan had been referring to the Sparta Ring when he congratulated Harry Wargrave in the White House, to the special intelligence unit based outside the United States in Montreal, Canada. To explain how this unique outfit came into existence, it is necessary to go back a year earlier—to the time when Vice-President Moynihan had recently assumed the presidency after his predecessor was killed suddenly in a skiing accident in Colorado.

3

Prague, Czechoslovakia

At that moment in history Matt Leroy—who later guarded
Elsa Lang on her monthly journeys from Basel to Zürich
Airport—was just completing his tour of duty as security
officer at the American Embassy in Prague. It was December 8, the weather was mild, although snow had fallen in
the High Tatra, and the American ambassador was holding an evening reception for certain Soviet Politburo members visiting Czechoslovakia. For Leroy his last night in
Prague before returning to the States the following day
looked eventful.

"My first chance to see the top enemy at close quarters," as he confided to an aide.

The ambassador was not so enthusiastic. He had just received a personal instruction from Joseph Moynihan, who
had recently succeeded as President, a message couched
in typically pithy terms, which were later to become so
familiar. "Don't play footsie with the Kremlin crowd. A
firm politeness is the order of the day. And on no account
initiate any toasts to their goddamn fake détente. . . ."

As he circled among the guests under glittering chandeliers, Matt Leroy had a vague look while he held a glass of
bourbon he sipped at occasionally. In fact he was examining everyone present with the utmost care, missing not
even the smallest detail. Among the senior Politburo guests
was Anatoli Zarubin, minister of trade and commerce. It
was Zarubin who pounced on Leroy, clinking glasses with
the American.

26

"To continuing détente, my friend," Zarubin proposed in perfect English.

"To détente," Leroy agreed without enthusiasm.

Zarubin was a small, dark-haired Russian with a neat mustache and a cheerful manner, and was reputed to be something of a ladies' man. Despite his doubts Leroy had found himself liking the talkative, joking minister, who expressed a fanatical devotion to the jazz of Dave Brubeck. "I have all his records, play them over and over again," he chattered on. "*Take Five*—that's my all-time favorite. . . ." Leroy had found other Soviet guests less likable.

The party was warming up by nine o'clock and the vodka was flowing most freely in the vicinity of Marshal Gregori Prachko, Soviet minister of defense. Prachko, a large barrel-chested man of fifty-eight, had arrived in full uniform and covered with row upon row of medals. "Enough to stock a First Avenue pawnshop," Leroy thought sourly. He was quite obviously trying to get everyone else drunk, insisting upon toast after toast.

"Détente! Détente! Is there anyone here who refuses to drink that toast with me? Then let him show himself as the enemy of peace!"

Leroy studied him unobtrusively, noted the brutal nose, the aggressive jaw, the bristles of hair projecting from ears and nostrils. "All of the bastard he's supposed to be," he was thinking. "And God help the men who serve under him." Leroy kept circulating slowly, looking for one particular man, a man, oddly enough, whose appearance he had no description of. Was it possible that somewhere among the large crowd Colonel Igor Sharpinsky was present?

Deputy chief of the KGB, Sharpinsky was a shadow to Western security chiefs, so much so that he had been nicknamed Colonel Shadow. Literally all that was known about him was that he existed and Washington's dossier on him occupied only one page containing a few lines. Even the few lines were vague and insubstantial. "It is rumored that he is the KGB officer who liaises with GRU, Soviet military intelligence. . . . It is believed that at different times he has served with different Soviet embassies in the West under assumed names." And that was about it.

A moment later Leroy saw another senior Politburo member who was not his favourite pinup. Surprised—this man had not appeared on the advance guest list—Leroy pretended to sip more bourbon while he watched one of the most feared men in the world: General Sergei Marenkov, head of the KGB. The secret police chief was hovering at the edge of the crowd as though observing everyone present.

Wearing a dark blue business suit, Marenkov was a short, stocky man of fifty-five with wide shoulders. He stood quite still, his strong-jawed face showing no expression. As he gazed around the room from under bushy eyebrows, he seemed to be cataloging everyone at the reception, which probably was exactly what he was doing, Leroy thought. Unlike his mysterious deputy, Colonel Sharpinsky, Washington had a dossier three inches thick on Marenkov. The general was known to have an encyclopedic memory. "I'll bet he knows every man inside our embassy—what his job is and when he pees," Leroy told himself.

Marenkov suddenly started moving slowly around the fringe of the crowd. By now the room was filled with noise, loud voices, the never-ending clinking of glasses, with Anatoli Zarubin tirelessly chatting and joking. Leroy seized his opportunity as Marenkov was passing him. He lifted his glass. "Peace and goodwill, for God's sake, General." Marenkov said something in Russian, and clinked glasses, and his brown eyes stared hard at the American, then he moved on. It had not been a too friendly encounter but Leroy had not been able to resist the chance to study the KGB chief at close quarters—even if only for a few seconds.

By the end of the evening Leroy felt he had achieved nothing. Certainly he had caught sight of no one who might be Igor Sharpinsky, no one who kept close to Marenkov. It had been interesting, something to put in his final report, but nothing more. The shock came when the party was over.

Returning to his room after midnight to complete his packing—he was due to catch the morning plane to Frankfurt—he felt in his jacket pocket for his cigarettes and stiffened. Tired with the anticlimax that so often ends a party, Matt Leroy became suddenly very alert. Inside the pocket his fingers touched something unfamiliar, something that shouldn't be there. He slowly drew out a sealed envelope. On the outside was written in English capital letters FOR THE PRESIDENT'S EYES ONLY.

Leroy got to bed that night much later than he had expected. Waking up his technical assistant, he had the envelope subjected to a series of tests. It was negative for explosives, for any kind of poison. He had the envelope, still sealed, X-rayed and the clear outline of a cassette showed up on the film. On the outside of the cassette someone had scratched the letters *AN*.

"Where did you get it?" West, the technician, inquired at one stage.

"It was delivered to me," Leroy replied and left it at that. "Incidentally, this is top security—so you mention it to no one after I've gone. . . ."

Back in his bedroom at 5 A.M., his packing completed, Leroy sat propped up against his pillow fully clothed while he thought. He knew the envelope could only have been slipped into his pocket—and very skillfully—by someone at the reception. He had put on a fresh suit only minutes before the reception had started. The only possible conclusion—fantastic as it seemed—was that the envelope had been slipped to him by one of the Russians at the reception. And right under the eyes of General Sergei Marenkov, head of the KGB. He shuddered at the thought. Whoever it was must have an incredible nerve. Or maybe he was desperate.

But the more he thought about it, the more plausible it seemed. It was no particular secret that he was ending his tour of duty, that he was on his way back to the States

—a fact that would certainly be known in Soviet circles. So someone had taken this fact into account, that the cassette would stay in Prague for only a few hours after it had been passed to him.

"And how the hell do I get it into the President's hands?" he asked himself.

It was typical of Matt Leroy that he should suspect the need for the utmost secrecy, which meant bypassing his own chief in Washington. He had still not solved the problem when he landed in Washington the following day. Instead, the problem solved itself.

Twenty-four hours after Matt arrived in Washington the Chancellor of the Federal Republic of Germany flew in as President Moynihan's guest. And Matt Leroy was invited to the White House reception to report direct to the German Chancellor on his assessment of the political situation inside Czechoslovakia. It was not an idea that greatly appealed to Leroy's chief, Chuck Grant.

"Why the hell he can't take his briefings from me God alone knows," he informed Leroy savagely.

"Maybe he likes on-the-spot reports," Leroy suggested with an owlish blink of innocence.

But it was President Joseph Moynihan who liked on-the-spot briefings. As he remarked in typical unorthodox fashion to one of his aides, "It's the man in the field who knows. The bureau desk johnnies over here love interpreting intelligence. For 'interpreting' read 'fouling it up.' It's their rationale for holding down a job that probably isn't needed anyway."

At the Washington reception, Leroy was introduced to Moynihan, who took him by the arm to guide him over to the Chancellor. "Just a moment, Mr. President," Leroy said quickly. In a few words he explained about the cassette. "I have it on me," he continued quickly in a low voice. "It could be dynamite. . . ."

"Really?" Moynihan gave a great big beaming grin. "Dynamite, you said? I'll look forward to opening that."

"I've had it checked for explosive content," Leroy said hastily, "both here and in Prague."

"I assumed that—I was joking. Now, do you think you

could slip it into my pocket as skillfully as it went into yours in Prague? And the place is crawling with Secret Service men. . . ."

"Done, Mr. President."

"You have one hell of a nerve coming direct to me with this—bypassing your superiors."

"I would agree with your evaluation of my action," Leroy replied.

"And your name is Matt Leroy? Correct? I might just need an insubordinate bastard like you in future. Some people," Moynihan went on with the ghost of a smile, "call it initiative. And now we'll go and talk with our distinguished guest."

Late that night Moynihan listened to the cassette alone in the Oval Office. The unknown man who had made the recording opened by saying that his code name in future would be Angelo, that he would communicate only by cassette, that the authenticity of each cassette would be shown by the letters *AN* he would scratch on the outside. He then gave information about Soviet policy, about the views of the most influential members of the Politburo, about the present Red Army order of battle in Eastern Europe.

What followed was even more extraordinary. He gave the President instructions that an entirely new intelligence unit must be set up outside the borders of the United States to transport cassettes from Europe to North America. "Your existing intelligence agencies have been exposed and destroyed by your own press and Congress in a way the Soviet KGB could never have achieved," the voice continued in English. "To protect me you must set up this special unit, commanded by an American, I suggest, but staffed by Europeans—they will be operating in Europe, remember. Because they are islanders, British personnel may well prove to be the most reliable. . . ."

And so it went on, giving details that cassettes would be dispatched by the Moscow Express concealed in the sleeping car that arrived in Basel, Switzerland, on the first Wednesday of each month. More details followed—the compartment number in the sleeping car, the precise place of concealment. On each Friday following the arrival of a cassette on Wednesday receipt of the cassette should be acknowledged over the Voice of America program beamed to Eastern Europe—by the playing of a record he would specify and which was to be played at 5 P.M. Moscow time. Receipt of this first cassette was to be acknowledged by playing Count Basie's *One O'Clock Jump.* The cassette ended with a warning.

"No attempt must be made by any of your special unit personnel to identify me. That is mandatory. As to my motives, these are my own affair. The next cassette will travel aboard the Moscow Express sleeping car that reaches Basel on . . ."

The previous President, a consensus man, would undoubtedly have consulted the Secretary for Defense, the new CIA chief Moynihan had appointed to try and revive this organization, and God knew who else. But Angelo had judged his man correctly. The following morning Moynihan made certain discreet inquiries without revealing the reason for them. At the end of the day he was convinced that the top-secret data given over the cassette were genuine, that Angelo could only be a member of the Soviet Politburo. He sent for Julian Haller of the National Security Agency.

Moynihan, an ex-Navy man, had known Julian Haller since the Vietnam war and they had remained friends ever since. Haller was also a Navy veteran—he had served aboard the U.S.S. *Savannah* during the Second World War and had later been transferred to naval intelligence. It was in this capacity he had first met the man who one day by accident became President. "Haller," Moynihan was fond of saying, "is one of the few men who really tell me what the score is. He isn't normal—he has no political ambition. . . ."

Julian Haller listened in absolute silence while Moynihan told him what had happened, that he proposed to go along with Angelo. "The information in that cassette you have listened to can only come from a senior member of the Soviet Politburo," Moynihan pointed out. "I've had it checked out."

"It could just be a subtle trap," Haller warned. "To influence you with false information—giving you enough genuine data to fool you."

"I've considered that. Angelo has given too much."

"It would seem so," the cautious Haller replied. "And he has predicted certain things which—if they come true—would reinforce our confidence. What do we do now?"

Moynihan, dressed in slacks and an open-neck shirt, stood up and assumed his favorite position, perching his backside on the front of his desk in the Oval Office. "First, Julian, let me tell you something of my philosophy. My predecessor tried the soft option with the Soviets—with everything. Open government was his call. Let's all be buddies and love each other. Rot!" He took a quick drink of scotch and banged the glass down on the desk.

"He was a sincere man," Haller suggested dubiously.

"He was naïve. The people only feel secure when they have strong, honest leadership—both qualities are equally important. The whole of the Western world has been sinking into a state of neurosis—almost a psychotic state—of fear."

"So how do we remedy that?" Haller inquired.

"I'm not a nice guy. . . ." Moynihan's mobile features formed a grin. "I'm a cynical bastard who believes only a strong lead will cure that psychosis—and stop the Soviets in their tracks. Leonid Sedov is no Stalin, but just so long as we present a weak profile he has to go on pushing, pushing—otherwise Marshal Prachko and his lackeys will take over in the Politburo. They may do so even yet—unless I can outmaneuver them—and God, it's going to help me if I have an ear inside the Kremlin—Angelo's ear. There's something else," he added casually.

"Top-secret? Sure you want to tell me?"

"Yes to both questions. It will help you realize just how vital your secret unit could be. Not yet, but when the time is ripe, I'm thinking of offering to conclude with the People's Republic of China a mutual defense treaty."

"That would be something else again," said Haller, startled.

"It would put the squeeze on the Soviets."

"So what do we do now?" Haller asked again.

"You disappear. Officially you retire from the NSA. You get the hell out of the States and set up this special unit. Angelo is right—the existing agencies are busted flushes for this kind of work. Certain congressmen, certain newspaper reporters have gone too far—they have destroyed our intelligence shield." Moynihan's face darkened and he hammered his clenched fist on the desk. "Meantime the KGB goes marching on in full strength and power—spying, sabotaging, subverting—and all with the full backing of the Politburo. When I took on this job, I swore on oath to defend the United States—and by God I'm going to do it!"

"The CIA is being reorganized—"

"CIA. Club of International Amateurs! That's what those initials stand for in my book."

"It could all be called pretty unconstitutional if ever it leaked," Haller warned again.

"I've thought of that. Any President who—for the sake of his country's security—won't risk personal impeachment isn't fit to sit in this chair."

"That's certainly a novel interpretation," Haller admitted. "Canada is the place," he went on briskly. "And can I use your name to get the cooperation of William Riverton, the Canadian industrialist? He was concerned with Allied intelligence in the last war and could provide the cover we need—maybe even the base?"

"Do that. I know him. Give the old warrior my best wishes." Moynihan paused. "Isn't this going to play hell with your domestic life? All the time this operation lasts you won't ever be able to set foot in the States. What about Linda?"

Haller had a stable marriage; he had been married for thirty years to Linda, who was a fashion designer in New York. Using the Metroliner service, they spent as much time together as they could even though they worked in different cities. It was Moynihan who answered his own question. "We'll find some way of financing frequent trips to Montreal for her. Now, what about personnel?"

Haller grinned. "That could come easy. There's a friend of mine called Harry Wargrave, a Britisher. Ex-naval intelligence, and he's got top U.S. security clearance. I see him as the link man between Montreal and here—maybe something more than that. He's in Canada now, fishing in the Lake of the Woods area." The grin broadened. "He's thirty-six. And he thinks he's retired."

4

Montreal, Zürich, Moscow

Under the energetic impetus of Julian Haller, the special unit to bring Angelo's cassettes out of Europe to North America was set up in seven days. But despite Haller's energy, this was only made possible by the cooperation of the Canadian millionaire William Riverton. Haller's interview with the Canadian was surprisingly short. Sitting behind his desk in the office on the tenth floor of the Baton Rouge Building, Riverton read Moynihan's letter of introduction only once.

"I have to burn this," he informed Haller, who sat smoking opposite him. "Back in a minute." When he returned to sit down again, Haller felt compelled to apologize.

"This is asking a great deal—"

"My understanding is," Riverton interrupted, "that you are to set up a highly secret intelligence unit aimed against the KGB. That is all I will know—or wish to know. Correct?"

"Correct."

Riverton went on speaking rapidly, staring straight ahead as though Haller were not there, and the American listened in fascination. He could almost feel the waves of intense concentration inside Riverton's brain as the Canadian solved problem after problem before Haller had even raised them.

"You need a base that is absolutely safe. Beyond that side door to my left is the suite of rooms I used in the Second World War. They will be at your disposal for as long as you need them. I will immediately have installed electronic devices that will defeat the most sophisticated bugging systems available to the KGB. On the roof of this building is a complex of radio antennae I use to communicate with my network of worldwide companies. I can supply you with the most advanced transmitter. My entire communications system will be available to you."

"We could import our own equipment," Haller began.

"Unwise. Nothing should cross the border. The man whose letter I have just burned suggested supplying funds through a series of untraceable bank accounts." Riverton smiled for a second and then resumed his poker-faced expression. "All accounts can be traced if you dig deep enough. I will put the sum of one million dollars in an account for you to draw on as you see fit—"

"Which will have one day to be repaid," Haller interjected.

"Never. One question. Will personnel of your unit be coming here regularly?"

"I foresee certain people—two or three—arriving at monthly intervals only. They will probably be the same people."

"Warn me the day before if you can. I will change around my receptionists outside—I have offices in other parts of the city. That way the same girl will never see these people twice. . . ."

Installed in Riverton's suite of offices, Haller made a series of phone calls. Harry Wargrave was the first man the American brought into Montreal. Warned in advance that discretion should be observed, the Englishman arrived wearing Canadian clothes and he spoke to the receptionist in a Canadian accent. It was a knack of Wargrave's to pick up in a few days the local accent of whatever part of the world he might be in.

"I need Elsa Lang," the tall, dark-haired Englishman said crisply when Haller had explained the situation. "She will be the courier who brings out the cassettes—a girl attracts less attention. Her father was a British admiral, she speaks French, Italian, and German fluently, she has a lot of nerve, and since she once worked under me with naval intelligence at the Washington Embassy she has top security clearance."

"You will come out of retirement to help, then?" Haller asked as he watched the Englishman closely. Wargrave gave a lop-sided grin, which the American remembered; it normally indicated Wargrave was under stress. "Something's gone wrong?" he inquired quietly.

"When you phoned I was on the verge of marrying an Irish-Canadian girl. I told her a job had cropped up I was considering that would take me away pretty regularly—your job, I was referring to. She flared up and said I stayed home or forget the marriage. So I said we'd forget it. . . ."

"I don't like this, Harry." An exceptionally humane man, Haller was troubled and he lit a cigarette—he was a three-pack-a-day smoker—before he went on. "Maybe if you went back you could make it up with her. God knows, you've had a bellyful of this type of work—"

"You've missed the point," Wargrave snapped tersely. "She had a lucky escape. I was already getting bored—sooner or later I would have got restless for something more exciting than nine-to-five behind a desk. You know me. . . ."

"If you say so. . . ."

The next recruit was Haller's choice—Matt Leroy might be an American, but he had plenty of experience of European underground warfare against the Soviets. And during a stint at the American Embassy in London he had perfected an English accent that enabled him to pass himself off as British. Also he had triggered off the whole operation by bringing back the cassette from Prague.

And there was another detail Haller had not overlooked in connection with Prague. West, the technician who had tested the sealed envelope slipped into Leroy's pocket at the Prague reception for explosives and poison, had already been flown out of Czechoslovakia. At the moment in Washington, West was about to board an aircraft for his next posting—the most remote part of the United States Moynihan could think of. Fairbanks, Alaska.

But Haller still had to interview and approve one of the key people who would form part of the unit operating inside Europe. Wargrave had already received a positive reply to his cable inviting Elsa Lang to fly to Montreal and she was due to arrive that afternoon.

"Elsa is a natural for this one," Wargrave had assured him, but Haller was reserving judgment. An Anglophile, the American wondered whether she would measure up in his eyes.

In London, exactly one week before Harry Wargrave arrived in Montreal, Elsa Lang was driving her Ford Escort automatic from Pinewood Film Studios back to a block of flats on the edge of Regent's Park. She was excited, on top of the world, exceeding the speed limit when she dared, impatient when traffic lights stopped her less than a quarter of a mile from her destination. Glancing to her right, she briefly caught the eye of a young man pulled up alongside her behind the wheel of a Porsche.

"Doing anything tonight, luv?" he called out.

He saw a fair-haired girl of twenty-seven, gray-eyed and with superb bone structure, a hint of hauteur in her expression that immediately aroused his hunter's instinct. Under her powder-blue cashmere sweater firm breasts were silhouetted, and he shrugged regretfully as she turned away and stared at the traffic lights. Then she was turning left away from him and passing Madame Tussaud's waxwork museum. She was almost there; within minutes she would be using the key in her handbag to let herself into Jerry's flat.

It was Friday afternoon, only three o'clock but almost dark—so dark that cars were traveling with their lights on. Elsa glanced at the passenger seat beside her where the black case containing her film makeup kit lay. For a year now she had been chief makeup girl at Pinewood and this was how she had met Jerry Gifford, the production manager she was going to marry. But her glance fell not on the makeup case; affectionately she had looked at the small package tied in silver ribbon, the package that contained the jeweled tiepin that was her engagement present for Jerry.

Parking her car by the curb, she checked the doors, got out holding the makeup case and the package, locked the car, and glanced up at the windows of the fourth-floor flat where Jerry lived. She frowned briefly, then smiled to herself. Curtains were drawn across the windows; he must have woken late and had a hell of a rush to get to Pinewood this morning. He was working on a different film from her and she hadn't seen him all day. Deliberately she hadn't sought him out to let him know her boss had allowed her to leave early. She wanted to be inside the flat when he arrived, to surprise him.

Outside the flat door she inserted the key, turned it, walked half inside, and paused. The stereo was on in the living room, playing a Spanish love melody. Jerry must have got back early. Closing the door quietly behind her, she heard something else above the stereo sound. Voices. From behind the half-open bedroom door. She froze. Her face lost all its color. Without making a sound, she walked slowly toward the door, forcing one foot in front of the other.

She felt she was sleepwalking, that this couldn't be happening. She could recognize both voices now. Jerry's. And the girl was Sheila, the six-foot redhead from Texas, her roommate. Like someone hypnotized, she paused close to the door, listening. Sheila said, "You like it like this?" Then giggled. Elsa felt as cold as ice, heard Jerry use foul, erotic words he had never used in her presence even in bed. Sheila responded with equally filthy language, which didn't so much shock Elsa.

She took one brief look through the door, closed her eyes, and backed quietly away. The bedclothes were all on the floor, the two naked figures were writhing as one. The full shock would come later, she knew. She placed the wrapped package with the tiepin on the living-room table, the package that contained the card carrying the words *For Jerry, from Elsa with all my love.* By its side she dropped her key to the flat. Then she left, quietly closing the door behind her for the last time.

She drove back to her own mews flat in Chelsea on automatic pilot, the flat she shared with Sheila Colston, stopping for traffic lights, moving forward again without being aware of what she was doing. All reflex actions. She still felt terribly cold as she turned into the cul-de-sac, as the wheels wobbled over the cobbles. The mews seemed horribly empty when she got out of the car, but contrarily she was also thankful: she couldn't have faced some meaningless chitchat with one of the neighbors.

Inside the four-room flat—living-dining room, kitchen, two bedrooms—she poured herself a neat scotch, put it to her lips, then poured it down the sink, untouched. Going into her bedroom, she closed the door, took the photo of Jerry, and put it into a drawer. From the same drawer she took the loaded Smith and Wesson and lay down on the bed.

Elsa Lang, twenty-seven years old, her carefully combed fair hair spread over the pillow, lay on the bed staring up at the ceiling, the .38 Smith and Wesson revolver close to her right hand. Before lying down she had made herself up in front of the dressing-table mirror, not really seeing herself at all as she applied the last touch of lipstick. And she had done one more thing before lying down. Emptying the loaded revolver, she had spun the chambers and inserted two bullets at random, then spun the chambers once more.

She was going to aim the muzzle at her temple three times, spinning the chambers after each aim—if she were still alive. And if she had survived after pressing the trigger for the third time she would go on living. Somehow. Which gave her a three-to-one chance. Or did it? She was too keyed up—or too empty, she wasn't sure which—to work out the odds.

At four in the afternoon it was dark inside the bedroom even with the curtains still drawn back. As she lay there, images of her past life came into her distraught mind. Her schooldays at the Godolphin, the exclusive public school near Salisbury. The ridiculous straw boaters with red bands. The navy-blue cloaks, red-lined and with hoods worn when they moved about inside the grounds. She remembered so well the evening she had been late leaving for supper, seeing ahead of her a column of cloaked and hooded figures wending their way from the boarding houses through the twilight toward the school, along the paths between the trees and the grass. Just like a coven of witches, she had thought.

She had hated school, with its lack of privacy in the dormitories at night, the emphasis on the team spirit. Even in those days she had been a loner—and alone—seeing her parents only at vacations. She had never revealed this to her father, Admiral Sir Geoffrey Lang, chief of naval intelligence. And since then she had met so many girls who would have given their back teeth to go to the Godolphin! Including her roommate, Sheila. Her hand clutched the familiar butt of the revolver. Time to press the trigger for the first round.

Later, that god-awful secretarial college where they taught you nothing except how to be a lady. Except that she had perfected her languages. Elsa had a natural talent and liking for foreign languages. Then the never-to-be-forgotten night when she had pleaded with her father only a few months before he had died. Her mother, whom she had never known, had died when she was born.

"So you want me to get you a job in naval intelligence?" he had growled over his bifocals.

"It would be different," she had pleaded without hope.

"Bore the pants off you," he had replied. Then he had

given her one of his rare smiles and hugged her shoulder. "Still, if that's what you want. . . ."

Everything had changed from that moment: life had savor. After a stint at the Admiralty she had earned swift promotion and been attached to the Paris Embassy. She had traveled all over Europe, sometimes acting as a courier, which was very unusual for a girl in those days. Then, out of the blue, had come the posting to Washington—and Harry Wargrave, Commander Harry Wargrave, R.N., who controlled naval intelligence in the United States. Her hand tightened on the butt of the revolver.

It was Harry who had given her the gun after a cipher clerk had been kidnapped from the French Embassy by the KGB. Or so it was assumed: his mutilated body had later been found in a used-car lot. It was Harry who had taken her to the FBI target range and trained her to be a crack shot. She certainly shouldn't miss at this range. . . .

She aimed the muzzle at her temple calmly. The metal felt cold against her skin. She wasn't supposed to possess the weapon—she had no permit. But at the end of her tour of duty in Washington she had flown back with secret papers and diplomatic immunity that bypassed the metal detectors at Kennedy Airport. No one had asked her for the weapon when she had resigned, bored with the idea of working once more at the Admiralty.

"Never aim a gun unless you intend to fire if necessary. . . ."

It was Harry who had told her that. Since leaving Jerry's flat near Regent's Park, Elsa had steeled herself not to cry; now, at the remembrance of Harry Wargrave, of his kindness and friendship, a single tear formed in her right eye, ran down her cheek. Something else he had once said came back to her.

"Life is never a bed of roses. Everyone has their ups and downs. If you get a big down, forget all that public school balls about not showing emotion. All right, do it in private—but let go just once. Cry it out of your system— but never give up. Never! Never!"

She let go of the gun and herself, twisting her slim

body as she sobbed and sobbed into the pillow for all of ten minutes. Then, drained of emotion, she got off the bed and went to the bathroom to clean herself up. This time she looked directly at herself in the mirror. "Get a hold of yourself, you stupid idiot," she told her mirror image.

She emptied the revolver of cartridges before she wrapped it in newspaper and put it into the trash can. And before she did that she broke the firing pin with a hammer so the weapon was useless. The cartridges she would drop into a public mailbox later; harmless, they would be collected by the mailman, who would doubtless hand them to the authorities. Strange that the memory of Harry Wargrave had brought her back to sanity.

Sheila did not return to the flat that night. Instead she phoned Elsa the following morning, her Texan accent nervous, unsure. "Elsa, I'm so sorry—it just happened, I don't know how. . . ."

"I shall be out of the flat between ten and noon," Elsa replied. Her voice was crisp and devoid of emotion. "So you have two hours to get over here, collect your things, get out."

"That's not much time—"

"And leave the rent money on the sideboard," Elsa informed her in the same calm voice. She replaced the receiver, ate a quick breakfast of coffee and toast, and was out of the flat before ten.

The following morning the postman delivered a package. She knew what it contained before she opened it and she dropped the tiepin from Jerry in the trash can—the contents of the previous day, including the revolver, had already been collected by the garbage disposal man. By now the weapon would be pulp in the crusher. There was no note with the tiepin.

"Gutless swine," she murmured.

She had already phoned Pinewood Films, giving them her resignation. She never wished to see the damned place again. Making herself up in front of the mirror, she took a lot of trouble over the process, then surveyed the result. She knew she was attractive to men. And she had made up her mind how she was going to live her life from now on. She was going to play the field, manipulate men, lead them on, and then drop them when they were crazy over her. She was going to be a thoroughgoing bitch, get her own back. It could even be fun—playing the deception game as once she had played it professionally with naval intelligence in Washington.

Above all, she was going away somewhere. Paris? Rome? It didn't make much difference. Five days later the long and cryptic cable from Harry Wargrave arrived, offering her the chance of a job. ". . . Something like the old days," was the only clue he gave her as to its nature.

Within an hour of receiving the cable she was calling at the Midland Bank branch in Piccadilly to collect the money he had cabled her. The Pan Am office was only a few paces from the bank and she immediately booked a first-class seat on the first available flight to New York. The cable had instructed her to fly there first, then take a transfer flight on to Montreal.

"Round-trip or one-way?" the booking clerk asked her.

"A one-way ticket," Elsa replied firmly.

Smartly dressed in a two-piece navy suit and a cream polo-necked sweater, Elsa Lang sat in a chair Haller had drawn up for her alongside his own. It was typical of him that he had not confronted her from behind his desk, that he had introduced an air of intimacy to put her at her ease. Wargrave sat some distance away, staring at the large wall map of Europe.

"Film makeup girl is a long way from naval intelligence," Haller suggested with a broad smile. "Without going into details yet, this is a tough job."

"You mean you haven't even taken the trouble to check my dossier?" Elsa demanded and her tone was sharp. Still staring at the wall map, Wargrave repressed a smile. Haller was going to get more than he had bargained for.

The American met her gray eyes, her smiling face, opened a drawer, and dropped a dossier on the desk. "There it is—I know it backward. But you could have lost your touch," he suggested gently.

"Lost my fanny," Elsa blazed crudely. "And before we go any further, I need to know who I would be working under. You or Harry Wargrave? Even if you decide to take me, I'd then have to decide whether I'd accept the offer—and the question of my boss could be crucial. . . ."

She was still staring hard at Haller and the American was careful not to show she had rocked him back on his heels. My God, he thought, she's checking *me* out, wondering whether *I* measure up. He had no way of knowing what Wargrave had immediately realized: Elsa Lang had weighed up Julian Haller as a man who responded to a challenge, and within minutes of meeting him for the first time.

"You would take all your instructions direct from Wargrave," the American assured her quietly. "Incidentally, I also know my job," he added mildly. "Would it have made a difference had it been otherwise?" he inquired.

"Bet your sweet life it might," she responded. "What do I know about you, Mr. Haller? We might prove incompatible," she added with a quirkish smile. She crossed her very desirable legs and Haller looked at them. "It's a more comfortable position," she remarked. "I'm not trying to sex you up. . . ."

Wargrave turned his head away, almost choked as he repressed a grin. Haller stared at Elsa's legs a little longer, and then he beamed broadly and Elsa chuckled softly. "You'll want to know why I'm interested in returning to my old work, I imagine?" she suggested.

"It would help some," the American admitted. "Cigarette?"

"Not while I'm on the grill, thank you. I had over a year at the film makeup job," she explained carefully. "Once I'd met all the types there were to meet I developed itchy feet, maybe a desire to do something more . . . *meaningful* is an awful word, but"—she smiled ironically —"probably it expressed my meaning."

For the next ten minutes Haller cross-examined the English girl, using every trick in the book to bring to light a weakness, something that might make her a dangerous liability in an emergency. And gradually—when she had indicated that she really wanted the job—he gave her some hint of what she was involving herself in, watching her closely for any sign of doubt or uncertainty.

A past master at the art of probing character, Haller was unable to fault Elsa, whom he was rapidly coming to like—even more important, to trust. With one hand stroking her crossed leg she answered every question directly and with composure, her eyes meeting his levelly, and only once did her hand freeze for a second, a reaction that neither man noticed.

"You've never thought of getting married?" Haller asked casually.

"Often," Elsa replied instantly. "But so far I've never met the right man." She was careful not to glance in Harry Wargrave's direction as she replied.

Haller lit a fresh cigarette and sprang his shock question. "Can you use a gun? You may have to."

"Yes. I'm most familiar with a .38 Smith and Wesson. In Washington, Harry took me to the FBI range and I practiced a lot. At that time the KGB had kidnapped a cipher clerk from the French Embassy—he wanted me to be able to protect myself. . . ."

It was Wargrave, a veteran of Balkan intrigue since his tour of duty in Athens, who had suggested the name for the unit just before flying across the Atlantic to organize the European end with Elsa Lang and Matt Leroy.

"We need a code name for this outfit," Haller had pointed out. "The President will be Bruno. What will we be?"

"Why not the Sparta Ring?" the Englishman had replied. "It has a hard, stoic sound—and these monthly trips to Basel are going to call for something like stoic qualities. But the main thing in its favor is that it has a Greek sound. If ever a whisper of the name reaches the KGB it will divert their attention away from Switzerland."

"Sparta it shall be. . . ."

For the next twelve months the operation flourished. In Basel, Wargrave had organized a backup team for Matt

Leroy. One of them was Peter Neckermann, an ex–police sergeant of the German *Kriminalpolizei* the Englishman knew and trusted. Neckermann played the part of the white-jacketed "steward" who boarded the sleeping car to retrieve the cassettes. Wargrave chose Neckermann's protectors from other men he had known for many years; one was a French Secret Service man who had retired early, the other a Dutchman recommended to him by General Max Scholten, chief of Dutch counterespionage. All three men were dedicated anti-Communists, and none of them knew what the operation was really all about. Wargrave ran Sparta totally as a close-ended unit.

Operating regularly inside Switzerland, he even kept the activities of Sparta a secret from his old friend Colonel Leon Springer, assistant-chief of Swiss counterespionage. Here Wargrave was taking a calculated risk, as he once explained to Haller in Montreal.

"Sooner or later Springer is going to hear of our regular trips to Zürich and Basel. He knows me well. He'll instantly suspect an espionage operation."

"We'll have to risk that," Haller had replied. "We know now beyond any shadow of doubt that the information coming in from Angelo is priceless. It's uncanny—it's almost as though Bruno were sitting in on every major Politburo meeting."

"And Angelo has to be Anatoli Zarubin. . . ."

"From his pictures he looks like a charmer," Elsa interjected as she looked around the windowless room that always gave her a feeling of claustrophobia. "I bet I'd fall for him," she added wickedly with a glance in Wargrave's direction.

"If a girl isn't fussy. . . ."

Despite Angelo's warning in the first cassette there had inevitably been speculation about Angelo's identity behind the closed doors of the room adjoining Riverton's. "He is the most civilized and cosmopolitan member of the Politburo," Wargrave had pointed out. "Everyone who has met him finds him reasonable."

"He's the polished idol the Kremlin wheels out every time it seems the West might be getting suspicious of the détente racket," Haller growled. "That's his main job—to throw smoke in our eyes."

"Getting back to Colonel Springer," Wargrave persisted, "I may one day feel the time has come to contact him. I don't have to give him even a whisper of what is happening."

"Use your own judgment—the European end is yours."

The American's final comment was a reference to the fact that he never left Montreal—that the whole European operation was always handled by Wargrave, Elsa, and Matt Leroy. Wargrave had stood up to leave when Haller indicated that it was not his final remark. His expression was grim as he told them of an incident in Moscow that had been reported to him by an undercover Russian agent working for the West in a minor capacity.

"Anatoli Zarubin—whom we are damned sure now is Angelo—often visits the Moscow railyards in his position as minister of trade and commerce—with the apparent purpose of speeding up dispatch of goods to the West. They need the hard currency, of course—so his visits would seem normal."

"Which is when he slips the cassettes inside the sleeping car on the Moscow Express," Elsa pointed out.

It had been three o'clock in the afternoon of Monday, November 1, in Moscow when the incident Haller told them about had taken place. The temperature was ten degrees below freezing point, it was as black as night, and the rails were coated with ice as Anatoli Zarubin, heavily muffled in a fur coat and hat, walked alone in the marshaling yards alongside the Moscow Express minutes before it was due to move into the station prior to its departure for the West.

Climbing aboard the sleeping car that two days later would reach Basel in Switzerland, Zarubin began inspecting the compartments. It was known in the Politburo that he had a fetish for neatness and cleanliness. "The express is a mobile propaganda weapon," he often explained. "The West will judge us by our trains and civil aircraft they see." Zarubin continued toward the front of the sleeping car, then stopped. A figure, no more than a glimpse of a shadow, had emerged from a compartment ahead and slipped off the coach. Walking more quickly, Zarubin arrived at the car door, which was swinging in the dark. He looked out and froze with shock.

A shot rang out, deafeningly loud in the silence and the dark, then a second shot. So close that for a moment Zarubin thought he had been hit. He dropped to the track and crouched low. To his right a man walking with a lamp doused the light and vanished behind a line of freight cars. Still crouched low, Zarubin was suddenly blinded by a powerful torch shone direct in his face. He waited for the third shot that would kill him.

"Oh . . . it's you, Zarubin. . . ."

The voice was that of General Sergei Marenkov, head of the KGB. "Come over here and look at this," Marenkov continued grimly. Still dazed, Zarubin walked slowly alongside the express to where Marenkov stood over a crumpled body with his pistol still in his hand. The KGB chief shone the torch down onto the face of the man he had shot. "It's Starov of the GRU," he explained in a hard voice. "He's a saboteur—see that grenade in his hand? He was going to attach it to the coach." Marenkov frowned suddenly and looked at Zarubin. "What were you doing here?"

"Checking the coach."

The man with the lamp neither of them had seen was now over three hundred meters away, already wording in his mind the report that would later reach Washington before it was passed on to Julian Haller.

Inside the room on the tenth floor of the Baton Rouge Building in Montreal, Wargrave had listened in silence as Haller finished his account of the incident at the Moscow marshaling yard. "It could have been a coincidence—Marenkov being there at the same time as Zarubin."

"Except that I've had two other reports of our friend General Marenkov poking his nose around those freight yards on other occasions," the American replied. "There's a time limit on Angelo's survival and that time could be running out."

The next date for collection of another cassette was Wednesday, December 1. It would be the twelfth cassette Sparta was picking up. On Tuesday, November 30, Harry Wargrave was staying at the Hotel Schweizerhof in Zürich. And at that moment he had no inkling that this cassette would contain the news of Marshal Gregori Prachko's Operation Thunderstrike military maneuvers, the news that would decide President Moynihan to send overnight to West Germany the huge airborne force.

Elsa Lang and Matt Leroy were already in Basel, staying once again at a different hotel in the city ready for the morning pickup. On Wargrave's instructions they never stayed at the same hotel twice. And the Englishman had just taken a serious decision: he was going to see Colonel Leon Springer of Swiss counterespionage. Was it instinct that prompted the decision? Or was it Haller's recent reference to the fact that soon they could be coming to the end of the Sparta road? He wasn't sure. He just knew that when he had followed his instinct in the past he had always been proved right.

It was noon when he entered Springer's small, cramped office on the second floor of the building that overlooks the river Limmat. He had phoned from the hotel and the Swiss had made an immediate appointment. He rose from behind his desk and came forward to shake the Englishman's hand.

"Welcome to Switzerland, Harry. Times are a little less tense since last we met," he commented in excellent English.

Thirty-three years old, Colonel Leon Springer was the very opposite of the cold, precise Swiss so often caricatured in newspaper reports. Slimly built, he had the nose of a predatory hawk, smiled constantly, and was fond of cracking jokes during moments of crisis. Smartly dressed in a dark blue suit, the Swiss was amiable and talkative, a man who moved restlessly and chain-smoked. Fingering his neat mustache with one hand, he poured coffee with the other.

His reference to the last time they had met recalled to Wargrave a major incident in his career as he sat down in a comfortable leather armchair and accepted the cup of strong coffee. At that time he had helped Springer track down a Communist spy ring operating out of Geneva. Three of the Soviet agents had died, two of them shot by Wargrave himself.

"I'm passing through Switzerland now and again on business, Leon," he remarked. "I should have called on you earlier."

Sitting back in the swivel chair behind his desk, Springer again stroked his mustache as he gazed out of the window where snow fell gently over the ancient buildings and spires of one of Europe's most beautiful cities. Wargrave observed the gesture with a sense of heightened alertness; it indicated the Swiss was under some stress. "So you have deserted your old love for the more peaceful world of business?" Springer inquired. Do I detect a hint of skepticism, Wargrave wondered.

"Not so peaceful," he replied easily. "Business can be just as wild a jungle and the same law applies—the survival of the fittest." He sipped his scalding coffee. "The only difference is they don't shoot at you—not often, anyway."

"The survival of the fittest?" the Swiss repeated. "And vis-à-vis the Soviets, that is a lesson many of our Western politicians still have to learn—before it is too late, I pray fervently. At least I thank God that Joseph Moynihan is sitting in the White House."

"I couldn't agree more. . . ." Wargrave switched the conversation, anxious to steer it away from Moynihan. "How is life for you these days? Brigadier Traber is thriving, I hope?"

Springer's sharp eyes blinked: the Englishman had given him just the opening he was seeking. "I will pass on to him your best wishes." He paused. "We would both thrive more if we could solve a very worrying problem. I suppose that if I asked you to give us a hand with it, you would say you were retired—to the world of business," he added significantly.

"Just spell out the problem, Leon."

"You have so many contacts, Harry, so many people who are indebted to you from the old days. Could you still call on one of them to come here and investigate a tricky situation?" He paused again. "It is only fair to say the risk could be total—and I would not want to know the name of the person you chose. . . ."

"I said spell it out."

Springer's manner underwent a change. As he leaned forward across the desk, the eyes above the beaky nose became alert and intense." "We have reason to believe a major Communist cell is operating in the strategic Andermatt area. One of my men checking in that town was recently found dead inside the Rhône Glacier—inside one of the ice tunnels. He appeared to have died from natural causes—until my forensic people found the tiny hypodermic puncture at the base of his skull. We still don't know what poison was injected."

"But it proves something is going on up there in the mountains?"

"Exactly. The trouble is I need a fresh eye to look over the Andermatt area—a non-Swiss who, because he is a stranger, may see something we would overlook. It is not something I would press you to do—even more since it will involve calling in one of your friends—"

"Consider it done."

Wargrave swallowed his hot coffee in three gulps. He had no wish to linger with the shrewd colonel, much as he liked him. Too much conversation could be dangerous. When he left Springer's headquarters he was well satisfied: he had explained his frequent visits to Switzerland and had cemented his relationship with the Swiss counterespionage organization by agreeing to help it.

The moment the Englishman had left the building, Springer called his chief, Brigadier Arthur Traber, on the scrambler phone. On that day Traber was visiting his headquarters in Bern, the Swiss capital. "Any development on the Andermatt front?" he inquired as he heard Springer's voice.

"Wargrave has at last called on me. I knew he would—sooner or later. He's covering his frequent visits here. The important thing is he has agreed to send someone to Andermatt."

"Any idea who?" Traber asked.

Springer chuckled before he replied. "You don't really expect that he told me that, do you, sir? He's a lone wolf, which is what makes him so effective. He's capable of keeping three balls in the air at once without anyone knowing. But he may well succeed where we have failed —he's done it before." Springer chuckled again. "He told me he was in business these days."

"The intelligence business?"

"I'm certain of it. What I don't understand is these monthly visits to Zürich. He arrives from Montreal on the first—or the last—Tuesday of each month, takes a room—always at a different hotel—spends the night here and catches the Wednesday flight back to Montreal. Why Montreal?"

"You tell me."

"I can't. Our people at the airport check him in and out, and that's it. But I suspect it could be high-level, very high-level indeed. . . ."

Wargrave went back to the Hotel Schweizerhof by a devious route in case he was being followed. It was unlikely, but long ago deviousness had become second nature. Taking a cab to the Quaibrücke—the last bridge before the lake—he paid off the driver, waited until a tram was about to leave, and jumped aboard at the last moment. A few minutes later he jumped off again just as the automatic doors were closing and walked rapidly up the Bahnhofstrasse to the Hotel Schweizerhof.

Immediately when he reached his room he placed a long-distance call. He had to wait a long time; he smoked several cigarettes while the call was routed through a series of European exchanges. At three in the afternoon—lunch had been sent up to his room—the phone rang. He

53

spent less than three minutes talking in a roundabout way clearly understood by the person at the other end of the line. "Andermatt, yes," were the last words he spoke before replacing the receiver. And even Wargrave did not realize that he had just made one of the most decisive phone calls of his career.

It was Tuesday, November 30, when Wargrave made his phone call. On the following morning, Wednesday, December 1, Elsa Lang took the twelfth cassette from Peter Neckermann, the white-jacketed "steward," in the crowded Basel station only seconds before Neckermann was abducted by the two KGB men—the men who ended up inside a cabin trunk trapped in the Rhine Falls at Schaffhausen.

And it was this twelfth cassette that carried Angelo's urgent warning about Marshal Prachko's Operation Thunderstrike. It was this cassette that decided President Joseph Moynihan to dispatch overnight to West Germany the huge airborne force in the giant C-5A transport planes as a warning to the Soviet Politburo. The repercussions of the twelfth cassette were enormous and worldwide.

The emergency meeting of the Soviet Politburo was summoned for eight o'clock in the evening, Moscow time, of Friday, December 3. One by one the fleet of black Zil limousines turned into the Kremlin gateway. Each driver, a KGB man, wore a flat, short-brimmed fedora hat and a heavy blue overcoat. Leonid Sedov, First Secretary, was the earliest arrival, coming from his apartment in the nine-story building at 26 Kutuzov Prospekt. General Sergei Marenkov, who occupied the apartment above Sedov, was next to arrive, followed a few minutes later by Anatoli Zarubin, minister of trade and commerce.

The last to arrive, at three minutes to eight, was Marshal Gregori Prachko, as always in full uniform, his insignia of rank glittering on his shoulder boards, his chest ablaze with his rows of medals. Why did he always arrive last, the cynical Leonid Sedov wondered. To make a dramatic entrance, of course. He opened the meeting the

54

moment Prachko had eased his great bulk into his chair.

It was an acrimonious, bitter meeting as the moderates clashed violently with the hard-liners, and for once the moderates had the ammunition to launch an all-out attack on Marshal Prachko and his supporters. For a whole hour Prachko listened in unaccustomed silence as the offensive was mounted against him.

"You have provoked the Americans into taking action. . . . The morale of the Western capitalist countries has been lifted to unheard-of heights. . . . You have weakened the chances of our comrades in France and Italy infiltrating their way into the governments of those countries. . . . Your saber-rattling has backfired, has put us back a whole decade. . . ."

Prachko, no mean political tactician, deliberately waited until the offensive was petering out and, like an expert general, launched his counterattack. He made a great show of opening a folder and extracting a typed report, which he placed before him on the highly polished table. As he began speaking, the lights from the chandeliers overhead reflected off his medals.

"I have here a highly secret report prepared by Colonel Igor Sharpinsky, deputy to my comrade General Marenkov, who also has a copy. As you know, Colonel Sharpinsky acts as liaison officer between the GRU and the KGB —he therefore felt the subject was so dangerous to the security of the state that he should supply this report to me—"

"One moment!" It was Leonid Sedov, First Secretary, seated at the head of the long table, who intervened. Sedov, sixty years old, was a well-built man of medium height with thick graying hair and an oddly shaped jaw— it was rumored he had recently been operated on for some undisclosed illness. He turned to General Marenkov, head of the KGB, who sat watching Prachko from under his bushy eyebrows with an impassive stare. "General Marenkov, would you prefer to deal with this report yourself?"

"I have no objection to the marshal revealing its contents. As he has just said, its gravity can hardly be exaggerated."

"Then I will continue," Prachko growled. "Operation Thunderstrike was carried out hundreds of miles from our border with the NATO forces—so even under the terms of so-called détente it was not necessary to inform NATO of the operation. And there was no way in which American orbiting satellites could guess the true purpose of the maneuvers. They cannot yet read signposts from the air," he went on sarcastically. "And yet within days of its completion the American President reacts by sending a huge reinforcement of troops to Europe—"

"Excuse me," Sedov interrupted, "but I cannot see where all this is leading. Could you get to the point?"

"Only someone sitting at this table could have informed Moynihan."

Having dropped his bomshell, Prachko sat back as all hell broke loose.

"That is slanderous, mad," Anatoli Zarubin protested.

"You go too far," observed Pavel Suslov, the thin-faced party theoretician. He also, like Zarubin and Marenkov, had attended the Prague reception at the American Embassy over a year earlier when the original cassette had been slipped into Matt Leroy's pocket. A quiet man, his presence had largely gone unnoticed. Sedov, who spent half his life preserving the balance between the moderates and the hard-liners, intervened again.

"You will need far more evidence than that to back up what you have just alleged," he said grimly.

"It is here." Prachko produced a thick wad of papers out of his folder. "Sharpinsky has produced a meticulous analysis of our actions and American reactions over the past year. Time and again Moynihan has anticipated our moves. It is all here and points to only one conclusion— a top-level informer."

Marenkov leaned forward. "I have read the report," he said abruptly. "I find it not only disturbing—I find it convincing. I propose a task force should be formed at once to investigate this matter—that it should be directed by the First Secretary, myself, and Marshal Prachko—"

"We should all have access to that report," Zarubin snapped.

Sedov intervened for the third time. "I propose that General Marenkov's suggestion should be put to the vote."

By a narrow majority Marenkov's proposal was carried. The meeting broke up in some confusion and members were still arguing as they left the room. Three men only remained behind—Leonid Sedov, Marshal Prachko, and Marenkov. The hunting down of Angelo had begun.

5

Montreal

"This time I want you to take great care—Sparta is soon going to blow up in our faces. I can smell trouble coming," Julian Haller went on as he warned Wargrave and Elsa in the room next to William Riverton's office in the Baton Rouge Building.

It was Monday, January 3. On Wednesday, January 5, they would be in Switzerland again to pick up the thirteenth cassette from Angelo. Elsa Lang felt sure it was the weather that was depressing Haller. Europe was now reeling under the worst winter for over forty years as blizzards raged and one airport after another was closed down. She tried to joke the American out of his black mood.

"Unlucky thirteen? I didn't know you were superstitious, Julian. And you an agnostic—shame on you."

"Fly over in that frame of mind and you'll fall flat on your face," Haller snapped. He regretted the outburst as he saw Elsa's expression. "Look, I've been in this game a long, long time. I can sense when an operation that's gone smoothly for months could turn sour."

"He's got a point, Elsa," Wargrave warned. "Those

two KGB types turning up in Basel last time weren't a good omen."

"Matt dealt with them," Elsa flared. "We knew it wasn't going to be easy right from the start."

"I admire your spirit," Haller said quietly. "But I've had more reports that Marenkov keeps checking the Moscow railyards—and that is one tough, very smart professional. He's onto something." He leaned forward over his desk and spoke very emphatically. "He's found the end of a piece of string and he'll go on and on till it leads him to something. We're sitting over four thousand miles away from General Sergei Marenkov and I can feel him moving, probing."

'We'll watch it," Wargrave said. "Wednesday afternoon we'll be back with another cassette. Just don't sit here worrying your guts out. O.K.?"

The next forty-eight hours were a nightmare for Julian Haller. His wife, Linda, had come up to Montreal from New York and he was glad about that—and sorry at the same time. A cool, soothing woman, Linda Haller made regular visits to the Canadian city, where Riverton had arranged a contract with a fashion firm to explain her visits. She had no idea of the existence of the Sparta Ring and had long ago accepted that there were many things her husband couldn't discuss with her.

"There's a crisis coming up, isn't there?" she asked him in the middle of the night when she got up and found him helping himself to a glass of milk from the refrigerator.

"Let's just say at the moment I'm not having the time of my life."

"You'll solve it. You have before."

"Other people are involved. Good people."

"Then I'm not going to say try and get some sleep, because I know you won't. Let's sit up and play Scrabble."

"You always beat me," he grumbled.

She wrapped an arm around his neck. "Tonight I'll let you win. . . ."

Wednesday afternoon the flight from Zürich was delayed by bad weather. Outwardly composed, Haller was worried stiff. He did something he had never done before: he went into Riverton's office and asked if they could chat to pass the time. The millionaire waved a hand to a chair and began talking about his experiences in the Second World War. He told the American a story about how he had once sat up thirty-six hours waiting for news of a girl who had been parachuted into France and hadn't sent the signal reporting her safe arrival.

"I nearly went mad with the waiting," Riverton went on quietly, not looking at Haller, "but the waiting is always the worst in this business. I was fond of this particular girl—she had a lot of guts and a great sense of humor. She was a little like the girl who comes here each month. . . ."

Haller was astonished. Without a word being exchanged the Canadian seemed to have read his thoughts, and Haller also had grown fond of Elsa Lang. "What happened to the girl you are talking about?" he asked.

"After thirty-six hours the signal arrived—she was safe. Incidentally, that girl of yours came in here one day and we had a long talk. Nothing about her work, of course," he added quickly. "Did you know that just before she came over here to join you she was on the verge of getting married?"

"No." Haller had not even realized Elsa had ever talked to Riverton. Thinking about it, he wasn't entirely surprised: Riverton was one of those rare men people confided in; it was something indefinable in his personality.

"She had a raw deal," Riverton went on. "She was very much in love with this film production manager. I gather he was older than her—but she's the sort of girl who'd be attracted to older men. Everything was fixed—wedding date, where they would spend their honeymoon. Then she arrived at his flat early one evening. The fool hadn't locked the door and the bell was on the blink. She walked in and found him in bed with her best friend.

That's why she accepted whatever job you gave her—to get the experience out of her mind."

"And I never knew. . . ."

"Would you have taken her on if you had? She's clever—she kept it quiet." Riverton turned to stare hard at the American. "And if you ever let her know I've told you I'll kill you with my bare hands. But bear it in mind if your operation gets tough." He looked up as Elsa Lang came into the room, followed by Wargrave.

"Sorry to burst in on you," Elsa said quickly, "but the girl outside said you were alone and we knew Julian would be worried. . . ." She stopped as Riverton answered his intercom. "It's all right, Miss Russell, I was expecting these people."

Haller was already leading the way through the side door into the concealed suite of offices. Closing the door, he swung around. "Ed never phoned in your arrival from the airport."

"There's some kind of foul-up with the telephone system," Wargrave explained as he took the thirteenth cassette from Elsa and started inserting it into the tape recorder. "And our flight was badly delayed—in Europe only Milan, Zürich, London, and Schiphol airports are still open. The weather is unbelievable. A blizzard is raging over most of the continent. I hope to hell it's quietened down in time for our February trip."

Haller began organizing the coffee percolator for Elsa, who had taken off her fur cap and dark wig. There were flecks of snow on her raincoat even though she had dashed from the car into the Baton Rouge Building. The American poured a large scotch for Wargrave and placed the glass beside the tape recorder.

"Any interference this time at Basel?" he asked quietly.

"Not a quiver," Elsa replied as she sank into an armchair. "The whole operation ran as smooth as silk." She lit a cigarette while Haller poured coffee. "Thanks, Julian, I could drink it by the gallon—it is cold, cold out there. We saw the Saint Lawrence frozen solid as we came in." She took a gulp of the coffee. "That's much better. I wonder what Angelo has to tell us this time. . . ."

She stopped talking as the familiar, hoarse voice began speaking. Before Angelo had spoken for a minute she froze despite the warmth of the room.

"My usefulness here has come to a sudden end. . . . I must ask you to make immediate arrangements to airlift me out of Romania this coming Saturday, January 8, without fail. . . . The emergency is total. . . ."

Wargrave stopped the recording and stared at Haller, who calmly lit a fresh cigarette; it was an instinctive reaction to take the tension out of the situation. Elsa had lost all her color; Wargrave stood by the recorder with both hands splayed on his hips, his cheekbones very marked, his eyes half closed as his mind raced. "Bruno is available, I assume," he said quietly.

"Bruno is not available," Haller told him, referring to President Moynihan by his code name. "He flew suddenly to Peking today. He won't be back for a week, so we're on our own."

"So it's up to the Turtle," Elsa said with a forced smile. The Turtle was the nickname she had invented for Julian Haller because he wasn't afraid to stick his neck out, to take major decisions without referring them back to the White House.

"Looks like it," the Turtle agreed. "As one of our revered past Presidents once said, the buck stops here." He looked up at Wargrave. "Set the machine going again— let's hear the worst."

Angelo continued reporting: evidence had accumulated over the months that an informer existed at a high level; finally the source of the leak had been narrowed down to someone inside the Soviet Politburo. A triad of three men—Leonid Sedov himself, Marshal Prachko, and General Marenkov—had been entrusted with the tracking down of the informer. And just as had happened with the first cassette received a year earlier, Angelo again laid down precise instructions as to how he should be rescued.

". . . an airstrip just west of Bucharest . . . map reference . . . landing time for rescue aircraft 11:30 A.M. local Romanian time, repeat local Romanian time

. . . cooperation of certain Romanian personnel assured . . . expert pilot required . . . confirm agreement this arrangement by playing Dave Brubeck's *Take Five* Voice of American program 1700 hours Moscow time Thursday, January 6, repeat Thursday, January 6. . . . . Any delay will be quite fatal. . . ."

The recording ended with a repetition of the warning that any delay would be fatal. Elsa reached over and took a large swallow from Wargrave's untouched glass of scotch. The color came back into her face as she spoke slowly, determined to keep her voice steady.

"Today is Wednesday. He asks to be airlifted out Saturday. It's impossible."

"It presents difficulties," Haller agreed.

"Difficulties?" Elsa almost choked.

Wargrave had said nothing as he walked across to the wall behind Haller's desk where a large-scale map of Europe hung. Using the ruler he had taken from the Turtle's desk, he began making measurements, checking distances. One distance he checked carefully was the flight route from Milan to Bucharest; then, using a flexible rule, he double-checked the same distance on a large globe in the corner. Tapping the rule against his teeth, he hummed a little tune while he made calculations on a scratch pad, then looked up at Haller. "I need an up-to-date European rail timetable—and all the airline timetables."

"Will do."

Haller disappeared into a room beyond that Elsa and Wargrave had never entered. Inside sat a Canadian ex-seagoing radio operator Riverton had found for Haller, a man whom the millionaire knew as utterly trustworthy and who had once worked for Canadian intelligence. On one table rested a transmitter, on another the coding machine Haller personally operated. As an added security precaution the Canadian had never been permitted to see Wargrave or Elsa. In the room Haller had just left Elsa was arguing with the Englishman.

"Wednesday today, Saturday he expects to be taken

out—three days and we're here in North America. You'll never manage it."

"In seven days the Israelis planned and executed the Entebbe operation. We have cooperation at the Bucharest end—so in three days it should be possible." He gave a lop-sided grin. "It damn well has to be possible."

He spent the next few minutes studying the timetables Haller had brought back, making more notes on his scratch pad. Haller watched him in silence, smoking a fresh cigarette and drinking a glass of milk. The Englishman stretched his aching shoulders and looked at the American. "It will be a close-run thing, as one of our more celebrated generals once said, but I can do it. At the moment the only airports in Europe still open are London, Schiphol near Amsterdam, Zürich, Milan, and Vienna. According to the met people, Milan may close down soon and there's a question mark over Zürich, so we may have to bring Angelo out by train—"

"By train!" Haller was appalled. "For God's sake, we have to fly him out here direct to the States. If it is to be done, it is to be done quickly or not at all," he paraphrased Shakespeare.

Wargrave shook his head. "You've never been to Europe bar one brief trip to London, have you, Julian? Like so many Americans you think of movement only in terms of by car or by flying. In Europe they have the finest train system in the world, expresses that move at eighty miles an hour. The Atlantic Express may be the answer."

"I don't like it," Haller snapped.

"You don't have to—you may just have to accept it if Milan and Zürich close down at the wrong moment."

"And if they do?" Haller demanded belligerently. "What's with this Atlantic Express?"

"The position that may face us is quite simple," Wargrave explained. "The blizzards raging over Europe have bypassed one country only—Holland. So we can count on Schiphol Airport staying open. The Atlantic Express leaves Milan late in the afternoon for its ultimate destination—Amsterdam. It passes through Zürich, so if Milan is closed to flying and Zürich stays open we can fly out Angelo from there."

"And supposing Zürich is closed down?"

"Then it's the long haul aboard the express all the way to Amsterdam." Exasperation began to show in Wargrave's voice. "For Christ's sake, I can get total cooperation from every security service in each country the express passes through. Face it, Julian, that train may be the only way to get him out fast. And we'll need aircraft standing by at both Zürich and Schiphol to fly Angelo to the States. Any more damned roadblocks you want to put in my way?"

Haller's quick mind had digested the information Wargrave had provided and, characteristically, he immediately changed tack.

"Cool it, Harry. Point taken. I don't know how I'm going to do it in the time, but I'll have a Boeing standing by at Schiphol, another one at Zürich."

Wargrave's expression was grim as he made his next demand. "I'll want full control of the whole operation," he warned.

"On a day-to-day basis I'm willing to concede—"

"*Full* control," Wargrave repeated. "Europe is my backyard."

"O.K.," the American agreed. He tapped a file on his desk. "And I know why it's Bucharest. On Saturday a Soviet delegation is visiting Romania to try and patch up differences between the two countries. The makeup of the delegation is interesting. . . ." He drank more milk slowly.

"Oh, come on," Elsa protested, "don't keep us in suspense. Who is in the delegation?"

"The report reached me this morning. Led by Anatoli Zarubin; another delegation member is Pavel Suslov, the Soviet party theoretician. Saint Marx himself."

"Surprise, surprise," Elsa commented. She glanced at Wargrave. "How the hell do we get Angelo from Bucharest to Milan?"

"By airlift," the Englishman explained. "First we borrow a Hawker-Siddeley 125 jet from a wealthy Italian playboy I know—oddly enough he's a violent anti-Communist. It's about eight hundred miles to Bucharest from Milan, another eight hundred back again. The HS 125 has a 2,600-mile range—which leaves plenty of fuel to spare."

Haller was twisted around in his chair, staring at the wall map of Europe. "Why not fly Angelo direct to Zürich?"

"Because it would take me too close to the Hungarian border—the Russians might send up interceptors to shoot us down. Also, the weather being what it is, I can't risk crossing the Swiss Alps."

The American was still staring at the map. "If Zürich Airport does close down, it's going to be a damned long train haul clear across Europe."

Wargrave nodded and looked grim as he glanced at Elsa. "It will be a nightmare—and literally, because the express will travel through the night. I suppose you both realize that once Angelo is out of the Balkans General Marenkov will mobilize the entire KGB–GRU underground apparatus to kill him before we can fly him out to the States? It will be like threading our way through a minefield. But I still say it can be done. Damn it, it has to be done."

Haller had not overlooked Wargrave's glance at Elsa. "It won't be necessary for Elsa to come on this trip," he said firmly.

"Like hell it won't," Elsa replied quietly. "I was in at the beginning—I'm going to be in at the end."

"It's up to her," Wargrave suggested mildly. "But she could come in very handy."

"I forbid it," Haller snapped.

"I thought I had full control," Wargrave remarked. "And this is no time to break up the team. Incidentally, we have to fly straight back to Europe tonight." This time he didn't glance at Elsa, who kept her expression blank; she was still feeling the effects of jet lag from their flight across the Atlantic a few hours earlier. "There's an Air Canada flight this evening that gets us into Schiphol tomorrow afternoon," Wargrave went on. "From there we fly on to Zürich and then on to Milan, where we touch down tomorrow, Thursday evening."

"Isn't that rushing it a bit?" Haller inquired.

"It gives me Friday in Milan to organize final arangements. And I can do that better from Europe than I can from here. Saturday morning I fly the jet to Bucharest to pluck Angelo up from the airstrip."

"You're flying the jet yourself?"

"I've flown that very machine several times before on trips with my playboy contact."

"I hear the Italian girls are quite something," Elsa murmured.

"And he has the pick of the bunch," Wargrave assured her. He tore the used sheets off his scratch pad and looked at Haller. "Now, we have to use every minute before we catch that evening flight to Schiphol. I've got a whole series of cables that have to be encoded and sent to various European security chiefs alerting them— Scholten in The Hague, Franz Wander of the German BND, Colonel Springer in Zürich, and Colonel Molinari of SIFAR in Milan."

"Alerting them?" the American queried.

"That I may need their help—just that. Nothing about Angelo, of course. Not yet, anyway. They may have to know after I've got him out of Romania. . . ." He was writing on the pad as he spoke. "This could develop into something pretty murderous if we have to bring Angelo all the way by train to Schiphol. And don't forget the Voice of America to play that record *Take Five* to warn Angelo we're coming for him."

"As if I would." Haller leaned back in his chair, looked at the ceiling, and said something that stopped Wargrave scribbling his signals. "There's one more little detail I omitted to mention. A third member of the Soviet Politburo is accompanying that delegation to Bucharest. . . ."

"That's right, save the best bit till last," Elsa joked.

"General Sergei Marenkov, head of the KGB."

2

Escape Route

6

Schiphol, Zürich, Milan

Leaving Montreal aboard Air Canada Flight 866, which departed at 9:35 P.M. on Wednesday, January 5, Wargrave, Haller, and Elsa crossed the Atlantic overnight. At London Airport they changed to their connecting KLM Flight 128, which took them on to Schiphol outside Amsterdam. For Elsa—as for Wargrave—it was the second time she had crossed the ocean in twenty-four hours and her mind was dizzy with fatigue.

"I don't think my internal clock will ever tell the right time again," she remarked to Julian Haller, who sat alongside her as they approached the Dutch coast.

"You should have got some sleep."

"Very funny, Turtle," she replied acidly. "I damn near woke you up to share my misery. You slept like a dog."

"Always do," Haller replied complacently.

Elsa peered out of the window to look down on Holland as the plane lost height. The flat landscape was barely streaked with snow, as though some giant had scrawled chalk marks across the fields. But there was a fierce wind coming in off the North Sea that was hurling giant waves against the dikes. As she looked down she saw drifts like white smoke, which were wave spume caught up in the wind. Two rows behind them, Harry Wargrave occupied a corridor seat where he could keep an eye on his companions. Then the warning lights came on, seat belts were fastened, and the plane was landing.

General Max Scholten, chief of Dutch counterespionage, was waiting for Wargrave in the security office at the airport and the two men met alone. "Big trouble?" the Dutchman inquired as he warmly shook Wargrave's hand.

"In a word, yes. How are things here?"

"The situation could become explosive—literally," the counterespionage chief replied as he lit a cigar.

General Scholten, one of Wargrave's closest friends, was a small, sixty-year-old man who looked ten years younger. Plump-figured, with a comfortable paunch, he had a cherubic, pink-complexioned face, twinkling blue eyes, and the cheerful smile of a contented man. His cherubic appearance had been the downfall of more than one spy he had amiably interrogated until he had caught his target in a contradiction. His appearance also concealed the fact that he was the most ruthless anti-Communist security chief in Europe. "You do not converse with a viper," he had once told Wargrave in his impeccable English. "You creep up behind it and chop its head off with an ax."

Wargrave glanced around the bare room, which held only a table and two hard-backed chairs. The interrogation room, he guessed. "What explosive situation?" he asked.

"I have a whisper—very reliable—that the Geiger Group is about to cross into Holland. I have already alerted the Venlo Team." He puffed at his cigar. "The trouble is it is only too easy to cross the border into Holland. . . ."

"They're bad news," Wargrave commented.

The Geiger Group of terrorists had created havoc in West Germany during the past year. Banks had been robbed, hostages taken, a leading German politician kidnapped; they had even attempted to blow up a major power station. And all in the name of the movement of World Freedom and Revolution, whatever that might mean. Wargrave doubted whether the terrorists even knew themselves.

"I think they are financed by the KGB," Scholten remarked quietly. "By remote control, of course. The problem is to prove it. That would plaster mud all over Comrade Sedov's face."

"Why are they coming here?"

"The Germans have made things too hot for them—so they move on to what they hope will be a softer target. I would dearly love to get them in the sunsights of the Venlo Team." Scholten was referring to the special team of snipers he had personally organized for just such an eventuality. "But you haven't come here to listen to my problems. What are yours?"

"We are over here to bring out a key anti-Communist agent," Wargrave said carefully. "We may bring him aboard the Atlantic Express. I can tell you more later with coded signals—we'll use the Scarab system."

"A big fish?" Scholten asked casually. "Or do I talk too much at this stage?"

"A big fish—one that could draw a lot of KGB fire because of the information he is carrying."

Scholten's blue eyes gleamed. "If you bring out the Soviet underground apparatus in an attempt to assassinate him, that could give us a unique chance to chop off the viper's head."

"As long as mine doesn't get chopped off in the process, you bloodthirsty old bastard," Wargrave said amiably. "And the plane—"

"Your American friends' Boeing 707 landed ten minutes ago—just ahead of your own flight. It is now at a remote part of the airport under heavy guard. And now, since your Swissair flight for Zürich does not depart until 1640, perhaps we could have a drink with your friends—if it is not breaking security. I would like to meet that attractive girl. . . ."

Wargrave was amused. He had left the aircraft alone and Haller and Elsa were now waiting in the transfer lounge. Scholten's eyes twinkled. "I saw her glance back at you in a certain way when you were coming down the aircraft steps. She likes you very much."

"Let's go and have that drink—with my friends," replied Wargrave.

In the transfer lounge Haller had just received a message handed to him by an armed courier from the American Embassy in The Hague. Before leaving Montreal, Haller—with no way of communicating in code with President Moynihan—had taken a desperate expedient of phoning a trusted friend in the American Embassy at Ottawa.

He had asked for a simple message to be sent to Moynihan—at that moment flying over the Pacific aboard Air Force One on his way to Peking. The message had read: *Our friend is leaving for fresh woods and pastures new.* It had been signed *Turtle,* the nickname the President knew Elsa Lang had given Haller.

The message had been handed to Moynihan during his first meeting with the Chairman of the People's Republic of China. Towering over the short, tough man who controlled the destinies of over eight hundred million people, the President had instantly understood the message—that it meant Sparta was on its way to bring out Angelo and transport him to the United States.

The news could hardly have arrived at a more opportune moment. Scheduled to spend ten days in China, Moynihan immediately grasped how much the arrival in Washington of Anatoli Zarubin, a senior member of the Soviet Politburo, would impress the hard-headed Chairman—and in the fact that he would be able to reveal that for over a year he had benefited from a direct pipeline into the Kremlin.

Waiting until he was back at the American Embassy, changing for the great banquet to be held that evening in his honor, Moynihan drafted a short reply to The Hague embassy, ordering the ambassador to send it by courier to meet the flight Haller had told him he was taking to Holland. And this was the message Haller was reading while Wargrave was talking with General Scholten.

Timing perfect. But utmost speed essential. Repeat essential. Bruno. Haller's reaction was relief mingled with grimness. The enormous stakes at issue were escalating hourly.

General Scholten's statement that the Geiger Group was about to enter Holland was not entirely accurate. At the moment the Dutchman was talking to Harry Wargrave at Schiphol, Rolf Geiger, the terrorist chief, had already established his headquarters in Amsterdam.

It is still not generally known by the public that most terrorist organizations operating in the West are financed —and often armed—by the Soviet KGB or GRU, however indirect the links may be. And contact was often maintained through East Berlin.

For Soviet Russia the policy paid high dividends. By creating ceaseless ferment in the West it allowed Soviet propaganda to contrast conditions in the West with the "peace" inside Russia, a "peace" maintained by the tight police state control exercised by the vast KGB apparatus. The Geiger Group of terrorists that had carried out so many violent incidents inside the German Federal Republic was a prime example of this policy.

Rolf Geiger posed as a German anarchist, but his real name was Dikran Kikoyan, his real nationality Armenian. Born at Yerevan, midway between Lake Sevan and the Turkish border, he was a dedicated Soviet agent who manipulated his group of terrorists so skillfully that they had not the least inkling they were controlled by the Soviet GRU. And Kikoyan was hardly the public's idea of a terrorist chief.

A small, dapper man in his early fifties, he was lean-faced, with a long nose and a neat dark mustache that matched his carefully trimmed hair. In London he would not have been known as a snappy dresser and he was quite a ladies' man with his courtly manner and capacity for making girls laugh. At this moment he was standing by the third-floor window of an old house in Amsterdam overlooking a canal while he recalled his interview with

Colonel Igor Sharpinsky in East Berlin three weeks earlier.

"It is no longer safe for you to continue operations in the German Federal Republic," the soft-spoken KGB chief had explained. "This alone confirms my decision that you should move on to Holland." He pushed across the table where the two men sat a copy of the West German newspaper *Die Welt*.

"You have to expect casualties," Kikoyan replied almost insolently as he crossed his carefully pressed trouser legs and stared out of the window of the second-floor office of KGB headquarters in East Berlin. God, what a monstrosity the place was, he thought as he gazed at the concrete blockhouses that served as apartment buildings.

"The newspaper," Sharpinsky repeated, his pale eyes gazing blankly from behind his rimless glasses, eyes that terrified most of his subordinates. Kikoyan—Rolf Geiger —was not in the least intimidated by Sharpinsky, whom he disliked intensely. As he had once remarked to his assistant, Erika Kern, "The ghoul makes a vocation of himself, puffed up like a pouter pigeon with his own power." He lit a cigarette as he glanced at *Die Welt*.

The newspaper's headline story was about the Geiger Group's failed attempt to rob a bank in Hamburg. There was a large picture of one of the dead terrorists clad in his sinister "uniform"—his head covered with a woolen ski mask with slits for the eyes, his body clothed in a windcheater and ski pants—all in black. Geiger himself had chosen the uniform as the group's trademark. "The clothes alone create an impression of terror," he had once explained.

"So we move into Holland," Geiger remarked, wiping a speck of cigarette ash from the sleeve of his expensive business suit. "That can be accomplished overnight—I have already foreseen you would decide this and have the necessary contacts in Amsterdam." He tapped his gold-topped cane against a leg of Sharpinsky's desk, which further irritated the Russian. "You have the diamonds I asked you to provide?" He checked his Patek watch.

"The Intourist bus will be leaving soon for Checkpoint Charlie, so we'd better get on with it."

"One thing at a time." Sharpinsky controlled his cold fury with an effort. He would have liked to have disciplined this American dandy severely, but Geiger had been too successful, was too highly regarded by Marshal Gregori Prachko himself. Geiger proceeded to infuriate him even further by taking the words out of his mouth.

"As in the Federal Republic, we have a double task. One"—he tapped his cane hard against the desk leg—"to create havoc and terror with a series of kidnappings of prominent Dutch figures, bank robberies, explosions in The Hague and Amsterdam?"

"Correct," Sharpinsky replied in a distant tone.

"Two, we must reconnoiter strategic objectives ready for sabotage when the Red Army moves. The Maas bridge that carries the main rail link between Belgium and Holland, the dikes which hold back the sea, the Phillips works at Eindhoven . . ." Geiger checked his watch again. "Do I really have to go on? And where are the diamonds?"

Tight-lipped, Sharpinsky opened a drawer, took out a small black cloth bag, and spilled a small fortune in diamonds on the desk. "Thank you," Geiger said with exaggerated politeness. Unscrewing the top of his cane, he pulled out a thin spool of rolled cardboard from the hollow cane; then he extracted several pieces of silk from a pocket, wrapped the diamonds, inserted them inside the cane, and pushed back the cardboard spool before replacing the top of the cane.

"Rather amusing," he remarked. "We use the products of the capitalist system to help destroy it." He did not need Sharpinsky to tell him that the diamonds had been smuggled by a devious route from South Africa via Angola to Moscow.

"Which route are you using to reach Amsterdam?" the Russian asked, still staring at the dapper little man facing him. Geiger's quick dark eyes had hardly met his once since the interview had started, as though to emphasize his contempt for Sharpinsky's attempt to intimidate him.

"From West Berlin I fly to Frankfurt," he replied easily.

"From Frankfurt another flight to Paris—then the Trans-European Express direct to Amsterdam. Customs checks on that train are nonexistent—"

"I do know that." Sharpinsky stood up to indicate the interview was ended, but Geiger was already on his feet, slipping on his Savile Row overcoat. For the first time Geiger stared hard at the Russian, smoothing his mustache with one manicured finger before he spoke. "And I would prefer it if you did not summon me to East Berlin again for a long time. I know you have arranged for the Intourist guides to keep the other tourists from West Berlin in the department store until I rejoin them inconspicuously—but the risk is, in my opinion, unnecessary."

Three weeks later in Amsterdam, Geiger recalled his cold conversation with the KGB deputy chief as he stood by the window gazing across the canal to a line of warehouses opposite, where chains with hooks hung five stories up just above double doors. Once they had been used to haul cargo up inside the warehouses. He swung around quickly as a girl came into the almost dark room.

Erika Kern, an attractive, dark-haired girl with a full figure, was thirty-two and a native of East Germany. Cold-faced—which added to her attractiveness—she was the only other member of the terrorist group who knew it was controlled by the GRU. The rest—"peasants," as Geiger sometimes referred to them—had the idea they were fighting for the world liberation of oppressed peoples—which did include citizens of Russia.

"The diamonds are sold?" she inquired.

"So easily—this is Amsterdam." Geiger pointed to an executive's case on a table, and when she opened it the case was filled with neatly stacked Dutch guilder banknotes—untraceable funds to finance Geiger's activities.

"No more interference from Sharpinsky, then," Erika remarked. Geiger nodded, little knowing how wrong he was—and with no suspicion of the huge emergency already building up.

The great blizzard continued to rage over Europe. On television viewers watched dramatic pictures of the river

Elbe in Germany frozen from bank to bank, watched the snow plows fighting a losing battle in Austria, saw the Swiss skating on Lake Zürich for only the third time this century. And Swissair Fight 793 from Schiphol to Zürich was pure hell. Once over the German border, the DC-9 flew into ceaseless turbulence along with heavy snow. Elsa stopped looking out of the window and Haller stopped reading his novel. Behind them again, Wargrave sat with his hands clasped in his lap as he checked his watch frequently. He had a vital call to make as soon as the plane touched down at Zürich.

Leaving the plane at the airport, he was met by a police official who offered to escort him to Springer, who knew he was coming in on this flight. "Give me a minute," Wargrave said, "I just want to call my fiancée."

Dialing the Andermatt number, he had to wait only a few seconds before the call was answered; he had cabled Andermatt before he had left Montreal. He spoke very quickly, asked a few questions, then gave brief instructions. By his watch the call had lasted less than three minutes. Then he let the policeman take him to Springer.

He gave the Swiss colonel exactly the same information he had given Scholten at Schiphol, but he added something extra. "I have someone in Andermatt and they may be getting somewhere. Too early to say exactly where yet."

"I am profoundly grateful."

"There is something else. In case of emergency I have given them your open number—without telling them who they will be speaking to. They will ask for a Mr. Gehring and say Leros is calling. If that happens, can you arrange for them to be put through immediately to yourself—or to Brigadier Traber, if you're not there? I'd like any message Leros passes to you—however cryptic—to be passed on to me urgently. By then you'll know how to communicate with me."

"Leros calling Mr. Gehring," Springer repeated. "Our switchboard operator will be informed it is a top-priority call if it comes through. And now?"

"I'm catching the 1925 Swissair flight to Milan. What's

going to happen will happen in the next forty-eight hours."
Wargrave looked out of the window, where snow was
falling heavily. "Has the Boeing from the States arrived
yet?"

"It is due within two hours—soon after your flight for
Milan departs. We shall take great care of it," he promised. He paused as he lit a cigarette. "This agent you are
escorting out of Europe—he is of very great importance,
may I ask?"

"Possibly the most important since the war." Wargrave
decided to be a little more frank with Springer than he
had been with Scholten; the Swiss security chief was going
to feel the heat earlier than the Dutchman—and if Zürich
Airport stayed open they would never even move into
Holland. "My plan is to bring him here aboard the Atlantic Express Saturday night—the day after tomorrow—
because by then we predict that the Milan Airport will
be closed."

"As quickly as that? Then it might be wise if I issued
a discreet alert?"

"It might be wise," the Englishman agreed. "We shall
set up our own communications unit on the express to
keep in constant touch with you—Colonel Molinari in
Milan is giving me his full cooperation. And I'm just
wondering whether it might be a good idea if you arranged
something rather special for me when the express reaches
Chiasso." He outlined the plan and Springer immediately
agreed.

"Be careful, be lucky," the Swiss colonel instructed as
he took his leave of the Englishman.

The moment he was alone Springer used his scrambler
phone to call his chief, Brigadier Traber, in Zürich. He
reported briefly what he had been told, then added a
comment. "It could be this is the opportunity we have
been waiting for—to flush out the main Communist sabotage teams the Soviets are holding in reserve for an
emergency. Had you better consult with Bern?"

Without realizing it, Springer was adopting an almost
identical attitude to that of Scholten in Holland. There was
a pause on the phone before Traber replied; when he did

he startled his deputy. "I don't think I need bother Bern yet. Saturday you said? That means over the weekend when most ministers will be away from their desks and not too easy to contact. We may handle this on our own, Leon. . . ."

The revolt of the European security chiefs against their more cautious government ministers was beginning.

Five minutes after Wargrave had made his brief phone call from Zürich Airport to the Swiss ski resort, Robert Frey left the Hotel Storchen in Andermatt and drove his Volkswagen van westward out of the town to the farmhouse that was his home several kilometers along the road toward Gletsch. Even with chains on his wheels he drove carefully; it was night and the roads were like skating rinks. Turning off the road, he pulled up in front of the steep-roofed building and went inside.

Frey, a huge man with a weather-beaten face, a world-famous mountaineer and the dominant citizen in Andermatt, was met inside the polished, woodblock hall by his assistant, Emil Platow, a short, wiry Swiss who seemed even smaller as Frey loomed over him. "Anything to report?" Frey inquired.

"News has just come in from Athens—about your girl friend, Anna Markos."

"So?"

"Nothing tangible. She lives in an expensive apartment. It is rumored the rent is paid for by a Greek cabinet minister. . . ."

"So, she is his mistress. Now give me the meat."

"That's all," Platow replied with some embarrassment. "And the fact that two days ago she visited the Rhône Glacier area with another tourist, René Marchais—the French skier who is so good on the slopes—"

"Marchais talks a lot when he drinks," Frey remarked. "I was listening to him in the bar at the Storchen the other night." He frowned and listened carefully as the sound of a distant rumble came from somewhere outside, a rumble of falling rock. About five kilometers distant, he estimated. The whole area was fragile with potential avalanche slides.

"So," he concluded sarcastically, "we have learned more about Anna Markos here in Andermatt than you have gleaned from Athens. Great work, Emil, great work. . . ." He strode off into his study to pour himself a stiff drink.

What Emil Platow had failed to discover was that five days earlier, in the morning, Anna Markos, a strikingly handsome and well-built Greek woman, had driven with René Marchais in her hired Renault to Gletsch at the foot of the Rhône Glacier. It was only nine o'clock when Anna pulled up outside the tiny railway station at Gletsch as she saw a police patrol car approaching from the other direction.

"Nice to have company—even if only the police," she remarked, glancing around the desolate wasteland of snow. Sunlight was reflecting off the mighty glacier to the north, a greenish reflection from what looked like a tidal wave of ice about to plunge down into the valley below.

René Marchais, the slim, boyish Frenchman who had picked up Anna at the Hotel Storchen, grinned. "I was hoping the only company I would enjoy today would be yours. . . ." So far he had failed in his efforts to coax her inside his bedroom but he was confident it was only a matter of patience and time. The approaching police car pulled up and the driver got out to speak to them; he glanced at the pair of skis in the back of the Renault.

"It could be dangerous skiing, sir," he warned. "The snow is unstable, to say the least."

"This is René Marchais," Anna interjected with a warm smile. "He is well known at Chamonix as one of their stars." She looked up at the mass of ice to the north. "Isn't it up there where they discovered a dead man in one of the ice tunnels?"

The Swiss studied her. Normally it was not a subject he would have discussed, but his wife was away visiting relatives in Lausanne and he welcomed the chance to chat with such an attractive woman. He, too, looked up at the silent glacier.

"Yes, it is a mystery we have yet to unravel—how he came to be there." He shrugged. "Probably we shall never know what happened. . . ."

"Was there no one about at the time? He died alone—in this wilderness?" Anna chattered on.

"Only Robert Frey's helicopter," the policeman replied. "He had landed near here to check the snowfall—it is one of his duties to keep an eye on the avalanche situation."

"And he saw nothing?"

"No, that is what increases the mystery—from the ground he might have seen nothing, but checking from the air he was bound to have seen anyone else in the area. It was entirely deserted at the time."

Anna continued staring at the remote glacier. "I always love a mystery—you can start imagining what might have happened. . . ." She caught the change in the Swiss's expression. "I'm sorry—it must have been rather horrible."

"I would not advise you to drive any farther," the policeman warned them. He looked again at the skis. "Nor would I advise anyone to ski—even if they do come from Chamonix," he added tartly.

Anna turned the Renault and followed the police car back to Andermatt as Marchais grumbled in his boyish way. "They are so cautious, these Swiss. I shall certainly ski from Andermatt, whatever they say. I find that story of the body in the ice tunnel fascinating."

"I'm not sure they liked us talking about it," Anna replied.

"It would make a good topic in the evening over a drink. Who was the mysterious man? What was he doing inside the glacier? Was it an accident or was he murdered?"

"Your imagination is running away with you," Anna told him in her excellent French. "And unless you promise to drop the subject I will not join you for that drink this evening."

"My lips are sealed," Marchais promised with exaggerated solemnity.

Two days later René Marchais was killed while skiing on the slopes above Andermatt. The police were not satisfied with the results of their investigation; they began treating it as a case of homicide.

"Maybe we should have gone by train," Elsa said brightly.

Her double scotch had jumped off the fold-out tray as the aircraft bucked and then dropped over the Swiss Alps. The scotch spilled all over the sleeve of the Turtle, who sat alongside her. Taking out a handkerchief, she began to sponge the sodden sleeve. "My my, Mr. Haller, you smell like a distillery. And all these months I thought you were teetotal."

"You wouldn't like just to pour the next one over me instead of down your throat?" Haller growled.

Behind them Harry Wargrave occupied his normal seat two rows back, the gangway seat where he could watch his two companions and move fast in an emergency. As the turbulence increased, he congratulated himself on his decision not to cross the Alps, not to fly direct from Bucharest to Zürich. The HS 125 executive jet waiting for him in Milan was twin-engined, an excellent plane—but not one to cross the Alps in a raging blizzard.

Like Elsa, Wargrave had now made two flights across the Atlantic in twenty-four hours and the double jet lag was hitting him like a hammer. Haggard-faced, his cheekbones showing sharp against the skin, he thanked God he would get two nights' sleep in Milan—Thursday and Friday—before his hazardous Saturday flight to Bucharest. And again, like Elsa, he had not slept a wink on the flight from Montreal to Schiphol.

His brain had been racing over the problems ahead, over the multitude of details to be organized. At this stage it was so damned tricky—people like Springer and Molinari had to be told enough to prepare for what was to come without revealing the big secret: that it was a senior member of the Soviet Politburo they were bringing out.

As the plane lost height for the approach run into Milan he watched Julian and Elsa talking, their heads close together.

"If Milan Airport stays open we may be able to fly back to Zürich," Haller murmured.

"That would solve a lot of problems," Elsa agreed lightly. "Fingers crossed, hope and pray. . . ."

As she was speaking, the aircraft dropped without warning into an air pocket and her stomach flipped again. Outside the window nothing could be seen through the pall of falling snow and Elsa was wondering if they were going to have to land blind, to go through the hazardous process whereby the pilot was talked down with the aid of radar. Christ, I hope not, she thought as the warning lights came on and she leaned over to fasten Haller's seat belt with her deft fingers.

"Someone could lose a little weight," she teased him as she snapped the belt over the hint of a paunch. Then she fastened her own belt and stubbed out her cigarette with steady fingers. The truth was Elsa Lang was scared stiff of flying, a fear she had concealed from everyone—even from Harry Wargrave, who thought he knew Elsa better than anyone.

The Swiss plane landed at Milan Airport at 8:05 P.M. It was still Thursday, January 6. In less than thirty-six hours Wargrave was due to take off in the Hawker-Siddeley 125 executive jet on his flight to Bucharest to pick up Angelo. At the airport Haller was impressed by Colonel Molinari's organization; discreetly bypassing all customs and immigration formalities, they were hustled inside the back of a large plain van without windows. The interior of the vehicle belied its plain exterior.

Fitted with comfortable, leather-armed seats, well heated against the bitter night chill outside, they relaxed as the van left the airport by the cargo entrance. In the front seat Molinari sat behind a small table using a radio telephone into which he spoke rapidly in Italian. Haller had no idea what he was saying but Wargrave and Elsa, who spoke fluent Italian, gathered he was reporting their imminent arrival to their destination.

"This vehicle is quite something," Haller remarked as the Italian completed his call and swung around to face them.

"It is a command truck," Molinari replied in English, "mainly used in antiterrorist operations. I am taking you to a special base we rarely use that will be at your entire disposal."

"How far from the station—Milano Centrale?" Wargrave asked.

"Two kilometers—your signal specified somewhere close."

Colonel Luigi Molinari, the SIFAR chief, was a typical north Italian in appearance; born forty-three years earlier at Piacenza, he was short, stockily built, with a hard, round-shaped head and a calm, wary manner. Haller was impressed by him also; he exuded an air of competence and toughness. His next remark and action confirmed the impression. "You specified weapons," he told Wargrave. Opening a large case on the floor, he lifted out a .38 Smith and Wesson special and looked around. Both Haller and Elsa held out their hands at the same time.

"Ladies first. . . ."

Molinari handed the gun and a package of ammunition to Elsa. Stooping again, he brought out a Colt .45 with another package and gave it to Haller. To Wargrave he gave two Sten guns with spare magazines, and Haller frowned. "Pretty conspicuous, difficult to conceal, hardly the latest in armament," he commented.

"Three criticisms in less than thirty seconds," Wargrave replied. "That's pretty good." Taking an empty holdall from his case, he stowed the weapons inside. "But these are for my flight to nowhere." He phrased the reply carefully—Molinari had not been given the slightest clue as to the destination of the HS jet. "As to its history, I have never known the Sten to jam."

"I have alternatives," Molinari remarked. "Take your pick." Haller left his seat, watching his balance as the truck swayed around a corner, slapping his hand against the wall. "It's armored, isn't it—the truck?" he queried, and Molinari nodded. Inside the case was a minor arsenal: German Lugers, Walthers, Belgian Browning automatics, several Colt .45s, two Webley-Fosberys, and even a couple of machine pistols.

"Enough to start a small war," Haller commented, "but I guess we have what we need."

"I have the impression you may start a small war," Molinari replied.

He opened a small window in the front of the truck that looked into the cab, picked up a microphone, and spoke into the instrument. "You might like to see this," he told Wargrave. Extracting a map, he handed it to the Englishman. "This shows the location. Study it and burn it after we have arrived."

Behind Wargrave Elsa and Haller peered through the little window, which gave them a clear view beyond the truck's windshield. They were driving down a narrow cobbled street in a poor area of the city, with a wall of unlit buildings on either side. The truck had slowed as it bumped over the cobbles, and it had stopped snowing for the moment. In the glare of the headlights they saw they were moving down a cul-de-sac; at the end the way was barred by a pair of enormous wooden doors large enough to let inside a massive hay wagon, which was probably what had once passed through them a hundred years earlier. The truck rumbled on. Elsa tensed. They were going to smash straight into those massive doors. At the last moment—in response to Molinari's warning phone message—the doors swung inward and the truck rumbled into a huge stone courtyard and stopped. Men immediately closed the doors behind them. They had reached the base.

The courtyard they stepped into when the rear truck doors were opened was entirely enclosed by ancient six-story buildings, but Wargrave noticed there was an alternative exit through another pair of doors opposite those they had entered by. Molinari led the way up a curving stone staircase, carrying Elsa's bag as she clutched the sable close under her chin; the night air was bitter. She looked around curiously at the second-floor room he led them to.

It was split-level and had a strange semicircular window at floor level, which Molinari immediately drew a curtain over. In the middle of the large room a huge old-fashioned green stove was radiating waves of heat and the furniture was heavy and dark. "I'll show you to your bedroom," the Italian said to Elsa. "You must be tired and there is an adjoining bathroom. A meal will be served in about half an hour," he went on in Italian—earlier Elsa had suggested they converse in his language. "And this will help to soothe the tension of the flight." He picked up a bottle of Chianti. "It's one floor up. This way. . . ."

Returning to the room below where Wargrave and Haller were waiting, Molinari became brisk and businesslike, seating them around a table where scratch pads and ball-point pens were laid at intervals. "I gather from your signal," he said in English to Wargrave for Haller's benefit, "that you are bringing out a key Communist agent?"

"The HS 125 jet—" the Englishman began.

"Is already waiting at Milan Airport." Molinari smiled thinly. "Your lady-chasing friend Aldo Martino was only too ready to oblige you. My own men are guarding it. When do you leave?"

"Saturday morning, 0703 hours. I expect to be back about 1330 hours. I'll need transport to bring my passenger back here for a change of clothes. I can't give you exact measurements—can you get hold of a large selection in various sizes? A vicuña overcoat would help—I want him to look wealthy—"

"We'll pay for all this, of course," Haller interjected.

"Including the jet charges?" Molinari inquired with a straight face. "Martino is charging fifty thousand dollars per hour."

"Fifty thousand dollars!"

"He's joking," Wargrave hastily assured the American. "Once Mr. X has changed I'll drive him to Milano Centrale. The schedule is tight but we want to take him to

Zürich aboard the Atlantic Express—unless Milan Airport is still open and we can fly him there."

"That is very unlikely," Molinari replied. "My met people tell me the airport will close down within twenty-four hours. You may have trouble taking off in your jet."

"I have to take off, come hell or high water, but we must assume from what you've just said it will be the Atlantic Express. Now I'm going to ask a lot."

"Anything you wish, Harry. Remember, I owe you."

At that moment Elsa Lang came downstairs and one of Molinari's men guarding the building showed Matt Leroy into the room. Leroy gave Elsa a little salute and turned to Haller. "Sorry I'm late—when I came in on the train from Basel I spent time mooching around Milano Centrale. Seemed a good idea to familiarize myself with the layout."

"That's all right," Haller replied. He included Elsa in his glance. "You'd both better sit in on this—I'll fill you in later on what you've missed."

"It's a giant of a station," the droopy-mustached American warned. "Anything could happen there."

"My men will be everywhere," Molinari assured him. "In uniform to put on a show of force—and in plain clothes, too."

Wargrave began speaking rapidly. There was so much to be done, so little time. "I want two extra Wagon-Lit sleeping cars attached to the rear of the Atlantic Express —reserved for our exclusive use. You managed to get the communications equipment I requested, Luigi?"

"It is waiting at Milano Centrale," Molinari replied.

"I want a complete communications unit set up in the Wagon-Lit—the second one, not the rear car. We have our own operator who will run that, a man called Peter Neckermann. I gave him your number and he—"

"He is at this moment installed in a room on the third floor here—next door to the room where we have our own communications outfit."

"That's going to save time," Wargrave commented. "I'll have some urgent signals to send within the next hour. Going back to the express, I want a direct telephone installed from the communications compartment in the Wagon-Lit to the train driver. Can you manage all this?"

"We will manage it." Molinari continued scribbling shorthand notes on a pad. "Twenty-four hours is ample time and we have more. Next?"

"Now we come to the moment when I land back at Milan Airport with our passenger. I'd appreciate your help in throwing out a smokescreen to cover the tracks." He went into details and Molinari said he saw no problem there. The Italian also suggested a second diversion, which they immediately agreed.

Everyone was smoking and already a blue cloud hung around the single overhead lamp above the table. Elsa, changed into a blue woolen dress that hugged her neck, sensed the tension in the room. "We come back here with the passenger, I take it?" she asked. "His appearance must be changed before we reach Milano Centrale—I've brought my film makeup kit."

"Come back?" Haller repeated in an ominous tone. "And where did you think you were going?"

"I'll be flying in the jet with Harry," she informed him. "We've already agreed—"

"You will not!" Haller hammered his fist on the heavy table. "I absolutely forbid it. That flight will be one of the most dangerous—"

"You think I'm some damned butterfly?" Elsa flared.

Wargrave intervened quietly. "She may come in useful—"

"She won't!" Haller snapped. "Because she won't be in that plane. If he agrees, Matt can go—"

"Matt just agreed," said Matt owlishly.

Wargrave shook his head, still speaking in his quiet, laconic tone. "Matt I need to keep looking around Milano Centrale. He has a flair for spotting something out of place. As for Elsa, she speaks fluent French—the second language where we're going to—and a girl can provide a distraction at just the right moment."

"I'm not happy about this at all," Haller snapped again.

"But then I'm running this end of the operation, Julian. Remember?"

"A woman agent," Molinari suggested soothingly, "can complement a man with great skill—especially when they have worked together for some time, as I can tell these two people have."

Haller glanced at Matt Leroy, who was staring into space. "Don't look at me," Matt said. "Elsa is a big girl now."

"And now, before we eat," Wargrave said crisply, "I'd like to go up and see Peter Neckermann alone if I may."

"I will show you the room," Molinari replied. Neither man looked back into the smoky room below as they ascended the stairs; there was an atmosphere they preferred to ignore. Elsa sat flushed with annoyance, Haller was brooding, and Matt had resumed gazing into space.

Alone with Peter Neckermann in the third-floor room, Wargrave began giving him instructions as he wrote out a long signal. Neckermann was the ex-*Kriminalpolizei* sergeant who for twelve months had played the dangerous role of the white-jacketed "steward" who retrieved the cassettes from the Moscow Express sleeping car in Basel. A small, well-padded man of fifty-two, he had a gnomelike face, thick brown hair, and a perpetually mild expression.

But Neckermann's appearance was deceptive. Just prior to retirement he had been off duty and driving his car along the Konigsallee in Düsseldorf when he had run into the Geiger Group rushing out of a bank they had just raided. Driving onto the sidewalk, he had headed straight for one terrorist, who stopped and aimed his machine pistol at Neckermann point-blank. Neckermann had pressed his foot down, the windshield had shattered, and unscathed he had ridden over the terrorist. And for several years he had served at Wiesbaden as radio operator in the communications division.

"You have to be very careful with this signal," Wargrave warned. "Transpose it into one-time code using pages one to one hundred in this book." He handed to Neckermann a copy of Somerset Maugham's *The Moon and Sixpence*. "And here are the technical data you need."

It was Springer who had only a month earlier remarked to his chief, Brigadier Traber, that Wargrave was a lone wolf. And this signal the Englishman was carefully keeping a secret between only himself and Neckermann. The signal was going to a senior member of the Yugoslav Politburo.

Julian Haller deliberately held back his announcement until after dinner, until after Molinari had left to make the many arrangements he had to organize. Alone with Elsa, Matt, and Wargrave, he sipped the occasional glass of wine he allowed himself. Putting the glass down on the table, he looked around with a smile.

"One final detail I ought to mention. On this operation we're going to need all the backup we can muster. So I've arranged for another outfit to supply an extra man, a Phillip John. He's a killer—" He saw Elsa's expression and changed the description. "A crack shot, that is. He's coming in from Genoa tomorrow."

Wargrave suddenly became tense and leaned forward over the table. "Could I inquire from what other outfit?" he asked softly.

"CIA." Haller looked apologetic. "Now don't start worrying, for God's sake. He's British—and he's kept strictly for backup, so he's not known. And he was the only one near enough to call in at such short notice." Haller took a deep drag on his cigarette, watching the Englishman for signs of doubt. "He can apparently shoot the wing off a bee at fifty yards. He could even be better than you," he added with a grin.

"The CIA has no idea why we need him, I suppose?" Wargrave queried.

"Good God, no!" Haller's reaction was explosive. "Just that I need him for a local job. Just as they have no idea Sparta exists. I asked in my old capacity as a National Security Agency man."

"I'll want a quiet talk with him before I decide," the Englishman warned. "And when he arrives I'd like him sent straight to me—before he has time to get his bearings."

Elsa smiled to herself. Mr. Phillip John was going to wonder what had hit him; in the past she had seen Wargrave subject a new recruit to intensive interrogation. Haller tried again to reassure him.

"We shall have two Wagon-Lits to guard—and if it does turn out we have to go all the way to Schiphol we'll have to organize a duty roster so people get a little sleep. An extra man could make all the difference."

Wargrave thought about it. A backup man was not a normal field agent. He was held in reserve for very special operations and there was a ban on engaging the same backup man more than three times in a year. That way he was least likely to become known to the KGB. "I have heard of Phillip John," he remarked.

"You have?" Haller was startled. "Not through Molinari?"

"Definitely not!" Wargrave stubbed his cigarette. "Let's just say I have my sources—which don't in the least put Phillip John at risk. And, as you say, we may need all the help we can get." He checked his watch, took Molinari's map showing their location over the stove, lifted the lid, and burned it. "I think it's time for bed now," he remarked.

"Bed I like," Elsa agreed. She caught Wargrave's expression. "They do have a separate room for you," she told him saucily and yawned.

"Tomorrow will be a packed day—checking details," Wargrave warned. "Saturday will be something else again —it's a long way to Bucharest and back. . . ."

7

Bucharest

At precisely 7:30 A.M. Saturday, January 8, Wargrave's HS 125 jet took off from Milan Airport and disappeared inside the heavy overcast. Strapped into the copilot's seat beside the Englishman, Elsa Lang had a large-scale map of the Balkans spread over her lap. She had flown with Wargrave before in Cessna aircraft and had displayed a flair for navigation, often locating features on the ground, checking the flight route, and helping to keep them on course.

"What happens if we don't get the right landing signal when we arrive?" she inquired.

"We turn back and head like hell for home."

As always, in the final cassette Angelo's instructions had been very precise. On approaching the airstrip outside Bucharest, the runway lights would come on and a signal lamp would flash repeatedly: three longs . . . one short . . . three longs. . . . And Angelo himself would be identified by two silver letters pinned to his coat lapel. *A.N.* The aircraft gained height rapidly, heading east for Belgrade, which lay on the direct route to Bucharest.

"Did Phillip John pass inspection?" Elsa asked.

"Winchester and Cambridge. Then a spell with a London merchant bank. It all bored him stiff, so he went after something more exciting. He's got that," Wargrave commented dryly. "A quiet man, which I liked. Reflexes like a top racing driver's. I tested him with the old trick—place a gun on the table between us and when I use a certain word in casual conversation he goes for the gun."

"Who won?"

"His hand reached the butt first."

"He beat you?"

"My hand was on top of his, pinning him down."

"What is he like. Handsome?"

"Five foot ten tall, a hundred and fifty pounds in weight, white-faced, curly brown hair, very controlled in his movements. A professional."

Crossing the Yugoslav coast in a snowstorm, Wargrave made his first contact with the Belgrade government's radar scanners. Through the microphone headset he spoke to them in Serbo-Croat briefly. During his years in the Balkans, Wargrave had made some good friends and one of them was Stane Sefer, chief of the Yugoslav security police. It was to Sefer he had sent his secret signal via Peter Neckermann on Thursday evening. Late on Friday he had followed this up with a phone call to Belgrade requesting Sefer's permission to overfly Yugoslavia "on an urgent mission."

"Our radar will track you in and out," Sefer had promised. "And in this weather you'll need us to keep you on course."

The lean-faced Stane Sefer had asked no questions, but he had guessed that Wargrave was on his way to fly out an agent working against the Russians. And like the whole Yugoslav government, Sefer was only too ready to support anyone helping to hold back the massive surge of Soviet power. No one in Belgrade was under any illusion that Yugoslavia could well become the Red Army's next objective—after the occupation of Romania, whose independent leaders were equally wary of the Bear's intentions.

It was another bad flight—flying blind all the way across Yugoslavia—and without the help of Sefer's radar tracking stations, which guided Wargrave to the Romanian border, he might not have made it. Beside him Elsa Lang sat studying her map, constantly trying to catch a glimpse of the ground, trying to look as though it was all in a day's work. During the first hour the neat scotch she had swallowed just before she boarded the jet had helped, but it was a three-hour flight to Bucharest and the anesthetic quality of the drink had long since worn off.

"At least it looks as though we've kept our flight secret," she remarked at one point.

Elsa might have felt less sanguine had she been able to witness an episode at Milan Airport soon after the jet had taken off. In the control tower Toni Morosi, a sallow-faced assistant air traffic controller, complained to his chief of bowel trouble and was allowed to leave the tower. Instead of heading for the men's room, the supposedy stricken Morosi went to a pay phone and dialed a Milan number. The call was answered immediately by the man at the other end.

"Russo here," Toni Morosi said quickly. "A Hawker-Siddeley private jet took off at 7:30 flying on an easterly course."

"What makes that significant?" the somber voice demanded.

"It was waiting all Friday in a special hangar heavily guarded by security troops."

"Who was on board?"

"No idea."

"Keep me informed of developments."

The connection was broken as Morosi mopped his forehead and hurried to the men's room to sit on a seat for a few minutes before returning to the tower. The man inside a Milan garage who had received Morosi's message later encoded it and included the information in a signal he sent on his powerful transmitter to Moscow. Because he saw no special significance in the message he delayed the transmission.

"There's the river Arges."

Elsa was peering down out of the window at the flat Romanian plain, checking landmarks against her map. The jet was now flying at fifteen hundred feet and for the past half hour she had located landmark after landmark. They had been lucky; once over the Yugoslav border and

93

out of touch with Stane Sefer's radar tracking stations they had run into clearer weather. The plain below was a white landscape but it was no longer snowing in this part of the Balkans.

"We should soon be there," Wargrave replied. "Keep a close lookout for those landing lights."

It was close to 11:30 A.M. Bucharest time, which was one hour ahead of Milan time, and as they drew closer and closer to the Romanian capital Elsa felt the jangle of her nerves growing worse. She glanced at Wargrave, whose expression was intent but calm. Sensing her glance, he smiled reassuringly. "Not every girl gets a trip to the mysterious Balkans—and all expenses paid, too."

"Better get ready," Elsa replied.

Behind them was a roomy cabin that could comfortably seat six passengers, and Wargrave suspected there could well be more than one passenger coming aboard—Anatoli Zarubin had a wife and daughter and it seemed unlikely he would leave them behind. The equipment Elsa was collecting off the seat behind her was less reassuring than Wargrave's remark. Resting the Sten gun and spare magazines where the Englishman could snatch them off her lap, she picked up her own .38 Smith and Wesson and laid that also in her lap. Then—dead ahead in the semi-dark of the wintry day—the airstrip lights flared.

"Watch for the flashing lamp signal," Wargrave warned.

Strung up to the highest pitch of tension, Elsa stared down as Wargrave dipped the nose of the machine steeply. What was waiting for them down there? They were landing in the middle of a Communist state—a state that had often showed its mistrust of Moscow, but still Communist. "Don't forget the A.N. symbol Angelo said he'd be wearing," she recalled. And that was a damned unnecessary remark, she thought; as if he would forget. I must get my nerves under control. Then the signal lamp began flashing. Three longs . . . one short . . . three longs. . . .

Wargrave reduced speed as the parallel lines of lights flew toward them, there was a bump as he hit the runway, then he was taxiing the jet, losing speed as fast as he dared, having no idea of the length of the runway. The jet stopped and Elsa peered out of the window on her side, seeing nothing. God, she thought, I want to go to the bathroom. Wargrave kept the motors running and looked out of his window.

"Funny, doesn't seem to be anyone about. . . ."

"But someone turned the lights on."

"So someone has to be here," Wargrave agreed.

He took the Sten gun from her and she grasped the butt of her Smith and Wesson. Just holding the weapon gave her a little comfort. What the hell was going on out there in the semidark? Suddenly Wargrave switched on the searchlight mounted on the nose of the jet. The light stabbed the darkness, showed up clearly a man walking toward the plane along the runway, a short, stocky man with wide shoulders, wearing a heavy fur coat and no hat.

He came on, walking sturdily, carrying a briefcase. At the first flash of the light he had thrown up a hand to shield his eyes, but now he had removed his hand and walked with his head lowered. As he came close his face became clearer, a strong-jawed face with bushy eyebrows that Elsa recognized from the many photos of him she had studied. She gasped.

"My God, Harry! It's a trap, a damned trap."

The man coming toward them—who had almost reached the aircraft—was General Sergei Marenkov, head of the Soviet KGB.

8

Bucharest, Vienna, Milan

Wargrave realized instantly that it was hopeless. He could try and fly straight out again, but the runway ahead wouldn't give him the space to take off, there was no time to turn the machine, and in any case they would have the aircraft ringed with machine guns, maybe even small field pieces. It didn't stop him trying. A hostage might just get them out of the trap, a hostage of the importance of Marenkov. Throwing open the door, he waited until Marenkov stood below it looking up at him.

"Don't move a finger, General," he shouted above the roar of the jets. He spoke in German, not expecting to be understood, but the Russian would understand the Sten aimed point-blank at his chest.

Marenkov made a waving gesture, indicating that the automatic stepladder should be lowered. Wargrave hesitated, then told Elsa to press the button. The power-operated staircase emerged and slid to the ground. Marenkov started to climb the steps and then stopped as Wargrave gestured with the gun and shouted.

"Hold it there."

"What is wrong with your bloody eyesight?" the Russian bawled back in English.

"Christ!" Elsa whispered in Wargrave's ear. "His lapel. For God's sake, look at his lapel!"

Marenkov was now himself pointing to his right coat lapel in which two silver letters were pinned. *A.N.* Wargrave gazed at them bleakly. He leaned out of the machine and Marenkov took a step upward and leaned forward also until their faces were almost touching.

"What does it stand for?" Wargrave demanded.

"Angelo. I am Angelo. We must leave quickly. My friends run the most terrible risk—take me on board and fly me the hell out of here."

Figures in fur coats had not appeared out of the near-dark and Wargrave was sure that one of them was Ion Manescu, chief of the Romanian secret police. Scarcely a minute had passed since Elsa had recognized Marenkov, but in that short time Wargrave's brain had been racing, recalling the whole saga of Angelo. He could have kicked himself for not suspecting the truth earlier. Lowering the gun, he reached out a hand and hauled the Russian aboard. He didn't even have to give the order to Elsa; she had already pressed the button and the automatic staircase retracted. Wargrave slammed the door shut as Marenkov scrambled into one of the front passenger seats and leaned forward to shout.

"You are at a turn-around point, a large circle. Turn your machine left through one hundred and eighty degrees and take off in the direction you landed. It should be done quickly."

"You think I intended staying for tea?"

It was as Marenkov had described: he was able to turn the jet in a slow semicircle and then he was facing back the way he had come, looking down the runway between the parallel lines of lights. He began taxiing past the lights, built up speed, the lights raced past in a blur, and then he left the ground and was climbing rapidly, heading west for the Yugoslav border and Stane Sefer's friendly radar stations.

Hindsight. Always useless. But from start to finish the Angelo operation had all the marks of a professional, of a man skilled in the craft of espionage at the highest level. And Anatoli Zarubin, Soviet minister of trade and commerce, had not qualified for that kind of work. It's always what is under our noses we do not see, Wargrave thought wryly. Once he glanced back at General Marenkov, who stared back at him from under his bushy eyebrows with his arms folded, his face expressionless. As he looked ahead, the one thing Wargrave could not fathom was why a man like Marenkov had done this thing. Why?

Sergei Mikhail Loris Marenkov was twenty when he found himself fighting behind the enemy lines in the Ukraine in 1941 as a partisan leader. He showed natural gifts of leadership and by 1943 he was an assistant commissar attached to a tank unit at Kursk. It was Nikita Khrushchev, a fellow-Ukrainian, who adopted him as a protégé and arranged his exceptional promotion. After the war a KGB talent-spotter—recognizing his talent for organization, his encyclopedic memory and his industry—recruited him for the secret police.

Marenkov had only to read a page of a report once and it was committed to memory for all time. In his mind he could carry hundreds of names and addresses and telephone numbers, any amount of statistical data, and he never forgot a face or a name. His progress up the step-ladder of power was rapid for another reason: he never attached himself to any power faction, so he was trusted by all. Then, at the age of forty-five, Sergei Marenkov got married.

Irina Marenkov, a slim, frail-looking beauty, was entirely different from her husband. Intensely political, she had already begun to have doubts about the system before she married Sergei. Alexander Solzhenitsyn's writings completed her conversion. She decided that the Soviet state was a sham, had become a near-military dictatorship under the growing influence of Marshal Gregori Prachko and his Politburo supporters. She sowed the first doubts in her husband's mind.

But Marenkov himself was also beginning to worry about the way the system was developing. He personally detested the swaggering, overbearing manner of his colleague Marshal Prachko, but carefully concealed his feelings. He knew that the Soviet arms buildup far exceeded what could ever be needed for defense against the West. Then Colonel Igor Sharpinsky was appointed his deputy.

It was some time before Marenkov realized that

Sharpinsky was Prachko's protégé, maneuvered into position as his deputy to increase the power of the GRU—Soviet military intelligence. Sharpinsky's official task was to liaise with the GRU, but secretly he supported Prachko's every move. Then Marenkov came home to his apartment at 26 Kutuzov Prospekt late one night to find Irina dead. She had taken an overdose of sleeping tablets and left a brief note. *As a suspected dissident, I have become a liability to you. I love you too much to destroy you. Instead, I destroy myself.*

Marenkov, who had never shed tears before, wept for an hour. For three days he stayed alone in the apartment, refusing to see anyone. Then he launched his investigation. It took him only three more days to discover that during his absence in East Germany a campaign of rumors had been spread accusing Irina of subversive activity. The source of the poisonous rumors was Colonel Igor Sharpinsky.

The secretive nature—among other qualities—that years earlier had led Marenkov into the KGB now served him well. Overnight—he stayed up until dawn taking the decision—he decided to work against the perverted system that had destroyed his wife, that was destroying his country. He became Angelo.

A highly intelligent man, Marenkov knew that sooner or later time would run out for him. There had been the unnerving incident in November in the Moscow freight yards when—only a minute after he had placed the latest cassette aboard the sleeping car—he had stepped off the coach to face Captain Starov of the GRU about to board the sleeping car to examine it. With characteristic decisiveness he had shot Starov twice and then placed in his dead hand the grenade he always carried in his pocket, the grenade he would have withdrawn the pin from and blown himself up with if he had ever been discovered and faced with imminent arrest.

When the triad of Leonid Sedov, Marshal Prachko, and himself was formed to track down the high-level informer, he found he occupied the macabre role of hunting down himself. To gain a little time he gave the impression that he suspected Anatoli Zarubin, whom from the beginning he had seen as a useful cover. He had even exploited Zarubin's known liking for American jazz when he asked in the cassettes for certain jazz records to be played over the Voice of America station acknowledging safe receipt of the cassettes in Washington. And it was this pretended suspicion of Zarubin he had given as his reason for accompanying the Soviet delegation to Bucharest.

And now he was eight thousand feet over Yugoslavia in a jet piloted by an Englishman, knowing that every kilometer of his long journey to the United States would be fraught with danger—that the entire forces of the KGB and the GRU would be mobilized to kill him and his protectors. It would not be a safe journey.

Within minutes of Wargrave's being airborne again, a small convoy of cars left the Romanian airstrip and headed back at speed for Bucharest. When the news broke of Marenkov's flight, Ion Manescu, chief of the secret police, planned to launch an official investigation. His report would show that unknown capitalist agents had airlifted the Russian out of Romania. Anxious to return to the capital, Manescu, noted for his furious driving, sat behind the wheel of the lead car and soon outdistanced the other vehicles.

Alone in the rear car, one of his subordinates, Leo Ionita, pulled up at a villa behind a railed wall, ran inside and made a brief call, then ran back to his car. Accelerating, he reached Bucharest only a short distance behind Manescu, stopped again, and ran into the hallway of a large block of apartments. There he spoke a few brief words to a member of the Soviet Embassy who was waiting in response to the phone call. Minutes later, the Russian drove straight to his embassy.

As in Yugoslavia, so in Romania there was a hard core of Stalinists who secretly support Soviet Russia. Leo Ionita was one of these secret Stalinists. Within minutes of his Russian contact's reaching the embassy, a short, urgent signal was transmitted to Moscow reporting General Marenkov's departure. Within minutes of this signal reaching Moscow, a fresh signal was transmitted from KGB headquarters at 2 Dzerzhinsky Square to Vienna, where Colonel Igor Sharpinsky was paying one of his frequent visits to the Austrian capital. He heard of Marenkov's flight from Romania while Wargrave was airborne, still a long way from Milan.

It was 11 A.M. Vienna time—one hour behind Bucharest time—when the Moscow signal reached the Soviet Embassy in the Austrian capital. As usual, Sharpinsky had arrived in Vienna armed with a diplomatic passport under an assumed name. With the signal on the desk in front of him, he sat in his second-floor office staring through the lace curtains into the street below. It was snowing heavily and passersby muffled in overcoats and scarves were trudging through the snow with their heads down.

Colonel Igor Sharpinsky stroked the thinning hair over his high-domed forehead and behind his rimless glasses his eyes were motionless, hardly aware of the people in the street as his mind raced, checking over a whole series of contingencies he might have to deal with. Despite his deceptively mild appearance he was one of the most dangerous and able men in the Soviet Union; at this moment on a wintry morning in the ancient Austrian capital he knew he was at a crossroads in his career.

He was in the position of a gambler who stakes everything on one throw. The prospect did not daunt him; Sharpinsky was an audacious man who had not reached his present post without taking risks. And unlike his recent chief, General Sergei Marenkov, he had never disdained intrigue. He was an only child, born in Leningrad; his father had been a captain in the GRU. Exploiting this connection, Igor had worked his way up the ladder of power by switching his allegiance from one power faction to another according to who was winning and who was losing. Had he been born in the West he would undoubtedly have ended up as chief executive of one of the major multinational companies where a premium is placed on successful intrigue.

Sharpinsky had been one of the few men who had

spotted Gregori Prachko's potential before the Soviet marshal's lightning climb to supreme power. He had carefully attached himself to the military meteor and his gamble had paid off. Prachko had secretly exerted his influence to place Sharpinsky in the key post of deputy to General Marenkov for liaison between the KGB and the GRU. And it was Sharpinsky who had been sent to various key embassies in the West under a series of aliases to report on the real state of Western defense. It was these reports—officially submitted only to Marenkov but with a second copy quietly submitted to Prachko—that had convinced the Soviet marshal that the time was approaching when Western Europe could be conquered without the risk of American intervention.

On receipt of the brutal signal from Moscow, "Seek out and destroy Marenkov," a lesser man might have leaped into action, issuing a stream of orders. Sharpinsky had sat calmly thinking for some time while his cold, logical brain sifted the possibilities, while he tried to think himself into the minds of the opposition. And he refused to allow the fact that he was desperately short of time to hurry or disturb him. Only when he had analyzed the problem to his satisfaction did he take action.

Pressing a button on his desk, he summoned his deputy, Rudi Bühler, the East German who directed the GRU sabotage units in Western Europe. Quietly he gave him certain instructions, which Bühler put into operation over the phone. After he had made a series of calls, Bühler put down the receiver and looked at Sharpinsky, who was still staring out of the window.

"Golchack is still at Annagasse 821. A team is on the way there now, backed up by a motorcyclist who will report to us the moment they have done the job. Air reservations have been made on the Zürich flight. But why Zürich?"

Forty years old—ten years younger than his chief—Rudi Bühler was a heavily-built man of medium height, but unlike Sharpinsky there was something gross about the East German. And unlike the smooth-skinned Russian's, his heavy, pug-nosed face had a leathery complexion. Before replying to the question Sharpinsky left his desk and took several agile steps to a wall map where a series of pins traced a course across Yugoslavia.

"First, among a sheaf of routine reports that came in this morning from Milan was mention of a British jet taking off in an easterly direction. . . ."

"I don't follow—"

"Listen and you might learn something," Sharpinsky replied in his soft voice. "Second, reports from Yugoslav agents at radar-scanning stations refer to the jet's course continuing across the Romanian border in the general direction of Bucharest. . . ."

By "Yugoslav agents" Sharpinsky was referring to certain Stalinists who regularly sent Moscow reports through secret transmitters, Stalinists who waited for the day when the Soviet Union would absorb Yugoslavia.

"I begin to see," Bühler commented. "This links up with the machine our Romanian agent reported had airlifted Marenkov out of the country."

"You are learning," Sharpinsky told him dryly. "But there is far more: our camera-carrying satellites orbiting over the Balkans are at this moment tracking the jet's course and so far it is heading back along the same course —to Milan."

"I still don't understand why we go to Zürich," Bühler persisted.

"Because they will try to take him there from Milan aboard the Atlantic Express. Agents in the freight yards at Milan yesterday reported a lot of security activity— and two special Wagon-Lit coaches are to be attached to the Atlantic Express leaving Milan late this afternoon."

"Why not fly him from Milan to Zürich?" Bühler objected.

"Because I have just heard that Milan Airport had been closed down to all traffic," the Russian replied. "We can hope that the jet will crash, but we must assume they have chosen a skilled pilot who will land the jet blind. If he succeeds they will certainly not attempt another flight. And Zürich Airport is still open—from there they could fly him direct to the United States. He must—whatever the risk—never reach Zürich." Sharpinsky glanced at his deputy. "So now you know—proceed with checking the Annagasse operation."

Bühler left the room, once again impressed with the painstaking deductive processes of his chief, and when he had left, Sharpinsky permitted himself a thin smile of satisfaction. Because the Russian was something of a showman who took every opportunity to impress his staff with his extraordinary brain. The reason why Sharpinsky knew that Marenkov was definitely scheduled to travel aboard the Atlantic Express was, in fact, far simpler.

Only a short time before Sharpinsky had summoned Bühler to his office a gloved hand had lifted the receiver in a telephone booth in Milan Central Post Office to take the call he had placed to a number in Vienna. The owner of the gloved hand had spoken rapidly in German to the Hungarian in Vienna after identifying himself as Patros.

"They plan to transport the agent aboard the Atlantic Express leaving Milan this evening . . . the two rear Wagon-Lit coaches . . . the last coach will carry the agent. . . ."

The phone call from Patros was brief and he was worried that only now had he been able to slip away to make the call. Also he had no idea of the identity of the Soviet agent who was working for the West. The gloved hand replaced the receiver, and after paying for the call the individual who had used the code name Patros hurried out of the Post Office.

In Vienna the Hungarian, who occupied a flat close to the Soviet embassy—who was unknown to the Austrian security services to have any connection with the Russians—took the message straight to Colonel Sharpinsky. It had been as simple as that. And Wargrave's jet was still on its way to Milan.

During the next hour Sharpinsky composed a long series of signals in his careful script. While he wrote he listened to Beethoven's *Emperor* Concerto, which he had put on his record player. It seemed appropriate to the scale of the operation he was about to launch, which included use of major GRU sabotage units in the West held in reserve for the time when the Red Army invaded Western Europe. The message from Moscow had been explicit, a heady directive for a less-balanced man than Igor Sharpinsky: "You have full power to activate the entire GRU apparatus if necessary. . . ." His task completed, he spoke into the intercom.

"Send me the duty officer from the coding section."

While he waited, Sharpinsky took a suitcase from a cupboard that had remained packed for months in case of an emergency. Every three days a woman KGB officer unpacked the case, spread out the clothes, and later repacked it. The contents were innocent enough—winter clothing (a similar case was packed with summer wear), a rare book carefully wrapped in silk, and the latest copy of a catalog from Sotheby's, the London auctioneers.

"Come in," Sharpinsky called out as someone knocked on the door. Leo Scoblin, assistant cipher clerk in the basement code room, entered. A thin-faced man of thirty-five, Scoblin walked with a slight limp. Sharpinsky handed him the signals inside a sealed envelope; it was only after Scoblin had left the room that the Russian noticed that the two airline tickets for Zürich brought in earlier by Bühler were lying face up on his desk. He placed a notepad on top of them; even the smallest lapse of security annoyed Sharpinsky, a perfectionist.

In the basement the chief cipher clerk immediately began encoding the signals for rapid transmission to secret transmitters in various parts of Europe. There were signals to Zürich, Basel, Milan, Mulhouse, and Amsterdam. But the longest signal was for transmission to Andermatt, Switzerland.

The signals to Basel and Zürich arranged for the coming arrival of Sharpinsky in Switzerland. The message to Milan was received by a transmitter operating inside a garage close to Milano Centrale, the station from which the Atlantic Express would depart that same evening. In Mulhouse, Yuri Gusev, star executioner, received his orders. And in Amsterdam, Rolf Geiger, leader of the

Soviet-controlled terrorist group, was instructed to stand by in readiness for possible urgent action.

In Andermatt, where Sharpinsky's signal had been decoded, an expert hand was tapping out a signal on a transmitter concealed behind a roll-top desk. The signal was on its way to Franco Visani, the chief Soviet GRU agent in Lugano, the Swiss tourist resort just north of the Italian border and on the main rail route from Milan to Zürich. It gave instructions for the organization of an attack on the Atlantic Express—with special reference to the rear Wagon-Lit.

Immediately when he had decoded the signal Visani left his apartment, went to a nearby hotel, and made a series of phone calls. He spoke in a cryptic way and left the hotel as soon as he had completed his task. It was unlikely the calls would ever be traced, but if they were they would lead only to an anonymous hotel phone.

At this stage of the huge operation Sharpinsky was mounting to kill Marenkov before he could leave Europe, the most important signal was the one transmitted to Milan. Just as in this great Italian city Molinari had set up his own secret base, so had the GRU. The Soviet military intelligence unit was also located only a few kilometers from Milano Centrale and was controlled by an Italian with the code name of Sappho. Ever since he had served a spell of duty at the Soviet Embassy in Athens, Sharpinsky had developed a liking for Greek code words.

Sappho ran his thirty-man unit from the cover of a garage in a side street, a garage from which he operated a small fleet of radio-controlled cabs. It was Sappho whom Toni Morosi, the assistant air traffic controller at Milan Airport, had phoned, warning him of the take-off of the HS 125 jet under maximum security conditions. Now Sappho, a bony-faced man, lean-bodied, and with an abundance of suppressed nervous energy, was discussing the decoded signal with his deputy, Ugo Sala.

The word "deputy" was misleading; Sala, short and carrying a lot of weight, a forty-year-old man with a large head and a wide, aggressive mouth, had—unlike Sappho—undergone a course of training in Moscow. Technically, he outranked Sappho, but the two men worked well together. Sitting in the living room of the small apartment above the garage, Sala listened while Sappho explained.

"Marenkov has gone over to the West. Yes, I know it is incredible—certainly heads will roll in Moscow, so let us thank God we are here. From now on he will be code-named Peter. And where do you think Peter is at this moment?"

"Don't play games at a time like this," Sala replied with unaccustomed irritability. He was badly shaken and doing his best to conceal it. "I gather we are involved?"

"At this moment," Sappho said slowly, aiming for maximum shock effect, "he is aboard a British jet, which we estimate will land at Milan Airport at between one and two this afternoon."

"Then why thank God we are here?" Sala demanded. "It puts us in the firing line. What do we do—attempt to kidnap him back?"

Sappho shook his graying hair. "The order is more drastic."

"That means we have to kill him—if we can?"

"Before he can board the Atlantic Express tonight. Just who is involved we are not sure—or they have not told me. Probably a combined Anglo-American operation. I want you to track him from the airport to the station."

"You are not sure, then, he will be taken to the Atlantic Express?" Sala pounced.

"My instructions are to prepare for any eventuality. They may just change their escape route at the last moment. If we fix ourselves on just one plan we may be fooled. That we cannot afford."

Sala lit a small cheroot; his mind was moving into high gear. "If he does go through Milano Centrale that might be the best place to get him—if we can detect him."

Sappho shook his head again. "I disagree. Already I have heard that the station is swarming with Molinari's security men. I have something else in mind—but your

107

job is to ensure which route they take when they leave the airport."

"I'll use one of the cabs, then—that way I can keep in radio touch with you."

"Exactly. Use the special waveband—and simply refer to him as the passenger."

Sala stood up and stubbed out his cheroot. "They really have dropped one in our lap this time," he commented.

Inside his office at the Soviet Embassy in Vienna, Sharpinsky was changing into the winter clothes he had taken from the suitcase kept in the cupboard. Dressed again, he took off his rimless glasses, replaced them with a pair of thick pebble glasses, and studied his new appearance in a mirror. The face that stared back at him bore little resemblance to Igor Sharpinsky. Satisfied, he put the pebble glasses in his pocket, replaced them with the rimless pair, and sat down at his desk as he checked his watch. Soon he must leave with Bühler for the airport but first he needed to have confirmation from the motor-cyclist that the Annagasse operation had proceeded smoothly.

Sharpinsky had much to feel satisfied about. He had alerted agents all along the route the Atlantic Express would follow from Milan to Amsterdam. He very much doubted whether he would need the services of the Geiger Group in Holland; the net had been spread and he was confident Marenkov would be dead before the train ever reached the German border. But it was this exceptional thoroughness that had carried Sharpinsky to his present position, and now he felt almost excited as he contemplated what success in this mission might mean for him personally.

Inside the Soviet Politburo the division between the hard-liners and the moderates was finely balanced and First Secretary Leonid Sedov was desperately trying to restrain the growing power of Marshal Gregori Prachko, the leading hard-liner. Only recently Prachko had confided in his protégé, Sharpinsky.

"Pavel Suslov is wavering—soon he may join us."

"You will still be one vote short of a majority," Sharpinsky had pointed out. "And Anatoli Zarubin will never join you."

"I am not thinking of that two-faced, spineless pro-Westerner," the barrel-chested Soviet marshal had replied savagely. "All he can think of is creeping to the Americans. I am referring to Marenkov."

"Marenkov?" Sharpinsky had been startled. "He never takes sides. He is nothing more than a policeman."

"Who may yet resign, retire—he has not been the same since his wife committed suicide."

"You are wrong—he is tougher than he has ever been; I work under him . . ."

But now Prachko had been proved right, even if not in the way he had foreseen. And if Sharpinsky was appointed head of the KGB in succession to Marenkov, the West would face the most aggressive Politburo since Stalin's day. The issues at stake were indeed incalculable.

Heinz Golchack, the Austrian rare-book dealer who lived at Annagasse 821, caught Swissair Flight 433 from Schwechat Airport with only minutes to spare. The flight took off at 1325 hours—the last to leave before the airport was closed down. Leaning back in his seat, Golchack studied the Sotheby catalog through his pebble glasses as the DC-10 climbed. He was courteous but a little vague with the hostess when she asked him what he would like to drink. "Have you any . . . Schnapps? I am not a very good air passenger, you see. . . ."

"Certainly, sir. Don't worry—I'll bring it quickly."

Back in the galley the stewardess commented to her friend that it was a change to have a polite passenger aboard in weather like this. "He's rather a dear," she went on as she poured the drink, "the typical absent-minded professor."

Which was rather strange, since less than two hours ago at Annagasse 821 Heinz Golchack had received a visit from two men heavily muffled in scarves and fur-lined overcoats, with their hats pulled well down over their foreheads. He was expecting one man, not two. Thirty minutes earlier a man had phoned explaining that he was a private collector of rare books from Munich, and could he call to see Golchack?

"I have brought a friend," the shorter of the two men remarked as Golchack stood in the doorway of his isolated fifth-floor apartment.

"Please come in. I have some coffee on the stove so . . ."

Heinz Golchack, a short, well-built man, was a fifty-two-year-old bachelor who lived alone and was something of a recluse—Vienna has many similar people—and he valued his privacy so much he cleaned the apartment himself. He was walking toward the kitchen when the shorter man who had phoned struck him a savage blow on the skull from behind with a rubber truncheon. Golchack was dead before he slumped to the floor.

His two visitors then became very active. His attacker took out a gauze cap and wrapped it over the dead book dealer's skull to prevent blood seeping onto the carpet. His companion consulted a list and checked off items as they were dealt with. A suitcase taken from the bedroom was packed with the clothes Golchack would have needed for a trip. His shaving kit was collected from the bathroom, his passport from a drawer.

While one man packed the case his companion emptied the coffeepot he found on the stove, washed and dried it, and stowed it away in a cupboard together with the two cups Golchack had put out. Just before they left, the man who had killed Golchack took a typewritten slip from his pocket and left it on a desk. The slip was from a Swissair printed pad and typed on it were the departure and arrival times of Flight 433 to Zürich.

Locking up the apartment with keys taken from Golchack's pocket, they carried his body and the case down a back spiral staircase and shoved them into the rear of the old Mercedes they had parked in the cobbled interior yard on arriving. Then they drove across the yard and out through the massive double-doored exit leading into Annagasse. A motorcyclist parked by the curb watched them go, kicked his starter, and drove at speed back to the Soviet Embassy to report completion of the job.

In an isolated part of the Vienna Woods the two men backed the Mercedes up an old track until they reached the rim of a deep bowl in the snows. It took them less than five minutes to heave the case into the bowl, topple the body after it, empty cans of gasoline, and ignite it with a gasoline-sodden rag. When the flames had died to a smoldering, oily stench they shoveled snow over the relics. They then drove back to the Soviet Embassy.

It had all been planned months earlier when agents had spotted Heinz Golchack as a likely candidate for an identity switch in an emergency. During one of Golchack's rare visits to Salzburg they had used skeleton keys to enter his apartment and photograph his passport, which was then duplicated in the laboratory on the top floor of the Soviet Embassy, duplicated except for the photograph, which had been changed. Heinz Golchack was now a charred corpse in the Vienna Woods. Heinz Golchack was also a passenger aboard Swissair Flight 433 on his way to Zürich.

9

Milan and Zürich

When Wargrave's executive jet crossed back into Yugoslav air space Elsa's role as navigator ceased; from now on Stane Sefer's radar scanners were guiding him back toward Milan. She decided to take the opportunity to seat herself beside their Russian passenger to brief him on what would happen when they reached Milan.

The bushy-eyebrowed KGB chief swiveled in his own seat to stare at her and she met his gaze, surprised to see in his brown eyes an unexpected human expression. "You enjoy flying?" he inquired quietly, watching her closely.

"Love it," Elsa lied instantly. "Especially when I have so much confidence in the pilot."

Immediately she regretted adding the last remark. A curious expression appeared briefly in the penetrating brown eyes; Marenkov glanced ahead at Wargrave and then looked at her again. Instinctively she knew he had detected in her tone something of the concealed affection she felt for the Englishman. God, this one is quick, she thought; I'm going to have to watch myself.

"I hate flying," Marenkov replied. "It frightens me every time I board an aircraft." The plane lurched at that moment, then dropped a hundred feet before Wargrave regained control. With the Russian staring at her, Elsa made a supreme effort to look unconcerned as her stomach flipped. Marenkov took a flask from his coat pocket, unscrewed the flask, and handed it to her as he leaned forward and whispered.

"I think you are a brave little liar," he told her. His large left hand squeezed her arm as he offered the flask with the other. "Neat vodka. Drink some—but slowly. Come, I insist," he went on. "The only way to fly is drunk. . . ." He grinned and she found the grin attractive and comforting.

Taking a swig, she swallowed the fiery liquid. Already she was beginning to understand how this tough-looking Russian had risen to become chief of the world's most feared secret police. It was not simply hardness, as she had imagined; he possessed a most unusual insight into human nature. Within minutes of their meeting he had penetrated two of the secrets she had successfully kept from everyone else—her paranoid fear of flying and her affection for Harry Wargrave.

"Drink a little more," he urged as she started to hand back the flask. Meekly, she obeyed the suggestion. His hand was still gripping her arm reassuringly. When she returned the flask he upended it and took a great swallow.

"You see," he told her with another smile, "I also take the medicine I recommend to others. Now, tell me about Milan. . . ."

Comforted by the vodka, comforted also—strangely enough—by the stocky, wide-shouldered man by her side, she began briefing him crisply, keeping it short and to the point, determined to impress him with her own competence. To her surprise she found the Russian was a man who could listen without asking questions and she had the impression he was memorizing every single word she said.

Once, as the plane lurched again, her coat fell open to the knees and he glanced down at her legs approvingly but without a trace of lechery in his steady brown eyes. Hastily she covered them up. He smiled again, a warm smile that transformed his normally bleak, watchful expression.

"You have beautiful legs," he remarked simply. "So had my wife, Irina. . . ."

"I heard about her," Elsa replied quietly. "I'm sorry— I know she . . ." Not knowing what to say next, she said nothing.

"Know she committed suicide," the Russian completed the sentence for her. His mouth tightened, his eyes became grim. "Technically, that was so. In fact she was driven to kill herself—which is another way of saying she was murdered. It is one reason why I am now sitting beside such an attractive girl aboard this plane," he ended softly.

Only a short time later the plane began to lose height rapidly and Wargrave warned them they were approaching Milan. The Russian handed Elsa his flask again and gratefully she took another swig of vodka. Hell was coming up again; she loathed landings as much as she detested takeoffs.

Caspar is aboard.

"Jesus Christ!" Julian Haller muttered the imprecation to himself as he read the signal Molinari had just handed him in Milan Airport control tower, the signal Wargrave had just radioed in from his approaching jet. Before the Englishman had taken off from Bucharest they had, at Wargrave's suggestion, made a list of all members of the Soviet Politburo and given them code names. "We are, after all," Wargrave had pointed out, "assuming that Angelo is Zarubin—suppose he is someone else? I'll want to let you know at the earliest possible moment." And Caspar was General Sergei Marenkov.

"I have bad news for you," Molinari continued. "The air traffic controller says it is impossible to bring in your jet in this weather."

They were standing by themselves, out of earshot of the tower staff. Haller took a quick decision. Inevitably all the security chiefs whose territory Angelo would pass through would have to be informed of his identity. He stared hard at Molinari. "I can tell you now Wargrave is bringing in a senior member of the Soviet Politburo. We have to get him to the States. The passenger I'm talking about is General Sergei Marenkov, head of the KGB."

The tough Italian SIFAR officer stared back at him, nodded his head, and walked straight over to the chief controller, a sharp-eyed man in his early forties. "You will talk that jet down."

"Impossible!"

Molinari was not a man normally given to dramatics but the situation could hardly be termed normal. Extracting his revolver, he laid it on the controller's desk. "That says you will talk him down. This is a national emergency. Or do you lack the guts?" he inquired softly.

"That is an insult," the controller flared.

"For which I will offer my abject apologies—when you have landed that jet safely."

"I can only try. . . ."

"Do better than that—succeed."

Wargrave lifted the angle of descent slightly, less than he would have liked but the grave danger was that the jet would stall. The Milan controller was still talking him down, seeing him only as a falling blip on the radar screen, and under his desk the controller's left-hand knuckles were white and bloodless. Behind him Molinari stood absolutely motionless, his eyes fixed on the blip which represented three lives at extreme risk. Beside him stood Julian Haller, shoulders hunched forward, an unlit cigarette in his mouth. Haller had compelled himself to stay in the control tower—he would much have preferred to wait inside the security room where he couldn't see what was happening. For the twentieth time he cursed himself for allowing Elsa Lang to accompany Wargrave.

In the copilot's seat Elsa froze like a zombie. Normally the large swallow of neat vodka she had taken from the flask Marenkov had offered would have made her tight. But it had no effect; she might just as well have drunk water. Now the Russian leaned forward in his seat to give her a reassuring squeeze on her shoulder. He was also watching the altimeter. There was a jerky bump. The jet had touched down. Again the blur of lights—far more fogged than on the Bucharest airstrip—sweeping past, then gliding. The jet slowed, stopped. They released their seat belts. Wargrave swung around and reached for the Sten gun.

"Drop flat on the floor," he ordered the Russian.

"What's wrong?" Elsa snapped.

"Too many vehicles coming. . . ."

"And the Soviet satellites will have tracked our course from Bucharest," Marenkov warned from the floor of the cabin.

The instrument panel clock registered 1:57 P.M. Outside, it was almost dark. Through the gloom the headlights of numerous vehicles were rushing toward the stationary machine. Fire trucks, three ambulances, and the armored truck that had taken them to Molinari's secret base when they landed at Milan the previous Thursday. The armored truck arrived first. Its lights played over the aircraft and then it pulled alongside, leaving space only for the automatic staircase to be lowered. Wargrave pressed the button, threw open the door as the driver of the truck got out and shone a torch up the staircase.

"Drop that damned light," Wargrave roared in Italian. The driver dropped the torch in sheer astonishment

115

and fright. Wargrave made him mount the staircase and demanded his identity card. "We have come to pick you up," the man protested. "The airport is ringed with troops." Ignoring the protest, Wargrave checked the identity card, handed it back.

"We're traveling with you in the cab," Wargrave informed the driver. "Three of us. And I'll drive while you guide me."

"There's hardly room—we have armed guards in the back to protect you. . . ."

Elsa went down the staircase first at a run and waited for Marenkov, who scrambled down with great agility, clutching his briefcase, with Wargrave close behind him. They climbed up into the armored truck's cab and Wargrave shooed the driver ahead, climbed behind the wheel, and slammed the door shut.

"This is my truck," the driver protested again.

"So I want to be behind the wheel in case one of those vehicles out there is the wrong one," Wargrave snapped. "Now—guide me. Which way to Molinari?"

"Head for the tower—those lights you can just see."

Wargrave already had the armored truck moving, driving at accelerating speed as fire trucks and ambulances swerved to avoid his onward rush. "You're crazy," the driver protested. "You and your passenger"—he glanced curiously at the man between Wargrave and Elsa who was muffled in his fur coat with the collar turned up so it was impossible to see his face—"would be safer in the back. That was the whole idea. . . ."

"Crazy?" Wargrave gave a bitter grin without a trace of humor. "Crazy enough to land on an ice-bound runway when your controller said it was impossible. Crazy enough to know that if a reception committee is somewhere on this airfield they will expect us to be in the back, not here. And where now? I said guide me, for God's sake."

"Between those two flashing lights."

The carabiniere driver shrugged at his madman as he pointed toward two lights that were just visible, that winked on and off at frequent intervals. It was snowing heavily, visibility was appalling, and Elsa was flicking snowflakes off her coat. Across her lap lay the Sten gun and her .38 Smith and Wesson. Behind the armored truck one of the ambulances was following closely and in the murk, under cover of the rumble of the armored truck's engine, Wargrave wasn't aware of its presence.

Only as they came nearer did Wargrave realize that visibility was so bad the small winking lights were actually large searchlights, each mounted on an army vehicle spaced to leave a passage between them for the armored truck. As he drove closer he could see beyond them the vague shapes of a large convoy arranged in a large semicircle—police cars, motorcycle outriders, and a second armored truck that was an exact replica of the vehicle Wargrave was driving. He slowed down as his headlight glare picked out a group of waiting figures, one of them Molinari, he thought, the other Julian Haller. Immediately to his right the airport tower loomed and visibility was clearing. He stopped. Behind him the ambulance stopped, its headlights focused on the rear doors of the armored truck.

The rear doors of Wargrave's truck were thrown open as the four armed carabinieri inside prepared to leap out and run to the front. There was a sudden hideous rattle of machine-gun fire from the stationary ambulance as a hail of bullets sprayed the interior of the truck ahead. The four carabinieri never had a chance; within seconds they were dead. The ambulance began reversing away from the carnage of ripped bodies.

Standing beside one of the searchlight trucks, Molinari reacted instantly speaking rapidly into the walkie-talkie he held in his hand. One of the searchlights swiveled, lit up the ambulance in its massive glare. Out of nowhere a light tank appeared, grinding forward on its tracks until it hit the ambulance, toppling it over sideways. One man only appeared from the far side of the overturned vehicle and started running. The tank's machine gun chattered briefly. The running man jumped off the ground as though jerked by a string, fell, and lay still on his back.

117

"Don't move!"

Wargrave shouted the warning as he gripped the Sten and poked the muzzle out of his window. On the far side of the cab Elsa aimed the Smith and Wesson out of her window and found she was aiming it point-blank at Colonel Luigi Molinari.

"Get out this side—quickly!" the SIFAR chief ordered.

They jumped out just as the searchlights were doused on Molinari's instruction over his walkie-talkie, hands grasped them by the arm and hustled them inside the back of the second armored truck, the doors were slammed shut, and Molinari pressed a switch that illuminated the interior. He led Elsa to one of the leather-armed chairs. "Coffee?" he suggested. "Strong?"

"Black as the devil, please."

Molinari gave Marenkov only one quick curious glance and then poured coffee from a flask. "We wait here for a while, of course," he said to Wargrave. "Thank God you weren't in the back—and a requiem for my poor carabinieri. How did you guess?"

"I didn't, but I was suspicious. I saw three ambulances. Three people aboard the jet coming in, so one ambulance, yes. Two, still feasible. Three seemed one too many. If we'd had radio communication in the cab I'd have warned you. And thank God you armor the wall between the rear and the cab—I heard bullets thudding against my back. . . ."

"We do our best," Molinari replied.

There was a short silence while they all drank coffee in quick, long gulps. Reaction was settling in. General Marenkov, relaxing in his chair, seemed the calmest person present. "I am greatly sorry about your men," he told Molinari. "I fear it is only the beginning."

"I'm Julian Haller," the American interjected grimly. "I will be the man in charge of your debriefing when we reach the States. But a few names and addresses for Molinari might be in order right away—in view of what has just happened."

"Absolutely no debriefing until you land me safely in America," the bushy-eyebrowed Russian replied

118

brusquely. "That is the normal procedure." He paused and turned to Molinari. "For you I make an exception. KGB personnel in Milan I can give you—but not the GRU people, who have, I know, built up a powerful apparatus here. Are you ready?"

Molinari produced a ballpoint pen and sat behind the small fold-out table at the front of the truck, which held a telephone, the coffee flask, and a scratch pad. Expecting the Russian to take a list from his briefcase, unaware that this contained only the latest Red Army order of battle, he was startled as Marenkov leaned back in his chair, half-closed his eyes, and began reeling off a list of names and addresses from memory.

In the control tower Toni Morosi, assistant controller, had watched the arrival of the armored truck, had witnessed what followed. He walked over to the chief controller, who was still recovering from the stress of talking down the jet followed by the bursts of gunfire outside the tower. "I'm feeling terrible," Morosi complained. "My stomach's getting worse. Could I go home?"

"You'd better push off, then," the controller told him.

He was irked by Morosi's frequent visits to the men's room during the morning, and in any case the airport was closed for an indefinite period. When he left the control tower, Morosi's health seemed to take a sudden turn for the better as he hurried to a pay phone and dialed the Milan number. Again the somber voice of Sappho answered almost immediately.

"Russo here," Toni Morosi announced. "The jet landed safely at 1357. An armored truck brought the passengers to the tower."

"And then?"

"There was a shoot-out. The passengers weren't hurt."

"You're certain of that?"

"I saw it all from the tower," Morosi snapped. "I don't make mistakes, you know. They transferred the passengers to another truck. It should be leaving soon now."

"You know what you have to do," the voice interrupted.

"Of course."

"Do it."

The armored truck left by the main airport gate, preceded by two police cars. A third police car followed close behind. And a few minutes before the first of the two police cars moved through the gate three motorcycle outriders had ridden ahead of it. In that weather—on an early January afternoon—they had the highway almost to themselves. Almost.

Sitting behind the wheel of his Renault, which he had parked a short distance from the airport exit, Toni Morosi sat beating a nervous tattoo on the rim of the wheel. He had the heater on and ten minutes later he was nearly asleep. It was the high-powered purr of the three motorcycle outriders leaving the airport that jerked him into alertness. Morosi watched them disappear in a southerly direction and tried to start the engine. It took him seven attempts before the engine fired, then he kept the motor ticking over and waited. Two police cars swung out of the gate and again turned south, followed by an armored truck. The cautious Morosi waited a few seconds longer and then was damned glad he had as the third police car appeared and sped after the truck.

"Looks like Genoa," he murmured to himself and drove after the convoy, keeping the taillight of the rear police car just in sight. It was going to be a long drive.

It was exactly 1435 hours when Colonel Molinari's convoy left Milan Airport and headed south through the wintry afternoon in the general direction of Genoa. In the airport security room he was informed over the radio that a Renault—it was difficult to be sure even though the police officer in the rear car was using night glasses—appeared to be following the convoy. "*Bene*," was his only comment as he switched his transceiver to a fresh waveband and began speaking rapidly.

It was exactly 1450 hours when a second armored truck emerged from the Milan Airport exit, but this departure differed in several respects from the earlier one. First, it turned in the opposite direction, heading straight for the center of Milan. Second, it was entirely unescorted as it moved at speed—almost dangerous speed—along the snowbound highway. Behind the wheel Wargrave glanced in the rearview mirror and saw nothing but the deserted road. "It might just work," he remarked to Elsa Lang, who sat beside him in the passenger seat.

"You could sound more confident," Elsa suggested.

"In this business I always assume the worst," Wargrave replied amiably.

Beyond the amored wall behind them Julian Haller was sitting with General Marenkov and four plainclothes SIFAR men, who had automatic weapons across their laps. The Russian again seemed the calmest passenger as he went on reading an Agatha Christie novel Elsa had loaned him. Was it fatalism, Haller wondered? Or was it simply that years of living with the pressures of his job had trained Marenkov never to show his emotions? The truck rumbled on at speed into the center of Milan.

Behind them Ugo Sala maintained a careful distance between the truck and the radio cab he was driving. Earlier he had waited in a side road close to the airport exit while he observed Molinari's convoy turn south, followed shortly afterward by Toni Morosi. "And I've come up with four aces," he told himself as he moved closer to the truck. It was safe now to close up; there was more traffic about.

Behind the wheel of the truck Wargrave again glanced in his rearview mirror. He was nearing Molinari's secret base where they had been taken when they had landed in Milan. He was also moving more slowly because of the traffic and the trams. Less than a minute later he looked in the rearview mirror again. "Trouble?" inquired Elsa.

"We're being tailed by a cab, I think."

"Lots of cabs about. . . ."

"This one appeared soon after we left the airport."

"One cab looks like another. How can you tell?"

"He parked it only half under cover—one side of the bonnet is thick with snow, the other barely smeared."

"What do we do?"

"Lose him."

Elsa checked her watch. "It's 3:30. The Atlantic Express leaves at five past five—and I have to work on Marenkov to change his appearance. We can't chase all over the city."

"Maybe we won't have to."

In Milan, trams have the first priority; you give way for a tram. Wargrave was approaching an intersection, the road ahead was clear, he pressed his foot down. Elsa glanced to her right and stiffened. "Look out—trams!" The first of a whole convoy of trams was crossing the intersection as Wargrave rammed his foot down to the floor. Appalled, Elsa saw the first tram looming just beyond her window, its bell ringing frantically. The truck roared on. Pedestrians turned and froze in horror. The tram driver, still ringing his bell nonstop, braced himself for the collision. Wargrave stared ahead, his foot still hard down. Inside the back of the truck the SIFAR men, hearing the bell ringing, gripped the arms of their seats. The tram driver stared in disbelief as the rear of the truck passed him in a blur and the tram sailed on.

Inside his radio cab Ugo Sala swore foully as he braked so savagely he would have gone through the windshield but for his safety belt. As it was, the stop made him gasp. Still swearing he waited as the convoy of trams proceeded past, masking the view ahead completely.

Reaching the turnoff into the dead-end street, Wargrave swung the wheel. He had slowed down but he was still moving fast down the narrow street, rattling over the cobbles as he reached with one hand for the microphone Molinari had used on their earlier visit to the base. "Ronco coming in, Ronco coming in . . ." he repeated in Italian, using Molinari's code word. Elsa tensed as she saw the massive double doors ahead remain closed while Wargrave continued toward them at speed.

"For God's sake, we can wait," she snapped.

"Not until that cab reaches the end of this street and sees us."

The huge doors, still closed, rushed toward them as Wargrave went on repeating the warning message over the microphone. Here we go, Elsa thought. He was within twenty yards of them when they swung inward rapidly and he drove on into the courtyard and braked. In the rearview mirror he saw them close again. They had arrived.

As the last of the trams passed, Ugo Sala drove forward, saw that the truck had vanished, and slowed down while he glanced to left and right as he passed side streets. It took him only a few minutes to realize that he had lost the vehicle. Pulling into the curb, he spoke into the mike, which was not tuned to the normal cabdriver's waveband.

"Rome Three calling. Rome Three calling. Passenger now dropped, repeat, passenger now dropped. . . ."

"Where are you?" a voice answered, Sappho's voice calling from a garage that was the headquarters of a small radio cab rental firm.

"Via Pisani."

"Then it's Milano Centrale. Proceed there at once and await arrival of passenger. . . ."

10

Zürich

At precisely 1435 hours—when Molinari's deception convoy was leaving Milan Airport—Colonel Igor Sharpinsky, in his assumed identity of Heinz Golchack, landed aboard Swissair Flight 433 at Zürich in a snowstorm. Among the passengers who filed off the aircraft behind Golchack was Rudi Bühler, who had traveled separately. At Passport Control the Swiss officials checked papers with their usual thoroughness. The official facing Golchack glanced at the short, well-built man standing before him and then looked at the passport photograph.

"Could you please remove your glasses for a moment, sir?" the official requested politely.

"Of course. I'm sorry," Golchack replied vaguely.

He removed the pebble glasses, which he was not wearing in the photograph, and the official had a shock. The face matched the photo—as far as any passport picture matches its owner—but without the glasses the Swiss found himself looking into one of the most penetrating pair of eyes he had ever encountered: blank, still eyes. Golchack noticed that—as with the other passengers—the official made a quick note of the name and passport number, and then he was asked for his home address. He had no way of knowing that this was the first stage of the alert Colonel Leon Springer had issued to all entry points.

"Thank you, Mr. Golchack. Are you staying long in Switzerland?"

"One or two days, then I go to Germany."

Outside the airport hall Golchack ignored the airport bus other passengers were boarding and summoned a waiting cab. "The Baur au Lac Hotel, please." Settling back with his case on the rear seat, Golchack waited until they had driven a short distance from the airport, checked his watch, and then asked the driver to pull up for a moment. He seemed to be drawing attention to himself. Outside, the snow was falling heavily, the cab's windshield was frosting over, and only the fan shape kept clear by the wipers enabled the driver to see where he was going.

"I have been thinking," Golchack explained in excellent German, "is there a train I could catch which would take me on to Bonn? If so, I think I will return to Zürich later."

"At 3:30 a train leaves for Germany. We should get you there in time."

"Take me to the Hauptbahnhof, then. Please hurry— as far as that is possible." Golchack smiled vaguely, gesturing outside the window at the weather.

Arriving at Zürich Hauptbahnhof, Golchack paid off

the driver, noted that his cab had already picked up another fare, and walked into the huge hall of the Hauptbahnhof where a series of rail tracks ended. Then he did a curious thing; after waiting a moment he glanced across to where a man leaning against a newsstand stood apparently gazing into the distance, and descended an escalator leading to the underground shopping mall.

Carrying his case, he walked across the mall and mounted another escalator on the far side, which carried him up to the street on the opposite side to the Hauptbahnhof. As he trod on the rubber mat at the entrance of the Hotel Schweizerhof the automatic plate-glass doors slid aside and a wave of heat met him. At the reception desk he presented his passport for filling in the registration form.

"You have a double room with bath reserved for me."

The receptionist consulted a card index. "Yes, Mr. Golchack. The reservation was phoned through from Vienna. Room 201. . . ."

The professorial-looking guest took his time over filling in the form, printing everything in careful capitals. By the time he had completed the formality, Rudi Bühler, who had followed in his own cab, had entered the reception hall. Also, the man who had stood by the newsstand in the Hauptbahnhof had come into the hotel and was studying some jewelry in a showcase.

"Room 201, you said?" Golchack repeated for Rudi Bühler's benefit.

"Yes, sir. The porter will show you to your room."

"Have you . . . a railway timetable I could consult first?"

Patiently, the receptionist handed over the timetable and Golchack moved farther along the counter to study it while Rudi Bühler quickly filled in his own registration form. In the hall behind them the man from the Hauptbahnhof newsstand was still examining the showcase jewelry. Then, as if by chance, all three men moved toward the elevator at the same time, accompanied by the porter carrying Golchack's and Bühler's cases.

The elevator was small and the four men were just able

125

to squeeze inside it together. As the elevator ascended to the second floor the man from the newsstand held his room key in his hand with the number showing. Room 207. The porter assumed the three men were strangers as the elevator stopped at the second floor. "You are on the third floor," he explained to Bühler. "I shall only be a moment."

The guest for Room 207 entered his own room as Golchack proceeded along the corridor with the porter. Alone inside Room 201, Golchack allowed time for Bühler to arrive at his own room and return to Room 207. Checking the bathroom, he went back into the large double bedroom and peered through the heavy lace-curtained windows that overlooked the Bahnhofstrasse. He was staring down into the richest street in the world, the street where all the big Swiss banks had their main branches. It was still snowing as a tram passed below his window, and sparks flashed as the overhead traction brushed the frosted wires. Checking his watch, he opened the bedroom door, saw that the corridor was deserted, locked his door, and walked along to Room 207. He rapped on the door in a certain way and Bühler opened it a fraction, then let him inside. Golchack wasted no time on greetings.

"Everything is set up?" he inquired in German. He looked around the room. "I want to send several signals immediately."

"I am ready when you are, sir."

Heinrich Baum, the man who had waited by the Hauptbahnhof newsstand, was a Swiss dentist from Basel. A compact thirty-year-old, Baum was lean-faced, sported a pencil-thin mustache, and had a brisk manner. He opened a black case resting on a table. When he first opened the case it appeared to contain a set of dental equipment. Pressing two concealed catches, Baum elevated a telescopic aerial and inserted three plugs into sockets, and the disguised transceiver was ready for transmission.

"Two signals have come in for you," he informed Golchack, "one from Milan and the second from Moscow."

With a feeling of relief Golchack took off his pebble

126

glasses and replaced them with his normal rimless pair so he could see to read clearly. The Milan signal was brief. *Peter landed safely. Interception failed. Everything indicates he will travel aboard Atlantic Express departing Milan 1705 hours.* He handed the signal to Bühler.

"We arrived here just in time," he commented.

The Moscow signal was briefer. *Now use total apparatus to destroy Peter.* Although unsigned, Golchack knew this signal had been sent by Leonid Sedov himself and Marshal Prachko. Again he handed the signal to Bühler, carefully keeping his voice flat and toneless.

"All the GRU sabotage units are now at our disposal."

"Let's hope we don't have to go that far."

Golchack glanced at him with his pale blank eyes and Bühler wished he had kept his mouth shut. Hurrying to the bathroom, he burned both signals, flushing the embers down the toilet. In the bedroom Golchack took three slips of paper from the Sotheby's catalog and handed them to Baum. He had written out the three signals while he waited in his bedroom for Bühler to reach Room 207.

"Send them in the sequence I have indicated," he instructed. "Encode the first, send it, then the second, and so on." He turned to Bühler as the sabotage chief returned to the room. "Let me have a look at the map."

Bühler opened up a large-scale map of Switzerland he had brought from his room and spread it out over the double bed. Golchack bent over the map, took out a pen, and ringed two areas, being careful not to mark the map. "At one of these points between Milan and Zürich we eliminate Peter." He spoke quietly as though discussing a business transaction. Bühler was staring at the second location Golchack had ringed.

"We would attempt even that?"

"If necessary, yes. I have already alerted Andermatt. The destruction will be enormous—but so long as we destroy Peter what does it matter?"

While they talked, Heinrich Baum was already starting to transmit the first, very brief encoded signal. And before he began transmitting he had set a small pinger clock for two and a half minutes. It was unlikely that Swiss radio-detector vans would be in the vicinity, but Golchack never took a single unnecessary risk. Working together, it would take two radio-detector vans at least five minutes to take a fix on a secret transmitter—to plot from two locations the cross-point of the radio beams indicating where the transmission was coming from.

And Baum's signals had only to travel a few kilometers to the place where the main Soviet transmitter was based. Beyond the east bank of the river Limmat that divides the ancient city of Zürich the land rises rapidly to the Zürichberg, a heavily wooded hilltop that in summer is the favorite relaxation spot of the Zürichers. In winter it is deserted and few people wander along the winding tracks lined with great walls of log piles. It was close to the Heubeeri-Weg track that a large mobile trailer was parked.

Officially, Professor Georg Mohner, the well-known Swiss meteorologist who occupied the mobile trailer alone, was studying weather patterns, and the interior of the trailer was crammed with meteorological equipment. What Mohner, a tall, thin, ascetic-looking man, did not advertise to the rare visitors to his well-heated trailer was the concealed power-operated aerial that could be elevated—and withdrawn swiftly—at the push of a button. Nor did he show them the exceptionally high-powered transmitter which, from the heights of the Zürichberg, could send signals all over Europe.

Within two minutes of receiving the first signal from Baum at the Hotel Schweizerhof, Mohner had elevated his own aerial and was transmitting long-distance. And, like Baum, he had set his own time-clock for two and a half minutes. The first signal went to Milan, the second to Moscow. The third—and longest—was transmitted to Andermatt.

In Room 207 at the Hotel Schweizerhof, Golchack checked his watch. It was exactly 4 P.M. In an hour's time the Atlantic Express would start its long journey from Milan with its ultimate destination Amsterdam. And already the secret Soviet base Golchack had set up inside Switzerland was geared for action.

It was exactly 4 P.M. in Vienna when Leo Scoblin, assistant cipher clerk in the code room at the Soviet Embassy, came off duty. Hurrying out of the Soviet Embassy as fast as his limp would allow him, he climbed behind the wheel of his Volkswagen. The engine was cold and it was only at the eighth attempt that the motor fired. Sighing with relief, he drove off at speed, weaving his way through the traffic, his hands gripping the wheel tightly.

Perhaps it was the heavy traffic, maybe it was his sense of extreme urgency, that made him take only cursory glances in his rearview mirror. Certainly he never saw the old Mercedes following him, a vehicle occupied by the same two men who earlier that afternoon had in the Vienna Woods cremated the body of a rare-book dealer called Heinz Golchack.

It was to Leo Scoblin that Colonel Igor Sharpinsky had handed the sealed envelope of signals before leaving Vienna to catch his plane for Zürich in the guise of Heinz Golchack. It was Leo Scoblin who had noticed on Sharpinsky's desk the two air tickets to the Swiss city. And it was the meticulous Sharpinsky who had ordered a watch to be kept on Scoblin, but only as a precaution.

Reaching the main Post Office, Scoblin limped inside and whispered across the telephone counter the number he wanted. The girl did not hear him the first time and he repeated the Zürich number in a slightly louder voice, but still softly enough to make it impossible for anyone else to hear him.

"You will have to wait," she informed him. "I will call out the booth number."

"Just say 'your Zürich number,'" he pleaded.

In a fever of impatience he was careful to conceal, he sat on one of the benches with his back to the wall. The system wasn't very satisfactory from Scoblin's point of view. For an international call you gave the girl the number and then waited until the call was connected and she called out the booth number you could take the call from. Leo Scoblin was no amateur—he had chosen a seat in the open—but he failed to notice the quiet entry of the two men from the Mercedes who took up a position in a shadowed part of the hall out of his range of vision.

He had to wait ten minutes and then the girl shouted out the message. "Your Zürich call is on the line. Take it in Booth Three."

Scoblin limped quickly toward Booth Three, which was near the Post Office exit. Closing the door carefully behind him, he lifted the receiver and spoke rapidly in German. "This call is very urgent. Kramer speaking. Paul Kramer. Put me through to Arthur Petersen. Please hurry."

"One moment, please."

The girl operator at Brigadier Traber's counterespionage headquarters reacted quickly. The names she had been given were top-priority and she plugged in immediately to Traber's private line. "Mr. Paul Kramer on the line for you, sir—from Vienna."

"Put him through."

"Paul Kramer here."

"Peterson speaking. . . ." Traber, a small, plump man of fifty-five with quick-moving eyes, found he was gripping the receiver tightly. The line was good and he sensed the extreme tension in the voice far away to the east in Austria, a voice he only heard very occasionally. The voice began speaking quickly.

"I heard the news two hours ago but I have only just been able to get away. Crocodile is coming. He is on his way to Zürich. . . ."

Inside the telephone booth Leo Scoblin heard the squeak of the badly oiled hinges as the door opened behind him. He had no time even to turn his head as the short-bladed knife was plunged up to the hilt below his left shoulderblade. At the other end of the line Traber heard a short gulp. "Hello," he said. When there was no reply he replaced the receiver. He felt slightly ill. Leo Scoblin, the Israeli agent, had been a nice chap. And Crocodile was the code name for Colonel Igor Sharpinsky.

More than that—just before he took the call a signal had come in from Harry Wargrave in Milan informing Traber that the "key anti-Communist agent" the Englishman had referred to on his way through Zürich was General Sergei Marenkov, head of the Soviet KGB. "All hell is about to break loose," the Swiss said to himself. Picking up the phone, he asked to be put through immediately to Springer.

Springer was at that moment at security headquarters in Lugano, southern Switzerland. It had been decided that Springer would watch over the Atlantic Express's progress along the section of rail track south of the Gotthard; north of the Gotthard Brigadier Traber would take over. Traber got through on the scrambler phone very quickly.

"Leon," he opened the call bluntly, "I have just heard from Wargrave that the passenger they are bringing through is General Marenkov of the KGB."

"God Almighty . . ."

"We may need his help, too. Brace yourself—there is more to come. I have also just heard from an impeccable source that Crocodile left for Zürich about two hours ago."

"Any more details?" Springer asked quickly.

"None. I fear the source was chopped in mid-conversation."

"This," Springer pointed out, "may be a once-in-a-lifetime opportunity for us—the entire Communist underground sabotage apparatus could surface to wipe out a huge target like Marenkov. I suggest a red alert throughout the entire country with all leaves canceled."

"My next move," Traber assured him. "Now I must get off the line. Good luck at your end."

Breaking the connection, Traber began making a series of phone calls. From what Leo Scoblin had told him, Sharpinsky must have come in by plane. His first call was to Zürich Airport security.

"I want an immediate list of all passengers who came in on Swissair Flight 433 from Vienna. I want to know where they are now. Check the airport bus. Track down all the cabdrivers who picked up passengers off that flight. When do I want the list? On my desk thirty minutes from now!"

11

Milan, Moscow, The Hague

It was 4 P.M. Saturday, January 8, when Heinz Golchack had set up the Soviet base at the Hotel Schweizerhof in Zürich. It was 4 P.M. in Milan when Wargrave, returning to Molinari's secret headquarters behind the massive closed doors at the end of the cul-de-sac street, dispatched a series of coded signals to various European security chiefs. They had been prepared in advance, and his radio operator Peter Neckermann had only to substitute the name "Marenkov" for "Zarubin."

These signals were sent to Brigadier Traber in Zürich, to Captain Franz Wander of the German BND in Wiesbaden, to General Max Scholten, Dutch counter-espionage chief in The Hague. While he was sending these warning signals the tempo of the whole operation was accelerating and there was a sense of extreme urgency inside the building Molinari had placed at Sparta's disposal. The Atlantic Express was due to depart from Milano Centrale at 5:05 P.M.

In her bedroom Elsa Lang was transforming Marenkov's appearance with the aid of the makeup kit she always carried, using the expertise she had acquired during her year's stint with the film company in London as makeup girl. Marenkov, a white overall draped over his shoulders, sat patiently in a chair as she trimmed his bushy eyebrows and changed his hairstyle. Again the Russian seemed the calmest person in the building.

"You'll have trouble turning me into a film star," he joked as he stared at his new image in the wall mirror.

"Well, you may not be Gregory Peck," she responded, her hands working busily, "but you could pass as Lee Marvin if you were taller."

"He's a villain—like me."

Elsa grinned as the Russian shook with laughter. "Keep still, you oaf, I've work to do." A curious relationship had developed between the Russian and the English girl since, detecting her morbid fear of flying, he had passed her his flask of vodka during the nightmare flight from Bucharest. It could hardly be called friendship, but each felt for the other a certain affinity, the affinity of people who conceal a deep loneliness. Else had lost her husband-to-be just before joining Sparta; Marenkov had lost his wife.

"Now, clothes . . ." Elsa said briskly.

Molinari had excelled himself in the short time at his disposal, bringing to the building a whole selection of winter clothes in various sizes and styles, including three vicuña overcoats. Marenkov tried on several suits quickly until Elsa was satisfied with a dark blue business suit. And one of the vicuña coats fitted him perfectly. He struck a pose in front of the mirror. "I think I'm going to enjoy myself in America," he remarked genially.

"We're traveling as husband and wife," she went on briskly. "You're George Wells, an oil executive working for Shell International—there is such a man, but at present he's in Venezuela. The fact that the Atlantic Express is bound for Holland where Shell has its headquarters makes the role even more convincing. We're traveling first-class, of course, and will share a sleeping compartment."

"Ten years ago and I might not have behaved myself."

She smiled her appreciation of the compliment and then became businesslike again. "Your tie needs straightening." Competent fingers occupied themselves briefly with the tie. "We're very well fixed. . . ." She had to explain she meant wealthy. ". . . hence the expensive clothes. Your passport will be ready before we leave."

As soon as Elsa had completed changing his appearance Marenkov was photographed and one of Molinari's technical experts in the basement attached it to the passport—a document that had been prepared in advance, omitting only the photo and details of height and color of eyes. Elsa gave him the passport and two ticket folders.

"We need tickets?"

"To pass through the barrier at Milano Centrale— everything must look normal in case anyone is watching."

She swung around as she heard the door opening, slid her hand inside a half-closed drawer, and grabbed the Smith and Wesson. Marenkov, moving with extraordinary agility, took hold of a full bottle of wine by the neck, raised it ready to throw, and stood in front of Elsa. In the doorway Harry Wargrave surveyed them with his hands on his hips.

"Not bad," the Englishman commented, studying Marenkov's changed appearance. "In fact, quite remarkable. You have about fifteen minutes—we want to reach Milano Centrale just before the express departs." He left the room and Elsa spoke severely to the Russian.

"I am supposed to be guarding you. From now on, you do exactly as I say." She pointed to the two folders he held in his left hand. "The tickets are for Amsterdam in case we have to go all the way through to Schiphol if Zürich closes down, which I hope it doesn't. The sleeper reservations are for Coach 4, the rear Wagon-Lit—the first one we come to beyond the ticket barrier. But we actually board the Wagon-Lit beyond, then walk back."

"Wargrave has organized this well," Marenkov commented.

"One more thing," Elsa went on. "The easiest way to recognize a man—or a woman—in disguise is by their walk. You walk with a heavy, deliberate tread. You've got to alter that. Now let's practice—walk around this room and I'll criticize. And remember, the danger point could be Milano Centrale before we get on the train. . . ."

At 4:15 P.M. a droopy-mustached figure wearing glasses and a raincoat was wandering around the vast concourse of Milano Centrale, a rail terminal that in size rivaled Frankfurt Hauptbahnhof. Built of marble with huge pillars and a soaring vaulted roof overhead, it resembled a majestic mausoleum rather than a rail terminal. And as he continued wandering around with a folded newspaper in his left hand, Matt Leroy was worried.

By now very familiar with European stations, he didn't like the look of Milano Centrale. It was too big, there were too many places where snipers could hide. Not that there was so much really to worry about with Molinari controlling the security, he reminded himself. Mingling with the passengers already boarding the Atlantic Express —many of them Italian workers returning from their New Year's holiday at home to jobs in Switzerland and Germany—was a small army of SIFAR men in plain clothes.

More than that, there were a large number of uniformed carabinieri putting on a deliberate show of open force. And high up behind office windows, Matt knew, were stationed three of Molinari's well-trained snipers armed with rifles and telescopic sights. The folded newspaper the American held in his left hand was not there by accident; every SIFAR man in the station knew he might use it to casually point in a certain direction, to indicate something that had aroused his suspicions.

One man Matt Leroy did not notice was a short man carrying a lot of weight who had a wide, aggressive mouth. Ugo Sala, the Italian who had followed Wargrave's truck from the airport and had then lost him when the convoy of trams barred his way, was standing outside the restaurant drinking a cup of coffee close to the barrier beyond which the sixteen coaches of the Atlantic Express spread away into the distance.

Unlike Toni Morosi, the assistant air controller who had followed Molinari's deception convoy south toward Genoa, Ugo Sala, a senior KGB operative, had visited Soviet Russia and while in Moscow he had several times seen General Sergei Marenkov at close quarters. Glancing

135

up at the station clock, he saw the time was 4:35 P.M. In thirty minutes the Atlantic Express was due to depart.

In Amsterdam, Rolf Geiger swung his cane jauntily as he walked nimbly along the cobbled street beside the silent canal; he avoided the diabolically uneven and narrow sidewalk—far too easy to slip and find yourself tumbling down one of the flights of steps leading to basement entrances. He had just visited the famous red light district where surprisingly attractive girls displayed their wares in picture windows.

Geiger was well aware he could have enjoyed himself with Erika Kern; more than once she had indicated this. But like Harry Wargrave, strangely enough, Geiger never mixed business with pleasure, never made love to one of his subordinates: it led to complications that could be dangerous. Turning up the steps leading to the building where he had set up his headquarters, he inserted the key in the lock and paused.

One hell of a gale was blowing in from what the Dutch called the West Sea. Geiger could hear behind him the sinister clank and scrape of the hanging chains as they rattled in the gale high up on the warehouses opposite. It took some force of wind to move the ancient iron. Inside, he climbed the incredibly narrow and twisting staircase to the third floor and was met by Erika Kern as he opened the apartment door. One look at her face told him something had happened. She spoke the moment he had closed and locked the door.

"We are on standby alert."

"What the devil do you mean?"

"A signal has just come through from Sharpinsky in Vienna. All units are to stay where they are pending further orders."

Geiger checked his watch, his jaunty manner now businesslike and alert. "That's damned bad timing—we're in the middle of moving into Holland. Now, let's just think. . . ."

Erika, a trained radio operator who dealt with the transceiver hidden in the basement, brought him up to date with her normal efficiency. "I have contacted Wojna at Willich. I was in time to tell him to stay there for the moment."

Jacek Wojna was the leader of the main terrorist unit, a huge Pole who carried out the raids Geiger planned. And Willich was a small German village, little more than an estate of new houses, midway between Düsseldorf and the Dutch border. It had originally been chosen as the German center of operations by Geiger because of its isolation and its proximity to the Dutch border as an escape route in an emergency. Erika Kern had lived in one of the houses, pretending to be Jacek Wojna's wife.

"They still have the gasoline truck and the ambulance hidden away," Geiger recalled. "I could do with some coffee," he added and went on talking while Erika attended to the percolator. Behind the drawn curtains it had started to rain and the storm lashed at the window.

"They will bring out the explosives—and themselves—inside the truck," Geiger continued as he sat on a couch and lit a cigarette. "That way they will easily cross the border. The ambulance they will leave behind."

It was six months since they had hijacked both vehicles in West Germany, killing the drivers and secreting the vehicles for a raid they had never carried out. The small dapper man sat very still while Erika made the coffee and she was careful not to say anything. He was, she knew, trying to anticipate the reason behind Sharpinsky's totally unexpected signal.

"The signal said nothing else?" he inquired eventually.

"No, just to stand by."

She stopped speaking as the door opened and Joop Kist, a small, thin-faced man of thirty, came in, his raincoat dripping. From beneath the raincoat he produced a Nikon camera equipped with a telephoto lens. Ignoring Erika, he spoke to Geiger. "I have photographed the Maas bridge—two whole films," he said with a touch of pride.

"The guards didn't see you?" Geiger inquired sharply.

"Of course not. Shall I develop the film in the basement? Tomorrow I can go to Eindhoven to photograph the Phillips works."

"Develop the films by all means," Geiger agreed amiably. "But don't be in such a hurry to rush about all over the place—wait a few days before you do the Eindhoven job."

Erika waited until Joop Kist had left before she made her remark. "I'm not sure I trust him. There's something not quite right about Kist."

Geiger was amused and smiled. "Just because he's our newest recruit you don't have to get nervous. He's Dutch —so he speaks Dutch, which none of us does, and we are in Holland. Already he has proved invaluable in making the initial contact with our illicit diamond dealer friend."

"My instinct has not always been wrong," Erika flared.

"Of course, he hasn't shown immediate interest in your sexual attractions," Geiger commented. His voice sharpened. "I had him thoroughly checked out, you know that. A month ago he shot a policeman who almost died. He was carrying the gun when he joined us and I had someone break into police records to photograph his file. The ballistics record of the bullet they took out of that policeman matches the gun he brought with him."

Erika poured coffee into a cup and handed it to Geiger with a cold expression. "I want to go and check the transceiver, if you'll excuse me."

"By all means," Geiger agreed equably. He was still smiling as she left the room with her lips pressed tightly. In an hour her annoyance would have evaporated, and this was Geiger's way of reminding her who was boss. She was a strange girl, he thought as he sipped his coffee —promiscuous in a discriminating way. Geiger often suspected that her main motive for accepting her dangerous task in the West was to get away from East Germany where her liking for swift, ferocious affairs would never have been tolerated.

Taking out his passport, he glanced at the document. The Western world knew him as Leo Sanchez, wealthy Argentinian playboy who moved around on the fringes of the international jet set. He was best known in Paris, where he had lived for three years, directing the Geiger Group's outrages in Germany by remote control. His picture had even appeared in the gossip columns of a London paper. "Be conspicuous and wealthy and no one will suspect you," he had once told Erika. And she had certainly not relished the move to Amsterdam; in Paris, she had left behind too rich a variety of lovers.

Finishing his coffee, he began to wonder about the unexpected signal from the man they called in Moscow the Silent Colonel, Igor Sharpinsky. Something was on the move somewhere and Geiger had a premonition he wasn't going to like it; certainly he didn't like the long arm of Sharpinsky reaching out again so quickly to rest a hand on his shoulder. Could it, he wondered, be something to do with the sudden dispatch of the huge American airborne force to Germany? President Joseph Moynihan was still an unknown quantity, but this action suggested he could be formidable.

At Dutch counterespionage headquarters in The Hague a call had just come through for Scholten. Major Sailer, his assistant, took the phone call and then put his hand over the receiver before he spoke to his chief. "A man called Panhuys wants to speak to you urgently—he's used the special number."

"Scholten here," the general said calmly as he took the phone. "Are you safe? Good." He listened without saying anything more except good-bye at the end of the brief conversation. Then he turned to Sailer.

"The Geiger Group have arrived. And that information is top secret. Now we come to the difficult part—the waiting. . . ."

It was night at Willich, the tiny village midway between Düsseldorf and the Dutch border where the Geiger Group had their temporary headquarters. Outside the isolated village flat fields deep in snow spread away in all directions. The village was little more than an estate of good-class houses recently built, each with its own backyard. Inside one of the houses, which was built on several levels, Jacek Wojna, the burly, six-foot-tall Pole the neighbors knew as Erika Kern's husband, was cleaning a Uzi rifle in the living room as he spoke to Gaten, a short, wiry Norwegian.

"I don't know what Geiger thinks he is doing—holing us up here at the last moment just when we were moving on to Holland."

"Geiger always has his reasons," the bony-faced Gaten replied cautiously. He was reassembling a German automatic weapon. The small armory of weapons inside the house was a mix of many countries, but none of the weapons was Russian. It was a careful policy of Geiger's to use nothing that might link them with the Soviet Union.

"Stop creeping up Geiger's arse," Wojna snapped brutally. "I'm the boss around here and you'd better not forget it." He aimed the rifle at Gaten and the Norwegian stiffened as Wojna's finger curled around the trigger. He pressed the trigger and laughed as Gaten jumped. "You really thought I had one up the spout, didn't you?"

"I'll be as glad to get out of Germany as you," Gaten assured the Pole. "And do you have to play with guns like that?" He had trouble keeping a quiver out of his voice; the Pole was quite capable of shooting one of his own team the moment he decided anyone was expendable.

They were talking in French, their only common language, and Gaten had been born in Bergen. A Norwegian anarchist, he had worked on the oil rigs, and Geiger was holding him in reserve for the day when the order came to sabotage the giant floating platforms in the North Sea that were flooding oil and gas into Scandinavia and Britain.

"You checked out the ambulance and the gasoline truck this afternoon?" Wojna demanded.

"They are safe in the barn," Gaten told the Pole.

"Hell, I could have guessed that!" Wojna threw down the rifle and reached for a bottle of gin on the couch beside him. "Are they ready for instant movement, is what I'm asking you. Do I have to spell out every question like talking to a bloody three-year-old?" He took a deep swallow from the bottle.

"The tanks are full of gas—I tested the ignition and they both fired the first time. They're well insulated with canvas over the hoods and I left the oil heaters burning."

"I'll bet it's still like a goddamn refrigerator inside that barn," Wojna grumbled. He looked around the living room and spat on the carpet. Already there were signs everywhere that the house was now occupied only by men; dirty glasses littered a table, empty liquor bottles lay on the floor and on chairs. When Erika Kern had lived there the place had been kept as neat as a new pin, and she would have given them hell if she could see its condition now.

"This place is a pigpen," Wojna snapped. "Finish assembling that shooter and then get things cleaned up. And don't forget to keep your gloves on." Not that Wojna gave a damn about cleanliness, but it was his way of enforcing discipline on Gaten.

"I'm not the bloody housekeeper," Gaten began; then he saw Wojna's expression. "All right, if you insist."

Both men were wearing cotton gloves—something Erika Kern had ordered before she left for Amsterdam. "I've cleaned the place for fingerprints," she had warned Wojna, "so you see everyone wears their gloves while they're still here."

Upstairs in the bedrooms four more men were sleeping; it was part of Wojna's system that his men slept in shifts so some of the terrorists would be fresh for action at any hour of the day or night. And screw it, Wojna thought as he took another swig from the gin bottle—when are we going to see the action? He little guessed he would have one more job to do inside Germany.

At 6 P.M. in Moscow—still only 4 P.M. in Zürich and Milan—the three Soviet Politburo members charged with the responsibility of identifying the secret informer now faced a different and more terrifying task. At Marshal Prachko's urging the signal had gone out to Sharpinsky to use the entire Soviet apparatus in Western Europe to stop and kill Marenkov. And Anatoli Zarubin had

141

replaced the former head of the KGB as the third member. It was, oddly enough, the moderate Zarubin who had supported Prachko's suggestion, but he had phrased his support carefully.

"Since Sharpinsky, your personal protégé," the small, dark-haired Russian reminded Prachko, "failed to suspect his own chief in time, then I suppose we must give him his head to try and remedy his gigantic error."

Prachko, bristling like the hairs protruding from his ears and nose, grunted and kept silent. It was First Secretary Leonid Sedov who brought up the fearful question. Sedov, who held his position by balancing the moderates against the hard-liners in a tightrope act, was secretly pleased with Zarubin's reaction. If there was a great disaster the responsibility could be dropped squarely on Prachko's barrel chest.

"What action should we take," Sedov inquired, "about all the key KGB agents in Western Europe—agents whose names and addresses Marenkov carries in that remarkable memory of his?" He paused. "I am thinking particularly of West Germany. . . ."

Seated at the long polished table under the chandeliers in the Kremlin, no one spoke for a minute. It was a blockbuster question. Ten years earlier most of the four thousand Communist spies in the Federal Republic had been West Germans; later they had been found to be unreliable and had laboriously been replaced by dedicated East German Communists who had to be provided with fake identities—not a process that could be accomplished overnight. And now these enemy agents were being tracked down by the West German analyst, Dr. Richard Meier, with the aid of a giant computer in Cologne known as NADIS.

Into NADIS were fed the behavior patterns of suspected Soviet agents—drop points for the collection by other agents of secret material, money movements out of suspect bank accounts, clandestine meeting points between agents—and from the computer printouts Meier was able to relate apparently unconnected persons and events. If to this operation was added Marenkov's lists of names and addresses, the German BND could organize a vast dragnet scooping up the entire Soviet underground apparatus. It would take at least a decade to rebuild the apparatus. It was Leonid Sedov who broke the silence.

"If Marenkov should escape," he suggested, "might it not be better if the agents had been evacuated—later they could infiltrate back into West Germany. It takes at least five years to train an agent," he reminded them.

"You suggest we send out a preliminary alert?" Prachko asked.

"This is perhaps more your province," Sedov suggested smoothly.

Marshal Prachko was trapped and he knew it. If he said no and there was a catastrophe he would be blamed. If he said yes—evacuate them—and it proved unnecessary he would also be blamed.

"Only a preliminary alert," he said at last, hedging his bets.

"And with your protégé Sharpinsky in charge of the operation to destroy Marenkov," Zarubin observed slyly, "how can we fail?"

Zürich Airport has closed down.

The grim signal from Brigadier Traber reached Wargrave only fifteen minutes before he was due to take Marenkov to Milano Centrale. He showed the signal to Julian Haller in the odd split-level room with the semicircular window they had first entered on arrival at Molinari's secret headquarters. The American read it and pursed his lips, a rare betrayal of emotion under stress.

"That means we have to go all the way," the Englishman remarked. "All the way across Europe to Holland, since Schiphol is the only airport still open. Which gives the KGB more time to wipe out Marenkov. . . ."

"Any extra precautions?" Haller inquired tersely.

"Plenty." Wargrave glanced at his watch. "Molinari has installed a scrambler phone on the third floor, thank God. I'm going to be using that until the moment we leave here. And one more thing, Julian. . . ." He gave the American specific details as to how the Russian was to be guarded on the train. "And now I've got to make those phone calls."

On his way up, Wargrave stopped on the second floor to give more instructions to Phillip John, the backup man Haller had brought in from the CIA. The new British recruit to Sparta was giving his 9 mm. Luger pistol a final check when Wargrave entered. Five feet ten inches tall, thirty-three years old, white-faced, Phillip John had curly brown hair and level blue eyes that stared straight at the person he was talking to. He merely glanced up as his visitor came into the room and went on checking the weapon before he inserted it inside his spring-loaded shoulder holster.

"Alarm bells ringing?" he asked casually.

"What makes you think that?" Wargrave inquired.

"I've learned to sense atmospheres." John smiled faintly. "And I did hear you come up those stairs at a hell of a lick."

"Zürich Airport has closed down. So it's all the way to Schiphol."

"That should be fun."

"I hope that last remark doesn't indicate your general attitude to the task before us," Wargrave said slowly and deliberately.

"No point in getting into a lather." John had a soft-spoken voice and his whole manner was easy and casual. But his movements had been anything but casual when they had played who-grabs-the-gun first to test his reflexes, Wargrave recalled. Even John's clothes were casual; he wore a black-and-white-check sports suit, carefully cut to conceal the Luger under his left armpit. He smiled at the tense expression on Wargrave's face.

"I rather like the look of that girl agent of yours," he remarked. "With her along, the trip will pass in a flash."

"And that's another thing," Wargrave continued in the same even tone. "If I catch you fooling around, I'll break your arm."

"No problem," John assured him easily. "But I have eyes that can see and she has a superb pair of legs. Or haven't you noticed?"

Wargrave ignored the remark, gave him detailed instructions, and left the room. On his way upstairs he felt faintly annoyed with himself. Surely he couldn't be jealous of this good-looking character he had seen chatting with Elsa?

For the next few minutes, alone in the third-floor room with the scrambler phone, he was very busy. His first call to Brigadier Traber gave him a shock. The Swiss counterespionage chief in Zürich interrupted him.

"Yes, the met people expect our airport to remain shut down for days. And there's more bad news—I have every reason to believe that Colonel Igor Sharpinsky is at this moment somewhere in Zürich. I'm looking for him now—but with no description of his appearance, the outlook is not promising."

"He'll be directing the operation to kill Marenkov."

"I'm certain of it. Any news from Andermatt—from your agent? That could be crucial, since Andermatt sits on top of the Gotthard tunnel the Atlantic Express has to travel through," Traber reminded the Englishman.

"Not a word. These things take time. But don't forget I've given my friend your number and the code number is Leros. If you get a message from Leros rush it through to me—it could be a cryptic message but I'll understand. . . ."

Wargrave's next call was to Captain Franz Wander of the German BND, who was waiting in Wiesbaden. Wander had already received the coded signal warning him Marenkov was the passenger and characteristically had taken action. "In a few minutes I shall board a train for Basel," his cheerful voice told the Englishman. "I have already been in touch with Traber and I will take over security from there while you're passing through Germany. What's that, Harry? Sharpinsky is in Zürich? I don't like the sound of that. . . ."

"No one does," Wargrave admitted.

"One more thing," the German went on. "When it becomes clear to the Soviets that you're getting Marenkov safely out I foresee an attempted exodus of their key underground agents—so I have ordered a full alert along the border with the East. Oddly enough, this terrible blizzard makes it easier for us to clamp down on all crossing points. We could net a huge haul."

"When we're getting Marenkov safely out," Wargrave repeated. "I like your confidence—believe me, it's going to be a bastard."

The call to Springer in Lugano—the Swiss had left a message saying he had moved there—was briefer. Wargrave simply checked that the special arrangements he had earlier requested to be made at Chiasso would be carried out. "A flatcar will be attached to the rear of the last Wagon-Lit," the Swiss colonel assured him.

In The Hague, General Max Scholten, cherubic-faced and plump, was talking to his assistant Major Jan Sailer, who was the very opposite in appearance to his chief. Six feet tall, thin-faced, and wearing a perpetual expression of anxiety, Sailer was giving Scholten the latest reports on the movements of the Geiger Group of terrorists. Towering over his short chief, the thirty-seven-year-old Dutchman shook his head dolefully.

"Rumors, nothing but rumors—nothing solid I can get my teeth into . . ."

"But all suggesting the Geiger Group is coming into Holland? Right?"

"That's about it."

He waited while Scholten took the call on his scrambler phone from Milan. He had already received Wargrave's coded signal that Marenkov would be aboard the Atlantic Express. And he knew that Zürich Airport had closed down—which meant that Marenkov would eventually be airlifted out of Schiphol by the Boeing 707 standing by— if Marenkov survived. And he also knew that the Germans had closed the eastern border to shut the door against an exodus of key underground agents in that direction.

"We look forward to seeing you in Amsterdam," he concluded his conversation with Wargrave. "If necessary I can communicate with you aboard the Atlantic Express. One final word. Take care!"

Putting down the phone, Scholten stood up and walked over to the window. The rooftops of the distant Parliament Buildings were streaked with snow, no more than that. The great European blizzard was still bypassing Holland. And one virtue that Scholten possessed was the ability to see two moves ahead in the game.

"Do you remember reading that in 1951 the Soviet agents Burgess and Maclean were taken off from Dunkirk aboard the Soviet freighter *Marya Ulyanova?*" he asked suddenly.

"I think I heard about it, yes," Sailer replied. He couldn't understand his chief's remark at all.

"The interesting thing is that history may repeat itself," Scholten continued. "I have just heard that the 17,000-ton Soviet freighter *Maxim Gorky* has just passed Heligoland in the German Bight and is proceeding south through heavy seas. Soon she will be off the Dutch coast."

"Really?" commented Sailer, still not seeing in which direction his chief's mind was moving. "She's going to have a rough passage—the glass is falling rapidly." Which was true: a gale Force Eight was building up and alerts had already gone out to watch the dikes where huge waves were battering the sea defenses. Less than forty-eight hours earlier Elsa Lang, looking down from the KLM aircraft flying them from London to Schiphol, had seen the white froth of the waves hitting the Dutch coast. "Incidentally," Sailer inquired, "have you informed the minister of recent developments?"

"Not yet." Scholten turned away from the window and smiled. "After all, it is Saturday and we do not wish to disturb his weekend prematurely."

The truth was that—like Brigadier Traber in Zürich—Scholten had not the slightest intention of communicating with his government. The revolt of the European security chiefs against their indecisive politicians was accelerating.

In Room 207 at the Hotel Schweizerhof in Zürich it was 4:30 P.M. when Heinz Golchack also heard that Zürich Airport was closed down. He had taken the simple precaution of asking his deputy, Rudi Bühler, to phone the airport to inquire about a flight to Germany. He reacted instantly to the news.

"That means they will have to take Peter all the way to Schiphol in Holland. Just in case he reaches here alive we will make further preparations."

Golchack wrote out two further signals for encoding and transmission by his radio operator, Heinrich Baum, to Professor Mohner's mobile trailer on the Zürichberg, where, in turn, Mohner would retransmit them to their ultimate destinations. The first signal was to senior GRU operative Yuri Gusev, at that moment in Mulhouse, France, close to Basel. The second signal was to Rolf Geiger, controller of the Geiger terrorist group in Amsterdam.

At this moment, as the great blizzard continued to rage over Europe, the ether was alive with signals radioed from one transmitter to another, legal and illegal. And half an hour before the Atlantic Express was due to leave Milan on its long journey two great opposing forces—the Western security systems and the combined KGB–GRU apparatus—were moving on a collison course.

At 4:35 P.M. Sparta was ready to move Marenkov to Milano Centrale and aboard the Atlantic Express. Alone in a third-floor room with Molinari, Wargrave was checking last-minute arrangements with the SIFAR chief. Phillip John had already left for the station in his own car with Peter Neckermann, Wargrave's radio operator, who would control the special communications unit Molinari had installed in the second Wagon-Lit.

"All clear?" Wargrave asked.

"Absolutely. It is very ingenious," Molinari agreed. "I wish you exceptional luck."

"Time to get moving. . . ."

In the split-level room Elsa was waiting with Marenkov, who was carrying her Gucci case. "You look too expensive for me to keep," Wargrave commented. Elsa assumed a snooty pose, twirling on her Gucci shoes, showing off her sable and matching Gucci handbag. "I'm quite sure you couldn't afford me," she told him saucily. She slipped

148

her arm inside Marénkov's. "This gentleman, as you can see, is far more my style."

The Russian was the very image of the successful tycoon in his vicuña coat, handmade shoes, and smart, snap-brim hat. To demonstrate that he had learned his lesson he took a few brisk, light-footed paces around the room —so different from his normal heavy, deliberate tread. Elsa clapped her hands, applauding the performance. Wargrave nodded his approval as he moved toward the door leading down into the courtyard where the Mercedes 450 was waiting. Half his mind was on what was happening in the room, the other half checking to make sure he had forgotten nothing. And alone upstairs after talking to Molinari he had made one last call, but this time not on the scrambler phone. It had been a booked call he had arranged earlier through the Milan exchange, a call to Andermatt.

12

Andermatt, Switzerland

At 4:40 P.M. Robert Frey put down the receiver of the phone in the bar of the Hotel Storchen in Andermatt and looked up as a woman came down the stairs into the hall beyond. "Anna, I have a large bloody mary waiting for you," he called out.

"Drink it yourself—maybe it will choke you."

Andermatt is a winter ski resort, a small town of white-walled, steep-roofed houses with one main street, standing at the head of a long valley that leads to Gletsch and the Rhône Glacier. Its hostels and hotels were packed with a cosmopolitan crowd of visitors. Among those who had recently returned from the ski slopes was Anna Markos, a striking-looking woman of thirty-eight with a full-bosomed figure that at this moment was occupying the full attention of Robert Frey. The Greek woman stood at the entrance to the bar with her hands on her hips, teasing Frey.

"Come on," he commanded in French, "stop clowning about."

Carrying his own drink and the bloody mary, he went over to a couch to one side of an open fire where half a tree trunk blazed and crackled. Sprawling in front of the fire, he crooked his finger at her. Anna Markos shrugged her well-shaped shoulders, walked into the bar, and, avoiding the empty place beside Frey, settled herself in a chair opposite him.

"Why do we always have to fight?" Frey demanded.

"Because you think you only have to crook your finger and any woman will strip naked and lie down for you."

"Many have enjoyed that pleasure."

The *après-ski* crowd was filling up the hotel and bar, faces flushed with their exertions on the slopes, with anticipation of the wild evening to come—French, German, Scandinavian, a few British (the Swiss franc was hard on their pocketbooks).

Anna Markos stripped off her ski jacket, ignoring Frey as she stared around at the crowd. Taking off her ski cap, she shuffled her long black hair loose and presented her profile to the huge Swiss as she briefly checked her appearance in a wall mirror. It was a magnificent profile with a superb aquiline nose, high cheekbones, and a prominent, well-shaped jaw. And now he could see more clearly the thrust of her breasts against the tight azure blue shirt, the outline of her long, powerful legs, which she crossed with slow deliberation. Reaching across for her drink, she evaded the clutch of his hand and drank half the contents of the glass in one deep gulp. Her large black eyes flashed at him over the rim of the glass.

"And this doesn't even buy you an introduction."

"And yet we have known each other for over—"

150

"We were never introduced—you intruded on my privacy," she rapped back ironically.

In force of personality and appearance Robert Frey, famous Swiss mountaineer, matched Anna Markos. Frey dominated the town of Andermatt, engaged in all its activities; and the winter sports season was the climax of his year. Over six foot three tall, a large bearlike man of forty-five with a great beak of a nose and a shaggy mane of dark hair, Frey exuded physical vitality and enjoyment of life. He was something of a local hero.

As a mountaineer, Frey had climbed all the major mountains in Switzerland, including all the faces of the killer Eiger. An expert skier, a skilled pilot, he was also a geologist and an expert on avalanches; he was a member of the Federal Snow and Avalanche Research Institute located on the Weissfluhjoch eight thousand feet above Davos. At this time of the year he was always on the move: taking up his helicopter to check on the snowfall, searching for potential avalanche zones; running his ski school for the cosmopolitan collection of visitors; throwing himself into the *après-ski* revels after dark.

It was after dark that the joking, back-slapping Swiss was in his element. Robert Frey, separated from his wife, had a large appetite for women, and seldom an evening passed when his appetite was not satisfied with a fresh conquest. Anna Markos was—so far—one of his few failures. The healed slash down his right-hand cheek bore witness to Anna's vicious defense of her body when he had trapped her in a bedroom. So he wanted her all the more; sitting sprawled before the log fire, he stared at her magnificent thighs and pictured the moment when they would be pinned under his great bulk.

"Dreaming dreams again?" Anna inquired caustically.

Robert Frey did not reply as he glanced at a couple of French girls who had just entered the bar, stared at him insolently for a moment, and then ordered drinks. From the discothèque in the next room pop music began playing and several couples started jiggling. Things were just beginning to warm up. He sighed, finished his drink, and

151

stood up. Bending down, he took hold of Anna Markos' chin in his great paw. She stared up at him contemptuously.

"I will see you later this evening, my beauty."

She said nothing as he strolled away, taking his parka off a hook and donning it as he went out into the night and climbed behind the wheel of a Volkswagen van. As he drove off Anna Markos left her drink, pulling on her fur-lined ski jacket while she crossed to the hotel exit and peered out. At five o'clock it was pitch-dark and in the gently falling snow the lights in the windows of the small town were a blurred glow. She hurried to unlock her rented Renault and get behind the wheel. In the distance Frey's red taillight was vanishing as she started her engine.

Following it along the narrow street where couples strolled with skis shouldered like fearsome weapons, she pulled in to allow two army vehicles to pass her. Glancing back, she saw soldiers armed with automatic weapons peering out from between the drawn-back canvas covers. Another army truck was parked in a side street. Was there some kind of military exercise in progress, she wondered. Anna Markos had no way of knowing that from his Zürich headquarters Brigadier Traber had just issued a partial alert throughout the whole of Switzerland.

Driving on, she reached the abrupt end of the town. Beyond ran the rule-straight valley, which eventually led to Gletsch and the Rhône Glacier; it was inside the ice tunnels of this glacier that Colonel Springer's agent had recently been found murdered. Pulling up off the deserted road, she got out of the car, took a monocular glass from her pocket, and focused it. The view through the single lens was none too clear but the lights in the huddle of farmhouse buildings helped, and the snow was stopping. She was in time to see Robert Frey's van turn in through the gateway. Above the huddle of buildings rose the radio antennae that helped Frey keep in touch with the avalanche institute above Davos.

As she stood alone by her car, what Anna Markos could not see was the powerful pair of night glasses trained on her from a window in the farmhouse. Emil

Platow, the short, thin Swiss of forty with brown hair and sideburns, lowered the night glasses as Robert Frey strode into the darkened room and threw off his parka. He stood silhouetted in the light from the hall. "What the hell is going on?"

"That woman friend of yours drove after you. She's stopped just beyond the end of the town. It's the second time. I think she's observing us through glasses."

Without a word Frey took the night glasses from Platow and gazed at the distant parked Renault, at the shadowy figure standing beside it. Impossible to make out the face, but the posture, the general outline of the figure—and the car—were familiar. Platow went on speaking.

"I spotted her in the same position about this time two nights ago."

Frey lowered the glasses, closed the curtains. "Put the damned lights on," he snapped. Going across to a cupboard when the room was illuminated, he took out a bottle and poured himself a glass of wine. He stood drinking it before he spoke.

"Well, I agree—it looks as though we've found our spy."

13

Milano Centrale

Matt Leroy passed through the ticket barrier and climbed aboard the second Wagon-Lit at 1655 exactly—ten minutes before the train was due to depart. Moving back toward the rear of the train, he began checking each compartment. On Track 5 at Milano Centrale the Atlantic Express stretched away into the distance, a sixteen-coach train. At the rear were the two Wagon-Lit sleeping cars specially attached and reserved for the use of Sparta.

Beyond these were the two normal Wagon-Lit coaches and beyond them three first-class ordinary coaches. The rest of the train was made up of second-class coaches—already mostly filled—and the restaurant car. Inside the second rear Wagon-Lit, Leroy took charge of three keys handed to him by a SIFAR man dressed as a rail inspector. All the keys were the same and they locked the end door of the coach, sealing off the last two coaches from the rest of the train. Reaching the last compartment, he rapped on the locked door in a certain way. Peter Neckermann opened it a fraction and then wider.

"Got everything you need?" Leroy inquired.

"The radio equipment is most superb," the German replied in his careful English.

Leroy glanced inside. There was so much equipment it reminded him of the control panel of a Boeing 747. Giving Neckermann a little salute, he proceeded on to check the rear coach. In about five minutes Mr. and Mrs. Wells—Marenkov and Elsa Lang—were due to arrive.

Beyond the main concourse in the lower hall at the foot of the escalators Phillip John stood close to the exit. Once he checked his watch and then began marching up and down to keep warm as more passengers ascended into the huge station. He kept glancing down the Via Pisani, looking for a dark blue Mercedes 450 automatic.

Behind the wheel of the Mercedes, Wargrave could see the vast silhouette of Milano Centrale coming closer as he kept a steady but not too fast speed. Over to the left loomed the lozenge-shaped giant of the Pirelli Building, and behind him Elsa sat next to Marenkov. Nobody had spoken since he had driven out of the courtyard of Molinari's secret headquarters and he decided it was time to ease the tension.

"Molinari is already at the station controlling the security operation," he told Marenkov. "Elsa will lead you into the main hall and up the escalator into the concourse. Resist the temptation to hurry—the place is crawling with guards although you won't see them. I'll come after

154

you and wait at the top of the escalator to make sure no one is following."

"A well-organized operation, Mr. Wargrave," the Russian commented. "So far . . ."

"For the vote of confidence, many thanks," Wargrave observed dryly.

"I merely wished to sound a warning note," Marenkov replied quietly. "Somewhere they will make their first attempt—it could be within the next few minutes."

"That's right," Elsa said brightly. "Cheer us up."

"Whatever happens when we pull up, you just go straight on into the station," Wargrave instructed. "Whatever happens," he repeated.

He turned the Mercedes, swung it close in to the curb, and stopped the car. A porter opened the rear door with unusual speed; at least, the SIFAR man was wearing a porter's uniform. Taking the Gucci suitcase, he moved off up the steps. Marenkov was just following Elsa Lang out of the car when the incident happened. Two cars approaching the station collided with a grinding crash. The Russian stiffened. "Come on—diversion," Elsa whispered as she took his arm. "All according to plan."

All hell was breaking loose where the two cars had hit each other. The drivers were outside their vehicles, gesticulating, shouting as uniformed carabinieri ran toward them. Everyone's attention was diverted in that direction; several late passengers paused to watch the commotion. Elsa and her temporary husband were already at the top of the steps, moving into the lower hall, walking past Phillip John and three carabinieri with rifles in their hands, stepping onto the deserted escalator, which carried them up into the concourse.

"Track 5," Elsa said as they stepped off the escalator. At that moment, as they started toward the ticket barrier, a sleepy porter driving a luggage truck almost drove into Elsa. The Russian moved with great agility; grabbing Elsa around the waist, he hauled her clear and then, as she took his arm, he walked with several heavy, deliberate paces at his normal walk. It was the near-accident that had put him off his stroke. Recovering, he brisked up his pace, walking with a quick, light-footed tread, the tickets in his hand as they approached the barrier.

Outside the restaurant Ugo Sala, the KGB agent, was standing while he drank his second cup of coffee to keep out the bitter cold. He had been watching the prosperous-looking couple without much interest until the luggage truck incident. Now he froze. While training in Moscow he had seen Marenkov on several occasions and Ugo Sala was an astute observer. He had noticed the change in the walk and as he watched the man in the vicuña coat he was sure of his identity even though the change in appearance was astonishing.

Had Sala been carrying a gun—which he was not—and had he been a good shot—which he was not—he might have tried to shoot Marenkov. Not that he would have succeeded because two SIFAR plainclothes men with their hands in their pockets were standing only a few meters away. Instead he left the station and hurried to his parked cab. Once inside with the door shut he used the radio telephone.

"Rome Three calling. Rome Three calling. Passenger has now boarded train. . . ."

At the bottom of the escalator Phillip John stood waiting with Harry Wargrave while Mr. and Mrs. Wells, the Shell International oil executive and his wife, disappeared from view as they walked on into the concourse. Behind them outside the station the commotion caused by Molinari's staged accident continued. "You look tired," John said. Wargrave glanced at the white-faced marksman. It had been a simple statement, as though John didn't really give a damn.

"Time enough to feel tired when we reached Schiphol," Wargrave replied tersely.

But John was right. Wargrave felt bone-weary from the feet up. He had stayed up half Friday night double-checking plans with Molinari, and only a few hours ago he had flown all the way to Bucharest and back. The lower hall was deserted now; the carabinieri had disappeared,

156

the last passengers had scrambled up the escalator. The two Englishmen were alone as Wargrave lit a cigarette, said, "See you," and stepped onto the slow-moving escalator. Phillip John would board the Wagon-Lit independently.

As the escalator carried him up, Wargrave stood casually with one hand on the rail, waiting for his first glimpse of the concourse beyond. Elsa and Marenkov should just about be passing through the ticket barrier. Reaching the top, he stepped off and then paused, moving a few feet to his right until he stopped in front of the downward-moving escalator. Elsa and Marenkov had just passed through the ticket barrier and were walking toward the entrance to the second Wagon-Lit.

At the bottom of the escalator Phillip John whipped his 9 mm. Luger out of his shoulder holster, took swift aim, holding the pistol in both hands, and fired a single shot. Wargrave fell backward, collapsing onto the moving escalator, which slowly carried his slumped body back down into the lower hall.

Elsa and Marenkov heard the single shot; still holding the Russian's arm, she looked back in time to see Wargrave slump, to see his crumpled body slide slowly out of view as the escalator carried it down. Her grip tightened on Marenkov's arm. She had a feeling of constriction in her throat, she felt sick with shock, then her training asserted itself.

"We go straight on board. . . ."

Matt Leroy was waiting at the entrance to the second Wagon-Lit and started to ask a question, but Elsa interrupted him. "I need to see Julian immediately." Leroy, whose orders were to stay by the only open door to the two rear sleeping cars, told a SIFAR man in the corridor to escort them. Haller was waiting for them in Compartment 3—he had left the secret base with Molinari a few minutes ahead of Wargrave to check for himself security arrangements at the station—and the smile on his face vanished as he saw Elsa's expression.

"Oh, Julian—they've shot Harry. He was at the top of

157

the escalator when . . ." Her voice broke and it was Marenkov who wrapped an arm around her waist and lowered her to a seat as the American stood up quickly. "Lock this door," he snapped, "and only open it for the special knock." Marenkov locked the door; Elsa stiffened herself and took the Smith and Wesson from her handbag. She laid it on the seat beside her.

"I'll be all right," she told the Russian, "and I still have a job to do."

Marenkov sat beside her and spoke with unusual gentleness. "In Russia we have a saying: tears wash away all tensions."

"No tears . . ."

Outside, Julian Haller was striding along the corridor with a grim expression. All the blinds were lowered in the rear two Wagon-Lits to shield the coaches from the platform. At the end of the second coach Matt Leroy was still waiting by the open door. "Wargrave has been shot," Haller informed him. "Stay where you are," he ordered as Leroy turned toward the door. "No one leaves the train." At that moment Phillip John climbed aboard and faced Haller.

"You've heard the news?" he asked quietly.

"That Wargrave has been shot? Yes. How is he?"

"They took him to the Swiss Red Cross place here." John paused. "I have bad news, I fear. Harry Wargrave is dead."

Haller stared at him, his expression devoid of emotion. He knew already the reaction would come later. "How did it happen?" he demanded. "Have they got the killer?"

"Not so far. I was at the foot of the escalator when someone fired a single shot. I couldn't see where it came from. Must have been an expert sniper. The station is swarming with carabinieri and SIFAR men. They've closed off all exits and Molinari has taken personal control of the search operation."

"Take over here from Leroy," Haller ordered. "Shut that damn door and allow no one else aboard. You come with me," he told Leroy. "Mount guard outside our compartment." Taking a deep breath, he went back to

158

Compartment 3. If you have a lousy job to do, get it over with quickly, he told himself. He would have liked to have a word with Molinari but the express was due to leave shortly. In response to his special knock the door was opened a fraction by Elsa and through the narrow opening she was pointing her Smith and Wesson at him. All exactly as per Wargrave's specific orders, he thought sadly. Her eyes searched his as he came inside and locked the door.

"Is he alive?" she asked quietly.

Haller shook his head. She sat down very erect, holding the gun in her lap, staring at the compartment wall. Haller squeezed her shoulder, lit a cigarette, and inserted it between her lips. "I hate this bloody outfit," she said tonelessly. Marenkov, tactfully, folded his arms as he sat beside her and said nothing. She hates me now, he was thinking—if I had stayed in Russia the man this girl secretly loved would still be alive.

It was only two minutes before the departure of the Atlantic Express when the late passenger appeared, carrying a small bag in one hand while the other held the cane to help him walk. Six feet tall, he seemed shorter as he hobbled along with a stoop, his shoulders bent. He wore a heavy astrakhan fur coat, which gave the impression of a heavy-built man, and a Tyrolean hat with a tiny red feather in the hatband. His hair was shaggy and gray and he peered ahead through a pair of bifocals. Despite his slight limp he moved surprisingly quickly with an odd, shambling gait. From behind the window of the closed door Phillip John guessed his age at sixty and never gave him a second thought.

Boarding the third Wagon-Lit coach, the passenger presented a ticket in the name of Joseph Laurier and the attendant ushered him to a double sleeping compartment reserved in this name. Laurier spoke not a word to the attendant, who heard him lock the door on the inside. "A sourpuss," the attendant thought as he returned to his post at the end of the coach. There was always one on every trip.

A minute later, the express, hauled by a single Bo-Bo 111 electric locomotive—a sixteen-coach train weighing over seven hundred tons—glided out from under the immense vault of Milano Centrale, rattled over the maze of switches and gathered speed as it headed north. The station clock registered exactly 1705 hours.

3

Avalanche Express

14

Chiasso, Lugano

The coaches swayed from side to side as the express built up speed crossing the flat, snowbound plain of the Po. In one hour it would reach Chiasso, the Swiss border point. Inside his double sleeping compartment in the third Wagon-Lit, Joseph Laurier, the last man to board the express, lifted the blind to look out into the night. The lights of Milan's outer suburbs had gone; by the light of a rising full moon he saw snow falling on the endless plain. Unlike most passengers who have just boarded a train, Laurier seemed restless.

Closing the blind, he left his compartment and began wandering toward the front of the train with his shuffling tread. Walking slowly, gripping the handrail to keep his balance, he passed through the two normal Wagon-Lits and then peered into each compartment as he progressed from coach to coach.

Sometimes passengers looked up as he passed, but from his vague glance no one guessed that he was noticing every single person aboard the express. Moving through the dining car, where tables were being laid—the first dinner sitting was at six o'clock—he continued his slow progress toward the front of the train. Long before the express was approaching Chiasso he had walked the full length of the train and back again to his own compartment.

In the communications compartment at the rear of the second Wagon-Lit, Peter Neckermann removed his headphones and looked up at Matt Leroy. "I have reported to Springer again that everything is O.K. so far."

"O.K.?" Leroy stared at the gnome-like little German who spoke good English. It was one of the qualifications that had enabled Neckermann to obtain his old job as international radio operator with the *Kriminalpolizei* in Wiesbaden. "O.K.?" Leroy repeated. "With Harry Wargrave dead?"

"You saw the body?" Neckermann inquired.

"For Christ's sake, no—I wasn't allowed to leave the train."

The droopy-mustached American was irritated. Neckermann had been a friend of Wargrave's and he had shown no emotion on hearing of the Englishman's death. These goddamn Europeans, Leroy was thinking. Stiff upper lip and all that crap.

"Did Haller or anyone else see the body?" Neckermann persisted.

"No."

"I see. . . ."

Unsure whether he could control himself, Leroy left the communications compartment and went back to Compartment 3, where Haller and Elsa were guarding Marenkov. Phillip John stood aside to let him enter the rear coach. "You look as though you've swallowed a bee," the Englishman commented in his soft voice. "Missing the Coca-Cola?"

Leroy punched him on the arm none too gently. "I did just that, fellow, so watch the smart remarks. And your extra nipple is showing." He tapped John's shoulder holster. There was a blur of movement and Leroy found himself staring into the muzzle of the Luger. "O.K.," he conceded, "so you're red-hot with the shooter." As he disappeared into the rear coach John slipped the gun back in place and unfastened the top button of his coat, which had tightened it to expose the outline of the weapon. John was a man willing to learn from anyone.

Knocking on the door, Leroy faced the set procedure —the door opened a fraction, Haller stared out holding a Colt .45 and let him inside. Leroy was relieved to see that outwardly, at least, the atmosphere of gloom had lifted. Everyone was making an effort. Marenkov was playing a game of solitaire with a pack of cards; as he entered, Elsa reached over and moved a card into place.

"Neckermann just reported again to Springer," Leroy informed Haller.

"We'll reach Chiasso soon," the American commented.

He lifted the blind a fraction as the express passed Como station and then lowered it. He had no way of knowing that outside in the night the passage of the express was being observed from the fourth-floor window of an apartment block close to the railway line. Inside the darkened room the owner of the apartment watched the long glowworm of lights speeding past. Closing the curtains, he switched on the light, opened a closet, and pressed a concealed catch, and a flap dropped open revealing a high-powered transceiver. He began transmitting.

As the express approached Chiasso, Joseph Laurier lay reclining on his berth inside his sleeping compartment in the third Wagon-Lit. Checking his watch, he became restless again. He swung his long legs onto the floor, took the bone-handled knife he had kept under his pillow, and slipped it down inside the thick sock of his right leg. The train was slowing down as he slipped on his astrakhan coat and Tyrolean hat. As the express stopped, he picked up his cane.

It was 6:05 P.M. when the Atlantic Express stopped at the Swiss border point, where there were huge marshaling yards, and where Swiss Passport Control and Customs board trains. And it was no longer snowing. After the steady rumble of the fast-moving wheels an uncanny hush descended on the interior of the train. Outside, the platform was deserted. Inside Compartment 3 Elsa picked up her revolver and rested it in her lap.

"You are expecting trouble?" Marenkov inquired.

"It's Chiasso. Every stop is a potential danger point.

Would you mind not playing with your cards until we're moving again? I don't want any distractions."

"Then you will have to conceal your legs—if you wish my attention not to be distracted."

Elsa forced a faint smile: the Russian was trying to cheer her up at a moment of tension. Haller had gone out into the corridor to keep watch and she felt her sole responsibility for guarding Marenkov—and again intuitively he had sensed her mood.

Outside on the platform, Joseph Laurier was trudging up and down alongside the third Wagon-Lit like a man who feels the need of fresh air after an overheated train. And he saw signs of growing activity. Three new passengers appeared from the waiting room, all men and all well protected in fur coats. Obviously traveling together, and carrying cases, they entered a second-class car and slammed the door shut. Laurier watched them and then turned to look toward the rear of the platform.

A huge canvas screen over seven feet high blocked off the platform near the end of the express. Somewhere in the distance Laurier could hear the rumble of approaching wheels. He glanced to his left again as a fourth passenger emerged from the waiting room and strolled toward the express, a far more striking-looking person than the three nondescripts who had boarded the second-class car.

Hatless even on that bitter cold evening, the newcomer was six foot two tall, wore a long blue coat, and was smoking a pipe. As he passed close by, Laurier observed his prominent cheekbones, his strong nose, the neat mustache as black as his thick hair, his hard jaw, and the dark, alert eyes. He walked with a steady, controlled tread and everything about the man suggested hidden reserves of strength. Tucking his slim executive case under his arm, he tugged with both hands at the semifrozen door handle and disappeared inside a first-class car.

For about ten minutes nothing more happened and then there was a resounding thump and the express shuddered. Something had been attached to the rear of the train. Laurier climbed back on board and a few minutes later, leaning out of the window of his compartment, he saw a dozen uniformed Swiss Passport Control and Customs officials boarding the train. Which was most unusual, Laurier reflected; normally only two men from each service came onto northbound trains at Chiasso.

Inside Compartment 3 Elsa was startled as the train shuddered under the heavy thump. "What the hell was that?" she asked Haller, who had just returned to the compartment.

"Some kind of shunting, I guess. There's a big marshaling yard here."

A few minutes later the express began moving again, heading for the eastern shore of Lake Lugano and the causeway that carried the railroad over to the west bank. And no one inside Compartment 3 was aware of the significance of the great thump that had hit the train. Attached to the rear of the last Wagon-Lit was a flatcar —and perched on the flatcar, held down by snap chains, was a large Alouette helicopter, its rotor blades folded parallel with the flatcar.

"I think I'd like a bit of exercise," Elsa said. "Do you mind?" she asked Haller. "I'm getting claustrophobia locked up inside this compartment."

"Just so long as you stay inside the rear two Wagon-Lits," the American replied.

"It's not just the exercise. . . ." Elsa had opened her case and was putting on her dark wig. "It might be an idea if I had a look at the passengers—I could just spot something." She put on her horn-rimmed glasses and the military-style raincoat she had always worn while waiting to collect the cassettes from Neckermann in Basel. "No one is going to recognize me looking like this. At least, I jolly well hope not," she added in mock indignation.

"Well, take care," Haller said reluctantly. "Maybe it is a good idea," he added.

Haller had changed his mind quickly. Not because he really thought she would spot anything significant—but it might help to release some of the tension out of her system after the shock of Wargrave's death.

166

It was Harry Wargrave Elsa was thinking about as she moved along the swaying corridor and waited while Phillip John unlocked the door of the second car. Planning out the journey back in Milan, Wargrave had given her an instruction. "After Chiasso put on your Basel gear and take a walk through the train. Take a good look at the passengers—you might spot someone. You suggest it—Julian will jump on me if I do."

Several cars ahead of her, six men dressed in Passport Control and Customs officer uniforms were just entering the compartment occupied by the trio of men who had boarded the train together at Chiasso. The three swarthy-faced men looked up in surprise at this invasion and then produced their passports. The compartment was so crowded now it was difficult for anyone to move.

"Baggage!" snapped one of the officials.

Heaving down a case off the rack, he snapped the catches open, stared inside, and whistled. Inside the case on top of some clothes were three Walther pistols. One of the Italians grabbed for a pistol and was knocked back against his seat by a chopping blow from a Swiss. A second Italian tried to punch another Swiss in the groin, and a fist slammed into his jaw. Within a minute all three men were handcuffed and two more cases had been opened. Again one of the Swiss whistled and showed the contents to his companions.

"Explosives, too. Hand grenades, gelignite sticks . . ."

Elsa entered the corridor of the car as the first Italian was brought out and hustled toward the front of the train. Walking more slowly, she saw the second two handcuffed Italians escorted from the compartment and taken away in the same direction. As she passed the compartment one of the Swiss inside pulled down the blind, but not before she had seen the open case on the seat with the pistols lying inside. Turning around, she went back toward the rear of the express to report what she had seen to Haller.

Walking into the Wagon-Lit ahead of the two sealed cars at the rear, she saw a gray-haired man with a cane emerging from a sleeping compartment; then he changed his mind and went back inside. Still walking rapidly, she passed the compartment, noticed that the door was only half-closed, heard something, started to turn. A hand grasped her around the throat, a second hand gripped her handbag as she reached for the gun and dragged her savagely back inside the compartment. "Try to scream and I'll throttle you," a voice hissed in her ear.

Half-choked, Elsa went on fighting inside the compartment, kicking viciously behind her, aiming for her captor's shins. The handbag containing the gun was wrenched out of her hand. Laurier gave her a hard shove in the back that sprawled her face down on the berth. Slamming the door shut, he locked it as she spun around on her back and prepared to launch herself with one hand crooked in a claw. Then she froze with shock as Laurier pulled off his gray wig and glasses.

"You really wouldn't want to kill me? Or would you?" Harry Wargrave inquired quizzically.

She stared up at him, all the color drained from her face. Wargrave grinned down at her. "Sorry I had to knock you about, but I had to get you in here fast—someone could have been coming down the corridor."

"What . . ." Her voice choked, this time with emotion. "God, I thought you were dead."

"That was the whole idea—I fixed it with Phillip John and Molinari. It was John who fired the shot—deliberately just nicking my shoulder. He's a crack shot, thank God. Then they rushed me to the Swiss Red Cross unit in the station. I changed into this outfit in a room next door and boarded the express with a minute to spare. Cigarette?"

She ignored the extended packet, her expression bleak. "I couldn't ask why you did all this, I suppose?" she asked in a strangely icy tone.

"Something's wrong aboard this express—I can't put my finger on it yet. I needed to work alone without Haller breathing down my neck. And I wanted to check all the passengers without being recognized. I've been in this business a long time and I reckon the KGB have my picture."

"You didn't warn me," she said very quietly.

"I couldn't."

"You bastard!" She stood up suddenly, swung her right hand, and struck him hard across the face. Then she gave way, buried her face in his chest as he hugged her to him. "Harry, you bastard . . . bastard . . . bastard." Her body, thrust against his, was trembling and shuddering. He lifted her chin until their eyes met. "No tears," he warned. "You have to go back to Haller looking normal. No swollen eyes." He held her tight until the trembling quietened, and then held her at arms' length. Her gray eyes were glossy but she had fought back the tears. "Good girl."

"I'm a mess." She turned away and studied herself in the wall mirror. Her black wig was awry; her horn-rimmed glasses had fallen onto the floor in their struggle, but they were unbroken. She fixed herself while they went on talking. "You said no tears—you mean I'm to go back and not let them know?"

"Exactly that, for the moment."

"Julian is pretty broken up about you. He hasn't said much but I can tell. Surely you can't suspect *him?*"

"Julian Haller is the best operative who ever came out of Washington. Just trust me. At this stage a man on the outside—outside the sealed coaches—could be a distinct asset."

He wasn't telling her everything, Elsa guessed, but by now she had accepted the situation. Harry Wargrave—always unorthodox, a loner—had so often been proved right in the past. "But Phillip John knows," she pointed out.

"Only that I'm alive. He thinks I'm still back in Milan, running the operation by remote control. And," he went on gently, "I couldn't warn you—are you sure you could have reacted convincingly when you heard the news if you'd known the truth?"

"No," she admitted. "Do I come along and see you secretly every now and again?"

"Definitely. And at regular intervals. I need to know anything that happens in the rear Wagon-Lits. One more thing: at any time Traber may transmit an urgent signal

169

to me from Zürich. The signal will come from someone called Leros. That you get to me fast."

"Your radio operator, Peter Neckermann, thinks you're dead—at least, I think he does." She frowned. "You didn't tell him? No? It was funny—I went in to see him and, come to think of it, he took the news very coolly." She smiled faintly and looked at Wargrave with a hint of pride. "As though he didn't believe they could knock you off that easily." She glanced at herself finally in the mirror and put on her horn-rimmed glasses, then turned to face him. "If I really looked like this would you ever notice me?"

He took hold of her chin and kissed her full on the mouth. "And that's something else you don't report back to Julian," he said with mock severity. "He doesn't believe in cohabitation between agents."

"I'd better go," she said hastily. "Oh, God, I nearly forgot to tell you. Three assassins came on board at Chiasso, but Swiss security nabbed them." She told him quickly what had happened and Wargrave's reaction surprised her. Listening with half-closed eyes, he then questioned her.

"A bit obvious, wasn't it?" he commented. "The KGB are better than that. It stinks to high heaven of a diversion —something to put us off our guard." His tone became urgent. "Try and convey to Haller that your instinct tells you we're moving into a danger zone. The arrest of those three thugs may make him relax." He rapped an irregular tattoo on the basin. "Knock like that when you come back—then I'll know it's you. And for God's sake get the message over to Haller—I sense big trouble coming."

As the Atlantic Express stopped at the station of Lugano, perched high above the city, three different pairs of radio detection vans were patrolling the streets below. The vehicles were under the direct control of Springer from his local headquarters in the tiny Piazza Cioccato.

"If some secret transmitter is going to radio progress to the Soviet base Sharpinsky has set up in Zürich, that transmitter has to be near the station," Springer informed his deputy, Captain Theodor Horner.

Horner, a short, round-shouldered man of forty with reddish hair and eyebrows, was looking down from the second-floor office into the deserted square. Surrounded with ancient stone buildings, on the western side was the entrance to the funicular that climbed to the station. "And what progress would it report?" he inquired.

"Lack of progress," Springer replied cryptically. "And now I'm going to meet the express. It is due two minutes from now."

Running downstairs, the agile colonel waited while the guard opened the front door, and then hurried across the beautiful little square to where the funicular was waiting for him. The doors closed the moment he stepped inside and the car ascended through the tunnel to the station. "Lack of progress . . ." Springer had already been informed by Peter Neckermann's radio aboard the express that three Italians armed with weapons and explosives had been arrested. First round to us, he was thinking as he stepped out of the car and walked onto the Lugano northbound platform. The Atlantic Express glided past him, halted.

No passengers were waiting to board the train. Springer wondered whether Wargrave might step off to have a word; on Haller's specific instructions, the Englishman's "death" had not been reported. The American saw no reason to send negative news at a time like this. The Swiss watched while a train door opened; two men in uniforms stepped out followed by the three handcuffed Italians, who had to be helped down the steep drop. Another uniformed officer left the train and the three Italians were hustled away to three waiting police cars.

On the far side of the road, almost out of sight, a green Volkswagen was parked without lights. Springer waited until the express started moving again, glanced across at the Volkswagen, which he imagined belonged to one of the night rail staff, and went back down inside the funicular to the Piazza Cioccaro. Within a matter of minutes

171

his staff would be subjecting the Italians to intensive interrogation.

Slumped behind the wheel of the green Volkswagen, Franco Visani, assistant manager of one of the smaller banks in Lugano, a small, portly Swiss of forty-seven, watched as the three handcuffed Italians were hustled inside the police cars. He went on watching as he saw a slim civilian return to the funicular and wondered who he was. Waiting a little longer until the police cars had gone, he switched on his lights and ignition and drove rapidly down the curving road into the city.

It took him only three minutes to reach his apartment. Once inside, he opened the wall closet that contained a concealed transmitter and began sending his prepared signal. Visani was a supremely confident man. Although he checked his watch, he omitted to set his time clock for two and a half minutes. He ignored his training. In any case, this was a maximum priority signal and he had to complete it. Also, he was a slow, pedantic operator.

Springer had just returned to his second-floor room, after chatting briefly with the guard downstairs, when two radio detector vans working in conjunction began picking up Visani's coded signal. Inside each van the operators turned their aerials with care, plotting their courses until they crossed, pinpointing the transmitter's location. A phone rang inside Springer's operations room. Horner listened for a moment, then replaced the receiver.

"A transmitter. In the Piazza Dante, for God's sake."

Springer ran down the stairs for the second time within ten minutes. Accompanied by three men dressed in civilian clothes like himself, he continued running along a side street. When he reached the Piazza Dante uniformed policemen were already there. One had used a skeleton key to gain admittance.

"The fourth floor, I think," he informed Springer. "One of my men is up there already."

On the fourth floor a skeleton key was used again. Two policemen with drawn pistols burst into the apartment and Springer followed calmly with his hands in his coat pockets. Visani was just ending his transmission, had just signed off and was closing the cupboard. He turned to face the policemen's pistols. Keeping out of sight, Springer caught sight of the Communist agent's face in a wall mirror. He withdrew from the apartment and returned to the Piazzo Cioccaro to tell Horner.

"Franco Visani, of all people! I have already sent out a call from a police car to pick up all his known associates. I suspect we have just cracked a major cell. I wonder what signal he sent?"

Springer might well have felt less happy with his success had he known the contents of the signal Franco Visani had just transmitted to Mohner's mobile trailer on the heights of the Zürichberg—a signal that in turn Mohner had retransmitted to the Hotel Schweizerhof.

Deception operation has just been completed. Three men in handcuffs taken off Atlantic Express by police at Lugano. . . .
In Room 207 at the Hotel Schweizerhof, Heinz Golchack read the signal and grunted. It was hardly a model of conciseness and he made a mental note to reprimand Visani through his immediate superior. He handed it to his deputy, Rudi Bühler.

"It's working," Golchack remarked placidly. Checking his watch, which registered 7:10 P.M., he walked over to the large-scale map of Switzerland spread over the bed and indicated a certain point on the railway between Lugano and Bellinzona, the next stop. "It will happen there."

"We should be out of here in half an hour, then," Bühler replied.

"We shall see." In any case, Golchack was thinking, I always have another card up my sleeve, something that even Bühler knows nothing about. As a piece of insurance it was useful to have a trained assassin aboard the train.

15

Vira, Bellinzona

Height: six foot two; color of eyes: black; name: Jorge Santos. Citizenship: Spanish.

At Lugano the Passport Control and Customs officials had entered the first-class compartment occupied by the fourth passenger who had come aboard at Chiasso. The tall Santos sat in his corner seat with his long legs stretched out while the Swiss checked his passport and then handed it back to him. Relaxed, still smoking his pipe, the Spaniard stared back at the official with unmoving eyes while he drew a thumbnail across his dark, neat mustache.

"Where are you traveling to, sir?" the Swiss inquired.

"I go all the way to Amsterdam," Santos replied in careful French.

There is something magnetic about this passenger, the Swiss was thinking, some feeling of pent-up tension despite his casual posture. He felt uncertain but could not pin down the reason for his uncertainty. And the official in uniform was one of Springer's men. A search of the Spaniard's case by his colleague in Customs uniform produced nothing unusual.

"Thank you, sir."

The two officials withdrew and proceeded along the train. Puffing gently at his pipe, Santos glanced out of the window where three men in handcuffs were being escorted out of the station. During the lap from Chiasso, Jorge Santos had observed several things. A rather drab-looking girl with dark hair and glasses had passed his compartment, glancing in. He had the impression she was looking for someone. And then a late-middle-aged man with shaggy gray hair and carrying a cane had passed, who also glanced in.

Soon after the Swiss officials had left, Santos stood up, opened the door, saw the corridor was empty, and slipped inside the next empty first-class compartment. His movements were anything but casual as he reached under a seat, wrenched loose the 9 mm. Luger attached with adhesive tape, and slid it inside his pocket. Returning to his own compartment, he sat down again in the corner seat, stretched out his legs, and puffed contentedly at his pipe.

At the small military subunit just back off the road that led across the high plateau on the way from Lugano to Bellinzona, the uniformed Swiss guard stamped his feet to keep them from freezing. God, what a night to be on duty! Behind him was a closed gate in a high barbed wire fence protecting the huddle of concrete buildings which, basically, were a series of sheds where army vehicles were stored. Then he stiffened and unlooped the rifle off his shoulder.

A large Mercedes traveling along the deserted snow-bound highway had suddenly turned off and headed for the gate. Blinded by the headlights, he jumped to one side and then the car drew alongside him and halted. The driver climbed out, a tall, loose-limbed man wearing a heavy overcoat who had his right hand inside his pocket as he began speaking rapidly in Italian. The guard interrupted him.

"This is military property. You are not allowed—"

"For God's sake, it's my daughter. And you have a phone." He pointed to the overhead wire the car had stopped under. "Look in the back. She's desperately ill—we need a doctor, a hospital, and quickly. . . ."

The guard glanced at the man in the front passenger seat, then peered into the back where a man in the rear seat had lowered the window. The Swiss guard had a daughter of his own, but it was not a child he saw next

175

to the man, it was a dark-haired girl in her late twenties, a girl doubled over in pain as she grasped her stomach and groaned horribly. He was still looking inside when the tall driver rammed a knife deep into his back. The soldier collapsed, dead.

The next stage of the operation proceeded with a precision that might well have been admired by a Swiss military commander. The girl, suddenly perfectly fit, jumped out of the car with a pair of wire cutters and proceeded to cut a hole in the wire fence large enough for a man to walk through. The tall driver climbed onto the roof of the car, took the long-handled wire cutter handed to him by another of the men, and severed the overhead phone line. The man who had sat by the girl in the rear bent over the soldier's body and relieved him of his military greatcoat and cap.

Three minutes later there was a furious hammering at the guardhouse door beyond the wire fence. The off-duty Swiss soldier inside who was sleeping with his legs perched on a chair woke with a start. Befuddled with sleep, he still had the presence of mind to pick up his rifle before he opened the door. Outside, a Swiss-uniformed soldier he assumed was Giulio stood bent over holding a limp girl in his arms. "What the hell . . ." He was still speaking when the girl shot him with a Mauser pistol. Dropping to the ground, she rushed inside, crossed an empty room, and stood in the doorway of an inner room where a third Swiss soldier was reaching for the phone. She shot him twice.

"Was that necessary, Luisa?" the man in uniform asked.

"It was quickest. Now, get on with it."

The dark-haired Luisa had a very pointed chin, sharp eyes, and a dominating manner. Urging the three men to hurry, she checked her watch. It was 6:50 P.M. In four minutes the Atlantic Express would reach Lugano. Satisfied that they were moving fast enough, she rushed back to the hole in the fence.

Six minutes later all three men were wearing the uniforms of the dead Swiss soldiers, two of them ill-fitting, but this was a detail that would be noticed only in the light and at close quarters. None of the three men aboard the army vehicle they were now driving through the gate they had unlocked—using one of the keys hanging from the guardroom wall—had any intention that they would be seen at close quarters. The vehicle they had taken from one of the sheds was a light Jeep mounted with a heavy machine gun—mounted on a swivel so it could be fired at any angle.

The Mercedes had already left the army post manned by only three men—as the attackers had known long before they arrived. With Luisa behind the wheel, the car was speeding along the highway northward; to her right ran the rail line over which the Atlantic Express would pass on its way to Bellinzona. In the distance she could just make out the square silhouette of the signal tower at Vira. Pulling up on the deserted highway with a violent jerk of the brakes, she flashed her headlights on and off, on and off, on and off. . . .

Inside the signal tower Emilio Valenti, a short, frog-faced man who had been surreptitiously staring south down the highway for the past ten minutes, saw the flashing headlights. He walked back up the tower to where his colleague was bent over the control panel. Signalman Carli was giving his full attention to the control panel; the Atlantic Express was due to pass over his stretch of the line. "Cigarette?" Emilio suggested. His colleague shook his head; he had one burning in the ashtray by his side, a fact Emilio had already observed. Emilio took a deep breath, hefted the heavy wrench he was holding, and brought it down on the back of Carli's skull. Carli, killed instantly, was still sliding to the floor when Emilio pressed a button on the control panel. On the northbound track a signal at green turned to red.

Snatching up his coat, Emilio put it on as he left the signal tower and hurried down the steps. Panting, he ran like a rabbit across the track and over the verge to the highway as the Mercedes arrived. Pulling up with a screech of brakes, Luisa screamed at him. "Not the front door—get in the rear." She was moving again before he could shut the door.

"I think I killed him . . ." Emilio began nervously.

"Shut your mouth, you creep. I've got a job to do."

In the rearview mirror she could see the lights of the Jeep slowing down. And half a kilometer behind her the three men in the Jeep could see the lights of the Atlantic Express approaching as they parked by the roadside.

"The last Wagon-Lit, remember, Marco," the man behind the wheel of the Jeep reminded his companion. "We know he's in that car."

"Think I don't know my job?" Marco snapped. "You handle the driving—I'll handle this." He took a tighter grip on the heavy machine gun as the driver switched on the ignition.

"Why are you so nervy?" Haller demanded. "They took off that bunch of thugs at Lugano. Sure, they'll try something else later."

"I've just got this feeling," Elsa persisted. "Call it a hunch, call it what you damn well like—I've got this feeling something nasty is about to happen. . . ."

The express had left Lugano, was now picking up speed as it approached the plateau beyond the city which the railway crossed before it began descending the great drop to Bellinzona, where the track clings like a thread to the mountainside. Inside the compartment Haller sat alongside Elsa while Marenkov stood with his back to the window, easing the stiffness out of his limbs. With the blind closed, from outside the train the Russian's bulk made a perfect silhouette. He was watching Elsa closely.

"What happened while you were going through the train?" he inquired softly.

"I saw those three gunmen being arrested."

"I think you saw—or experienced—something else. Am I wrong?" Marenkov held up a warning hand. "Think before you speak. I am a man who respects a clever woman's intuition." As he spoke Marenkov was thinking of his poor, dead wife, Irina; of the times when she had sensed coming shifts in the Moscow power factions and had warned him.

"Thanks," Elsa replied somewhat ungraciously. Marenkov was beginning to get to know her a little too well. Risking what must seem a touch of insolence, she looked sideways at Haller. "I just think we can't afford to relax for a single second."

"What the hell makes you think I'm relaxing?" the American snapped. "We're running a deadly gauntlet all the way to Schiphol. What I can't understand is what's got into you at this particular moment."

"Fear," Marenkov said quietly. He was still standing with his back to the window, still watching Elsa curiously. "I can always smell fear." The Russian shrugged and gave up his probing of the English girl. "The express is slowing down," he remarked.

Haller checked his watch, although he knew they couldn't possibly be approaching Bellinzona yet. "Must be a signal against us," he commented.

In the main signal tower at Lugano the chief signal-master, Alois Reiter, a forty-year-old man with restless eyes, was staring at his control panel. He was staring at the Vira stop signal, a stop signal for which there was no reason. Another man might have hesitated while he thought of reasons, might have phoned the Vira tower. Instead Reiter instantly obeyed instructions. He dialed a number that put him straight through to Springer's headquarters. Horner took the call, listened briefly, put his hand over the receiver, and reported to Springer.

"There's an unexplained stop signal on the line—the tower near Vira. The express will be halted in less than two minutes from now."

Springer's reaction was electric. "Warn Haller—major alert." He glanced at a map on the wall, turned to another officer. "Red alert for sector 431. All vehicles to be stopped—civilian, police, military, the lot. Set up road-blocks around the entire sector. Seal it off. Nothing moves in or out."

"Military vehicles, too?" the officer queried.

"Everything, I said," Springer snapped. "Everything that moves. And don't forget the Locarno airstrip."

The officer was already using the phone, issuing a

stream of orders. All over sector 431 Swiss Army and security units began moving through the night, helicopters were taking off, light army planes were moving out of their hangars. And, using the transceiver himself, Horner was sending out the top alert. *Guisan . . . Guisan . . . Guisan. . . .* The name of the Swiss commander-in-chief during World War II who had, at a critical moment, ordered total mobilization of the Swiss armed forces against the vehement objections of his government. In Traber and Springer the spirit of Guisan still lived.

The Atlantic Express was hardly moving when there was an urgent rapping on the door of Marenkov's compartment. Unlocking the door, Haller opened it a fraction. In the corridor Matt Leroy found himself staring into the muzzle of Haller's Colt .45. "A top alert just came over the radio," Leroy snapped.

"Get back to the end of the car." Haller stepped out to run along to the communications compartment in the next Wagon-Lit and saw Peter Neckermann—against all all orders—standing in the corridor. "Guisan," Neckermann shouted. "Guisan—Guisan. . . ."

Haller swiveled on his heel, went back inside the compartment, where Marenkov was still standing with his back to the window. "Down on the floor," he rapped out, grabbing the Russian, pushing him down. Elsa was already on the floor as Marenkov sprawled alongside her. "Under other circumstances I would appreciate this position," he told her. Realizing he was reassuring her, she took his hand, squeezed it. "They'll handle it."

"We can be sure of that," Marenkov replied, concealing the extreme tension he was feeling.

Haller had left the compartment and Elsa reached up to lock the door. The express was now stationary as the American ran along the corridor to where Phillip John stood on guard. He grabbed the Englishman by the arm. "Come with me," he ordered and went inside an empty compartment. Switching off the lights, he raised the blind a few inches, then all the way. He couldn't see anything that attracted his attention. It wasn't snowing, the sky was clear, and a full moon shone down on a deserted highway that ran close to the railroad track. Haller lowered the window and a wave of ice-cold air filled the compartment. He glanced north, saw the red light, looked south, and dropped to a kneeling position.

"Here they come. . . ." He had hardly spoken when they heard the drum-fire rattle of a machine gun. In the stillness of the night the sound was appallingly loud. "An army Jeep," Haller said quickly. "Aim for the driver. Stop him. Get the driver. . . ."

John squeezed in front of Haller, calmly took up a position huddled in the corner, and steadied his Luger, aiming for a point on the highway the Jeep had not yet reached. The machine-gun cannonade was a roar now, ripping across the windows of the rear Wagon-Lit as it drove along the highway. The man behind the gun was an expert, moving the barrel up and down a fraction as he sprayed the Wagon-Lit. John waited, his Luger steady, his body motionless. A hail of bullets thudded into their compartment and then the Jeep came into sight as it passed the window. John fired three times in rapid succession. The rattle of machine-gun fire ceased as the Jeep drew level with the second Wagon-Lit. Then it disappeared into the night, heading north along the highway.

"Missed them. Damnation," John said bitterly.

"Moving target," Haller commented sympathetically. He had jumped up off the floor, aimed his Colt .45 out of the window, fired one shot. The Jeep's machine gunner slumped over his weapon. Haller ran back down the corridor, used the special rap on the door, which was opened by Elsa, her revolver aimed through the gap. Marenkov was on his feet and behind him the blind was ripped to pieces, the window shattered. Had he remained standing a minute longer he would have been dead a dozen times over. The Russian crunched glass as he stepped forward.

"My congratulations on your security system, Mr. Haller. Were any of your men hit? No? Thank God for that.

181

They will, of course, make a fresh attempt to kill me, but I am considerably reassured by this little happening."

Haller kept the surprise out of his expression. The Russian seemed the calmest person in the Wagon-Lit. At the far end of the corridor Haller saw Leroy giving a thumbs-up sign, indicating that the second Wagon-Lit had escaped unscathed as the Jeep had fled off down the highway. "We're moving into the next car," he told Marenkov. "Elsa, escort him there." He stared over their shoulders through the smashed window into the night. "And that's a damn fast reaction. . . ."

Along the highway a convoy of Swiss military vehicles had appeared and was stopping. Troops armed with automatic weapons leaped from the trucks and fanned out to surround the halted express.

From his Lugano headquarters Springer had already dispatched chief signalmaster Alois Reiter and two other railmen by fast car to the tower of Vira. By now the whole of sector 431 was alive with military and security vehicles on the move. Roadblocks had been set up. Large choppers were landing troops at strategic points. The entire wartime antisabotage system was in operation and one unit had already reached the military subpost where the gang had hijacked the Jeep. By radio they reported back to Springer the finding of the bodies of the three dead Swiss soldiers. The colonel ordered that the news be immediately circulated to all units operating in sector 431.

The three Communist agents who had sprayed the express had abandoned the Jeep inside a copse of trees and were riding in the Mercedes with Emilio Valenti, the signalman who had stopped the express. Behind the wheel sat Luisa, her face tense as she drove at high speed along the northbound road leading to Bellinzona. With a deserted highway ahead, she rammed her foot down; the speedometer needle crept up to a hundred and eighty kilometers, a dangerous speed on the ice-patched road.

"You'll kill us at this speed," warned Marco, who had

used the machine gun, who had been shot by Haller in the forearm.

"Shut your trap." Luisa spoke as though in command. "You did your job, now I'll do mine—get us away."

She skidded as she took a bend, the car started to go out of control, she fought with the wheel, regained control, accelerated along the next stretch. Behind her she heard Marco gasp. "Scared?" she inquired. "Then open the door and get off"

"There's a chopper coming toward us," the loose-limbed man beside her remarked. "How soon before we change cars?"

"Three minutes. Maybe four. Then we lose the bastards. In half an hour we'll be at the airstrip."

"The longest half hour of our lives," screeched Marco behind her. "Mother of God! Look ahead. . . ."

The Mercedes was moving at top speed down an incline with wooded verges on both sides. Ahead was a road-block made up of police cars parked broadside on. As Luisa lost speed a searchlight came on, shining direct in her eyes. Ducking her head, she lost more speed, turned onto the verge, moved into reverse gear, backed, turned, and started to drive back the way she had come. Then she swore foully and jammed on her brakes.

An army tank had emerged from the trees, was now holding the center of the highway as the barrel of its long gun was depressed and then held in a fixed position aimed point-blank at the car. Luisa reached for her pistol in the dashboard alcove. At the same moment a soldier smashed open the window by her side and aimed his rifle. The rear windows were broken, rifle muzzles poked inside the car.

"Stay exactly where you are," a voice shouted in Italian.

The doors were hauled open. The four men put up no resistance but Luisa began clawing and kicking at the officer, who had grabbed the pistol from the alcove. Dropping the pistol, he struck her a savage blow with the back of his hand and she fell back against the wheel. She was bleeding, groggy, barely half-conscious as he dragged her out. "That will teach you to murder Swiss soldiers," he said calmly. "Handcuff the bitch," he ordered a subordinate.

Many kilometers away down in the Lake Maggiore delta, army vehicles making a routine check on a private airstrip had surrounded a light plane. The pilot put up no resistance. Within thirty minutes Colonel Springer had destroyed the key Lugano Communist underground sabotage apparatus.

The Atlantic Express was moving again, heading for the great drop where the rail track clung to the mountainside as it descended to Bellinzona. Elsa rapped on the door of Wargrave's compartment. He opened it a fraction, let her inside, and relocked it. "Fun and games," he commented. "They didn't get Marenkov, of course? Cognac?" He offered her a metal flask. "You look as though you need it."

She studied the Englishman as she drank from the neck of the flask. He was still dressed as Joseph Laurier, wearing his shaggy gray wig and bifocals. Even allowing for the disguise, he looked damned tired.

"No, they didn't get Marenkov," she confirmed. "Nor anyone else—although I don't see how you could be so confident."

"The time element. The express had stopped a whole minute before the machine gun opened up. It was an unscheduled stop and Haller is no fool. Tell me about it."

He listened intently, noticing once again how Elsa could compress a complex incident into a few words. She had taken off her black wig and glasses as though she wanted to make herself as presentable as possible for him. "So you were right," she said as she ended her report; "those three so-called assassins who came on board at Chiasso were a diversion—to make us drop our guard before the real professional attack."

Wargrave shook his head. "Not so professional as I feared. They botched the job. Well planned up to a point—but they missed their opportunity."

"Really?" Sometimes she thought Wargrave was a little

too sure of himself. "Well, all right, how would you have done it?"

"Machine-gunned the whole Wagon-Lit as the express was still slowing down—it could have been done in a fast-moving Jeep. They gave Haller just enough time to react. You say John tried to shoot the driver? Roughly what distance was there between the window and the Jeep?"

"We were about fifty meters away from the highway. Julian said the Jeep took its time—moving at about twenty miles an hour."

Wargrave made the same comment as Haller. "But it was a moving target—and at night, to. How is Marenkov being guarded, by the way?"

"Exactly as you specified." She stood up to fix her wig and glasses. "I'd better get back—Julian let me out to see what was happening farther up the train. Most of the passengers are pretty jittery. Inspectors are going through the cars telling everyone it was a Swiss Army exercise—no one has seen what happened to the rear Wagon-Lit, of course. I don't think everyone is swallowing the story."

Wargrave produced a thin spool of cardboard used for sewing thread. "One more thing. When we stop at Bellinzona step out on the platform with this concealed in your glove. A man in Swiss railroad uniform will approach you and warn you to get back on board, that the train will soon be leaving for Airolo. In French. Slip him this spool. It's a message for Springer."

"He knows about Joseph Laurier?"

"No, but you told me Julian hasn't reported my supposed demise." He squeezed her arm. "And watch it. That Vira attack was just for openers."

"More is on the way?"

"You can bet on it. Colonel Igor Sharpinsky has yet to serve up the main course."

Elsa looked at the tiny spool Wargrave had given her to hand over to Springer's man at Bellinzona. "Why not get Peter Neckermann to send a signal? I can pretend the signal is from me."

"Because the message asks for a fast double-check to be made on Neckermann himself."

In Lugano Springer had taken one of his split-second decisions that so often startled his subordinates. He had decided to board the Atlantic Express at Bellinzona. Leaving Horner in charge, he was driving through the outskirts of the city, heading for a military airstrip that had already been alerted. And before his sudden departure he had issued fresh instructions.

"I want radio detector vans patrolling every place the express stops at between here and Zürich—Bellinzona, Airolo, Göschenen. . . ."

"You think we may repeat our success here in Lugano?" Horner suggested.

"Sharpinsky will need to know what is happening so he can plan his next move. That means a Soviet agent aboard the train must in some way pass a message—or indicate by a gesture—whether Marenkov is still alive. After the attack at Vira I am sure some signal must be passed at Bellinzona."

"I will arrange it."

"We will extend the operation," Springer hurried on. "Between here and Zürich very few passengers will leave the train. Those that do are to be followed by unmarked police cars.

"I will arrange that also."

"And if any locals are hanging around a station when the express arrives, they are to be followed also."

Springer was thinking about these instructions as he accelerated, knowing that he was short of time. At least the train would be delayed at Bellinzona while the shattered rear Wagon-Lit was unhitched, with the flatcar behind it. Then they would have to bring back the flatcar with the Alouette helicopter aboard and link it to the express again. And why had Wargrave asked him to have the chopper hauled behind the train?

As he approached the airstrip Springer felt he had some cause for satisfaction. He had heard that Franco Visani, who had operated the secret Communist transmitter in the Piazza Dante, was showing signs of weakening under interrogation. "Before the express reaches Basel I could just enroll the entire Soviet underground network," he told himself. "The farther the train goes the more moles will emerge from their burrows."

The military pilot of the light aircraft, who had seen the headlights of Springer's car approaching, had his engine tuned up as the colonel left his car, ran toward the machine, and climbed into the passenger seat. Equipped with skis, the aircraft moved down the runway, lifted off. Again Springer checked his watch. With a bit of luck he would make it.

The hard-faced woman wearing a shabby coat and hat stood in the shadows of the hall of Bellinzona station as the Atlantic Express pulled in and stopped. At the southern end of the platform a large canvas screen had been erected, a screen similar to the one at Chiasso that had masked the attachment of the flatcar with the Alouette. The screen meant nothing to her—she was watching for something quite different.

Unusually, many windows were lowered even though the night was bitterly cold; restless passengers, unconvinced by the story of a "Swiss military exercise," wanted to see what was going on. The woman's eyes sharpened as a door opened and a passenger descended to the platform. Joseph Laurier, wearing his astrakhan coat and carrying his cane, began to walk idly up and down the platform. A moment later her eyes switched as another door opened.

Clad in her sable and Gucci shoes, clutching her Gucci handbag, Elsa Lang strolled along the platform near to the entrance hall, paused to light a cigarette. Noting the attractive fair-haired girl's clothes, the woman's mouth pursed. Then someone else got off the train and her eyes switched again.

Phillip John, looking like a male model in his smart camel's-hair coat, strolled along the snow-crusted platform watching Elsa, his left hand tucked in his pocket. His right hand—his gun hand—swung free. A moment later

Jorge Santos, the six-foot-two Spaniard, smoking his pipe, descended to the platform near the station exit. Elsa watched him as he stood staring around, studied the confident way he held himself, his striking face, which reflected an almost animal magnetism. God, she thought, what a handsome brute. She had glimpsed him earlier inside a first-class compartment but she had not realized how tall he was. Santos caught her eye for a second and glanced away. His pipe had gone out. Very deliberately he bent down, lifted a foot, and knocked his pipe against the sole of his shoe to empty the relics.

"Madame Wells?" Elsa turned and faced a man wearing Swiss railroad uniform. "It might be best if you got back on board. The express is due to depart shortly," he murmured. They were very close together as she passed over the spool Wargrave had given her and he took it from her with such skill no one noticed the exchange. Leaving her, the Swiss walked back into the darkened hall, Elsa lingered on the platform—getting straight back onto the train might appear a little obvious.

The Swiss dressed as a railroadman had just reached the exit when a car pulled up and Springer, muffled in a scarf, stepped out. "Is the Atlantic Express still here?" the colonel asked the railroad man. "It will be here at least ten minutes," the man replied as he slipped the spool to Springer. Walking into an office that had been reserved for his use, the colonel closed the door and nodded to one of his staff, Major Jurgen Thall, who was waiting for him. Extracting the message from the spool, he read it quickly and handed it to his subordinate.

"Top priority to Captain Franz Wander of the German BND. He should by now be waiting at security headquarters in Basel. The answer must—*must*," he emphasized, "come to me over the radio telephone aboard the express. It has to bypass Peter Neckermann, the radio operator on the train. And I want the reply thirty minutes from now. . . ."

Walking back into the hall and out onto the platform, he passed a woman in a shabby coat and hat who was being questioned by one of his men in a Swiss rail inspector's uniform. "Can I help you, madame?" he had suggested a moment earlier.

"I have been waiting for my husband," the woman explained. "This is the five o'clock express from Milan?"

"This is the Atlantic Express, yes, madame."

"Surely he should have got off by now?"

"Assuredly," Springer's man agreed. "You are certain he was traveling on this train?"

"He expected to—unless he was delayed by a business meeting."

"Then he must have been delayed. You will see, he will arrive in the morning."

"I'm sure you're right. Thank you."

The shabbily clothed woman walked back through the hall and outside to where an old Fiat was waiting by the curb with a man behind the wheel. She got inside next to him and closed the door and he drove off. "He gave me the signal," she said. "They didn't kill him. Marenkov is still alive somewhere on the express."

On the Bellinzona platform Joseph Laurier was still limping restlessly about, but Jorge Santos had returned aboard the train. Now he stood leaning out of a window with his dead pipe projecting from the right-hand corner of his mouth. Elsa was walking back to the rear Wagon-Lit with Phillip John trailing a few yards behind her. At that moment Springer appeared from the hall, followed by his assistant Major Thall, crossed the platform, and entered the train.

Nothing in Laurier's expression or movements betrayed his extreme surprise. He had recognized the colonel instantly, had caught the brief glance Springer gave to the north—toward the Gotthard the express would soon be approaching. Had Springer foreseen—as Laurier had— that soon the Atlantic Express could be moving into a gigantic geographical trap as it climbed the mighty gorge where the mountains on both sides closed in like pincers on the rail track?

Behind the canvas screen at the end of the platform the Swiss railroad staff, working with their normal speed and

189

efficiency, had already unhitched the bullet-riddled Wagon-Lit and the flatcar. Backing them onto the side spur to Locarno, they had separated the two cars and had brought back the flatcar carrying the Alouette helicopter, linking it with the Wagon-Lit now occupied by Sparta. Laurier climbed aboard the train, gave one last glance toward the Gotthard, closed the door. One minute later the Atlantic Express left Bellinzona.

A short time before, as the woman in the shabby coat and hat left the station hall and climbed into the Fiat, one of Springer's men made a note of the car's number. As the car drove off he shook his head at the driver of a police car parked by the side of the station. With the snowbound streets of Bellinzona deserted at this hour it would be impossible to follow the Fiat without being detected.

After leaving the station the Fiat drove less than a kilometer before it turned inside an open garage. The doors were shut immediately by a waiting man. Hurrying up inside his apartment, followed by the woman, who was lighting yet another cigarette—she was a chainsmoker—the driver opened up the transmitter concealed inside the television set and began sending one of two signals prepared in advance. Unlike his banking colleague in Lugano, Franco Visani, the driver sent his signal to the Zürichberg in less than two minutes, so the patrolling detector vans did not get a fix on him.

Less than an hour later, traced by the car registration number, the couple were under arrest and subjected to intense interrogation. Deprived of food, allowed only water to drink—but, above all, deprived of tobacco—it was the woman who cracked. Eighteen men and women comprising the Bellinzona Communist underground sabotage apparatus were apprehended. But that was sixteen hours later. The vital factor was the signal that had been sent to Zürich.

16

Zürich, Andermatt

At 7:45 P.M. in Zürich Traber received a signal telling him that the Atlantic Express had just left Bellinzona. He passed on the news to his assistant, Major Kurt Dobler, who sat at another desk in the same room. Dobler, an alert man of forty with a lean face and long jaw that gave him a foxlike appearance, got up from behind his desk and marked the time next to Bellinzona on a wall map.

"Any further developments on the passengers from Vienna who came off Flight 433?" he inquired.

Traber himself had handled the check in his search for Colonel Igor Sharpinsky since the tragically broken call from Leo Scoblin in Vienna warning him that Crocodile —Sharpinsky—was on his way to Zürich. Holding his pen poised over the passenger list, the counterespionage chief shook his head.

"We have traced most of them and they appear genuine. I've just heard that this Heinz Golchack checks out."

"Wasn't that the Austrian passenger who changed his destination?"

"That's right. We found the cabdriver who picked him up from the airport. Apparently Golchack asked him to take him to the Baur au Lac, then decided instead he would catch a train for Bonn. It sounded an odd note to me, so I phoned Lorenz in Vienna and asked him a favor. Lord knows he owed me one."

"What happened?" Dobler asked.

"Lorenz cooperated more than I could have hoped for.

191

He went with some of his security men to Golchack's apartment, let himself inside, and checked the place. Golchack wasn't there but they found a Swissair printed slip giving the times of Flight 433 to Vienna. So, that's that."

With an expression of resignation the portly Swiss used his pen to cross out one of the few remaining names on his list, that of Heinz Golchack.

Peter still alive. Still aboard Atlantic Express. Positive. In Room 207 at the Hotel Schweizerhof in Zürich— less than two kilometers from Traber's headquarters— Heinz Golchack read the signal that had just been relayed from Bellinzona. He checked his watch: 7:45 P.M. Taking off his rimless glasses, he began polishing them, although they were perfectly clean. Bühler, his heavy-built, pug-nosed deputy who knew his chief so well, noted the gesture. Golchack was beginning to feel the pressure.

"It is a disappointment," Bühler ventured.

Golchack glanced at him briefly with his pale eyes and the East German wished he had not spoken. Replacing his glasses, Golchack studied the map of Switzerland spread over the bed. On a nearby table his transistor radio was on, the volume turned down low; it was important to hear the news bulletins, to be sure that Zürich Airport remained closed. Taking out his pen, Golchack ringed an area on the map, again without marking it.

"Bellinzona was merely Phase One," he said calmly. "Now we will launch Phase Two. . . ."

Without moving, Bühler stared at the area Golchack had ringed. He was, after all, GRU chief of sabotage operations in Western Europe. This time he did not allow Golchack's stare to intimidate him. "That means uncovering one of our main sabotage plans if it ever comes to invading Switzerland."

"So?" Golchack inquired softly.

"I thought I would just mention it. . . ."

"So you have mentioned it—for the record in Moscow later, no doubt," Golchack continued in the same mild tone. "And I will consider whether to include it in my own report—that you hesitated at a decisive moment."

"You misunderstand me," Bühler said hastily.

"That I will also consider later—whether I misunderstood you, Rudi." Golchack held his subordinate in suspense to discipline him, walking over to the window to stare down into the street. It was snowing very heavily, a dense white curtain of snow that blurred the view. Zürich Airport would certainly remain closed. Turning around suddenly, he issued a crisp order.

"Send the signal to Andermatt. Phase Two. Immediately!"

At his headquarters Brigadier Traber was taking short puffs at his small cigar. He was not satisfied. Ever since the days before the Russian Revolution in 1917 Switzerland had been a refuge for Communist agents because of her neutrality—ever since Lenin had waited in Zürich with his comrades, hoping for revolution to break out in a Western country; Russia had been low on his list of priorities. So the Russians were very familiar with Switzerland, which Swiss security never forgot. Picking up his phone, Traber asked to be put through on the scrambler radio telephone to Springer aboard the Atlantic Express.

It was no secret in Swiss military circles that the brilliant Springer was being groomed to take over from Traber on his retirement, that he had Traber's full backing. When the call came through Traber explained the position to the colonel.

"My suggestion is that we start again from zero in Zürich," Springer said briskly. "Send out teams with the Flight 433 passenger list to all hotels—to check the registration lists."

"One hell of a job," Traber commented. "There's so little time."

"Start at once," Springer urged. "Put every available man on the job. If there's one chance in a thousand of our tracking down Sharpinsky we mustn't miss it."

"I'll start at once," Traber promised.

"One other thing: send out every possible radio detector van. Sharpinsky has to have radio communication to keep control of this operation I'm convinced he's personally directing. . . ."

"Consider it done."

"And put a pair of vans close to the Hauptbahnhof," Springer went on. "It worked at Lugano and it could just work in Zürich. Incidentally, has any message come in from Wargrave's agent Leros in Andermatt?"

"Negative."

Ten minutes later one of Traber's radio detector vans was parked in a side street just below the first-floor restaurant of the Hotel Schweizerhof.

Less than three hours earlier in Andermatt, as Anna Markos stood by her parked Renault watching the farmhouse through her monocular glass, it was the closing of the curtain by Robert Frey that warned her she had been seen. Climbing back inside the car, she drove the short distance back to Andermatt, reversed the Renault in the narrow street, and left it where it could not possibly be seen from the farmhouse. Then she walked back to the edge of the town and waited.

Clad in her ski jacket and tight ski pants, she felt the bitter east wind slice through the back of her fur-lined hood like a knife. But Anna had endured the Athenian winters and Greece is closer to the Siberian winds than Andermatt. Keeping close to the corner of the last house in Andermatt, she continued her watch on the distant farmhouse, then checked the time: 5:30 P.M. The Atlantic Express should now be halfway between Milan and Chiasso. Then she heard the sound she was waiting for.

The throb of the helicopter's motor was faint but distinct in the cold night; as on earlier occasions at this hour she noted how quickly Frey's men had manhandled the chopper out of the barn that housed the machine. Angling up her monocular glass, she saw the whirr of its rotors as the Sikorsky helicopter climbed, following the snow-blurred silhouette more by its lights than its bulk.

It flew straight down the valley toward her, gaining height all the time, passing over Andermatt at an altitude of one thousand feet as it headed east in the general direction of the Gotthard and the giant Wasserhorn peak. Later, Robert Frey would return to enjoy the *après-ski* revels, but now he was attending to more serious duties, checking the general avalanche situation before he made his routine report to Davos.

Brushing snow off her clothes, Anna Markos climbed back behind the wheel of her Renault. She had left the engine running; in temperatures like these it often took five minutes to get the damned thing started again. Driving at speed along the deserted valley road, she pulled in around the back of the huddle of farmhouse buildings, which were in darkness. Not a light anywhere. It was a risk she was taking, but if a guard had been left behind she would say she had come out to visit Frey.

At the rear of the farmhouse she found a back door with glass-paneled windows. Thrusting her gloved hand against a pane, she crushed the glass and felt inside. She was surprised to find the key had been left in the lock; had it not been she would have used the skeleton keys in her pocket. And it was not amateurishness that had caused her to smash the glass pane first; Anna wanted her break-in to be discovered later.

She explored the interior of the deserted farmhouse with the aid of a torch, moving from room to room until she came to Robert Frey's study, the room on the western side where Emil Platow, Frey's assistant, had earlier watched her through a window with his pair of night glasses. Here she spent longer.

A large oblong-shaped room measuring about fifteen by twenty feet, the polished wood-block floor was carpeted with expensive Persian rugs. In one corner on a steel table stood the transmitter Frey used to communicate with the avalanche institute near Davos. She read a few words typed on a printed form next to the transmitter. *Slow buildup of snow on the Wasserhorn. No sign of a dangerous situation developing so far. . . .*

It was a desk built into a wall that eventually attracted her attention. Dropping the flap, she studied the interior. In the pigeonholes were two books on mountaineering, but otherwise the desk was remarkably free of the papers and clutter normally found inside such a piece of furniture. Anna's deft fingers began feeling around inside the pigeon-holes, probing, pressing. Suddenly the index finger of her right hand pressed in against something. There was a faint machinelike hum and the entire pigeonhole structure slid toward her over the dropped flap. Behind was a second transmitter.

It could just be a spare, a backup in case the main transmitter broke down, she speculated. And it was an advanced design, possibly secreted against the possibility of vandals breaking into the farmhouse. Just possibly . . . She pressed her finger inside the same pigeonhole and the false front retreated back into its original position, concealing completely what lay behind it.

For a whole minute she stood in front of the desk. She had closed the flap. Then she did a curious thing. Taking hold of one of the teardrop earrings she was wearing, she held it in her hand and used the torch to find a bare patch of wood-block floor. Dropping the earring, she left the farmhouse by the back door, climbed into her Renault, and drove back to Andermatt.

Once inside her bedroom at the Hotel Storchen, she went to the drawer containing her jewel case, unlocked it, and took out a bracelet and a string of imitation pearls. Adding to these her other teardrop earring, she screwed up her collection inside her large motoring glove, left the bedroom, and went downstairs. The bar was unusually crowded for that hour and Anna thought she sensed a feeling of tension, a lot of nervous laughter and heavy drinking. A lithe, quick-smiling Frenchman got up hurriedly from a table and came toward her. It was Louis Celle, a friend of René Marchais, who had recently been killed on the ski slopes. And this time he was not smiling.

"Anna, come and have a drink with me," he pleaded.

"Sorry, Louis. . . ." She kept her gloved hand tightly closed. "I have to go out for a few minutes." She genuinely regretted her need to refuse him; he looked so miserable.

"I went along to the police station again," Louis continued. "Did you know they are not satisfied that René's death was an accident? At my urging they checked with Chamonix, and they know he was an expert skier."

"You know how sorry I am." Anna kissed him on the cheek. "But who can tell? Even the most expert skiers can—"

"It was an easy slope," Louis insisted. He gestured toward the bar. "Everyone is talking about it. Hardly anyone will go on the slopes now."

"Because of René?"

"Well, not entirely." Louis hesitated. "Since then conditions have deteriorated and people are beginning to fear avalanches. They say a snow buildup is developing."

Anna stroked his cheek. "Go back and have a drink, Louis. Maybe later I can join you. . . ."

Leaving the hotel, she paused a short distance from the exit and listened. It was bitterly cold and very dark, but overhead the sky was clear again and the tip of the moon appeared behind a mountain. But what had caused her to pause was a low, sinister rumbling sound, which echoed from one side of the valley to the other. Avalanche sounds. No wonder most tourists were steering clear of the slopes.

In a deserted side street she found a drain coated with ice. The distant rumble continued as she used the heel of her boot to smash the ice and dropped the jewelry between the drain slots. And as she walked back to the Storchen she could hear the familiar voice in her mind. "Detail, Anna—never overlook the small detail that can kill you. . . ."

After taking off in his Sikorsky helicopter, Robert Frey had pointed its nose straight for the giant Wasserhorn peak, which rose above the Gotthard railroad track far below. Beside him sat Emil Platow, who peered down as they passed over the glittering lights of Andermatt.

"I hear the police are investigating René Marchais's death," he said and something in his tone made the huge Swiss piloting the machine glance at him sharply.

"You are losing your nerve?" he inquired quietly.

"Of course not." Frey's question had shaken Platow badly; it was not safe for a member of Frey's organization to betray any sign of demoralization. In fact, it could be damn dangerous. "It's just that all Andermatt is talking about the accident. . . ."

"So there's nothing to worry about—and the police can never prove it was anything but an accident. But it was necessary," Frey said calmly as he increased altitude. "I realized that when Marchais was talking his head off in the Storchen bar about my chopper being the only thing around when they found that counterespionage agent's body in the glacier tunnel." The subject went clean out of his mind as he maneuvered the machine toward the Wasserhorn summit.

Among all the top GRU agents who controlled secret sabotage apparatuses in Western Europe, Frey was—in the opinion of his master, Colonel Igor Sharpinsky—the cleverest and most ruthless, with the possible exception only of Rolf Geiger. Why had the Swiss, who already enjoyed so much prestige as a mountaineer internationally, betrayed his country for over fifteen years? Certainly he was no perverted idealist; he had read very little Marxist theory, which he thought a thundering bore. His dual motives for his treachery were far simpler.

Shrewdly, as he believed, weighing up the likely outcome of the endless struggle between the Communists and the West, he was convinced that in the end Soviet Russia must win because of its superior and aggressive leadership. As he had once remarked to Platow, "Since Churchill, Adenauer, and de Gaulle there has been no leader worth a damn in the West." Recently he had begun to have doubts since President Joseph Moynihan had taken over in the White House, but it was too late to turn back now.

The second motive was Frey's greed for power. He reveled in the fact that he personally controlled a secret organization, that within the past few hours he had sent to Franco Visani, the Soviet agent in Lugano, detailed orders for an attack on the Atlantic Express. Now, losing altitude as he prepared to land on the summit of the Wasserhorn, he was checking on the second, far vaster contingency plan Sharpinsky had suggested in his signal to Frey from the Hotel Schweizerhof in Zürich.

With expert touch he landed the machine carefully on the center of the flat-topped peak, well clear of the brink. Adjusting his snow goggles after switching off the motor, he opened the door and dropped to the ground, followed by Emil Platow, who carried the measuring instruments.

From the summit the view was intoxicating in its moon-lit grandeur, but Frey hardly noticed it, nor did he approach the brink from where he could have looked down on the railroad track over which the Atlantic Express was due to pass later that evening. The two men worked quickly, measuring the depth of the recent snowfall, and then climbed back into the machine, which was airborne again within minutes.

"My God," Platow exclaimed as the helicopter headed back for Andermatt. "Another fifty centimeters of snow since the last check—the whole slope could start a gigantic slide any moment."

"So if we have to resort to the ultimate weapon the timing is perfect," Frey replied calmly. "And don't start worrying about Davos—nothing like that has fallen in Andermatt. So they won't suspect the report I send in. . . ."

At 6:15 P.M. Robert Frey's Sikorsky landed again at the farm. It was Emil Platow who discovered the break-in. Frey had entered by the front door and gone straight to his study, where four other members of his sabotage team were waiting. Throwing down his parka on a chair, he sat down to write out for the avalanche institute above Davos: *No further appreciable buildup of snow on the Wasserhorn. Have compared last year's records and if these can be taken as standard. . . .*

Frey became aware that someone was peering over his shoulder. Looking up, he saw Erich Volcker, a short, fat, bald-headed man of forty-five standing behind him. "Damn it, I can't write out this damn report with you standing there watching me," he boomed.

"Sorry."

"There's been a break-in." Emil Platow came running into the study in a state of great excitement. "Someone

199

was here—must have been before you arrived," he said, looking at the four other men. "A pane in the back door is broken."

"Calm yourself, Emil," the huge mountaineer reprimanded.

Standing up, he put his large hands on his hips and looked around the room, noted that the desk flap was closed, let his eyes go on wandering. The other five men, dominated by his presence, remained quite still, quite silent. Frey's eyes continued his search, moving across the furniture, then they dropped to the floor. He took two long paces, stooped, stood up dangling the teardrop earring from his fingers. He smiled at Erich Volcker.

"I know this. Foolish of her to leave her calling card, wasn't it?"

17

The Gotthard

In its awesome grandeur this gigantic gorge that carries the main north–south rail link from nordic Europe to the Mediterranean south is one of the wonders of the world, rivaling the Grand Canyon in Arizona. As the rail track continues its endless climb, passing through spiral tunnels turning through three hundred and sixty degrees as the ascent goes on, crossing bottomless ravines and gulches, the immense Alpine peaks close in on either side.

Awe-inspiring in summer, it has an atmosphere close to terror in winter. High up on the near-vertical slopes millions of tons of snow hang poised—often needing only the passing of a single skier to bring them down. Close to

Airolo, the small town at the end of the strategic tunnel passing under the Alpine range—passing under Andermatt—huge crags overhang the rail track. At frequent intervals the track is lined with great steel snow barriers. This is avalanche country.

It was the Gotthard that worried Wargrave. It was the Gotthard that so concerned Springer that he had flown from Lugano to board the Atlantic Express at Bellinzona. And in the guise of Joseph Laurier, Wargrave was still restlessly moving about the train. Ahead in the otherwise deserted corridor he saw the six-foot-two-tall Spaniard, Jorge Santos, leaning against the passenger rail while he puffed at his pipe. He paused next to Santos, hanging his cane by the handle on the rail.

"You, too, my friend, find this a disturbing journey—and soon we shall move into a region fit for the Greek gods, a veritable Olympus," Laurier remarked in fluent French.

Santos' black eyes glanced at the newcomer sharply, then he shrugged. "These long train journeys by night are full of stress." He paused, puffing on his pipe. "And that strange business after Lugano when the express stopped. A Swiss inspector told me it was an army exercise. You believe that?"

"I think it was something far more sinister," Laurier replied. "I can recognize live machine-gun fire when I hear it."

"And now we are moving into the Gotthard," Santos remarked. "A frightening place."

"Who can tell what may happen on a night express?" Laurier mused. "So many strangers all crammed together for so many hours." He glanced at the profile of the man standing beside him, a striking profile with its aquiline nose, its high cheekbones. "I am traveling all the way to Amsterdam on this trip," he remarked. "Are you?"

"All the way. So it will be a very long night. . . ."

There was a growing tension inside the express as it headed up a gentle incline on its way to the great gorge. In the dining car they were serving the second sitting and more drink was being consumed than food. Passengers in their compartments who might have been settling down for the night sat up staring out the window at the moonlit landscape. In the rear Wagon-Lit food was being served to the occupants from a compartment that in Milan Molinari had had converted into a makeshift galley.

"Why could not food have been brought along from the dining car?" Marenkov inquired as he sank his teeth into a pizza.

"Because poison is one of the weapons of the KGB," Haller replied bluntly.

"Don't you like pizza?" Elsa asked the Russian.

"I can eat anything," Marenkov replied ambiguously.

Springer sat opposite him, eating his own pizza off a cardboard plate and drinking coffee from a cardboard cup. He had already asked the Russian for a list of KGB agents in Switzerland and Marenkov, glancing at Haller, had tapped his forehead. "The moment I am aboard the Boeing at Schiphol, the moment that aircraft is thirty thousand feet over the Atlantic, I will provide all the information you need."

"I need it now," Springer told him sharply. "It is, after all, for your own protection."

"It is the normal procedure," Marenkov replied brusquely. "It is my passport to America—the information I carry in my brain. All previous KGB agents who have fled to America have waited until they set foot on United States soil before they talked—"

"It's useless," Haller interjected. "I've been through all this with the general earlier—and as he says, it is normal procedure."

Springer's face was set and grim as he stared at Marenkov, who looked back at him impassively. Elsa decided it was time to defuse the rising tension between the two men. "Do let him get on with his food," she said lightly to the Swiss colonel. "We've got enough on our plates," she punned, "without fighting among ourselves."

They had finished their meal when Matt Leroy knocked on the door. "Colonel Springer is wanted on the radio telephone urgently," he announced. He looked at the relics of the meal. "Nice to see no one is going hungry," he remarked. Haller looked appalled. "God, it's time you changed duty with John—drag him out of his compartment and then get back here and eat."

Elsa, complaining of stiffness, accompanied Springer to the communications compartment; she had guessed this signal could be the reply to Wargrave's request for a double-check to be made on their radio operator, Peter Neckermann. And since Springer had earlier been told by Haller of Wargrave's "death" in Milan she didn't want the reply to be passed on to Haller. Inside the communications compartment the gnome-like Neckermann had just finished his own meal. Springer took the call on the phone and without looking at Neckermann said "yes" several times and finally, "You are sure?" Breaking the connection, he took Elsa into the corridor and waited until he heard the German lock the door on the inside.

"I don't understand what's happened," he said gravely. "I had a message signed by Wargrave at Bellinzona and Haller says he died in Milan. The message said I was to give you the reply. That call was from my chief, Brigadier Traber, in Zürich. He has heard from Captain Wander of the German BND, who is now waiting to take over the train's security in Basel. Peter Neckermann is cleared. Wander says he would vouch for him with his life."

"Don't tell Haller—or anyone. I'll join you later."

"As you say. . . ."

Springer had a curious expression as he studied Elsa for a moment, an expression that could have been a hint of hope. "I thought Haller's story was odd," he murmured. "I leave the entire matter in your hands."

Phillip John had replaced Matt Leroy as guard at the forward end of the Wagon-Lit as Elsa approached him. The Englishman, smart and cool-looking as ever in his check sports suit, smiled faintly. She had the impression that during his rest period he had freshly shaved. "Can't keep away from me?" he chaffed her.

"Strange as it may seem, by making a massive effort I can manage it for an hour or two," she replied. "And now perhaps you would let me into the next car."

"What for?"

"Because I damned well say so," she rapped back.

"The lady only has to ask—her request is granted," John replied, not in the least fazed. He reached up and made a show of straightening the dark wig she had donned before leaving Haller's compartment. Then he perched her horn-rimmed glasses higher on her nose. For a second his hand touched her cheek. "Sooner or later, when all this is over, you and I ought to—"

She passed through the door he had opened without replying, heard him lock it, and hurried to Joseph Laurier's sleeper. Inside the compartment Wargrave checked the position of the bone-handled knife he had earlier slipped inside his right sock before he opened the door and let her inside. She told him about the signal clearing Neckermann and he nodded. He was still wearing Laurier's shaggy gray wig and bifocals and again she thought he looked horribly tired.

"What about food?" she asked. "You got something in the dining car, I hope?"

"No." He gestured toward his case. "I brought a flask of coffee and sandwiches from Milan. What is the atmosphere like back in Marenkov's compartment?"

"Lousy. Springer tried to get a list of Swiss KGB agents out of Marenkov and he wouldn't give. Haller is acting as peacemaker. But there's something more."

Lighting a cigarette, he placed it between her lips as she sat on the berth. "What is something more?"

"Tension—getting worse all the time. Only Phillip John, who's on guard duty, by the way, seems unaffected, the cocky bastard. The trouble, as I see it," Elsa continued, crossing her legs and taking off her horn-rims, "is nothing more has happened. It's getting on their nerves —the waiting, the inaction. And yet they feel sure something big is coming. They're worried about the Gotthard."

"Me too."

Turning off the light, Wargrave lifted the blind. The express was climbing steeply now, moving around endless curves as it headed toward distant Airolo. And the big mountains were closing in on the train, great peaks;

Wargrave had to crane his neck to look up and see their moonlit summits. Out of the shadow of a ravine a long spear of ice hung motionless in the night, the spear of a huge waterfall frozen in midair. The wheel rumble changed as the express moved onto a bridge spanning a dark drop. He lowered the blind, switched on the light. "Any met reports come in?" he asked. "I'm thinking of the weather north of the Gotthard."

"Terrible, Springer says. A raging blizzard. It's just this section between Airolo and Chiasso where it's stopped snowing—and that isn't expected to last for long. Oh, and just to cheer you up: a *föhn* wind's expected here soon."

"I think it's started already—you can feel it hitting the side of the train."

Wargrave was stripping off his gray wig. Removing his bifocals, he tidied himself up, combing his hair briefly. Elsa watched him with concern now she could see his real appearance. "God, you look tired—your eyes are bloodshot. When did you last sleep?"

"Can't remember," Wargrave said cheerfully. It was Saturday night. Friday evening he had been up until the middle of the night going over operational details with Molinari. Saturday morning had brought the arduous flight to Bucharest and back, including two rather tricky landings. And since boarding the Atlantic Express he had not slept a wink. He checked himself in the wall mirror. "Back to normal—that's better."

"Why are you dropping the Laurier cover?" she asked.

"Because the time has come to emerge into the open— from what you've just told me morale back in the Wagon-Lit doesn't sound too good."

"Is that all?" she asked quietly. "You're expecting something to happen, aren't you? And you'll give Julian one hell of a shock. He'll blow his top," she warned.

He took her by the shoulders. "Just stop fretting and get back to them. Don't say a word about me. Not one word."

"If you say so. . . ."

Wargrave waited a few minutes to give her time to get

back to the compartment and then opened the door. Peering both ways to make sure the corridor was empty, he walked back along the car, which was swaying around another endless curve. At one point he raised a blind and the ice-bound walls of the Gotthard loomed in his face, their dark shadows flecked with more spurts of waterfalls frozen in the moonlight. Pausing by the locked door to the rear Wagon-Lit, he lit a cigarette, then rapped in a certain way.

Phillip John opened the door, holding his Luger pistol in his right hand. His white face showed shock, then he recovered and slowly slid the Luger back inside the spring-loaded holster. Wargrave put a hand against his chest and gently pushed him back against the toilet door.

"Don't I gain entry?" he inquired mildly.

"I thought you were still in Milan. . . ."

"Will-o'-the-wisp, that's me," Wargrave told him amiably as John relocked the door. "People never know where I'm going to turn up next—it's helped to keep me alive all these years. Let's have a chat while we're alone."

They were hemmed in the narrow space between the end of the car and the toilet door, out of sight of the corridor beyond, which was empty. "Why, in the name of God?" demanded John. "There's been a wake going on for you ever since we left Milan."

"Because it was necessary, old man," Wargrave explained, mimicking John's public school accent. He saw a flush of color in the white face. "And now it's time to bring up the reserves—me. We have a job to do. There is what used to be called a fifth columnist in this car. KGB or GRU man to you."

"In this car?" John said slowly. "You have to be joking." He stared at Wargrave. "No, you're not joking. Who is he?"

"I don't remember saying it was a he."

John stared hard again, a flicker of surprise in his eyes for the second time. "You can't possibly suspect Elsa Lang? I gathered she's been with your outfit since way back when."

"The best moles have been on the inside, implicitly

trusted by their employers for a long time, John. It is the key to their success. Surely you've learned that by now?"

"Elsa Lang? I'm staggered. Jesus Christ, Haller will go berserk when he hears." He frowned. "You really do have proof? You have the reputation of never trusting anyone."

"I have proof." Wargrave stubbed his half-smoked cigarette under his foot and immediately lit a fresh one. The train was rocking from side to side as it negotiated a long, steep curve. Peering out of the window, Wargrave could see the glow of the front cars behind the engine, the flash of the overhead traction wires.

"What are you going to do about the Lang girl?" John asked.

"Nothing."

"But you said you had proof. . . ."

"I said that, yes," Wargrave agreed laconically. "But I didn't mention Elsa was the agent. You were the one who brought her name up. The GRU put a man aboard."

"The GRU?"

"Definitely. Marenkov would have recognized a KGB man. He is one of Colonel Igor Sharpinsky's people. Neckermann was a prime suspect—he had access to the communications system."

"Was?" John inquired.

"Yes. He was cleared only a few minutes ago. Springer gave Elsa a message to bring to me. You see, John," Wargrave went on affably, "I was certain when I heard that machine-gun gang at Vira riddled the rear Wagon-Lit. Only the rear Wagon-Lit, mark you—not the second one Marenkov and Elsa boarded at Milan. They *knew* he was in the rear car."

John looked thoughtful and leaned back against the toilet door. "It is suggestive," he admitted. "So who is the candidate for the GRU man?"

"You are."

"You must be out of your crazy mind."

"Because you're a marksman," Wargrave explained.

"Then I could have killed you at Milano Centrale."

Wargrave shook his head. "You knew you couldn't do

207

that. You knew Colonel Molinari was in on the fake shooting. And you wanted to get aboard the Atlantic Express. Incidentally," he went on, "if you had shot me and tried to run, three of Molinari's trained snipers had you in their gunsights all the time you were in the hall—just as a precaution."

"Crazy like a fox you are. . . ." John's mouth twisted in a sneer. "Why haven't I shot Marenkov by now?"

"Because you haven't had one single chance. Every time that compartment door opens, someone's revolver is aimed point-blank at you. Haller's, Elsa's—it makes no difference. And you're a professional, John—you know if you fired at them the reflex of their trigger finger would get you. I made very special arrangements to protect Marenkov before I came aboard."

"This is all pure speculation," John protested. "You said you had proof—show me your bloody proof, you bastard."

"Vira," Wargrave replied simply. "Elsa described to me exactly what happened. From a stationary position you aimed your Luger at a target of three men moving at no more than twenty miles an hour. You fired three shots. You missed with every one."

"It was a moving target."

"At a range of fifty yards. Three men bunched together. You were waiting for them. And Haller shot one of them. You aimed to miss your own men."

John, the man who had phoned Vienna from Milan, using the code name Patros, to warn Sharpinsky that Marenkov would be aboard the Atlantic Express, sighed. "This is beyond me. I need a cigarette, too. . . ." His right hand slid inside his jacket, started to withdraw the Luger at speed. Wargrave's hand holding the cigarette pressed the burning end down on the back of John's wrist. John winced, let go of the gun, which slid to the floor as he hit Wargrave a hard, chopping blow on the side of the neck. A little late, Wargrave realized John was ambidextrous, that he could use his left hand with the same force and agility as his right. Fog swam in front of his eyes as John kneed him savagely in the groin, but

Wargrave anticipated the attack and turned, taking the blow in the side of his leg. He aimed a blow at John's lower belly, but John also turned and took the impact on his hip.

As they struggled, confined in the small space between the toilet and the outer door, Wargrave was still groggy from the unexpected blow, seeing his opponent as a blurred figure, and John was stronger than he had expected. Suddenly, John lowered his head and butted Wargrave hard in the face while he pressed down the handle of the door, which flew open. Wargrave fell outward into the night, but as he fell his left hand reached upward, grabbed at the top of the door, and then he was hanging in space by one hand from the swinging door.

The express had just started to cross another curving bridge spanning a deep gorge, which yawned below Wargrave. Only the swing of the train stopped his hand from being crushed by the door smashing back against the side of the train. The swing began to move the door inward again. John waited, the Luger he had rescued from the floor in his hand. He had no intention of shooting Wargrave—the sound of a shot could never be explained. Wargrave was simply going to disappear. He had a reputation as a loner, so who would be surprised when he vanished again? All this went through John's quick brain as he waited to hammer the Luger barrel against Wargrave's half-frozen knuckles, to smash those knuckles.

The door swung slowly toward John as Wargrave groaned with pain, reached out, and then dropped his hand and doubled up. John watched clinically, his white face showing no excitement, nothing. The door swung closer and John raised the barrel of his Luger, his eyes on the clenched knuckles that were all that held the Englishman from oblivion. He aimed the barrel with deliberate care. The door swung in. Wargrave's right hand holding the knife he had hauled from his sock lunged, entering John's stomach. The express lurched. John fell out the door; his body missed the guardrail and plunged over a hundred feet to the almost frozen river in the gulch below. He landed on his back and slow-moving water creeping down from the high Alps froze over him, forming first a thin film of ice. From the express, Wargrave, clambering safely back inside the corridor, looked back at the gulf before he closed the door. His nose was running with blood from where John had butted him. Twelve hours later, Swiss troops who arrived at the bottom of the gulf found a macabre sight—John spread on his back staring upward, embalmed in ice. They had to use electric power drills to get at him.

18

The Wasserhorn

In the side street alongside the Hotel Schweizerhof in Zürich the radio detector van operator was smoking a forbidden cigarette to keep himself awake. Ever since the van had arrived there had been no sign of illegal signals being transmitted in the district. A kilometer or so away a team of Traber's men was checking a hotel's register; they had four more hotels to visit before they arrived at the Schweizerhof.

In Room 207 Heinz Golchack mopped beads of perspiration off his high-domed forehead. Certainly it was hot inside the well-heated room but it was more than the temperature that was causing Golchack to sweat. In a very short time a historic "natural" catastrophe of gigantic proportions was about to take place in the Gotthard. Not that this concerned Golchack. The only question in his mind was, would it kill General Sergei Marenkov?

And he was aware of the rising tension in his two companions, a tension he pretended not to notice. It was

Henrich Baum, his radio operator, he was most doubtful of. Baum, after all, was a Swiss. Let him sweat, Golchack thought. And Golchack was a man who always hedged his bets. "Never rely on a single plan," he was constantly drilling into his subordinates. "It is always vital to have a backup. . . ." Aboard the Atlantic Express, Golchack had two secret backup men.

One of them—Phillip John—had been infiltrated into the CIA three years earlier. John had actually carried out several executions on behalf of his American employers to cement his credibility. In the meantime he had waited for the moment when Golchack would order him to act on behalf of his real employer, the GRU. It was by no means unlikely that John would be able to seize the opportunity to wipe out Marenkov at some stage of the journey.

"Baum," Golchack said suddenly, "when I tell you, these two signals are to be transmitted." He handed the Swiss two slips of paper. "The shorter one for Basel is to be transmitted first. Then you send the Amsterdam signal. Encode them."

Golchack forced himself to sit still in a chair as he thought. He had dedicated his life to climbing the rungs of the Soviet ladder of power. Although he had never married, he was not indifferent to the attractions of women, but he had satisfied his natural urges in brief encounters that held no danger of distracting him from his life's ambition. And even after ordering the massive Andermatt Phase Two operation he was still hedging his bets.

The long signal to Amsterdam worried him a little—it was perhaps a little too lengthy for safe transmission—but it was necessary. It gave very detailed contingency instructions to Rolf Geiger, head of the Geiger terrorist group, now close to the Dutch border. And, of course, there was always the second backup man aboard the Atlantic Express. There was always Nicos Leonides. . . .

Nicos Leonides. In certain Balkan circles the name kept men awake at night: prominent anti-Communists who thought they heard a footfall on the stairs, men who feared they might have been "put on the list," as the phrase was so innocently termed. It would have been quite wrong to use the designation "hit man" where Leonides was concerned. The crude phrase conjures up a picture of a hired killer who completes contracts to kill an individual for a large sum of money. Leonides, a dedicated Communist from Salonika, only terminated the lives of well-known anti-Communists. The curious thing was that his employer—Colonel Igor Sharpinsky—had never met him.

Leonides had first offered his services to Sharpinsky when the Russian was pretending to act as military attaché at the Soviet Embassy in Athens under an assumed name. And Leonides always communicated by phone through public call boxes. At first skeptical, fearing a trap and mistrustful of Leonides' idealistic protestations, Sharpinksy had ignored the Greek's offer to serve as an executioner. Several phone calls later, the Russian had agreed to Leonides' suggestion that it might be "convenient" if the editor of a certain Athens newspaper, a late-middle-aged man, should be eliminated.

Three days later the skeptical Sharpinsky was astonished to read that the Greek editor's car had been discovered burned out at the foot of a steep cliff and half-submerged in the sea, the body washed away by a storm. Two years and three deaths later, Sharpinsky was convinced that he had an ideal human weapon for emergencies. Shrewdly—since the targets were always suggested by Leonides—Sharpinsky guessed that the Greek combined his Communist dedication with personal vendettas. So typical of the Balkan peasant mentality. But by a devious route there had always been a line of communication whereby the Russian could contact the Greek. And fortunately, at just the right moment, Nicos Leonides had been in Milan. He was now aboard the Atlantic Express.

Sprawled in the corner seat of his first-class compartment, his long legs crossed at the ankles, Jorge Santos relit his pipe and glanced up as Harry Wargrave hurried past along the corridor on his way to see Phillip John. Like Wargrave, the Spaniard had not eaten in the dining car; he had brought with him aboard the express a bottle of wine and some food, which he had just finished consuming.

Puffing at his pipe, he checked his watch, then changed his position to ease the stiffness out of his limbs. There was, he sensed, an air of uneasiness aboard the train, which was now moving much more slowly as it climbed the great ascent toward the distant Gotthard tunnel. Outwardly at least, Jorge Santos was one of the most relaxed passengers aboard the Atlantic Express.

"I still think you might have told me, Harry."

Elsa was using a gauze pad from her first-aid kit to wipe blood from Wargrave's nose when Julian Haller, grim-faced, had issued his second rebuke. They were sitting in the Wagon-Lit compartment—with Marenkov and Springer—and Wargrave was quite unrepentant, even aggressively so.

"It worked," the Englishman snapped. "I winkled out the GRU man they'd placed on the inside. And don't forget," he went on emphatically, "that before we left North America you agreed I would control this end of the operation."

"You could have trusted me . . ." Haller began again.

"Too much play-acting would have been involved," Wargrave insisted. "You had enough on your mind as it was. So let's stop wasting time and get on with the next stage of the operation."

"Which is?" Springer inquired.

"I'm taking off in that Alouette chopper you've got aboard the flatcar. Elsa's coming with me. And I need that special radio you brought onto the train, Leon—to keep in communication with the express while we're aloft."

"That's out," Haller snapped. "Taking Elsa . . ."

"Do I have to remind you once more, Julian," Wargrave inquired quietly, "that I'm running the European end?"

"Why use the Alouette now?" Springer asked curiously. "I have troops placed at strategic intervals along the line between here and Airolo."

"Maybe because I'd like to check the points between the intervals." Wargrave grinned sardonically as Elsa put away the gauze. "If you don't like that, call it sixth sense—nothing has happened for a while now and I reckon Sharpinsky is due to make his next attempt very soon."

Marenkov had remained silent during the discussion but the mention of his deputy, Colonel Igor Sharpinsky, stirred him. It was only recently that Haller had decided to tell him of the GRU man's suspected presence in Zürich. "I agree with Mr. Wargrave," he said quietly. "It has been too quiet for too long. Like him, I sense something is going to happen."

Fifteen minutes later Wargrave helped Elsa across the swaying gap from the rear of the Wagon-Lit to the flatcar where the Alouette helicopter, guarded by a unit of Swiss troops, was chained down. Climbing up inside the cabin, Elsa reached down for the automatic weapon and spare magazines a Swiss soldier handed up to her. "Good luck," he called out in French.

Elsa was dressed in ski pants, a fur jacket with the hood pulled over her head, and fur-lined boots—all of which she had borrowed from one of Springer's ski troopers aboard the train. Already on board the machine and sitting in the copilot's seat was Springer's Swiss radio operator, Max Bruder, a short, thin man who spoke English. Wargrave was the last to climb on board and settle himself in the pilot's seat as two Swiss soldiers on the swaying flatcar bent down, ready for his signal to release the snap chains.

From the open door of the rear Wagon-Lit Springer, his face chilled with the cold, was watching anxiously. He was alone—Haller had stayed behind in the compartment to guard Marenkov while Matt Leroy patrolled the corridor. And the Swiss colonel was none too happy about the maneuver Wargrave was about to attempt. He had to gauge the moment of takeoff with unnerving precision.

The flatcar was swaying considerably—the maximum sway is always with the last car of the express. He had to build up sufficient lift-off power for instant elevation the moment the snap chains were released. He had to avoid any risk of stalling the motor, which would bring him crashing down on the flatcar—or on the track behind it. And there was a strong sidewind blowing from the east.

Behind him in the heated cabin Elsa found herself clutching the automatic weapon tightly as Wargrave started the motor, as the rotor above them started to spin erratically and then increased into a steady whir. Glancing down, she saw her white knuckles in the glow from the instrument panel. The machine was throbbing with power, straining to lift off. She took a deep breath, forced herself to relax. At that moment Wargrave raised a hand, dropped it, signaling for the release of the snap chains. The flatcar chose this moment to give a sudden lurch and a gust of wind beat against the side of the machine.

"Oh, God . . ."

The machine ascended vertically, was above the train as the side wind beat against the fuselage with such force that the chopper was hurled westward. Then Wargrave regained control and Elsa peered down out of the window. The lights of the Atlantic Express were visible far below, a curving chain of lights as the train moved around yet another endless bend. Elsa relaxed back in her seat, adjusted her headset, checked her watch. It was 8:15 P.M. She spoke into the microphone under her chin.

"What is that huge peak in the distance—way over to the northwest?"

"That," Wargrave replied, "is the Wasserhorn."

It was 8 P.M. in Andermatt when a heavy farm tractor hauled Robert Frey's Sikorsky out of the barn among the huddle of farm buildings west of the ski resort; Anna Markos had been mistaken when she had assumed Frey's team manhandled the chopper into the open. As the machine emerged, Robert Frey stood beside his deputy, Emil Platow, towering over him.

"Hurry it up," Frey ordered the tractor driver. "We don't have all night to do the job."

He climbed up inside the chopper as the tractor driver released the machine, which was equipped with skis. Emil Platow and four other men jumped into the machine behind him. And within three minutes Frey, sitting in the pilot's seat, was airborne, gaining altitude rapidly as he headed southeast toward the huge summit of the Wasserhorn, which overlooked the Gotthard railroad track.

The lights of Andermatt passed below them as Frey continued on course. He had already informed the avalanche institute at Davos that he had decided to make one final check because there had been a rise in temperature of several degrees. *A routine precaution . . .* his signal had worded it. Behind him the cabin was crowded—and not only with the five-man team, which included his explosives expert, Emil Platow. Sometimes a very small quantity of explosives is used to set off a minor snowslide to prevent a dangerous accumulation later. But the machine was carrying almost a ton of gelignite, was, in fact, a veritable flying explosives depot as Frey continued to head for the massive peak of the Wasserhorn.

A short time before Robert Frey had driven at speed from Andermatt to board the Sikorsky he had visited Anna Markos in her bedroom at the Hotel Storchen. Anna was sitting in front of her dressing table, apparently making herself up for the *après-ski* revels, when someone knocked on her door. Getting up, she went over to the door and spoke through it. "Who is there?"

A deep, familiar voice replied. "It's me, Robert. Robert Frey."

She unlocked the door, let him in, and returned to the dressing table, watching the huge, shaggy-maned Swiss as he stood behind her looking at her mirror image with open admiration. Bending over her, his hands clasped her ample bosom and squeezed. "And who did you think it might be? I have a rival?"

"Dozens." Her nails clawed at his exploring hands and

he removed them with a grunt. For a moment in the mirror she caught an expression of near-savagery in his face as he wiped a streak of blood from one hand, then he smiled and shrugged. "Someone has stolen my bits and pieces of jewelry," she informed him. "Look." Opening the drawer, she lifted the lid of her empty jewel case. "I took them off yesterday evening, and tonight when I came to put them on . . ." She shrugged her well-shaped shoulders. "I know they are not valuable—but even so . . ."

"You should inform the police. I'd go right away if I were you. The station is very close—take the first street on the left after you turn out of the hotel."

"You think so?" she asked doubtfully.

"In Switzerland the police take theft very seriously. Let me help you on with your coat."

She slipped on a thick sweater and let him help her into the coat. "They'll get annoyed if you don't report a theft," Frey said easily as he accompanied her downstairs. The bar was packed, filled with smoke and the sound of raucous pop music. He went with her to the exit and repeated the directions. "I would come with you but I'm expecting a phone call from Davos," he remarked casually.

He remained standing outside the hotel entrance as she walked away, rubbed his face vigorously as though the keen bite of the wind was chilling him, then got into his Varu and drove off at speed toward the farm. A few yards up the street a Peugeot stood parked without lights. Behind the wheel Erich Volcker noted the signal Frey had made by rubbing his face and waited until Anna Markos had disappeared down the side street. Then he switched on his lights and tried to start the engine.

Walking slowly down the deserted side street, Anna Markos pulled up her ear muffs; now she had full use of her acute sense of hearing. The street was dead straight and narrow, so narrow it allowed the passage of only one vehicle. On either side of her the houses were shuttered and silent and flakes of gentle snow drifted lazily down. In the night hush the only sound was the crunch of her

217

boots on the crusted snow. And this, she knew, was not the way to the police station.

Then she heard the car turn into the street behind her. She began walking more quickly, her long, powerful legs covering the ground at speed. She was careful not to run: one slip on the ice and she would be finished. Behind the wheel of the Peugeot sat a grotesque figure. Erich Volcker was short and very fat, but it was hard fat. He had plump legs and small, neat feet. His round skull was entirely hairless and his pouched lips tightened as he trapped the Greek woman in his headlight beams. Taking a deep breath, he pressed his foot down.

Anna Markos heard the change of the engine sound. In the lights of the car she saw a few paces ahead a large round rock lying by a doorway. She risked running the few paces, stooped, picked up the rock, and swung around. Behind his wheel Volcker stared in astonishment as he saw her turn and face him. He kept his foot down. The rock sailed through the air, and struck his windshield a smashing blow, and the glass crazed. One moment he had ten-tenths vision, the next second he was blind. Holding the wheel steady, he looked out of the side window and watched the walls of the houses rushing by, maintaining the same distance from them, waiting for the bump and thud as he rolled over her.

Pressed inside the doorway, Anna watched the car flash by her, proceed on down the street, slow at the end almost to a crawl as it turned a corner and disappeared. She went back swiftly up the street the way she had come and turned right into the main street, where there were lights, people. As she reentered the Storchen there was the same curious smile on her face as when she had collected the jewelry to throw it down the drain.

Anna Markos, the agent Harry Wargrave had sent to Andermatt, was a very brave woman. Suspecting that Robert Frey was the head of the Communist cell operating from Andermatt, she had not been sure. At the risk of her life she had sprung a trap using herself as bait—and now she was sure. The attempt to murder her had proved her case. As she entered the crowded reception hall, Louis Celle grasped her arm.

"Come and have a drink, Anna. For a start . . ."

"Louis, I'm looking for Robert Frey."

"He just drove off."

"In which direction? Do you know?"

"Yes, he went that way. . . ."

Louis waved his arm toward the west, toward the cluster of farm buildings beyond Andermatt where the helicopter was housed. Anna ran upstairs, locked herself inside her bedroom, and used the phone to call Göschenen station for the second time in an hour.

"Can you tell me when the Atlantic Express is expected to reach Göschenen?"

"There has been a delay, madame, but the express is making up time. We expect it here at 8:49."

"So if I catch the 8:31 from Andermatt on the Schöllenen I should be in time?"

"Assuredly, madame—it is a connection."

It took Anna Markos much longer to get through to the Zürich number she had memorized. The girl who answered the phone at the other end merely repeated the number. "This is Leros calling," Anna said quickly, "Leros calling Mr. Gehring. It is very urgent."

"One moment, please. . . ."

Behind his desk at counterespionage headquarters in Zürich, Traber stiffened when he heard who was calling. It was the very first time Wargrave's agent in Andermatt had approached him. "Put him straight through," he replied. He was even more surprised when he heard the voice of a woman speaking to him in faultless German. "I am Gehring, yes," he said immediately.

"Please give a name urgently—very urgently—to Mr. Roose. You heard me—to Mr. Roose? The name is Robert Frey. Repeat it, please. That's right. . . ."

The connection was broken before Traber could reply. Mr. Roose was Harry Wargrave. The reference to Robert Frey the Swiss counterespionage chief didn't understand at all; Frey was one of Switzerland's most respected citizens. But Traber did not waste time on speculation.

Pressing a button on the intercom, he asked to be put through to the duty officer of the communications section. Within three minutes the signal was on its way to the communications compartment in the Wagon-Lit at the rear of the Atlantic Express.

Robert Frey was a perfectionist, never satisfied, and he was not satisfied now with the progress of his sabotage team—although they had, in fact, worked swiftly since disembarking from the Sikorsky perched at one end of the rocky plateau that formed the summit of the Wasserhorn. The initail shoveling away of snow to reach the hard-core ice layer below had not taken long; the wind from the east that had caused a near-disaster when Wargrave was taking off from the Atlantic Express flatcar had scoured the summit of the Wasserhorn almost clear of snow, leaving only a thin coating.

"Hurry it up," Frey ordered. "Move your bloody muscles—we're behind schedule."

"We're damn well not," Emil Platow murmured to the man he was working with as he checked his watch.

"What was that, Emil?" Frey demanded, his huge figure looming over the stooped Platow.

"We're on schedule," the Swiss snapped irritably.

"This part we can hurry over. The next part, no. Do you never use that bonecase you call a brain?"

And Frey was right. At distant intervals, they had shoveled open five separate holes. Now they were beginning to use the drills powered by the portable generator on board the helicopter. Cables trailed like lifelines from the Sikorsky to the drills the team were using, drilling through the ice core deep into the rock of the mountain summit. It was a calculated risk, using the drills, but the sites chosen were well back from the precipitous edges of the plateau.

Frey had chosen the drilling sites long ago—and Frey knew something he had not included in the reports he passed on to Davos after each flying expedition to check the stability of the mountain slopes high above the Gotthard. Zigzagging across the Wasserhorn was an immense fracture, a fracture whose depth Frey had once privately checked with seismological equipment. The chief of the Communist cell based in Andermatt knew that the apparent impregnability of this giant towering above the Gotthard railway was flawed.

The drilling completed, they began the mind-chilling climax to the operation, the lowering of the explosives into the prepared cavities. Frey himself supervised this part of the operation; while Emil Platow handed him the small dome-shaped shells, he gently lowered them into position. The other four men carried the explosive shells gingerly from the chopper. As Frey !owered the last one inside its cavity, all that remained was to link up the electrical system that would cause detonation—at intervals of several seconds rather than simultaneously. Frey was aiming for nothing less than a chain reaction; as one part of the mountain shifted, so it would release the next section, and then the next—until the deep fracture opened up and sent half the mountain down onto the railroad track in an avalanche of unprecedented magnitude.

"There's a chopper coming," Platow said suddenly.

Frey looked up; Platow surpassed his chief in only one quality: the exceptional acuteness of his hearing. And Emil Platow was right. A chopper was coming toward the Wasserhorn.

Wargrave's Alouette helicopter was now a long way north of the Atlantic Express as he followed the line of the railroad, still uneasy and not sure what he was looking for. A movement of civilian vehicles, a movement of men, something that shouldn't be there? In the moonlit night the view ahead was fantastic—in the distance he could see the panorama of the main Alpine line, half-obscured in clouds and the terrible weather north of the Gotthard.

Behind him Elsa was swiveling her night glasses through a wide arc to the northwest. She paused, her lens locked on the Wasserhorn peak. She waited a moment before she spoke; Wargrave liked people to be certain before they expressed an opinion. Then she lowered her glasses and spoke into the mike below her chin.

221

"There's a chopper landed on the Wasserhorn."

"Are you sure?" Wargrave demanded.

"If I hadn't been sure I wouldn't have said so. And I think there are several men moving about on the peak."

"That is the Wasserhorn," Max Bruder, the Swiss radio operator, confirmed.

"Report it to Springer," Wargrave snapped. "I want a top priority check—which means a reply within minutes. Repeat: within minutes."

Wargrave changed course away from the railroad track, heading directly for the huge summit gleaming in the moonlight. Behind him Elsa inserted a magazine into her automatic weapon and released the safety catch. Bruder was sending his signal. Elsa reached for a spare magazine and laid it in her lap. Wargrave was straining to see what was happening on the summit. In less than a minute he saw that Elsa was only too damned right. There was a chopper—and men moving around it.

Aboard the express Springer reacted instantly on receiving the signal. Through Neckermann he was urgently contacting army headquarters at Andermatt. There was only a brief interlude before the reply to his query came back from Andermatt. As usual, before taking off in his Sikorsky, Frey had informed the local military commander of his flight to check the snow situation. Springer read the reply and dictated a signal for immediate transmission to Wargrave.

Chopper on the Wasserhorn commanded by Robert Frey, the highly respected and able mountaineer. His departure for routine avalanche check passed and approved by military commander at Andermatt. Springer.

"So that's that," Elsa commented as she read the signal Bruder had handed her. "False alarm. And I've taken us away from the rail track. Sorry, Harry."

"You must never apologize for vigilance, Elsa," Wargrave said sharply. "It could have been something."

"Robert Frey is a remarkable man," Max Bruder commented as Wargrave changed course again to head back for the railroad track. "I met him once—it was an honor to shake the hand of such a man."

"Some sort of local hero?" Elsa inquired.

"Only one of the world's top mountaineers," Wargrave replied. "Now let's go on checking the track."

"The chopper's going away," Emil Platow said, unable to keep the relief out of his voice. "Funny—it wasn't any army machine. No markings. . . ."

"Some idiot civilian pilot lost his way, trying to find the airstrip," Frey replied.

"At this time of night?" Platow beat his gloved hands around his body to bring back the circulation. It was bitterly cold but the view was magnificent, a vast panorama of range upon range of snowbound peaks. From where he stood perched on a boulder Platow could see, far below, the glint of the moon on great spears of ice, great waterfalls frozen in midair, dark shadows that hid the gashes of bottomless gorges.

"You worry too much," Frey remarked as he made a connection with two wires. When he had finished, it would merely require the turn of a single switch on the control box to set off the series of massive detonations. Completing the connection, Frey glanced at his watch. They were ahead of schedule. By only a few minutes, but they were ahead of schedule. And only because he had driven hard his well-trained team. Now nothing could save the Atlantic Express.

Nor was Robert Frey worried about the aftermath of the huge catastrophe he was precipitating. In all probability the Bern government would appoint him inspector in charge of the investigation later; once the avalanche started to roll, who would remember the muffled sound of the previous detonations on the peak—even assuming they were heard? And should anything go wrong, Frey already had his escape route planned.

"I think I can see it coming!" Platow called out.

"Are you sure?" Frey queried as he joined Platow on the boulder.

"For God's sake, of course I'm sure!"

"Then tell the others to get back on board the chopper fast. Move, man, move!"

Almost delirious with nervousness and excitement Platow scrambled across the plateau to pass on the order to the other men, who stood in a huddled group as though seeking warmth from each other against the penetrating cold. On the boulder Frey lifted the glasses slung around his neck and focused them down the Gotthard. And Platow was right. The distant lights of the Atlantic Express had appeared around a bend far below.

The Alouette had almost returned to a position above the railroad track when Bruder reported that an urgent signal was coming through from Springer aboard the train. Taking down the message, he handed it to Wargrave, who glanced at it and then swore. The words came clearly through to Elsa, craning her neck to look down at the railway.

"Bloody hell. . . ."

Message from Leros, the signal read, *Robert Frey. Repeat, Robert Frey.*

"Those men on the Wasserhorn," Wargrave snapped —through the microphone his voice crackled with urgency—"it's a Communist sabotage team."

He had already changed course violently, swinging the Alouette sideways so Elsa had to grab the arm of her seat to keep her balance, accelerating as he changed course, as he ascended, building up a speed of eighty miles an hour as the rotor system above them whirled into high gear while he headed directly back for the Wasserhorn summit. The whole cabin was suddenly charged with tension as Bruder, bewildered, protested.

"But that is Robert Frey. . . ."

"Able and respected mountaineer," Wargrave said viciously, recalling Springer's earlier description. "Elsa, get ready to gun those men down—every single man on that peak. Shoot to kill."

Elsa reacted instantly: dropped her night glasses and grabbed her automatic weapon. They were approaching the mighty peak at great speed as she lowered a window and the cold, bitter night air flooded inside the heated cabin. Kneeling down, she rested the barrel of the wea pon on the window edge as her face froze, as the machine rocked and swayed in the turbulence of the sudden ascent that was taking them to a height above the peak. It was going to be damned difficult to aim at anything under these circumstances, she was thinking. Wargrave seemed to read her thoughts as he continued climbing, his cheekbones sharply outlined in the glow from the instrument panel.

"Spray them—elevate the gun up and down a fraction and then sideways back and forth a fraction. Only a fusillade will get them."

On the Wasserhorn summit four of the men had almost reached the stationary Sikorsky, running across the light snow in their anxiety to reach the machine, but the fifth running man had stopped, turned, and pointed upward. A shot rang out, then another, both of them missing Wargrave's chopper, which was now descending toward the summit. Elsa let loose a long tracer burst, moving the muzzle in a slight arc.

On the peak bullets riddled across the snow, reached Emil Platow, who had fired. He slumped in the snow. Twenty meters away Frey cursed the stupid, crazy reaction of Emil, bent down to the controls box, and turned the switch. For a moment nothing happened. For a moment even the supremely confident Frey wondered whether the electric circuit had failed. Then he felt the first tremor, the first terrifying rumble. He ran toward the helicopter and then stopped, his mind blank for several seconds, unable to take in what he saw.

The Sikorsky with the four men aboard it toppled as the rock under it collapsed. Frey had miscalculated the extent of the accumulated detonations. For a second or two the Sikorsky remained poised on the brink, then it went down. Smashing against a crag, it broke off the rotor system, losing the whole system as the fuselage with the men inside spun down the mountain until—hundreds of feet down—it struck a protruding crag. The machine detonated, exploded in a brilliant flash of flame, vanished in a whirl of disintegrating fragments. By pure chance only Robert Frey was left alive on a tiny platform of surviving rock, staring up at the Alouette hovering over him.

"I want that man alive," Wargrave snapped. "Lower the hoist cradle, Elsa."

He had no need to give instructions to Max Bruder, who was already radioing Springer. *Avalanche coming. . . . Huge avalanche heading for railroad track. Started by Frey. . . . Repeat, avalanche heading straight for express. . . . From the Wasserhorn . . . the Wasserhorn. . . .*

From the hovering machine they had distinctly heard the explosive detonations, followed by the terrible rumble as the Wasserhorn came apart at the fracture, sending millions of tons of snow and rock in a slow, gradually increasing slide of mammoth proportions. From the air, it was like watching an ocean inclined at an angle of forty-five degrees in motion as half the mountain came apart and began its gigantic descent to the Gotthard far below.

Elsa, who during her stint at the Washington Embassy had flown in helicopters with Wargrave when he had taught her to use the hoist, was already lowering the harness cradle from the open door while Wargrave held the machine in a hover above the relic of the summit. It wasn't easy; the cabin was littered with equipment, with pairs of short skis, sticks, and climbing boots. At one moment she damn near fell out of the door as her foot tripped over a rope with a large grapple hook.

"Just stay aboard," Wargrave commented through his mike.

"Just let me concentrate on the job," Elsa flashed back. "You might keep the bloody machine level, for a start. . . ."

Wargrave smiled briefly; Elsa Lang was on form, full of guts and spit, which was just as well considering what she was trying to do. He almost issued a warning about how to handle Frey when he reached the cabin, then decided to keep his mouth shut. The swaying hoist cradle was now within feet of the huge Swiss mountaineer, swaying backward and forward. Unnoticed by Elsa, who was concentrating on her tricky job, Frey took a small .22 pistol out of his coat pocket and rammed it barrel first up the tight cuff wrapped over his left wrist. Then he reached up, grabbed the swaying cradle, held it while he adjusted and fixed the straps firmly. Then he signaled with an upward gesture.

Elsa began hauling him up as the helicopter continued its hover and Frey swayed below, coming up closer to the machine foot by foot. Max Bruder was continuing to send his urgent warning signal to Springer nonstop. Below, the mountain continued its vast collapse, spreading as it gathered momentum, spreading a kilometer-wide wave of falling rock and snow, heading for the tree line, the fir forest that lay in its path. Below that, far below, the Gotthard railroad track still gleamed in the moonlight as the Atlantic Express came closer and closer.

"Another minute and he'll be aboard," Elsa reported.

"I want him alive—but watch the bastard. I can't help you."

Wargrave was none too happy about what they were attempting. On the one hand he had guessed how important it could be for Springer to be able to interrogate Robert Frey—Anna Markos' message had indicated she had identified him as the top Communist agent in Andermatt. On the other hand he was worried that, confined as he was by his need to control the machine, Elsa was going to have to deal with the mountaineer on her own.

Elsa was preoccupied with the last tricky stage of getting Frey inside the cabin. Using one hand, she detached her headset and microphone. Her Smith and Wesson was ready—tucked inside the top of her ski pants. It was up to her to cope with this giant Swiss on her own and now she could see his face clearly as he stared up at her. Was there a flicker of surprise when he saw that it was a girl who was hauling him to safety? She kept her eyes fixed on the large, hawklike nose, the eyes she could hardly see behind the snow goggles he wore. Something warned her this was a formidable man, that she had better be pretty damned careful.

Then she was swinging the cradle inside through the open door and Frey was aboard. Glancing around, the mountaineer saw the pilot, trapped by his need to control

227

the machine, the radio operator next to him absorbed in repeating his urgent signal. His right hand tugged at his left cuff to extract the pistol as the girl slammed the door shut. The pistol stayed where it was, caught by the tightness of his sleeve. Elsa faced him with the Smith and Wesson in her hand and then the machine lurched, and threw her against the side of the cabin, and she dropped her weapon. Frey hurled his whole bulk against her, throwing her on her back at the rear of the cabin, falling with her, pinning her down underneath him. His right hand grasped her throat, squeezed.

As she lay pinned under the great bulk of Frey, Elsa's right hand scraped over the floor, felt the grapple hook, grasped it, and hooked it around Frey's thick neck. Startled, he let go as he felt the point pressing against his throat. Half-choked, her eyes blazing with fury, she screamed at him in French, "Get off, back off me, or I'll rip your fucking throat open. . . ."

Frey was frightened—and not only by the piercing point of the hook pressed against his throat. The look in the girl's eyes was terrible. She would do it. He knew she would do it. "Back off slowly—but very slowly," Elsa hissed through her teeth. Frey climbed up slowly as Elsa came up with him, holding the grapple at his throat. Then he felt the barrel of a gun rammed hard into his back and heard Max Bruder's voice.

"One mistake and I'll blow your spine to pieces."

Within two minutes they had Frey bound and tied with his wrists behind him. Elsa, who had jerked Frey's .22 pistol from his cuff, was none too gentle as she tied the final knots. Then she rolled him to the back of the cabin, leaving him face up so he could breathe. Before she left him she bent over him with the hook. "One peep out of you and I'll use this. Understand?"

Wargrave had already swung the machine in a half circle and was heading out across the Gotthard valley at high speed for the train. At that time he had no idea he had captured the chief Soviet sabotage agent inside Switzerland; nor did he know that Colonel Springer, receiving the news from Bruder, had already sent two top priority signals to Andermatt and to Brigadier Traber in Zürich. Within hours patrol cars, armed with lists of Frey's known friends and associates, were speeding through cities as far apart as Geneva and Lugano; officers were knocking on doors in the middle of the night, taking people in for intensive interrogation. Within five days the entire Frey sabotage ring had been rounded up. But at that moment all Wargrave was concerned with was the steady fall of the mighty avalanche toward the railroad track as the Atlantic Express continued up the incline.

19

Avalanche

Robert Frey was a brilliant organizer who believed in taking out insurance against the possibility that even the best-laid plans can go astray, and the operation to destroy the Atlantic Express—adapted from the Communist contingency plan to block the Gotthard in wartime—hinged on precise timing, on the express being in the right place to take the full force of the avalanche he had unleashed from the Wasserhorn.

So at intervals along the track—and always at places where the express would be moving slowly up a major incline—he had placed individual members of his wide-spread sabotage organization. Frey had calculated carefully the likely course of the avalanche, the section of the track it would take out. It was essential the express should be moving over that selected portion of the track when the avalanche struck. And it was because these were single men spaced apart that Wargrave had found it impossible to spot them from his aerial survey.

Springer reacted with his usual energy and decision when he received the first warning of what was coming from Wargrave's helicopter. In the compartment he occupied next to the compartment containing Marenkov and Haller, he bent over a map with his assistant, Jurgen Thall. "The Wasserhorn is there." He drew a circle over a stretch of track. "If the avalanche reaches the track I estimate it will hit somewhere inside that ring."

"And we are now traveling just about in the middle of it," Thall pointed out.

"A little nearer to the northern end of the danger sector," Springer replied. "Get on the phone to the engineer—tell him I need maximum speed."

Thall left the compartment, ran down the corridor to the communications section where a special phone had been installed to link them directly with the engineer's cab. Alone inside his own compartment, Springer switched off the light, raised the blind, and lowered the window. Ignoring the blast of cold air, he stared out at the terrifying moonlit spectacle.

There was no dramatic roar, no rushing momentum, only the steady slide of a whole mountain on the move toward the railroad track. It was like a great wave coming toward him in slow motion, a tidal wave of tumbling rock and snowslide, a slide of millions of tons of snow. As Springer watched, it reached the top of the tree line, the first trees of a great fir forest spreading down the lower slopes. Like an oceanic tidal wave it simply passed over the firs, and Springer knew that under that white wave great trees, scores of years old, were being crushed to pulp like matchsticks. Then he saw something that made him freeze. The slide reached an immense crag. Instead of pouring over it, the slide jerked the crag off the mountain and took it down with the mounting torrent. Springer then realized this was no ordinary avalanche, huge though it might be: the Wasserhorn was flawed; this was an avalanche to make history. He turned as Thall slammed open the door.

"We can't get through to the engineer."

"Why the hell not?"

"He's not answering."

At that moment the slow-moving express, lumbering up an incline, lost more speed, then stopped. A few seconds later it began to creep backward down the incline, back down into the sector of maximum danger.

There were two men inside the cab of the Bo-Bo locomotive hauling the Atlantic Express up the incline. They had little to do except watch the gauges, check the signals ahead. And the throb of the motor had muffled all sound of the oncoming avalanche. Enrico, the chief engineer, was cleaning his hands with a rag when Frey's man jumped aboard, hauling himself inside the cab. Enrico stared in disbelief as the man struck his colleague a brutal blow over the head with the barrel of his gun, splitting his skull. The man aimed the gun at Enrico. "Turn around." The chief engineer turned around and the saboteur struck him a grazing blow, which he imagined had eliminated Enrico, who sank to the platform, dazed and only half-conscious. Frey's man, Anton Gayler, studied the controls briefly, then moved a lever, then two more levers after the express had stopped. The Atlantic Express started moving backward.

Gayler, a short, burly man with buck teeth, had no fear he would be caught in the avalanche; on the eastern side of the track, only a short distance away, a driver was waiting behind the wheel of his Fiat with the engine running, waiting to pick up Gayler and drive him up the eastern side of the gorge well clear of the avalanche. As the express continued its slow retreat down the incline, Gayler peered out of the western side of the cab. Several uniformed men were running up the track toward him. One of them, a civilian, was streaking far ahead of the others. Gayler took aim with his gun.

"Get troops to the cab," Springer ordered as he pushed past Thall into the corridor. But it was the colonel who was first out of the train, opening a door at the end of the car, dropping onto the lower step and then jumping carefully from the slowly reversing express to the track. He had fourteen coaches to pass before he reached the locomotive as he streaked along the track, his nine-round .32 Browning automatic in his hand. But he had one advantage in his race against time—the express was moving backward past him, hauling the locomotive steadily toward him.

He was close to the motor when he saw the silhouette of a man lean out of the motor cab, a silhouette without railroad cap or uniform, a silhouette that aimed something at him. Springer ducked as he continued running, heard a shot, then a second shot as gravel spurted up beside him. Springer suddenly stopped running, whipped up his automatic, calmly gripped it in both hands, and fired. Something—it was the gunman's pistol—spun out of the cab and fell on the track.

Inside the cab Gayler, the knuckles of his right hand shattered and bleeding, swore and stumbled to the other side of the cab. Using his left hand, he lowered himself from the cab to the track and stumbled across the verge onto a nearby road. A dozen yards away stood a Fiat with a driver behind the wheel and the car's engine running. Gayler gasped with relief at his luck in getting off so close to the escape vehicle.

Aboard the train on the east side a compartment window had been lowered. There were no lights inside. A shadow of the upper half of a man appeared at the window, which was shielded by the train's bulk from the moonlight. A hand protruded. As Gayler stumbled on toward the parked Fiat a single shot was fired and Anton Gayler fell dead in the road. A second shot was fired. The man inside the Fiat slumped dead behind his wheel. It was marksmanship of the caliber the dead Phillip John had been reputed to possess. The shadowy figure withdrew from sight and the window closed.

The express was still moving backward when Springer climbed into the cab. He took in the scene at a single glance: one man probably dead; Enrico, the chief engineer, stirring feebly on the floor as he slowly recovered from the grazing blow. Springer knelt beside him, shook him none too gently.

"Get a grip on yourself—quick. I have to get the train moving forward at speed . . . an avalanche is coming. Get a hold on yourself, man, for God's sake. How do I do it—get the express moving forward?"

Enrico made a supreme effort, sat up with his back to the cab, and began pointing. Springer reached for one lever. A shake of the head. A gesture. Springer reached for another lever. Enrico nodded, tried to call out, "Careful . . ." Springer moved the lever and the express jerked to a grinding halt. More gestures. Springer's hand moved from lever to lever until Enrico nodded. The stalled express began moving slowly forward, so slowly Springer was appalled at the lack of pace. Two Swiss soldiers had boarded the cab after him and one was trying to apply first aid to Enrico. But the engineer, a sturdy man from Basel, waved him aside and clambered to his feet to help Springer.

"Who are you?" he asked.

"Military intelligence." It was not the answer Springer would normally have given but he wanted to impress the man with a sense of extreme urgency. "I want the motor opened full throttle," Springer said vehemently. "An avalanche is heading straight for us."

"Could be dangerous on this stretch. . . ." The engineer was moving the controls despite his warning; perhaps it had struck him that avalanches can be even more dangerous. The wheels began to move a little faster; Springer felt the vibrations of enormous power quivering the plate under his feet. The engineer had reacted totally to his instruction and the Atlantic Express started to crawl up the steep incline, but still agonizingly slowly, rumbling over threads of bridges spanning great gulfs, swaying as it swung around great curves, as the needles on the gauges shuddered. Several needles, Springer noticed, had passed above red markings, indicating the tremendous pressures building up. He went over to the western side of the cab.

The great forest had gone, obliterated under the tidal sweep of the oncoming avalanche, which was level with

233

the train, less than one kilometer away now, the vast wave of tumbling rock and snow so high that Springer had little doubt it was going to overwhelm the express. Normally it would have stopped in the narrow valley floor, but this time too much was coming, too high, too fast. . . .

Many thoughts raced through Springer's mind as he watched the disaster coming closer: about his wife, Clara, and his eighteen-year-old son, Charles, a student at Lausanne University—both of whom would be at home now in their Zürich apartment, whom he might never see again. And then he realized the true magnitude of what was approaching—it was a *triple* avalanche that fiend Frey had unleashed to kill just one man—never mind about the other three hundred and fifty souls on board the express. . . .

At first he had identified what he knew was the fall of a major powder-snow avalanche, which makes little more than a hissing sound as it slides downward, a vast wave of snow glistening in the moonlight with a certain majestic splendor. But now above the rumble of the laboring locomotive he heard a sound like thunder reverberating among the peaks that warned him that gigantic quantities of ice were on the move. And as if this were not terrible enough, he could see huge rocks bounding down amid the white dust of the powder snow. It was also a rock avalanche.

September 11, 1881. The village of Elm overshadowed by the Plattenbergkopf. Millions of tons of rock had fallen, a great wind had preceded the impact, whirling people into the air, carrying whole houses into space, smashing others to pieces under the shock of the blast wave. That, too, had been a rock avalanche. And there were three hundred and fifty people on board the express, Springer thought again. Oh, my God. . .

Throughout the length of the train stark panic had gripped the passengers, who filled the corridors despite the efforts of the Swiss railroad staff and security men to keep them inside their compartments. The thunderclap of the ice fall completed the panic. Some, in their terror,

234

opened doors and dropped to the track, running back past the train as though escape lay that way—when they were running *toward* the avalanche.

It was even more frightening at the rear of the express where, with the lights turned out, Haller and Marenkov stood looking out of the window. And Julian Haller, glancing at his watch, thought of his wife, Linda. In New York it would be 2:35 P.M., local time. She would be working in the fashion design office on Madison Avenue. Would he ever see her again? He doubted it. At least she would benefit from his generous pension rights. Suddenly a girl with long hair came running past them under the window—running toward the avalanche—her face distorted with terror. Marenkov leaned out, grabbed her by the hair. As she screamed, he used his other hand to grip her under the armpit and hauled her bodily up inside the compartment. He slapped her across the face to stop the hysterics. Haller opened the compartment door and faced Matt Leroy, who was on guard outside.

"What's happening?" Leroy demanded.

"Nothing much," Haller replied with bitter irony. "Take this girl back up the train; hand her over to one of the security people and tell him to keep her inside a compartment."

On the western side of the track, railroad officials and men from Springer's detachment had rounded up most of the fleeing passengers, were pushing them back on board the slow-moving train with the aid of other passengers, who helped hoist them aboard. Haller returned to the window beside Marenkov and saw something horrific. From distant houses in the path of the avalanche people were running. In the moonlight both men saw a child rushing down a field, pursued by a woman, presumably its mother.

As the child continued running, a boulder descended from out of nowhere and crashed down on the child. Haller felt physically sick as he watched the distraught mother reach the boulder, running her hands over it in a hopeless attempt to move it—the rock must have weighed a quarter of a ton. The American glanced at Marenkov and his gall rose as he saw the impassive expression on the Russian's face. He could have hit him. Then Marenkov spoke in a low growl.

"The bastards . . ."

"Your people," Haller snapped.

"Kindly inform Springer," Marenkov continued in the same growling tone, "that as soon as he is ready I will provide a complete list out of my head of every KGB agent in Switzerland. The GRU people I do not know. . . ."

In the corridor of the first-class car next to the third Wagon-Lit Jorge Santos stood among a crowd of people staring out at the avalanche. He had noticed something, and as he stood with his dead pipe clenched between his teeth he was trying to make a calculation. The two eastern faces of the Wasserhorn were angled toward each other, separated by a gulch, so now two separate waves of the avalanche were advancing toward each other. If they met in time, their massive collision might just halt the entire landslide.

Inside the Alouette, five hundred feet above the avalanche, Wargrave had noticed the same phenomenon. Holding the chopper in a hover, he was now engaged in a highly dangerous task. Among the equipment Springer had put aboard the helicopter at the Englishman's suggestion was two hundred kilos of gelignite; as long ago as the previous Thursday Wargrave had foreseen a situation where he might need to bomb a hostile vehicle approaching the express. Wargrave had now assembled the explosive cylinders on his lap into one large bomb, which he had fused. If he could slow down the right-hand wave of the avalanche it might give time for the other wave to collide with it.

"You should know," he warned Elsa and Max Bruder, "that this is highly tricky. It's a short fuse—it has to be —and if it detonates too early . . ."

"There are several hundred people aboard that express," Elsa said quietly. "Only four of us up here. . . ."

Her throat felt parched and she was sick with fear as

Wargrave opened the window, ignited the fuse, and dropped the homemade bomb. The moment he had dropped it Wargrave elevated the chopper at maximum speed. The bomb detonated the second it reached the ground just yards ahead of the right-hand wave. It slowed the wave for only seconds, but by then the left-hand wave met it in frightful collision. The sound of the impact reached them inside the Alouette as the chopper rocked under the shock wave, as a storm of snow hurtled up and enveloped the Alouette. Then the snow dust cleared and Wargrave was descending toward the train.

The avalanche ended in the normal cone shape. A tongue of snow swept over the track behind the express, flooding over the track just below the overhead traction wires, too weak now to bring down the traction pylons. The Atlantic Express continued on its way, heading for Airolo, the last stop before it entered the Gotthard tunnel.

20

Schöllenen Trap

Immediately after phoning Traber in Zürich from Andermatt to send her warning signal—the signal that had been instrumental in saving the Atlantic Express from destruction—Anna Markos had packed her case in her room at the Hotel Storchen. She estimated she just had time to catch the 8:31 train from Andermatt to Göschenen, where she would wait to board the Atlantic Express.

Before leaving the room—she had earlier paid her bill—she took one precaution. Feeling under her left armpit, she checked to make sure the sheathed knife concealed there was easily extracted. Unlike Elsa Lang, who had been trained to use pistols and automatic weapons by Harry Wargrave on the FBI shooting range in Washington, Anna was a child of the Balkans, where women use knives.

And again unlike Elsa, the daughter of a British admiral who had been educated at the Godolphin public school in Salisbury, Anna had been brought up in the back streets of Athens. She was only seven years old when both her parents had been killed by the Communists at the time of the Greek Civil War—the war the Greek anti-Communists had partly won owing to the military aid sent by President Truman. And in the Balkans passions are stronger and last longer than in the West. Since she had been eighteen years old Anna had devoted her life to fighting the underground Communist apparatus. It was in Athens that she had originally joined forces with Harry Wargrave.

Going out the back way to the garage, she removed the blanket she had draped over the hood of her rented Renault to prevent the engine freezing up. Within two minutes she was driving out of the archway and into the main street. It was only a short distance to the station just beyond the eastern outskirts of Andermatt but she drove carefully. This was not the moment to skid into a wall. There were one or two other cars about, and a hundred yards behind her a small gray Fiat followed at a discreet distance. Behind the wheel sat the fat, bald-headed Erich Volcker, the man who earlier had unsuccessfully tried to run her down in a side street.

Anna was heading for the Schöllenen railroad, which descends from Andermatt to Göschenen on the main Milan to Zürich rail route. It is one of the strangest and most sinister railroads in Europe. With a gradient of 1 in 5½, it creaks and rumbles its way down over a rack-and-pinion system as huge cogs suspended below the coaches turn over the ratchet rail. In less than three miles it drops over a thousand feet and the journey takes fifteen minutes.

In that time it grinds its way down through a series of tunnels and avalanche shelters and at one point crosses the river Reuss where that ferocious stream plunges and winds its way through the terrible gorge and over a great waterfall. Traveling it by day is a weird experience; by night the experience becomes eerie and frightening as the grind of the slow-moving cogs reverberates and echoes inside the dark tunnels.

At intervals windows in the rock and short open stretches outside the tunnels reveal an awesome view—the drop into the gorge, the tumble and froth of the foaming torrent below. At the moment the Reuss was frozen. As Anna pulled up outside the station she was not surprised to see that apparently she was the only passenger. In a week's time the train would be crowded with returning vacationers. Leaving the Renault parked outside—she could inform the car rental people later—she went into the booking hall to buy her ticket.

"You will have about three minutes to catch the train at Göschenen," the ticket clerk informed her. "Hurry across to the main station when you get down."

"Thank you," Anna replied in German. "I know the way—I came up only two weeks ago."

Choosing a compartment in the middle of the short train, she perched her bag on the seat ready for a quick exit and sighed with relief. She had got away from Andermatt in one piece. And she had done the job: she knew who was controlling and directing the secret Communist cell from Andermatt. Then the door was opened and a man climbed inside as the train began to move. Sitting down in the seat diagonally opposite to her, Erich Volcker took out a cigar and paused.

"You mind if I smoke my cigar, miss?"

Anna glanced at him and shrugged her shoulders without replying as she looked away. The grinding of the cogs was beginning and she had the feeling the strain on the train was enormous as it angled downward, that maybe the cogs would slip and the train would plunge down

239

through the tunnel. It was an irrational fear; she knew the Swiss rack-and-pinion system was an engineering marvel, that in its whole history it had never failed to operate smoothly and safely.

"Some people do object to cigars," Volcker continued as he puffed until the end was a glowing red.

Anna was tense and her nerves were strained. In that brief glance she had noted a great deal about Erich Volcker, had observed his hard fatness, his obscenely bald head, and his small watchful eyes. Some men who were bald have a magnetic attraction for women; Erich Volcker did not fall into this category. And she was suspicious. Why, when the train was empty, had he chosen this compartment?

It could be that she faced nothing more harmless than an amatory approach from this hideous man. That was an experience Anna Markos was only too familiar with. And when Volcker had tried to drive her down in the Andermatt side street before she smashed his windshield she had no chance to catch even a glimpse of the driver with the headlights glaring in her face. Surreptitiously she checked her watch. Another thirteen minutes alone with this creep. And he was carrying no baggage. Was he a railroad official going home? If so, why was he not in uniform? With an unencouraging expression of arrogance on her face, Anna went on checking the possibilities as the train ground down through another tunnel. Through a cavernous window in the rock she caught a moonlit glimpse of the ice-bound river Reuss.

"You have had a pleasant holiday, I hope?" Volcker persisted in his throaty voice as he moved to the seat opposite her. "Everyone has a great time in Andermatt."

Anna Markos stared directly at him for the first time, her full lips curled in an expression of contempt as she loosened her fur coat as though feeling the warmth of the compartment. She noted his very large hands, the backs of his fingers sprouting black hairs. He could use some of that up top, she was thinking. She sat with her own hands clasped casually in her lap as he went on staring back at her while he pulled on the cigar until the end was again a fiery, glowing tip. Then he removed the cigar from his mouth, leaned forward quickly, and stabbed the burning end on the back of her right hand to shock her— to throw her off balance for a few seconds.

At least, that was what he tried to do. Anna's hands moved with a movement so quick it was a blur. She knocked the cigar out of his hand, there was a shower of sparks, some of which touched his cheek. "You bitch . . ." His huge hands grasped her around the throat, half-encircled her strong neck in a vicelike grip. His long fingers held her like a restricting necklace, his thumbs jammed deep into her windpipe. She clawed the right side of his fat face, drew blood as she carved a deep gash, but Volcker ignored the pain, knowing it would take only thirty seconds. Twisting around on the seat, she dropped backward, but he held on and came down on top of her with the whole of his bulk. Her vision was swimming, she felt her consciousness ebbing away.

With a sudden violent movement she swung her powerful body sideways off the seat, carrying him with her, and he landed underneath her on the floor of the compartment with her on top. But still he held on with his strangling grip. She could feel the cogwheel vibrations coming up through the floor as the train made its laborious twisting way down the Schöllenen. With a supreme effort of will she stopped herself fainting. Volcker's fat, bald-headed silhouette was a fading blur.

With her right hand thrust between them, she seized the handle of the knife, jerked it clear of his throttling embrace. Gritting her teeth, she gripped the knife with all her strength and thrust it upward and deep into his side. He let out a muted, animallike gulp and his hands left her throat. There was a peculiar thudding sound. Panting for breath, Anna hauled herself back up on the seat. The sound was the thudding of Volcker's tiny feet on the compartment floor. The sound stopped. Volcker lay very still, his eyes open and staring.

Anna checked her watch: 8:40 P.M. Six minutes to Göschenen. Bending over the dead man, she heaved and strained to extract the knife. It took all her strength to free the weapon. Using a large handkerchief she found in one of his pockets, she wiped the handle clean of prints, after donning a pair of gloves. Then she wiped the blade clean of blood, mopped up a few spots off the compartment floor, and stuffed the handkerchief back into his pocket.

Inside his wallet she found a card with his name on it. Printed under the name in German were the words "aircraft mechanic." Another visiting card bore the name of Robert Frey. She replaced the wallet and stared out of the window. The train, still moving at a snail's pace as it continued its steep descent, had moved out of the tunnel and was passing under an avalanche shelter. Below the shelter roof the railroad track was open—there was a sheer drop, a glitter of ice a long way down. She unlatched the door, left it bobbing gently against the door frame with the cogwheel vibration.

Standing behind the dead man, she stooped and hoisted him by the shoulders. He seemed to weigh half a ton as she hauled him upright, her hands under his armpits, and forced the body forward until it was touching the opened door. Her chest heaving with the exertion, she took another deep breath and pushed with all her strength. The door flew open; Volcker dropped through the opening, missed the track, and fell out of sight into the gorge. The compartment was suddenly icy cold with the night air flowing in. Leaning out, looking to her left, she saw a fresh tunnel coming up. She hauled the door inward and closed it.

After a quick check of the compartment floor for traces of blood, she checked her appearance in the mirror. Her neck was bruised and swollen. Opening her case, she took out a scarf and wrapped it around her neck, refastened her fur coat, and pulled up her hood. Taking a lipstick from her handbag, she applied it freshly. That made her feel much better. Then she remembered the cigar. She found it smoldering under a seat and pitched it out of the window.

As the little train emerged from the end of the tunnel and stopped alongside its own special station she was standing by the door. At Göschenen, north of the Alps, a blizzard was raging. She checked her watch: 8:46 P.M. Once again a Swiss train had arrived precisely on time. Picking up her bag, she opened the door, stepped down into the snowstorm, and hurried across to the main station. She gave not a single glance backward to the mouth of the Schöllenen tunnel.

21

Göschenen, Zürich

By the time the Atlantic Express had reached Airolo, Wargrave, guided by his Swiss radio operator, Max Bruder, had landed the Alouette at a nearby airstrip ringed by what seemed to be half the Swiss Army. Springer drove the short distance to the airstrip and, as Robert Frey was taken off the machine, he faced hostile and armed men—so hostile that Springer himself escorted the hitherto respected mountaineer to a police van. Weather conditions being so appalling north of the Gotthard, the chopper would be useless, so it was left at the airstrip. Springer then drove Wargrave, Elsa, and Bruder back to the waiting express, which started up as soon as they were on board.

The train had only just commenced its ten-minute journey through the Gotthard tunnel when Wargrave called what he termed "a council of war" in the Wagon-Lit compartment where Marenkov remained under guard. Besides Elsa and Julian Haller, Springer was present. It was Wargrave who opened the meeting with a typical remark. "I suspect that what has happened so far may only be the beginning. As they say on British Rail, after the soup the worst is yet to come. . . ."

"What I do so love," Elsa interjected, "is your eternal optimism."

"My eternal realism," the Englishman corrected her with a laconic smile. "We know that Traber has reported the arrival of Colonel Igor Sharpinsky in Zürich and I don't think that gentleman is going to give up easily."

"I can give you a description of him," Marenkov said suddenly.

Springer stared at the Russian; since the avalanche a radical change had taken place in Marenkov's attitude that he would provide no imformation until he was airborne and on his way to the States. "That we could use," the Swiss agreed. "In the West he is known as Colonel Shadow because no one has ever been able to photograph him."

"And I could build up a sketch from your description," Elsa suggested. She was already taking a large notepad from her case. "When I was makeup girl with a film company I used to pass my spare time sketching people."

"Leave that for a few minutes," Springer suggested. "We have almost two hours before we reach Zürich. There is a mystery I do not understand. The man who attacked the engineers in their cab was shot—once by myself, but I only winged him. He managed to escape from the cab on the other side of the train and was making his way to a waiting car when someone shot him dead. That same someone then shot dead the driver of the escape vehicle."

"One of your people?" Haller inquired.

"No. That is the whole point—I have checked. But one of my people who was scanning the express from a crag on the eastern side says both shots were fired through an open window by someone on board the express."

Wargrave stirred in his seat. "Any idea what range the shots were fired from?"

"The report I have received estimates the first shot was at a range of about one hundred meters—and the saboteur who was killed by a single shot was moving at the time.

As for the man behind the wheel of the car, the range was even greater."

"That's some shooting," Elsa exclaimed.

"Precisely," Springer interjected. "Which is exactly what worries me—we have, somewhere among the three hundred and fifty passengers aboard the express, an outstanding marksman. Who is he? Why is he on the train?"

The train roar as it moved through the tunnel was very loud and Elsa had to raise her voice to make herself heard. "But if he shot down two of Sharpinsky's men he has to be on our side."

"I admire your recognition of the obvious, your logical turn of mind," Wargrave remarked dryly. "I find it so reassuring."

"I have the strangest feeling someone is cocking a snook at me," Elsa replied caustically. "It couldn't be I'm displaying an element of naïveté, I trust?"

Wargrave grinned as she glared at him. "Naïve, you're not. But the unknown marksman could have had an excellent reason for shooting down those two men—if he were sufficiently ruthless. By killing them he ensured that if caught they would never talk under interrogation. It could also mean something else more sinister. . . ."

"That he is important," Springer said quietly. "Important enough to have the power to shoot down his own people to protect his identity."

"Then the list of possible names is very narrow," Marenkov suggested.

"Narrow it," suggested Haller.

"Boris Volkov. Simovitch, the Bulgarian. Leitermann, the German from Leipzig. All of them are KGB marksmen of exceptional caliber."

"I go along with that," Haller said. "The question is: which one is sitting within fourteen cars of where we're sitting now?"

Marenkov shook his head. "Leitermann is in the United States waiting for an assignment. Within ten minutes of the Boeing's taking off from Schiphol with me aboard you will have details and he will be under arrest." He waved a hand as Haller started to speak. "No, that is what was agreed—a complete debriefing to start once I am over the Atlantic. Volkov is under treatment in a Moscow clinic for a liver complaint. I cannot add to the list GRU personnel because I don't know them."

"So that leaves Simovitch," Haller pointed out.

Wargrave intervened. "Simovitch was secretly killed in Brussels eighteen months ago by the British Secret Service."

"Which cancels out everyone you have mentioned, Marenkov," Haller observed irritably.

"Not quite," the Russian replied. "There is a fourth man." He turned to Wargrave. "You once operated in Greece?"

"If you say so."

"Then you may have heard the name Nicos Leonides?"

"No."

"He is Sharpinsky's favorite executioner—although, as far as I know, he has worked only in his native Greece. I have no description of him—but it is a possibility."

"And no description of any kind—even a reference to his habits, likes, dislikes?" Elsa inquired.

"Nothing." The Russian stared around the compartment and his expression was grim. "Of one thing I am certain—so much is personally at stake for Sharpinsky that when he learns I am still alive I am convinced he will board the express himself—at Zürich." The Russian clenched his fist. "You can count on it."

"So we need your description of him quickly," Elsa said emphatically.

"That may not help—he is a master of the art of disguise, a natural-born actor. But he will board this train before it leaves Switzerland—I stake my life on it." He smiled without humor. "In fact, come to think of it, that is what I am staking—my life. . . ."

Wargrave left the compartment and moved up the train away from the Wagon-Lit as it approached Göschenen. Unlike previous night trains bound for Holland, the new Atlantic Express would be continuing north to Zürich instead of bypassing the city and heading northwest for Basel via Lucerne. And despite all the efforts of Swiss rail officials to reassure passengers, there was still a sense of nervous tension aboard the train after the avalanche experience.

As he passed compartments Wargrave noticed that some had the blinds drawn where people were trying to get some sleep, but in others passengers were still wide awake, staring fearfully out although they could see nothing but the tunnel. As it approached the exit and Göschenen station, the train slowed down, then glided past the platform and stopped. A snowstorm was raging and the platform was deep with a white carpet as a single passenger climbed aboard.

Anna Markos had a first-class reservation and she was relieved to see the compartment was empty. In the next compartment Jorge Santos watched her pass as he sat alone, his long legs still sprawled, his pipe between his teeth. When the express began moving again he stretched, stood up, and went out into the corridor. He stood for a moment outside the next compartment where Anna Markos was taking off her coat, displaying in profile her magnificent figure. Glancing sideways, she caught sight of Santos observing her. The Spaniard gave her a wink. She turned her back on him and when she sat down, crossed her legs, and looked again he had gone. Two minutes later Harry Wargrave entered her compartment, closed the blinds on the corridor side, and sat down opposite her.

"Thank you, Anna," he said simply.

"My message—it reached you?" Like Wargrave, she was conversing in little more than a murmur.

"In the nick of time, thank God. I can tell you now—you probably saved the train from total destruction. Frey set off an avalanche from the Wasserhorn."

"Oh, my God. . . ."

"You saved us all, Anna," Wargrave repeated gently. "Was it very tough in Andermatt?" He leaned forward. "You look strained. Something happened, didn't it?"

Anna shrugged. "Yes, something happened." Very briefly she described her experiences and the expression on Wargrave's face grew grimmer as she continued. "I got on to Robert Frey partly by instinct. Also by luck and digging." She took a deep drag on her cigarette. "He was just a bit too much the local hero. But that proved nothing. I checked on who was near the Rhône Glacier the day Springer's agent was found dead in the ice tunnel. Robert Frey's chopper had landed at Gletsch nearby early that morning. Still not conclusive. . . ."

She described what had happened since. ". . . Even the hidden transmitter in his farmhouse wasn't conclusive. There were no code books left lying around, of course. So, as I told you, I set myself up as human bait. . . . when he guided me into that deathtrap of a street, I knew."

"And the man on the Schöllenen who tried to kill you," Wargrave reminded her. He squeezed her right leg above the knee so hard his grip hurt. "For Christ's sake, your brief was to take care, not to push it over the edge."

"But you admitted I saved the express, Harry. We took chances in Athens, remember. . . ." His hard grip on her leg comforted her. There was a time when she had suggested they become lovers and Wargrave—reluctantly—had told her it was madness for agents to become emotionally involved. She had seen his point but even now, with his hand gripping her, she felt the old feeling. "What do I do now I'm here?" she asked as he released his grip.

"Stay under cover. I'm not telling anyone about your being on the train—I may still need a secret backup." He leaned forward and gently removed the scarf from her neck. He winced when he saw the bruising, which had now developed into ugly blue welts.

"That needs medical attention."

"Later. It's a little sore but I'll survive. Is there anything else I should know?"

"Yes. Colonel Igor Sharpinsky is somewhere in Zürich."

"That bastard! God knows we spent time trying to track him down in Athens a hundred years ago."

Wargrave explained how Traber had heard that Crocodile—the code name for Sharpinsky—had arrived in Zürich and that Marenkov was convinced the KGB colonel would board the express at Zürich. "But at least we do have a description of him," he went on, "and Elsa Lang is building up a sketch portrait that may help."

"He is very clever, very ruthless," Anna warned.

"Even so, for all we know, Traber may already have tracked him down."

The gigantic Wasserhorn avalanche that might have engulfed the Atlantic Express just missed it. . . . The train is now proceeding on its way to Zürich. . . .

It was 8:40 P.M. in Room 207 at the Hotel Schweizerhof when Heinz Golchack switched off his pocket-size transistor radio, which had just broadcast the news flash. Aware that Rudi Bühler and Heinrich Baum were watching him, Golchack kept his face expressionless as he polished his rimless glasses.

"What the hell do we do now?" Bühler demanded aggressively when he could stand the silence no longer.

"We destroy that map for a start. . . ."

He waited while Baum was burning the map in the bathroom and then waited again as Baum hurried back to receive a signal that was just coming in from Moscow via Mohner's transmitter on the Zürichberg. He read the signal in silence and went to the bathroom to burn this message himself. When he returned, his high-domed forehead was glistening with sweat.

"Send the short signal to Basel," he instructed Baum, "then the long one to the Geiger Group in Amsterdam." The signal to Basel was going to Yuri Gusev, the GRU executioner, who had now arrived in that city from Mulhouse in response to Golchack's earlier signal.

Heinrich Baum, the Swiss dentist from Basel, looked dubious. "The Amsterdam signal is a very long one," he suggested tentatively. "Can we not abbreviate it?"

Golchack stared at him with his pale eyes, but the Swiss stared back defiantly. They had been locked away inside the room for five hours now without food and only a flask of coffee Bühler had brought to drink from. Golchack, who was a teetotaler—"Alcohol clouds the brain and distorts judgment"—ate very little and saw no reason why his subordinates should not confirm to his habits.

But there was a feeling of claustrophobic tension in the room and Baum would have given anything for a brief walk along the Bahnhofstrasse, even in the snowstorm that was enveloping the city.

"If it had been possible to make it shorter I would have done so," Golchack replied coldly. "Are you questioning my instruction?" he inquired softly.

"Of course not."

"Then why are you not already sending the signals?" Golchack inquired in the restrained voice Baum found so unnerving. The Swiss sat down in front of his transmitter and began sending the shorter signal to Basel.

The operator in the radio detector van parked in the side street under the second-floor restaurant of the Hotel Schweizerhof reached for the radio telephone that put him in direct communication with Traber's headquarters. It was Traber himself who answered the call.

"We have a radio fix, sir." He was careful to keep the excitement out of his voice. In an emergency Traber did not appreciate any display of emotion. "The Hotel Schweizerhof. Yes, sir. Positive."

"Continue listening. I'm coming myself."

The police patrol team checking hotel registers had just arrived at the Schweizerhof when the plump figure of Traber, puffing a small cigar and with hands thrust deep inside his overcoat pockets, walked into the reception hall. Behind him followed six of his men, also in civilian clothes and all of them armed.

"Anything?" Traber asked, glancing at the register.

"Heinz Golchack never went on to Germany," one of the policeman said quickly. "He's registered here—Room 201."

"I see." Traber took another puff at his cigar. "Any other arrivals since lunchtime, say?"

"Heinrich Baum, a dentist from Basel—Room 207. And a Rudi Bühler—also from Vienna, whose arrival could coincide with Flight 433—in Room 316."

"Golchack's room first," Traber ordered. He looked at the receptionist. "Passkey, please. And if anyone in the hotel tries to use the phone—no matter from which room—your switchboard is temporarily out of action." He turned to the hotel porter, who was lapping up every word. "Take us to Room 201 first."

The two policemen remained in the reception hall as Traber ascended in the elevator with two of his men while the other four went up the staircase. Outside Room 201 Traber waited while one man inserted the key quietly, turned it, and then burst inside holding his pistol, followed by his colleague. When they found the room unoccupied they proceeded along the corridor to Room 207, registered in the name of Heinrich Baum. Again they adopted the same procedure, but here the outcome was different.

Heinrich Baum had just finished sending his overlong signal to Amsterdam, was just closing up his disguised transmitter, when the door burst open. He grabbed for his pistol lying next to the transmitter and was still turning around when Traber's man shot him dead. He fell to the floor, his right hand dragging with him the encoded Amsterdam signal. Previously he had destroyed the signal to Basel. Traber stooped down and retrieved the piece of paper.

"Pity we couldn't have interrogated him," he remarked.

"And God knows how long it will take our cryptanalysts to decipher this, if ever. It's probably Soviet one-time code. Unless the code book is here. . . ."

"Sorry, sir," the man who had shot Baum apologized, "but he was reaching for his gun."

"You did well. And I can't say I'm sorry to see a dirty Swiss traitor get his."

A brief search produced no sign of any book, but in the bathroom Traber sniffed. "Smell of burning. Previous signals going up in smoke and down the toilet, of course." They found that Room 316—registered to Rudi Bühler—was also empty and Traber then went back down to the reception hall. His tone was crisp when he spoke to the receptionist.

"Golchack and Bühler have gone. Surely you would have seen them if they left by the front entrance? My men are searching the hotel but I'm not optimistic."

The receptionist looked doubtful. "Unless they left when my colleague took over the desk for a few minutes while I used the bathroom. That was less than a quarter of an hour ago . . ."

Less than fifteen minutes earlier Heinz Golchack had indeed left the hotel, explaining to the temporary receptionist that he had a migraine and that the night air might help to clear it. During this brief chat Rudi Bühler had also slipped away through the exit. Leaving the hotel, Golchack had walked the few yards to the escalator that led down to the underground shopping mall.

At that hour the underground cavern was deserted and he had quickly taken off his pebble glasses and slipped them into his pocket. From another pocket he had taken an old peaked cap of the type worn by chauffeurs and pulled it well down over his head. Crossing the shopping area, he had mounted another escalator that brought him out onto the other side of the Bahnhofplatz from the Schweizerhof, and hailed a cab.

"Pelikan-platz, please," he had instructed the driver in faultless German.

Getting out at the Pelkian-platz, he had waited until the cab disappeared before crossing the road and walking at speed through a series of side streets. Even though it was snowing heavily Golchack was enjoying himself. He loved the city of Zürich with its spires and ancient buildings and twisting streets, just as he loved Vienna for the same reasons. He would, in fact, have happily lived in the Swiss city for the rest of his life. And the girls were marvelous, with their erect walk and their slim figures. There was nothing like it in Soviet Russia. Then he arrived at Lindengasse 451, a villa near the end of a deserted cul-de-sac.

Taking a key from his pocket, he opened the door and went inside. At the top of a flight of steps in the split-level hall a tall, dark-haired girl in her mid-thirties met him.

She was holding an automatic, which she slipped back inside her handbag as she recognized her visitor.

"Get rid of that, Ilse," he ordered.

He had handed her the passport made out in the name of Heinz Golchack. She took him into a large, heavily curtained room full of somber furniture and antiques. Taking off his snow-covered cap and coat, which showed he had been outside recently, he handed these also to her; then he sat down and took off his soaked shoes. "And get rid of that lot, too. What time will the express arrive?"

"The last time I phoned the Hauptbahnhof—ten minutes ago—they said 2233 hours. Expected departure time is 2300 hours."

"Then we shall have to hurry—there is a lot to do. I am going aboard the Atlantic Express."

"The security cordon at the Hauptbahnhof will be massive, Mr. Vogler."

Mr. Vogler . . . Traveling from Vienna to Zürich, Colonel Igor Sharpinsky had assumed the identity of a real person—or poor Heinz Golchack, rare-book dealer whose cremated relics were now hidden in a bowl of snow in a remote part of the Vienna Woods. Now he was temporarily assuming the identity of Edward Vogler, Swiss antique dealer, who did *not* exist—but whose pretended existence had been carefully built up by Ilse Murset, an expert in antique dealing.

In the quiet backwater of the Lindengasse no one took much notice of neighbors, but it was understood that Edward Vogler spent much of his time abroad, that he was something of an eccentric, a night owl who returned to the villa late and worked through the early hours. On the odd occasion—always after dark—a man somewhat resembling Sharpinsky in build had been seen hurrying into the villa, but it had been established he was rarely home.

Taking away the wet clothes and shoes, Ilse returned with a dressing gown and slippers, which Sharpinsky put on; he then settled himself in a chair behind a desk covered with invoices. It was most unlikely the police would check this address, but if they did they would find Edward Vogler

253

attending to his business affairs. "Is everyone here?" Sharpinsky inquired. "Good. Then bring them in and we will make plans to deal with Traber's massive security cordon."

And it was not by chance that Sharpinsky had moved from the Hotel Schweizerhof just before the Swiss security men had arrived. On the rare occasions when Igor Sharpinsky operated abroad underground he never stayed in one place for more than five hours. As he waited for Ilse to fetch his subordinates from upstairs the Russian thought grimly about the signal from Moscow Baum had handed him before he left to the Schweizerhof. *All key agents now being advised to leave Western Europe. . . .*

The signal was a terrible blow to Sharpinsky because it implied that Moscow was contemplating the possibility that he might fail in his attempt to kill Marenkov. And the fact that the signal was unsigned told him it had been dictated by Leonid Sedov himself. They had heard over the radio that the avalanche had not destroyed the Atlantic Express.

At 8:40 P.M. in Zürich, when Sharpinsky had heard the news that the Atlantic Express had survived, it was 10:40 P.M. in Moscow when First Secretary Leonid Sedov sat in session with the other two Politburo members charged with handling the Marenkov crisis—Marshal Prachko and Anatoli Zarubin. Prachko, normally so aggressive and confident, was strangely silent as they digested the news. It was Zarubin, the small, dark-haired minister of trade with his sophisticated manner, who subtly turned the blame on Prachko.

"Your protégé does not seem to be shining in this supreme emergency," he suggested amiably. "So far all he has done is to uncover our main underground sabotage apparatus inside Switzerland."

"He has to try something," Prachko bridled, pulling at the hoglike bristles protruding from his nostrils.

"He also had to succeed," Zarubin observed. "How much longer do we allow him before they fly out Marenkov and he starts uncovering all our agents—men it has taken years to train and infiltrate? I am thinking particularly of West Germany," he added.

"Sharpinsky will think of something," Prachko blustered.

"But if he doesn't?" Leonid Sedov intervened as he rubbed his jaw. The recent operation had left him with a tickle that irritated him in moments of tension. His voice was firm and decisive as he stared directly at Marshal Prachko. "Is this not the time to order a general evacuation of all our key agents from West Germany, France, and Belgium—before it is too late? They can always return later."

"My information," Prachko replied, playing for time, "is that the German border controls on the east have been alerted and fully mobilized. And in this weather it will be even more difficult for them to slip over the frontier into the German Democratic Republic."

"Then they will have to try and reach the freighter *Maxim Gorky,* which is now proceeding south from the Baltic and will soon be off the Dutch coast."

"If that is *your* recommendation," Prachko agreed slyly.

"No!" Sedov's voice was sharp. "As minister of defense, it is your advice we seek."

Prachko was trapped and he knew it. There had already been a débâcle in Switzerland that could be laid at his door and now he was faced with two impossible alternatives. If he said no and Marenkov reached America, the Communist underground apparatus in Western Europe would be shattered. If he said yes, the agents would escape but it would take time to infiltrate them back into Western Europe. He opted for what seemed at that moment the less dangerous alternative.

"I recommend they should be evacuated."

Zarubin, he noted, recorded in a minute that the decision was that taken by the minister of defense. He didn't like it but there was nothing he could do about it. He made one final comment.

"At this moment Sharpinsky is probably making plans that will eliminate the traitor Sergei Marenkov. . . ."

255

22

Zürich Hauptbahnhof

It was 9:10 P.M.—less than two hours before the Atlantic
Express was due to depart from Zürich—when Sharpinsky
sat looking at three photographs on the desk in the living
room of the Lindengasse villa. He had already given
specific instructions to four men, who had left the villa,
and now he was alone with Ilse Murset he felt the tension
rising inside him. The waiting was always the worst part,
but everything had been dealt with. And Rudi Bühler
should by now be in Basel waiting to board the Atlantic
Express later.

When Bühler had left the Schweizerhof Hotel a few
seconds ahead of Sharpinsky he had crossed to the
Hauptbahnhof and caught a train for Basel. The hotel
receptionist would have provided Traber's men with his
description—if they had by now tracked down the
temporary Soviet base—and it was only prudent that
he should leave the city immediately. As Sharpinsky
studied the three photographs, Ilse's slim white hand
touched his neck.

"What can the photographs possibly tell you?"

"Study the enemy," Sharpinsky replied. "Looking at
these pictures, I believe it is possible to foresee how these
men will react under pressure."

The first photograph, the least clear, was of Springer,
the brim of his hat pulled low, a picture taken with a
telephoto lens from a window in the Bahnhofstrasse. The
second picture—much clearer—was of General Max

Scholten, chief of Dutch counterespionage, his cherubic face easily identifiable, and taken outside the Hotel Astoria opposite the railway station in The Hague. The third, taken several years previously in Athens, was of Harry Wargrave. Sharpinsky's finger stabbed at the third photo. "That man is the most dangerous."

"You feel tense. . . ." Ilse's fingers continued to caress the Russian's neck. "Shall we go upstairs?" Her tall, slim figure was taut as she unzipped the front of her dress. The Russian hesitated; he checked his watch.

"There's no time to go upstairs."

"Then let's do it here on the floor."

Two of the men who had left the villa immediately on receiving Sharpinsky's instructions walked to a Citroën parked farther down the street. Klaus Jaeger, tall and heavy-built, a native of East Germany, got behind the wheel while his smaller, slimmer companion, Hans-Otto Nacken, also from East Germany, sat beside him. Both of them were carrying faked West German papers. Within a matter of minutes they were approaching the Hauptbahnhof.

Jaeger did not pull up in front of the Hauptbahnhof; he took the Citroën around to the end of the station and parked it in the shadows. Leaving the car, both men strolled into the station through the side entrance past the baggage counter. For the sake of appearance Jaeger was carrying a case. They spent several minutes while they walked around studying the Swiss rail porters who were waiting for the arrival of night trains.

"That one over there," Jaeger said as he stopped and lit a cigarette. "He's just about the right height and build."

Separating himself from Jaeger, Nacken walked over to the porter, who was a short, well-built man of a similar physical makeup to Sharpinsky. "I see from the indicator board that the Atlantic Express isn't due to leave till eleven o'clock. I've got my times mixed up—so I'm due for a long wait. The board is correct, I suppose?"

"Yes, sir. And it's a miracle it's making up time. Have you heard the news?"

"What news?"

"There was an avalanche south of the Gotthard—the worst this century, they say. It almost overwhelmed the express."

"My God! No. I hadn't heard. Well, at least there won't be one between here and Basel." He offered the porter a cigarette. "Must be boring work for you—hanging around here all night. How much longer do you have on duty?" he asked casually.

The porter took a deep drag on the cigarette. "I go off at eight in the morning. You get used to it."

Nacken chatted for a few minutes and then drifted away, putting his left hand in his coat pocket. It was the signal Jaeger, watching from a distance, had been waiting for. He walked over to the porter. "Can you fetch my other bags from the car? It's parked at the end of the station." He dumped the case he was holding on the porter's trolley and followed him. They were moving along an ill-lit cavern past the baggage storage department and no one else was in sight.

Reaching the Citroën, Jaeger opened the rear door after glancing around to make sure no one was about. "The bag in there," he explained. "Be careful, it's heavy." As the porter leaned inside, Jaeger took a small steel truncheon encased in leather from his pocket, leaned over the porter, and smashed it down on the man's skull with considerable force. The porter collapsed, dead.

Nacken appeared from the shadows and helped to heave the body completely inside the back of the car. "The trolley," Jaeger reminded his companion as he pulled a traveling rug over the corpse. Nacken moved the trolley back against the wall into the shadows. It would be needed later. Then they were both moving into the front seats, closing the doors quietly, and Jaeger drove away over the Limmat bridge.

He drove to a quiet part of the lake beyond the Quaibrücke and pulled up by the shore under a copse of trees, switching off his engine and lights. It took the combined efforts of both men to undress the dead man, to divest him of his uniform, cap, and boots. Jaeger took his wallet, checked with his torch to make sure the porter's rail pass was inside. "That's it," he said. "Now, let's lose him."

They fastened heavy chains around the body—the chains from the case Jaeger had warned the porter was heavy—and between them carried the body to the edge of the lake. At this point the ice on the lake was thin and the water below was sixty feet deep. Swinging the body between them, one man holding the shoulders, the other the feet, they cast him down. The weighted corpse broke through the ice with a splintering crunch and sank.

Getting back behind the wheel of the car, Jaeger drove to the Quaibrücke, crossed it, and headed for the Lindengasse. They now had what they had been sent for, a railway porter's uniform, and the porter would not be notified as missing by his wife—if he had one, Jaeger thought callously—until long after the Atlantic Express had departed. After all, as he had told Nacken, he was not due off duty until eight in the morning.

The second team of two men who had been dispatched from the Lindengasse at the same time as Jaeger and Nacken had a simpler task. Getting into another car, they drove to the western side of the city until they reached a large garage in an industrial suburb. One of the men got out, opened the double doors, and then closed them after the car had been driven inside. It pulled alongside a huge furniture truck that carried on its side the legend *Möbel—Salzburg*.

Getting out of the car, the driver switched on the garage lights and took a case out of the car. When he opened it the case contained nothing more sinister than liverwurst sandwiches and a flask of coffee. "No alcohol," Sharpinsky had warned. "If I find you have disobeyed me you will be recalled at once." The second man went to a wall phone and dialed a number. It was Ilse Murset who answered.

"André here," the man reported. "The consignment is now ready for delivery."

"Understood!" Ilse broke the connection.

Inside the garage the men who had phoned Ilse climbed up into the cab of the furniture truck, pulled aside the canvas cover, and checked the load. Here again the truck contained nothing more sinister than a full load of furniture, but it was very heavily laden and the tail gate at the back tilted outward at a perilous angle. Also there was a curious cable and pulley device that linked the tail gate through the full length of the truck to the cab.

"Alfred, here are yours."

The man in the cab threw down some overalls, climbed down from the cab, and made his way to the back of the garage where there was more room. Within a few minutes, both of them dressed as furniture delivery men, they sat down on a bench to consume their sandwiches and coffee. At regular intervals the driver checked his watch.

As soon as they had delivered the porter's clothes to Lindengasse 451 Jaeger and Nacken drove off again in the Citroën and recrossed the Quaibrücke. But this time, instead of proceeding south along the lake shore, they drove north along the banks of the river Limmat and then turned uphill along the main road toward the Zürichberg. They were driving through an expensive district of neat villas and well-kept gardens when Jaeger swung the wheel and turned into a drive.

Behind them a man who had been waiting in the bitter cold closed and locked the wrought-iron gates. Pulling up in front of the two-story villa where icicles hung from a balcony, Jaeger switched off the ignition and alighted from the car. "Check the limousine," he ordered Nacken. "And above all check the engine."

A severe-faced woman of fifty who had heard the car arrive opened the front door, let Jaeger inside, and closed it. She had her hair tied back in a bun and wore a long dark dress that gave her the appearance of a housekeeper.

'All your clothes are ready for you in the main bedroom," she informed him.

"Get rid of this." Jaeger handed her his identity card. "And where is the passport?" They were speaking to each other in fluent Russian. The woman took a passport from her pocket and handed it to him. He checked it quickly. The Soviet diplomatic passport, carrying his own picture, was in the name of Boris Volkov; rank, captain. He went upstairs to change.

The business suit laid out on the bed was Russian in style and made of Russian cloth. He even changed into Russian underclothes, shirt, tie, shoes, and hat. When he went back downstairs he found Nacken had already changed into his own uniform, that of a Soviet chauffeur. "The car," Jaeger said, "I want to check it for myself." Following Nacken, he entered the garage by a door directly from the back of the villa.

Inside the garage stood a gleaming Mercedes that had recently been polished to a glasslike sheen. And that won't last long in this weather, Jaeger thought. The car was carrying diplomatic plates, those of the Soviet Embassy in Bern. He made Nacken get behind the wheel to test the ignition and the engine fired immediately. Satisfied, Jaeger went back into the house and dialed the number of Lindengasse 451. Again it was Ilse Murset who answered the call.

"Bernard here," Jaeger reported. "The collection is now ready for delivery."

"Understood!" Ilse broke the connection.

"All the arrangements are complete," she told Sharpinsky as she zipped up the front of her dress. "Everyone is in position and I will be ready to drive you to the Hauptbahnhof."

Colonel Igor Sharpinsky, sitting only in his shirt, nodded.

"Soon now, Traber," he said. "Very soon now . . ."

The Atlantic Express was making up lost time rapidly as it continued its nonstop descent north of the Gotthard through a blinding snowstorm. In the motor cab of the

261

powerful Bo-Bo locomotive, Enrico was being assisted by a fresh chief engineer Springer had insisted should accompany him from Airolo. It was not an arrangement that pleased the sturdy Swiss from Basel.

"It takes more than a bump on the head to knock me out," he grumbled as he watched the gauges and checked the signals. "And we are going to make Zürich on time. Damn it—my reputation is at stake."

Inside the compartment of the rear Wagon-Lit where Marenkov was under guard the atmosphere was tense and growing worse the closer they came to Zürich. For the third time—to Julian Haller's intense irritation, but he was now feeling very fatigued—the Russian repeated the same remark.

"I am convinced that Sharpinsky will board the express at Zürich. . . ."

"Will attempt to," Elsa corrected him. She held up the portrait sketch of Igor Sharpinsky in her notepad that she had built up from Marenkov's description. "Now, for the first time, we know what he looks like."

The stocky, wide-shouldered Russian waved an impatient hand. "That won't help—I keep telling you he is a genius at altering his appearance."

"Don't be so pessimistic," Elsa snapped back. "I told you I spent a whole year as film makeup girl changing actors' appearances. If anyone can spot him coming on the train, I can."

This both Wargrave and Springer, who also sat in the compartment, had agreed. So the plan was that when the train arrived at the Hauptbahnhof Elsa would stand close to the ticket barrier examining everyone who came aboard. And the Swiss colonel, at least, had reason for satisfaction: Marenkov had already out of his encyclopedic memory provided a list of names and addresses of all KGB agents in Switzerland—although not of the GRU agents, whom he knew little about.

"Which areas outside Russia did Sharpinsky work in when he was attached to different embassies under various cover names?" Wargrave inquired.

Marenkov checked off the posts on his fingers. "Paris,

for six months. London, for another six months. Washington, for two years. Athens, for a year. Finally, The Hague, for another year."

"So presumably in languages he is fluent in Greek, French, English, and American?"

"I was under the impression the last two were the same language," Haller interjected tartly.

"We all have our illusions," Wargrave replied with a grin. "Am I right, General?"

"Correct," Marenkov replied. "Sharpinsky is a remarkably accomplished linguist—it was one factor in his being moved around so rapidly, in his swift rise to become my deputy. Unlike most Russians he is a natural cosmopolitan. He is fluent in German, also," he added. "He spent some time in East Berlin maintaining contact with terrorist groups."

Haller stretched and yawned. "Well, we'll just have to wait and see what happens when we get to Zürich"—he checked his watch—"which will be soon now."

"Sharpinsky will come aboard this train," Marenkov repeated obstinately. "I know him."

"When the time comes, let's just hope I know him, too," Elsa said fervently as she studied her sketch.

The Atlantic Express, its cars crusted with snow, glided inside the huge cavern of Zürich Hauptbahnhof, moved alongside Gleis 4, and stopped. Traber's security ring mounted around the station was one of the tightest he had ever organized. Inconspicuous in a heavy coat and a shallow-brimmed hat, he stood near the ticket barrier puffing at his short cigar as passengers began filing off the express, haggard-faced from fear and lack of sleep. But it was not the passengers getting off that Traber was quietly studying; it was the huddle of passengers waiting to board the express.

Thirty security officials, armed and in civilian clothes, were at various points inside the Hauptbahnhof. There were also an unusual number of uniformed police strolling around the concourse. Outside in the snow a dozen patrol cars with reinforcements were parked at strategic points, all of them in radio contact with Traber's assistant, Major Kurt Dobler, who stood close to his chief with a compact walkie-talkie in his hand. Showing his identity card in the palm of his hand, Springer came through the barrier to meet Traber.

"How are things aboard the express?" Traber murmured.

"Tense. But under control. Our VIP is convinced that Sharpinsky will try to board the train."

"Seems unlikely now you have a description." From the express Springer had informed his chief that Marenkov had told them what the KGB colonel looked like. "On the other hand," Traber continued, "we have not yet located the main Soviet control base."

At the barrier there was exceptional security. Alongside the ticket collectors stood security men waiting to check passports and just behind them stood a group of uniformed police. A few yards to the right a second barrier was open—reserved for porters to take luggage aboard. Each porter was stopped while a dog handler allowed a German shepherd trained to sniff out explosives to check the baggage.

"Who is that attractive girl in the fur coat waiting on the far side of the barrier?" Traber inquired.

"One of us. Elsa Lang. She may be able to recognize Sharpinsky if he tries to board the express."

On the far side of the barrier, her fur hood pulled up against the cold, Elsa stood smoking a cigarette, studying the waiting passengers openly as though waiting for a friend she had arranged to meet. From her experience as a makeup girl she knew how easily a person's appearance could be transformed. So she was concentrating on height and build, looking for a short, well-built man. Forget everything else, she reminded herself—mustaches, beards, clothes, apparent age—fix your eyes on what can't easily be changed. A civilian near to her moved closer, spoke behind his hands as he lit a cigarette.

"Security. Colonel Springer told me about you. If you see him, tell me—even if you only think it might be him. Don't look at him again."

"I know my job."

"I can tell that already. And move well away from me as soon as you finger him. There could be shooting."

"Thank you for the warning," Elsa replied more graciously from behind her handkerchief, her eyes still fixed on the crowd penned behind the barrier.

Leaning out of the window from his first-class car, Jorge Santos was still smoking his pipe. Only someone who knew him well would have noticed something slightly odd as he stood there with the window down, watching the last of the passengers disembarking, who were passing through the barrier. Normally he smoked with his pipe clenched at the right-hand corner of his mouth; now the pipe was projecting from the left-hand side. A few paces from where he stood Wargrave opened a door and stepped down onto the platform. He took up a position where he could cover Elsa Lang, his hand inside his overcoat pocket gripping the Smith and Wesson.

On both sides of the barrier the security men had a sense of waiting for an imminent emergency as passengers began moving through the barrier slowly while their passports and tickets were checked. And porters were now passing inside their own separate barrier, waiting while the German shepherds sniffed the baggage. At the moment a large furniture truck carrying the legend *Möbel—Salzburg* was moving along the east bank of the river Limmat. The driver checked his watch and swung the huge vehicle over the bridge leading direct to the Hauptbahnhof.

"Nothing so far," Traber murmured. Major Dobler was just receiving a message on his walkie-talkie. "My God!" he muttered. "Are you certain? Check it with Bern. Top priority. . . ."

"What has happened?" Traber asked calmly as Springer moved closer.

"A Mercedes with Soviet diplomatic plates has just drawn up outside. One passenger—here he comes."

Striding into the station, his back erect, walking with a distinctly military bearing, was a tall, heavy-built man wearing a fur coat and hat. Behind him one of Traber's men removed his own hat, a signal to alert his chief. The new arrival joined the line.

"What the hell is going on?" Springer hissed.

"I don't like it" Traber replied crisply. "Keep your eyes open."

When the passenger from the Soviet diplomatic car reached the security officials the line stopped and there seemed to be some confusion. Another security official slipped quietly away from the barrier and hurried over to Traber. "What do we do, sir? He's carrying a diplomatic passport. Military attaché at the Soviet Embassy in Bern. A Captain Boris Volkov. . . ."

"Who?" Springer exploded. "Boris Volkov is a top trained assassin! To hell with his diplomatic passport. Delay him at the barrier." He stopped as there was an appalling crashing sound from the front of the station. Outside the Hauptbahnhof the large Salzburg furniture truck had run up onto the sidewalk. Inside the truck's cab the driver had released the cable attached to the tail gate, which collapsed, spilling out a torrent of furniture on top of a line of people waiting for cabs. The scene that followed was too horrific to describe as men and women buried under the heavy furniture began screaming. From under a wardrobe a woman's projecting hand shook feebly and then fell still. Inside the station all eyes turned in the direction of the sound, all except those of Springer, who continued to watch the barrier where Klaus Jaeger, in the guise of a Soviet captain, was protesting violently.

Through the second barrier a short, well-built porter, whose trolley had just been checked by a German shepherd, pushed the trolley along the platform, his cap pulled down over his forehead. As he passed Jorge Santos, who was still leaning out of the window, he glanced briefly sideways at the Spaniard and then moved on down the platform with the single blue suitcase he was carrying.

"Can you not recognize a diplomatic passport when you see one?" Jaeger was shouting in German. "My embassy will hear of this, I promise you."

He was still protesting when the security official disappeared with the passport. Reaching Springer, he handed the passport to the colonel. "It looks genuine," the official commented.

"I don't give a damn if it's gold-plated," Springer told him viciously. "He's not going aboard that express. Go and tell him it doesn't seem genuine, that we're checking with Bern." He looked at Traber. "And it's going to take an incredible amount of time to get through Bern. . . ."

"A lot seems to be happening all at once," Traber observed, looking toward the front of the station where Major Dobler had run to check the furniture truck incident. "Almost as though someone planned to divert our attention."

"To give time for Volkov to slip aboard, of course," Springer snapped. Then he frowned. "No, that can't be right. If this man was Boris Volkov himself he would never use his own name. There's something here that I don't understand—don't trust. . . ."

The Hauptbahnhof was in an uproar. Police cars had converged on the furniture truck where people trapped under the deluge of furniture were still screaming. An ambulance, its siren screeching, pulled up alongside the truck. The driver and his mate, the perpetrators of this brutal diversion, had been confident they could escape in the resultant confusion. Diving down an escalator leading to the underground shopping mall, they separated, heading for different escalator exits. Each man emerged on the far side of the Bahnhofplatz with a pistol in his hand.

They found themselves facing a mixture of passersby and policemen. To make more confusion, they started firing at random and several pedestrians, running for cover, collided with policemen. But two policemen ignored the confusion, raised their own pistols, steadied them with both hands, and took careful aim. Each of the policemen fired twice. The truck driver was still running when he fell dead. His mate died five seconds later.

Inside the Hauptbahnhof, Klaus Jaeger, still playing his role of a Soviet military captain, stormed up to Springer and snatched the diplomatic passport out of the Swiss's hand. "You will hear more about this from Moscow," he shouted. "It may well cause a major diplomatic incident with your government." Springer let him go with the passport as Jaeger walked swiftly back to his parked limousine, where Nacken, dressed in his chauffeur's uniform, had remained behind the wheel of the Mercedes. As Major Kurt Dobler returned to report about the furniture truck horror Springer grabbed the walkie-talkie off him and began speaking rapidly, his voice now matter-of-fact.

"I want all unmarked cars and trucks—repeat, unmarked—to follow the Soviet limousine on a shuttle system. Follow, but do not intercept. And all available radio detector trucks will carry out the same instruction. Now, move it!"

He handed the walkie-talkie back to Dobler and looked at Traber. "May I leave it to you now, sir? I'd better get back aboard the express."

Even as Nacken—with Jaeger sitting in the back—drove the Mercedes away from the Hauptbahnhof, the huge dragnet Springer had set in motion was operating efficiently. A laundry truck that had taken the Zürichberg route was actually driving ahead of the Soviet limousine when the driver saw its headlights in his rearview mirror. His colleague beside him reported its position over the radio and detector vehicles followed them up the road toward the Zürichberg.

Arriving at the villa on the hillside—confident that he had not been followed because there were no cars behind him—Jaeger turned in between the wrought-iron gates, which again were promptly closed behind them. Inside the villa Nacken, who doubled as radio operator, started sending the previously encoded signal on a transmitter to Mohner on the Zürichberg inside his mobile trailer. The signal informed Moscow that Colonel Igor Sharpinsky had boarded the Atlantic Express.

Within ten minutes two radio detector trucks close to the Zoo at the top of the Zürichberg crossed their beams at a point on the Heubeeri-Weg track inside the woods on the summit. Mohner, the much-respected meteorologist, had just completed sending his overlong transmission when he heard a knock on the door of his mobile trailer. When he opened it, security officers were facing him with pistols in their hands.

"I wondered how long it would be before you came," he said.

Promptly at 2300 hours the Atlantic Express began moving out of Zürich Hauptbahnhof on its way to Basel and West Germany. In various compartments the considerable number of fresh passengers who had come on board were settling themselves, listening to the story of the avalanche from travelers who had boarded at Milan. As the platform slid past him, Jorge Santos, still leaning on the open window, noticed a porter's trolley standing by itself on the platform. His mouth tightened as he raised the corridor window and made his way back to his own compartment. As with many other compartments, the blinds were drawn on the corridor side and it was only when Santos opened the door that he saw the man sitting in his corner seat in the otherwise empty compartment. Santos went inside and closed the door, his pipe still in the left-hand corner of his mouth.

"Hello, Nicos," Harry Wargrave said. "I thought the moment had come for us to link up."

"I agree," Nicos Leonides replied. "Colonel Igor Sharpinsky has just boarded the express. . . ."

23

Basel, The Hague

Three years earlier in Athens it had been Harry Wargrave's idea that Nicos Leonides, secretly a dedicated anti-

Communist, should try to penetrate the Soviet Balkan underground by offering himself as a private Communist executioner. "I have a strong whisper that Sharpinsky is a member of the Soviet Embassy staff here in Athens," he had explained. "Try and get to him."

"It will take time and ingenuity," Leonides had warned.

"So we will provide him with bodies," Wargrave had gruesomely suggested, "bodies of prominent anti-Communist Greeks he would like to see dead."

Working at the time for the British Secret Service, Wargrave had typically run this private operation on the side while he continued with his regular work. Over a period of time Wargrave and Leonides—once the Greek had persuaded Sharpinsky over the phone to allow him to prove himself—had provided three major executions, three "bodies."

The first "victim" had been the late-middle-aged anti-Communist editor of a leading Athens newspaper, only one of Leonides' many personal friends—and in the Balkans friends are much closer than in the West. Realizing that in any case he was a target for Soviet gunmen, the editor had readily fallen in with the plan. His burned-out car had been discovered at the foot of a steep cliff after a stormy night and it was assumed the body had been washed out to sea. Instead, the "dead" editor, a widower, had secretly been transported by motorized caïque to one of the more remote Greek islands, where he was still enjoying his unusual retirement.

In due course two more "victims," both of them friends of Leonides in the clandestine Greek anti-Communist underground, had agreed to cooperate—again, both of them widowers, so there were no family complications. One, an aging politician, had "died" in a plane that had crashed into the sea after a bomb explosion—but only after the politician piloting the plane had earlier parachuted from the aircraft over land. The third, a senior security chief on the verge of retirement, had "expired" when his car exploded after he turned on the ignition. The relics of the body discovered spread over a wide area were those of a corpse Leonides had stolen from a morgue.

All three Greek "victims" were now living on the remote Greek island: living off the proceeds of a major bank raid that Leonides himself had pulled off without injuring a soul. And Nicos Leonides had established himself in the eyes of Sharpinsky as a singularly effective executioner who stage-managed "accidents" that could never be traced back to Soviet sources.

It was Harry Wargrave who, before leaving Montreal on his flight to Europe to rescue Angelo, had cabled Leonides to fly to Milan and phone the Vienna number Leonides had been given if he wanted to contact Sharpinsky. The KGB colonel had fallen for the bait and ordered Leonides to board the Atlantic Express—to kill Marenkov as soon as the opportunity arose.

"I suppose he's still counting on me," Leonides told Wargrave with an ironic smile as he sat down facing the Englishman in his compartment aboard the Atlantic Express.

"How do you know he's just come aboard?" Wargrave asked sharrply.

"Because I was instructed that at Zürich Hauptbahnhof I must signal from the train window whether Marenkov was still alive—by keeping my pipe in the left-hand corner of my mouth."

"So who is Sharpinsky?"

"I have no idea." Leonides spread his hands in a gesture of resignation. "I watched carefully and none of the passengers coming on board took any notice of me. That was my mistake. . . ."

"What mistake?"

"I think he came through the barrier disguised as a porter." Leonides described the solitary trolley he had seen on the platform as the express moved out of the Hauptbahnhof. "A porter always takes his trolley away with him," the Greek pointed out. "By now he will have transformed himself into one of the numerous passengers who came aboard. What do I do next?" he asked abruptly. "And what about Anna in the next compartment?"

It was Anna Markos, Leonides' sister-in-law, who had formed part of Wargrave's secret cell in Athens—

whose sister, once Leonides' wife, had been killed during a Communist bomb outrage in the center of Athens. I have a great deal of hate going for me, Wargrave thought as he stared back at the tall Greek.

"You both stay under cover," he decided. "Incidentally, I assume it was you who shot those two saboteurs when the express was stopped at the time of the avalanche?"

"My very meager contribution to our combined efforts so far," Leonides replied.

"Yes, you both stay under cover," Wargrave repeated. "I have a hunch that before this thing is finished I may have to adopt some rather unusual, not to say totally illegal, methods. So let us assume for the moment that we are all back in Athens."

"It is my intention to kill Sharpinsky once he is found," Leonides said quietly. "I want no exchange of this man for one of our people in prison inside Russia. I want to kill him. Is that quite clearly understood?"

Wargrave stood up and his face was bleak. "And until we reach Schiphol and get Marenkov aboard that waiting Boeing to fly him to the States I am in complete control of the operation and give all the orders. Is that clearly understood, Nicos?"

"I regret to say—yes."

Inside the single sleeping compartment reserved in the name of Waldo Hackmann, American citizen—the compartment had been reserved from Lugano—Colonel Igor Sharpinsky had divested himself of his porter's uniform. From the blue case he had carried aboard the train he changed into fresh clothes and had stuffed the porter's uniform inside a strong plastic bag weighted with bricks. Pulling down the window, ignoring the blast of cold air that flooded inside the compartment, he waited until the express was crossing a bridge over a river and then hurled the plastic bag out. It fell a long way down before it hit thin ice, broke through the surface, and sank. Closing the window and lowering the blind, Sharpinsky turned up the central heating to warm up the compartment before any Swiss officials arrived.

Now he was dressed in a checked sports jacket and slacks of American cut, his cheeks plumped out with cotton wool pads; his head had been shaven bald by Ilse Murset before he left Lindengasse 451. He tried on his horn-rimmed spectacles and checked himself in the mirror. Under his check sports jacket—the label inside bore the name of a Fifth Avenue store—he wore a very thick sweater, which gave him a portly appearance. He lit a large cigar, took out his American passport, and checked it. He was now Waldo Hackmann, a dealer in Old Master paintings from Boston.

His case, which he had left on the berth, carried several labels with a much-traveled look. The Hôtel Georges Cinq, Paris; the Dorchester, London; the Ritz-Carlton, Boston; and the Mark Hopkins, San Francisco. He had just finished checking his appearance when there was a knock on the compartment door. Hackmann opened the door and faced the sleeping-car attendant.

"This compartment was booked in the name of a Mr. Waldo Hackmann, due to board the train at Lugano," the attendant explained.

"I'm Hackmann," Sharpinsky replied in a perfect American accent. "I came on to Zürich by another train yesterday—change of schedule."

He presented his passport and ticket as a Swiss Passport official appeared behind the attendant, reached past him, and began examining the document. Sharpinsky noted that besides checking the document the official was writing down the name and passport number. He looked up at the passenger. "And your home address, sir?" Sharpinsky gave him an address on Beacon Hill, Boston. As the door closed and he was left alone, Sharpinsky took a deep drag on his cigar. As he had anticipated, a very thorough check of every passenger was now taking place. And probably, soon, they would be checking with the United States. . . .

Returning from Nicos Leonides' compartment to the Wagon-Lit at the rear of the express, it had been Wargrave's idea that an immediate check should be made on all passengers who had come aboard at Zürich. Waldo Hackmann's credentials were among the first to be subjected to this scrutiny.

From the communications compartment operated by Peter Neckermann an immediate signal with Waldo Hackmann's details was sent to Interpol headquarters in Paris, where a special night staff was waiting on duty at Traber's request. From Paris the information was instantly relayed to FBI headquarters in Washington; in the American capital it was 5:15 P.M., Eastern Standard Time. A phone call was immediately put through from there to local FBI agents in Boston.

Agents Crammer and Hinds drove at once to the Beacon Hill address Hackmann had provided, even though a check in the telephone directory had shown a Waldo Hackmann living at the address. The house in the quiet street of old and picturesque dwellings seemed to be empty, but Crammer and Hinds had strict instructions. Opening the front door with skeleton keys, they explored the interior. It was Crammer who found in a wastebasket a crumpled carbon copy of Hackmann's European schedule.

Saturday, January 8, Zürich; Sunday, January 9, Amsterdam; Monday, January 10, Paris; Tuesday, January 11, Brussels. . . .

The request for the check from Washington had been marked "brief—urgent," so Crammer immediately reported back to Washington, from where a reply was sent to Paris and then to Neckermann aboard the Atlantic Express. And no one suspected that the real Waldo Hackmann, a Communist sleeper, acting on instructions Sharpinsky had originally sent from Vienna before he left for Zürich, was at that moment spending a pleasant weekend at the St. Regis Hotel in New York, where he had registered under an assumed name. The Atlantic Express was approaching Basel when Springer crossed Waldo Hackmann's name off his list of suspects.

Three hundred and fifty miles north of Basel the 17,000-ton Soviet freighter *Maxim Gorky,* the new pride

274

of Soviet Admiral Gorshkov's spy ships, a vessel fully equipped with the latest sophisticated electronic devices and bound from the Baltic for the African state of Angola, was changing course. The vessel's captain, Josef Morov, had received an urgent coded signal from his home port, Leningrad, ordering him to anchor off the mouth of the Rhine near Rotterdam. The ship was plowing through heavy seas as he discussed this new instruction with Commissar Valentin Rykin, who had also received his own signal.

"How long do we have to wait, I should like to know," Captain Morov demanded. "I am responsible for the safety of this ship and the glass is falling rapidly."

Rykin, a short, broad-shouldered man with a thick thatch of black hair who outranked even the ship's captain, gave a shrug. "Twelve hours, maybe. Then we reverse course and head back for Leningrad at full speed."

"At full speed! In this weather!"

"That's your problem. You must be prepared to take on board a large number of key agents who may arrive in powerboats at intervals—possibly even pursued by Dutch torpedo boats."

"We shall be in Dutch territorial waters. If their coastguard people wish to come aboard—"

"They will be stopped," Rykin snapped. "I have already ordered machine guns to be mounted."

"You must be mad," Morov protested. "You can't open fire on Dutch ships—it will cause an international incident."

"Only if necessary. . . ." A huge wave hit the bridge and Commissar Rykin was hurled against the woodwork as the vessel's bows were submerged under green foaming sea. Rykin recovered his balance and stopped himself rubbing his badly bruised elbow; a Soviet commissar was indifferent to pain. "Only if necessary," he repeated. "In any case Holland is a toy state," he sneered. "How many tank divisions can they muster?"

It was midnight as the Atlantic Express approached Basel. It was also midnight in The Hague as General

Max Scholten at Dutch counterespionage headquarters stood staring out of the third-floor window of the old building that overlooks the Hofvijver Lake in the middle of the city. The Gale Force Eight blowing in the North Sea was whipping the surface of the lake, creating a turbulence similar to that in the mind of the Dutch security chief. His aide, Major Sailer, put down the phone and reported the news.

"The Atlantic Express reaches Basel in five minutes' time—and Marenkov has survived so far."

"Which explains the reports I am getting from Germany and France that top Soviet agents are beginning to run—and in this direction apparently. The Germans have sealed off their eastern frontier with the Zone."

"And you mentioned you had heard the Geiger Group of terrorists is definitely crossing our border into Holland," Sailer reminded his chief. "Not that there is any connection. . . ."

"I wonder. . . ." In the distance the cherubic-faced Dutch security chief could see the dim outline of the Houses of Parliament. Sailer joined him by the window. "Do you not think we should inform the minister, perhaps . . ."

"At this hour?" Scholten demanded in mock horror. "And it is the weekend—almost Sunday morning. No, I will handle this myself." He stopped speaking as Sailer answered the top-priority phone where the line was being kept permanently open. Sailer listened, said thank you, and replaced the receiver.

"The long-range marine radar people have just picked up that huge Soviet freighter, the *Maxim Gorky*. They say she has changed course, that she is heading direct for the mouth of the Rhine."

Scholten glanced at a wall map of Western Europe. "Now I do really wonder—I sense a pattern emerging that may link the Atlantic Express with that freighter. I want to speak to Harry Wargrave on the express."

"But the express doesn't pass anywhere near the mouth of the Maas." (Sailer was referring to the mouth of the

Rhine.) "It travels direct via the Rhineland to Amsterdam."

"Alert all the torpedo-boat patrols," Scholten ordered.

As the Atlantic Express stopped at Basel Hauptbahnof, Wargrave was talking to General Max Scholten over the radio telephone from Neckermann's communications compartment. It was a long conversation and when he said good-bye he privately thanked God that at the end of the line—controlling the Dutch sector—was one of the most dedicated security chiefs in Europe, despite Max Scholten's outwardly cherubic appearance.

And Neckermann had been very active sending signals since they left Zürich. One signal had gone to Captain Franz Wander of the German BND who was waiting at Basel Bad Bahnhof—the station beyond the Hauptbahnhof where German Passport Control and Customs board all trains bound for Germany. Even if intercepted by secret Soviet monitors, the message would have meant nothing to them. It read: *Inge is on board Atlantic Express. Please board train and effect arrest as soon as on German soil.* Translated, the signal referred to Marenkov as Inge, indicating he was still alive, and asking for total security precautions to be taken over from the Swiss.

Two minutes later the express moved in under the roof of Basel Hauptbahnof and stopped. Inside his compartment Waldo Hackmann had lifted the blind and turned off the lights and was sitting in the dark. It so happened that his window was facing the wired-off "cage" inside which passengers waiting to board the train were kept after they had passed through Swiss Customs.

Hackmann's teeth clenched tight on the fresh cigar he had not lit as he studied the people inside the cage. Among them he could clearly see Yuri Gusev, the GRU agent he had summoned from Mulhouse, and, standing well apart from the Russian, Rudi Bühler, who had earlier caught a train from Zürich to Basel. Bühler, heavily built and of medium height, had changed his appearance. Wearing French clothes, he was dressed in a long raincoat that seemed to add to his height, and inside his pocket he carried a passport identifying him as Pierre Masson, commercial artist.

Yuri Gusev was a short, large-chested man with big feet and he carried a suitcase. Expensively dressed, he had a Swiss passport in the name of a Geneva bank official who existed and he had arrived at the last moment. Convincing in demeanor, he had been hustled through into the cage by a tired Customs man who had not checked his case. A minute later the cage was opened and the new passengers came out onto the platform and headed for the waiting express.

Boarding the express, Gusev, star executioner of the GRU, went straight to the sleeping compartment number he had received in the radio signal sent earlier to Mulhouse by Sharpinsky from the Hotel Schweizerhof. Waldo Hackmann opened the door while he was still rapping on it, let Gusev inside, and closed and relocked the door. Gusev wasted no time as the pseudo-American began talking. Opening his suitcase, he took out a Swiss railway inspector's uniform and changed into it rapidly.

"Peter is in the rear Wagon-Lit," Hackmann told him as Gusev pulled on his uniform trousers. "He is well guarded—you can wait until the express is moving, until they are lulled into a feeling of overconfidence. They must be very tired."

"No!" Gusev was abrupt, certain in his reply. "We strike immediately—at Basel Bad Bahnhof the German BND are bringing aboard a small army."

"Here at the Hauptbahnhof?" Sharpinsky was startled, forgot for a moment that he was traveling as Waldo Hackmann, and had replied in Russian although hitherto they had conversed in French. Inwardly he cursed himself for the slip, which he would not have forgiven in a subordinate.

"The psychology of the situation is simple," Gusev explained as he put on his inspector's cap and checked his appearance in the mirror. "Swiss security is about to hand over to the Germans—subconsciously they feel their job is done, that they can relax."

"I still think it is too early," Hackmann snapped in French.

Gusev overrode his remark, talking at the same time as the KGB man. ". . . There is a lot of confusion while the express is here at the Hauptbahnhof. Passengers are getting on and off. There is a lot of movement—a fluid situation that I can take advantage of. Have I ever failed you yet?" he demanded as he straightened his uniform jacket.

"If you are sure . . ."

"I am more than sure—I am certain. I have been thinking of nothing else since I received your signal. Peter will be dead and I will be off the train before it leaves here."

"Get on with it—but do not fail," Hackmann snapped.

"I will check the corridor—"

"Not necessary," Gusev told him. "I am a Swiss official in uniform checking tickets. No one will think it odd if they see me leaving your compartment."

Opening the door, he listened for a moment, stepped out into the corridor, and Hackmann locked it behind him. He was glad the executioner had gone. Yuri Gusev had built up a formidable reputation and was something of a law unto himself; on his record of success he could afford to be. So highly was he rated that on two separate occasions he had been interviewed by Marshal Gregori Prachko himself. Hackmann lit his cigar and reminded himself that at the first opportunity he must throw Gusev's suitcase—which now contained the business suit he had divested himself of—out of the window.

The moment he had left Hackmann's compartment Gusev walked toward the rear of the train, standing aside to let passengers move along the corridor as they struggled with their cases to find their compartments. As he entered the second Wagon-Lit, the coach linked to the sleeping car where Marenkov was under guard, he came face-to-face with one of Springer's security men in plain clothes.

"Have any new passengers entered this car?" the security man asked him in German.

"That is what I have been sent on board to check,"

Gusev replied in the same language. "I have plenty of time before the express leaves the Hauptbahnhof. I was told you would have a list of passengers who came on board earlier. Is that so?"

The security man reached in his pocket and produced a list of names. "Give it back to me before you get off the train."

"And if I do find someone not on the list?" Gusev inquired. "Who needs to know?"

"I do. Be careful not to alert any fresh passenger," the security man warned. "Just find me, give me the details—I will take it from there."

Gusev's reference to the list of passengers had been an inspired guess, but he was very familiar with the efficiency of the Swiss security system. It was typical of the Russian executioner to take such a bold line. Unlike his professional colleagues of lesser caliber, Gusev was not a man who believed in intricate planning; an opportunist by nature, his technique was the swift, unexpected thrust—to take full advantage of the element of surprise. As he had once boasted to Sharpinsky, "There is not a security establishment in Europe I could not walk inside."

"Walk in . . . ?" the KGB deputy chief had queried skeptically.

"Confidence is the key. You give the impression that you belong there—aggressively so if challenged."

And it was true. Only six months earlier Gusev had penetrated one of France's top nuclear centers to kill a defected Soviet scientist. Now, as the express waited in the Hauptbahnhof, he walked steadily along the corridor toward the locked door leading to the rear Wagon-Lit.

Ahead he saw a woman passenger who had just boarded the train; behind her, a second Swiss security official again in plain clothes. You learned to recognize the breed. The short, large-footed Russian stopped the woman. "May I see your ticket, madame?" he requested in German.

"Can't it wait until I have found my compartment?" the middle-aged woman, who was carrying a case, demanded irritably.

"Your ticket, please," Gusev repeated firmly.

The security man squeezed past them as Gusev inspected her ticket. "Thank you, madame." He handed back the ticket and the reservation slip. "Your compartment is four doors along."

Arriving at the locked door to the rear Wagon-Lit, Gusev slipped inside the toilet, pushed the lock across to show the "engaged" sign, and waited with the door almost closed. A minute later Haller came down the corridor, rapped on the locked door in a certain way, and was admitted by Leroy, and the door closed again. Gusev waited, checking the second hand of his watch, then emerged, glanced back along the deserted corridor, and repeated the same rapping signal.

Leroy was opening the door, his revolver in his hand, when Gusev fired the small gas pistol through the aperture. The pellet of tear gas exploded in Leroy's face and he was aiming his weapon blind when Gusev flung the door wide open and hit him on the side of the skull with the barrel of the pistol, knocking him out. The amount of gas ejected by the specially designed pistol was small—enough to put the victim out of action briefly but not enough to affect the man who fired the pistol.

Closing the Wagon-Lit door behind him, Gusev stepped over the unconscious Leroy and peered along the next corridor. At this moment Wargrave was still inside the communications compartment, talking to Scholten in The Hague. Haller had entered the compartment containing Marenkov and Elsa and was reporting the latest news.

"They're checking everyone coming on board—double-checking them, that is. They have already made one check while the passengers waiting to board were inside the wire cage."

"So nice Springer is still alert even though his job is nearly over," Elsa remarked. "He gets off at Basel Bad Bahnhof, I assume?"

"Correct," Haller agreed. "Then the German people come on board and we'll be in equally good hands there—Franz Wander is one tough character. Since his appointment the KGB have had it rough in the Federal Republic. Where is Harry now?" he inquired.

"Still in the communications compartment." Elsa put her hand over her face to suppress a yawn. God, I'm whacked, she thought; if only I could snatch an hour's sleep.

Marenkov, who had stood up behind Elsa when Haller rapped on the door, still looked remarkably fresh and restless. "Since Sharpinsky didn't get on the train at Zürich, I'm convinced he will board the express here," he said dogmatically.

"Springer checked the passengers inside the cage. I think I'll go along and have a word with Harry," Haller replied. Elsa opened the door for him and closed it as the American walked down the corridor, rapped on the communications door, and disappeared inside.

Gusev, who had been waiting out of sight at the far end of the car, watched Haller walking away, entering another compartment. The moment the American was gone he padded along the corridor. His large feet moved quite silently as he moved with a cat-footed tread. He knew which compartment Haller had left—the window blind facing it was very slightly askew. He moved steadily along the corridor, not slowly, but neither was he hurrying as he listened carefully.

Reaching the compartment door, he did not hesitate for a second, repeating the rapping signal Haller had used to gain admittance to the car when he was hidden inside the toilet. The door began opening. Behind it Elsa stood with her Smith and Wesson and behind her stood Marenkov. She had opened it only a few inches when the pellet from Gusev's gun pistol hit her chest and exploded, sending the vapor into her eyes. The door was flung wide open by Gusev, who had dropped the gas pistol and was pulling the Luger from his shoulder holster with lightning speed.

Temporarily blinded, Elsa was trying to aim the Smith and Wesson when Marenkov hurled her aside onto the berth and leaped forward. His powerful left hand grabbed Gusev's gun hand, twisted it brutally, and smashed it against the door jamb, once, twice. Gusev felt his wrist break, the gun slip from his hand. He dropped to his knees; his left hand, pulling a knife from beneath his

282

uniform jacket, lunged the blade forward and upward. Considering the pain he was feeling, the knife thrust was extraordinarily swift, a flashing blur. Then he felt Marenkov's right hand lock around his left wrist as the Soviet general, bending down, again smashed his hand against the door jamb three times in rapid succession. Gusev's second wrist was broken and the knife fell from his nerveless fingers.

Marenkov was not finished with him yet. Using both hands, he hauled the broken Gusev up, grasping him under the armpits, and literally threw him out of the compartment. Gusev crashed against the metal passenger rail and slumped to the floor, then made one final effort to get to his feet again. Inside Marenkov's mind all the pent-up frustration and hatred he had concealed since his wife's suicide flooded out like a dam bursting. "Give me a gun," he had demanded of Haller hours ago and the American had refused. Farther along the corridor Wargrave had emerged from the communications compartment and now he watched, a revolver in his hand, unable to shoot for fear of hitting Marenkov.

As the incredibly tough Gusev clambered to his feet Marenkov smashed a fist into his face, driving his head back hard against the passenger rail; then, using both clenched fists, he hit Gusev blow after blow, and when the executioner sank to the floor for the second time he kicked him with vicious force in the skull and trampled on him. Wargrave grabbed him by the arm. "For God's sake, that's enough—he's dead . . . dead . . . dead. . . ."

The Russian turned and went back into the compartment, where an appalled Elsa was swabbing her eyes with a handkerchief she had dampened under the tap; appalled that she had failed in her task, as she believed. "That was for Irina," Marenkov said quietly, the ferocity ebbing away. "Are you all right? For a moment I thought he had killed you. . . ."

"He would have done—except for you."

Confusion filled the corridor outside. Leroy, recovered from the attack, was equally appalled at what he regarded at his own failure. It was Haller who calmed them down, who sent Wargrave to warn Springer of what had happened. On the platform outside, Waldo Hackmann, who had left the train as though to get some exercise—but in fact to be ready to leave the Hauptbahnhof if Gusev's lightning attack succeeded—was close to the rear Wagon-Lit compartment when the corridor blind, carelessly shut, flew up. Standing by a porter, he saw for a brief moment General Sergei Marenkov outlined by the light from inside the train—recognized his recent chief, despite the trimmed hair, by his bulk, by his movement as he bent over a girl sitting on a berth. Then Haller hauled down the blind and fixed it properly.

A few minutes later Hackmann witnessed the stretcher that Springer had arranged to be brought being carried off the train with a blanket drawn over the stretcher's occupant, who he knew could only be Yuri Gusev.

Returning to his sleeping compartment, Hackmann closed the door in a state of shock and stared at the single glove on his berth. The glove told him that Rudi Bühler had successfully come aboard the express. Sinking down onto the berth, he lit a fresh cigar and stared at the opposite wall. Having counted so much on the previously flawless record of Yuri Gusev, he was left now only with Bühler, who was certainly no trained assassin. And Nicos Leonides—whom he had seen for the first time at Zürich because he knew which window to look for when he had slipped on board the train disguised as a porter—no longer had the KGB colonel's confidence; otherwise he would have done the job before now.

As the train moved out of the Hauptbahnhof on its way to Basel Bad Bahnhof, Sharpinsky took a decision. The only possible solution now was for the Geiger Group to destroy the entire Atlantic Express, taking Marenkov with it.

24

Germany, Amsterdam, The Hague

"Look, for God's sake—Crufts Dog Show!"

Standing beside Matt Leroy, Elsa stared out in amazement at the scene on the snowbound platform as the train stopped at Basel Bad Bahnhof. On the platform stood forty German shepherds, each with its handler, straining at their leashes as though they couldn't wait to board the express.

"I don't get it," Leroy replied as the doors of the three Wagon-Lits were opened and the dogs scrambled on board. It was Captain Franz Wander of the BND, a large, smiling-faced German who spoke English with a Cambridge accent, who explained his tactics to Julian Haller and Wargrave inside the compartment next to the one where Elsa was guarding Marenkov.

"It is just after midnight. For most of the time the train will be traveling through Germany it will be night—and this means there will be no good reason for people to be moving about the train. I can average three dogs to patrol the corridors of each car. That will keep the passengers in their compartments. I want total control of movement until you cross the Dutch border."

"You could get a few complaints," Haller observed with a dry smile.

"Complaints I can deal with." Wander, very smart in a gray business suit despite his bulk, grinned broadly. "We shall tell them there is a bomb scare—that the dogs are here to sniff out explosives." He looked at Wargrave. "Any objections, Harry?"

"None." Wargrave spread his hands. "Brilliant, I call it. We might even get a night's sleep."

"Some people in the nonsleepers will want to go to the bathroom," Haller remarked.

"We shall royally accompany them there and back—with a dog. . . ."

Prepare contingency plan to destroy Atlantic Express. Wait for fresh signal before taking action. Skiros.

It was midnight in Amsterdam—the Atlantic Express was about to stop at Basel Hauptbahnhof, and a few miles south in The Hague Scholten had just heard of the change of course of the *Maxim Gorky*—when Rolf Geiger stood by the third-floor window of the old house in Amsterdam checking in his mind the plans he had made in response to the signal he had received earlier.

"Skiros" was the code name for Sharpinsky and the signal had been dispatched by the Swiss dentist, Heinrich Baum, from the Hotel Schweizerhof. As Geiger peered down between the almost closed curtains a police patrol boat puttered under an arched bridge and passed below along the canal beneath the building. Behind him his new recruit, Joop Kist, the thin-faced Dutchman, was talking on the phone to Amsterdam Central station. Kist said thank you and replaced the receiver.

"They expect the Atlantic Express to arrive here at ten in the morning," he reported.

"Good. Send Erika to me and stay downstairs on guard until I call you."

Closing the curtain, Geiger was sitting behind a desk when Erika Kern, his dark-haired confidante, came into the room. Despite his disbelief in Erika's mistrust of Joop Kist he still felt it wise to let the Dutchman know as little as possible about what he was planning. He came straight to the point as the girl sat provocatively with her superb pair of legs crossed. She never stops trying to rouse me, he thought cynically.

"Everything is arranged in case we have to go into action?" he inquired.

"Yes," Erika replied crisply. "First the express will have to be diverted through Belgium to ensure it crosses the Maas bridge. That is arranged."

"Go over it again."

"Jacek Wojna and the others are still waiting at Willich and they have been ordered to stand by for imminent action. They have the explosives, of course—so it only needs one brief signal for them to move."

"They know the exact section of the railway embankment to blow up north of Düsseldorf?"

"Wojna has already reconnoitered the area—he may be a brute but he has the unit under tight control and he can be relied on to do the job."

"He will have to move very fast, and the weather in Germany is appalling."

"That will help him," Erika replied in her most soothing tone. "Half the police are out trying to rescue people from cars caught in the snowdrifts."

"It sounds reasonably satisfactory," Geiger commented. A meticulous planner, he took nothing for granted, least of all success. "So if we are ordered to blow up the embankment the authorities will have to divert the express at Cologne via Brussels. It will continue toward here via the Maas bridge."

"Did you enjoy your walk earlier?" Erika inquired softly. She was only too well aware that Geiger had paid a visit to the red-light district and there was a hint of malice in her question.

The Armenian reacted instantly. Getting up from behind his desk, he walked around it and slapped her hard across the face, then returned to his chair. Erika said nothing, showed nothing in her expression, although inwardly she was delighted. At long last she had provoked the Armenian, and although she would have preferred Geiger to have sprawled her on the couch and whipped up her skirt, it was a step in the right direction: Erika enjoyed being manhandled.

287

"And the main base here?" Geiger asked in an even tone as though nothing had happened.

"The barn near Dordrecht is ready for them when they cross the border with enough explosives to blow three bridges sky-high. The whole express will go down into the river. What about uniforms?"

"The normal ones." Geiger was referring to the group's standard operational clothing—black ski masks, wind-cheaters, and ski pants. He smiled as he fingered his mustache. "If we are seen we want to leave our trademark."

"You do trust Joop Kist?" Erika inquired doubtfully.

"He is another peasant, an idealist, but he speaks Dutch, which is invaluable now we are here. In any case, I have seen to it that he knows very little of our plans."

"I'm still worried about him. If there is an emergency and I am proved right?"

"Shoot him," Geiger told her cheerfully.

The Atlantic Express was speeding through blizzard-stricken Germany as Elsa Lang made her way back from the front of the train toward the rear Wagon-Lit, almost exhausted now. It had been her own idea that, with the sketch of Colonel Igor Sharpinsky firmly fixed in her mind, she would check the passengers in the faint hope of spotting the KGB colonel. As she entered the next Wagon-Lit, Waldo Hackmann—after giving the attendant at the end of the car a large tip—was turning around to walk back to his compartment with a glass of brandy in his hand.

Their eyes met for a moment and then Hackmann walked on ahead of her and disappeared inside his compartment. As she passed the closed door Elsa automatically noticed the number. Compartment 19. She had noticed nothing familiar about the passenger. Passing one of Captain Wander's dog-handlers, she patted the animal, returned to one of the empty compartments in the rear Wagon-Lit, and said good-night to Matt Leroy, who was on guard.

"Pleasant dreams," the droopy-mustached American wished her.

"I'm going to sleep like a dog."

She flopped onto the lower berth in her clothes and fell instantly asleep. But she did not have pleasant dreams; instead she stirred restlessly as she experienced nightmares. She was at Basel Hauptbahnhof, collecting yet another of those bloody cassettes. . . . She was landing at the Bucharest airstrip with Wargrave, seeing Marenkov instead of Anatoli Zarubin approaching the plane . . . hearing the burst of machine-gun fire at Milan Airport as the fake ambulance fired into the back of the armored truck where she sat in the cab with Wargrave and Marenkov. . . . More machine-gun fire as she lay on the compartment floor at Vira while the Jeep riddled the train . . . watching the avalanche wave coming closer until it overwhelmed her and she woke up. Sighing with relief, she lay listening to the thudding of the express's wheels taking them to Schiphol, to safety. . . .

At 2:30 A.M. the express was approaching Karlsruhe, where it would stop briefly. Inside Compartment 19 Sharpinsky was sipping the last of his brandy as he talked to Rudi Bühler, who had entered the compartment ten minutes earlier when the German dog-handler was temporarily absent from the corridor.

"You have to get that signal transmitted," Sharpinsky told his deputy. "You have to get off at Karlsruhe—a car will be waiting for you—get to the house and make sure personally the signal goes off immediately to Amsterdam. Any questions?" He spoke as though there couldn't possibly be any.

"It is a very long signal," Bühler commented as he examined the encoded message the Russian had handed him. "If the Germans are using radio detector vans . . ."

"At this stage we are all expendable," Sharpinsky told him brutally. "Including myself," he added frankly.

"You propose to stay aboard the express, then?"

"Until the very last moment—in case I do the job my-

289

self. Although that I doubt, with all those damned dogs the BND have put aboard the train."

Bühler glanced at his chief, who had spoken with his normal self-restraint. He had never liked Colonel Igor Sharpinsky, but close to the moment of parting he had a grudging admiration for the KGB colonel. The bastard has guts, he was thinking. With the rolled-up signal concealed inside the partially hollowed-out cigar he was smoking, Bühler left the compartment as the express was slowing down, coming into Karlsruhe. The German dog-handler who had returned to the corridor saw nothing strange in a passenger disembarking.

Only a handful of passengers got off the train at that hour of the morning as Rudi Bühler left the station, walked a few hundred yards, and slipped into the rear seat of a waiting BMW, which immediately drove off. He stubbed out his cigar containing the signal. A minute later a radio detector vehicle disguised as a refrigerated truck followed the BMW—a little behind schedule because the driver had trouble starting his engine. Wander had surrounded Karlsruhe Hauptbahnhof with a variety of BND transport and every single passenger leaving the express was followed.

Reaching an apartment block, Bühler hurried inside and up to the sixth-floor where his radio operator was waiting with the transmitter. As he had commented to Sharpinsky, the signal was extended and two radio detector vehicles located its source just as the transmission to Amsterdam was completed. Bühler had destroyed the encoded signal when German police burst into the apartment. The GRU sabotage chief was inside a bedroom when he heard the outer door crashing open and he moved instantly and with great speed. Throwing up the bedroom window, he stepped out onto the fire escape, turned and fired his Walther five times at policemen coming into the room. Then he started to run down the fire-escape steps. But he overlooked one thing: the iron steps were coated with ice. Slipping, slithering, he tried to save himself as he pivoted over the low rail. He let out one long scream that only ended when he hit the concrete sidewalk five flights below.

At 3 A.M. in the old Amsterdam house overlooking the canal Rolf Geiger read the decoded signal from Karlsruhe. Looking up at Erika Kern, who was waiting with an expectant expression on her long-jawed face, he nodded.

"The operation is on?" Erika asked.

"Indeed it is," Geiger replied suavely. He was relieved, already looking forward to completion of the job, to the moment when he could return to Paris and its fleshpots, resuming his Argentinian identity of Leo Sánchez while he directed the group's operations in Holland by remote control. "Send the signal to Willich," he ordered. "And tell them to move fast—very fast. . . ."

At Willich, Jacek Wojna, the activist leader of the terrorists, reacted instantly on receiving Geiger's signal over the transmitter inside the split-level house where he had waited so impatiently. Within ten minutes he was driving his Mercedes 450 SEL out of the garage and eastward from Willich. Gaten, the Norwegian expert on sabotaging oil rigs, was by his side; crammed inside the rear were four other men.

Heading down the autobahn leading to Düsseldorf, Wojna soon turned off the autobahn on to a side road, and then swung the car down a track leading to a large old barn. Inside, an ambulance stood alongside a large gasoline truck. Wojna, Gaten, and another terrorist changed into ambulance attendants' clothes and scrambled inside the ambulance. As Wojna drove the vehicle away one of the three men he had left behind took the Mercedes under cover into the barn alongside the patrol truck.

With the siren screaming, Wojna drove at speed through the snowstorm that had started toward a point north of Düssseldorf where a deserted stretch of the main railroad track from Basel to Amsterdam crossed a long embankment. Gaten was terrified by the speed at which the Pole was traveling and once they skidded, but the Pole, an expert driver, brought the vehicle back under control.

"For Christ's sake watch it," Gaten snapped. "You're going to kill us all."

"Shit!" Wojna sneered. "Left your guts behind you in Willich?"

Wojna, born and brought up in the Paris slums of the Goutte d'Or district where he had led street gangs when he was twelve years old, despised the educated Norwegian anarchist and took every opportunity to put him down. "We're nearly there," he said after a few minutes, peering through the windshield.

It took them five minutes to place the explosive charges they brought from the back of the ambulance at several carefully selected points to wire them for time-fuse detonation. Then, their uniforms covered in snow, they left the isolated section of embankment and drove a short distance toward Holland, stopped, and waited.

The detonation was enormous. There was a brilliant flash, a great burst of snow as whole sections of railroad track were hurled into the air. And one hundred meters of embankment slid like a wave onto the nearby highway. The main line north from Düsseldorf to Amsterdam had been severed.

"Now for the next move—to cross the border," Wojna told Gaten.

The ambulance started moving at speed again toward Holland, its siren screeching nonstop, and a few minutes it passed a police car moving in the opposite direction. Gaten's hand clenched with tension but Wojna maintained his speed. The police driver never gave the ambulance a second thought as he remarked to his colleague, "Some poor bastard in trouble. . . ."

Arriving back at the barn, Wojna pulled up with a jerk that caused a slight skid, left the engine running, and jumped out of the vehicle. "Get the lead out of your feet," he snapped. "In five minutes we're away and I'll smash the face in of anyone who isn't ready."

Inside the barn the three men left behind had already removed the circular plate that had been skillfully cut out of the rear of the gasoline truck, forming a concealed entrance through which they could crawl inside. The interior of the huge truck was stacked with the large quantity of explosives, timer devices, and distant electrical detonation systems Wojna was carrying into Holland. Hidden ventilation ducts had been cut in the roof of the wagon, enabling men to travel inside the cylindrical space for long distances.

"Hurry it up, for God's sake," Wojna ordered as he tore off the ambulance driver's uniform and put on the boiler suit and cap of a gasoline truck driver. Gaten dressed himself in a similar outfit; he would travel alongside Wojna.

The other four terrorists climbed through the circular entrance into the bowels of the truck and Gaten then fixed on the plate, sealing them inside. While the Norwegian went outside to get behind the wheel of the ambulance, Wojna examined the closed plate, scooped dirt off the floor of the barn, and rubbed it around the circumference of the plate. Not that he expected any trouble with the Dutch Customs officials at the crossing point—not in this weather when they would be only too anxious to get back to the warmth of their hut. Satisfied, Wojna climbed behind the wheel of the truck and drove it out, then waited.

Gaten drove the ambulance inside the barn alongside the Mercedes, hurried outside, closed the barn doors, and climbed up inside the cab of the truck beside Wojna. He hardly had time to close the door before the Pole was moving down the track and turning into the road.

They crossed the border into Holland without trouble; the Dutch officials hardly glanced at the papers Geiger had prepared in advance. Long-distance gas trucks were constantly crossing the frontier from Germany. Once inside Holland, Wojna kept his speed down well within the limits—despite the lack of snow. The Pole felt pleased with himself; once again he had successfully completed another operation. And now they were heading for the new base Geiger had established for them, at Dordrecht, which happened to be close to the great railroad bridge over the Maas—the line the Atlantic Express would have to be diverted to.

At 4:20 A.M. the Atlantic Express had left Mainz and was on its way to Cologne when Captain Franz Wander woke everyone up in the rear Wagon-Lit and assembled them in Marenkov's apartment. Julian Haller, heavy-eyed from lack of sleep, was awake, but Wargrave and Elsa had slept for a while when they received the German security chief's summons.

"I thought you should know," Wander informed them crisply, "that the express is going to have to be diverted at Cologne to go via Aachen and Brussels to Amsterdam."

"Why?" snapped Wargrave.

"A portion of the rail track north of Düsseldorf has been blown up, so the train cannot proceed by its normal route direct to Amsterdam. We suspect more fun and games by the Geiger Group," he added, in his excellent English.

"I smell a rat," Wargrave commented, "a lot of rats. . . ."

"I don't see any connection with Marenkov's being on the train," Wander replied. "Would it have destroyed the whole train if we had been passing over that section at the time? I'm sure it wouldn't—some cars would have had a bad time but a lot of the express would have survived."

"Exactly," the Englishman replied. "They couldn't have been sure enough of getting Marenkov." He stood up. "I think I'd like to have a chat with Scholten on the radio telephone."

Going inside the communications compartment, Wargrave asked Peter Neckermann if he could use the phone by himself. Alone in the compartment, he called the Dutch counterespionage general in The Hague.

"Harry Wargrave here, Max. We're somewhere between Mainz and Cologne."

"I know that," Scholten replied instantly. "Wander sends me frequent reports about your progress. Our cooperation is total."

"What you probably haven't heard is that a section of track has been blown up north of Düsseldorf. I don't like this development one little bit."

"I know that, too. Which means you will be diverted via Brussels and Roosendaal. Not a coincidence, in my opinion. Also—and this is strictly between the two of us —I know the Geiger Group, who probably blew up the line, have now moved into Holland."

"So that's the next obstacle we face?"

"I'm sure of it. And a most formidable obstacle, Harry —but possibly also a golden, once-in-a-lifetime opportunity. If we are prepared to act with the utmost ruthlessness," he added. "You know that the Soviet freighter *Maxim Gorky* is at this moment lying at the mouth of the Rhine estuary, that she is taking aboard a great number of top GRU and KGB agents from France, Belgium, and Germany—especially Germany?"

"Wander did mention this, yes," Wargrave replied cautiously. "How far are you prepared to go? And surely your torpedo-boat patrols can intercept them?"

"In the prevailing storm conditions—and at night— that is not so easy as it sounds," Scholten replied casually. "Also, I have suggested to my good friend Commander De Vos that he does not exert himself too much in that direction."

"You're suggesting . . .?"

"I think I can locate the Geiger Group—it will be a race against time—but if I do I propose we go all the way." Scholten detailed his plan and the Englishman suggested certain modifications.

They spoke together for no less than twenty minutes, then Wargrave left the compartment and went along the train to see Nicos Leonides. Closing the door, he began speaking rapidly. ". . . so, be ready for me," were his last words to the Greek as he left and went into the next compartment to have the same conversation with Anna Markos. When he left her his expression was grim. In the end he was going to have to rely on his secret Greek cell to do the job.

Ten minutes before Harry Wargrave made his long phone call to General Max Scholten, a local call came through for the Dutch security chief. His deputy, Major

Sailer, answered the phone, and then spoke to Scholten.

"There's someone called Panhuys on the line."

"I'll take it," Scholten said quickly. He listened for only a brief time, saying yes and no at intervals, then replaced the receiver and walked over to the wall map. "That explosion on the line north of Düsseldorf will bring the Atlantic Express here via Aachen and Brussels," he remarked. "We know that already," Sailer replied. "We heard the news fifteen minutes ago."

Taking out a pencil, Scholten ringed a portion of the map with a decisive sweep. The circle he had described covered the general area of the Rhine delta. "Somewhere inside this ring the climax will take place," he predicted. "Alert the Venlo Team," he added casually. "For imminent action."

The instruction startled Sailer. The Venlo Team was a picked group of Dutch sharpshooters personally selected by Scholten for their marksmanship, a highly secret anti-terrorist section controlled by the Dutch security chief himself.

"Where do we place them?" Sailer inquired.

"At the secret base in Dordrecht."

Without realizing it, Scholten was sending his men to the same town where the Geiger Group was assembling, but this was not entirely a coincidence. Scholten proceeded to explain his line of reasoning.

"We know the Atlantic Express is being diverted through Brussels to Roosendaal and Amsterdam, Sailer. How would you destroy an entire train—to make sure you killed the one passenger aboard you wished to kill?"

"Blow up the railroad track—as they have done north of Düsseldorf."

"But then only a portion of the train would be wiped out. Marenkov might well survive. Think again."

"I've run out of ideas," Sailer confessed.

"I would blow up a whole bridge while the express was on it—say, the long Maas bridge. The whole express would then fall into the river."

"Oh, my God . . ." Sailer stopped speaking as the phone rang. He took the call and then handed the receiver to his chief. "Harry Wargrave wants to speak to you direct from the *Atlantic Express*."

"Leave me alone while I talk to him." Scholten spoke for twenty minutes with the Englishman over the radio telephone link-up, replaced the receiver, and then called back Sailer on the intercom. His deputy returned to the office in some excitement. "We are getting reports that a lot of powerboats have been observed moving at speed toward the *Maxim Gorky*. Most of them made it but two overturned in the heavy seas before they reached the freighter. There were no survivors."

"And all of them top Soviet agents clearing out. I like it when vermin eliminates itself," Scholten commented. "And now I have to ask you to enter into a conspiracy between the two of us. . . ." Scholten watched his deputy carefully. "Are you willing?"

"I have always fancied myself as a conspirator," Sailer replied with a dry smile.

"Then go and steal from two different sports goods shops four sets of Geiger Group outfits—black ski masks, black windcheaters, and black ski pants. You can use skeleton keys to avoid the appearance of a break-in and for God's sake don't let the police catch you at it. Two different shops, I said—the loss may not be noticed for months."

"Any particular sizes?"

"Yes, I was coming to that. Two outfits for tall men, two for men of medium size. We are going to try and strike a very heavy blow at the Soviets, Sailer. Oh, and two more things. Get hold of De Vos, the torpedo-boat commander—tell him not to try too hard to intercept any of those powerboats. Risky work in this weather," he added casually. "After that I want a quiet word with my friend De Vos myself. . . ."

About half an hour earlier, just after Scholten had taken the call from the man who had given the name of Panhuys, in Amsterdam Erika Kern had crept downstairs to the first floor with a Luger pistol in her hand. Opening the back door, which led on to a cobbled alley, she had come face-to-face with Joop Kist, also holding a Luger in his hand.

"What the hell are you doing out here?" she demanded in German.

"I heard a prowler—there's been an attempted break-in." Kist showed her where there were jimmy marks on the outside of the door. "I think they did the place next door and then tried here. I must have scared them off."

Still suspicious, Erika looked at the window of the neighboring house where the glass had been smashed. She peered inside and could see nothing. Joop Kist thanked God she had not brought a torch—otherwise she might have seen the phone he had used to call Scholten, even the jimmy he had left on the floor to fake the attempt to break into Geiger's house.

"Let's get back upstairs," Erika snapped. "And make sure you bolt this door."

Left by himself, Kist sighed with relief as he bolted the door. It had been a stroke of luck for Scholten that he had managed to plant a man inside the Geiger Group. The trouble was Kist had not been able to tell him much in the quick phone call—only that Geiger was planning a major operation, which was imminent, and that he had ordered Erika Kern to have the car ready to drive him south toward the Belgian border. In other words, as Scholten had immediately seen, in the general direction of Dordrecht and the Maas bridge.

At Schiphol Airport, the only airfield in Western Europe still open to flights to and from the United States, Dutch troops were guarding the Boeing 707 waiting inside a remote hangar. Jeeps carrying machine guns circled the hangar constantly; inside, more armed soldiers stamped their feet in the cold as they watched over the plane. It was already fully fueled and the air crew slept in a building close by.

The *Maxim Gorky,* heaving to at the mouth of the Rhine, was now taking aboard very heavy seas. Despite her size, the 17,000-ton freighter was taking cruel punishment and her captain, Josef Morov, was becoming increasingly outraged as he discussed the situation with Commissar Rykin in the privacy of his cabin.

"By forcing me to stay here you are endangering the ship and all my crew," he roared.

"My orders remain unchanged," Rykin replied coldly.

"You talk like a trained parrot!" Ignoring Rykin's bleak expression, he thundered on. "I have already lost one of my crew trying to take on board these crazy fools coming out to us in launches and powerboats."

"Those crazy fools are some of the Soviet Union's most important citizens. We have already rescued over a hundred men—key agents it has taken years to train, the élite of our European underground apparatus."

"And how long do you think it takes to train the crewmen of my ship?" Morov demanded. "We are heaving to in one of the worst seas I have ever encountered."

"I thought you were a skilled ship's master," Rykin sneered. "Surely you can cope in an emergency."

"It is not your responsibility," Morov rapped back furiously. "You just sit on your backside and then claim all the glory if we ever get back to Leningrad. Not that I give a shit for the glory," he went on. "And do not look too complacent—ships have been known to capsize."

"You are exaggerating," Rykin replied, but there was a hint of nervousness in his tone now.

"Look out of the porthole," Morov ordered him.

Clutching to furniture to keep his balance, Rykin went to the porthole and drew back the curtain. At that moment a gigantic green, foam-crested comber was sweeping toward the porthole. Rykin flinched as the monster struck the cabin. He was still lying on the floor when Morov stood over him and said something that terrified Rykin.

"You seem to have forgotten that our original destination was Angola, and what this ship is carrying."

It was the reference to the cargo that frightened Rykin. The *Maxim Gorky* was carrying in her holds arms and ammunition for guerrilla forces in southern Africa, including two thousand tons of gelignite and amytol. As Rykin picked himself up off the floor he knew he was standing on a floating platform of high explosives.

25

Maxim Gorky

At 6:15 A.M. the Atlantic Express left Cologne and turned west toward Aachen along the diverted route that would take it through Belgium on its way to Amsterdam. In the rear Wagon-Lit Elsa Lang sat with Marenkov and Julian Haller while she experimented with different sketch versions of Sharpinsky. Working from the original picture built up from Marenkov's description of the KGB colonel, she produced fresh pictures—of Sharpinsky with a beard, then with a mustache, then again clean-shaven and with rimless spectacles.

"What's the point of all these scribbles?" asked Haller irritably. He had refused to sleep all night and was close to a state of exhaustion.

"The general says Sharpinsky is an expert at disguise," Elsa replied, continuing her sketching. "We are all pretty sure Sharpinsky came aboard at Zürich. One of these sketches may match someone on the train."

"You've got a hope," Haller told her.

"I've got obstinacy, Turtle," she said, using her pet name for Haller. "You stick your neck out—I'm sticking mine out now that sooner or later I'll spot him."

She was still making fresh sketches when they arrived at the frontier town of Aachen, where Captain Franz Wander handed over to Belgian security. "A safe journey to Schiphol," the German said to Harry Wargrave as they shook hands. "I'm sure you will make it now."

"Thanks for getting us through Germany in one piece," Wargrave replied. "Probably largely due to your friends." He indicated the file of German shepherds streaming off the train with their handlers. "It was a damned clever idea."

Between Aachen and Brussels Nord the dining car was opened for breakfast. One of the first arrivals in the dining car was Waldo Hackmann, still wearing his checked sports suit and horn-rimmed glasses. He chose a corner seat at the far end of the dining car from the kitchen where he could observe all the other diners. In his American accent he ordered a large breakfast of bacon and eggs, lit a cigar, and opened a copy of *Time* magazine.

In the rear Wagon-Lit Wargrave had just suggested to Elsa that they should get some breakfast in the dining car. Julian Haller said he only wanted coffee and would they have it sent along with the meals they had ordered for Marenkov, Matt Leroy, and Peter Neckermann. A Belgian security officer would supervise the preparation of the food in the galley to avoid any risk of poison being introduced into the food.

Entering the dining car, Wargrave and Elsa chose the corner table nearest the kitchen. A few tables away Nicos Leonides sat facing Anna Markos, ignoring her as though they were strangers. "My God, what a feeling of freedom to be sitting eating breakfast," Elsa murmured as she broke a roll. "Sitting with everyday passengers and watching the countryside go by."

"Not much of a view," Wargrave observed.

As they passed through the fringes of the Ardennes Forest, it was still snowing heavily and the trees were crusted white with snow. While she ate her breakfast Elsa studied the other passengers, looking for Sharpinsky. At the far end of the dining car Waldo Hackmann had observed Harry Wargrave and it gave him immense satisfaction to see the Englishman sitting there. He glanced at his watch: 8:15 A.M. Within two hours the Englishman would be at the bottom of the Maas, drowned, his corpse carried out to sea by the swift-flowing Rhine. At the thought he savored his next cup of coffee.

He was still sitting there when Wargrave and Elsa walked past him on their way back to the Wagon-Lit. It amused Sharpinsky that the Englishman never gave a second glance to Waldo Hackmann, the American picture dealer from Boston, Massachusetts.

At 7:45 A.M.—while Wargrave and Elsa were breakfasting in the dining car—Rolf Geiger left his Amsterdam headquarters to drive south to the Maas. He sat alone in the back of his Mercedes 450 automatic, smartly dressed in a fur-lined overcoat, reading a copy of *Le Monde,* with an executive case on the seat beside him. Behind the wheel, equally smart in her dark blue chauffeuse's uniform, Erika Kern drove with verve and skill through the early morning traffic. By her side, silent and morose, sat Joop Kist.

It was an impressive performance Rolf Geiger put on; in the past he had noticed that police patrol cars never gave him a second glance when they had the attractive Erika behind the wheel to distract their attention. Within fifteen minutes they had left Amsterdam behind and were speeding south as Erika stepped on the gas. They passed a signpost and Geiger glanced up. The signpost read *To Schiphol Airport.*

Less than an hour later they were south of Dordrecht and close to the great Maas bridge. As in most of Holland there was hardly any snow—only a few thinning streaks among the birch woods they were passing on a lonely stretch of the road. It was at this moment that Joop Kist spoke for the first time.

"Stop the car. I've got to have a pee."

"For Christ's sake," Erika snapped, "we're nearly there."

"I've got to pee," Kist persisted. "Now!"

In the back Geiger sighed. "Stop and let him get on with it," he said. "And be damned quick about it," he told Kist.

The Dutchman got out and hurried behind a copse of

trees. Undoing the buckle of his belt, he took out the electronic signal capsule from behind it and laid it beside a rock. On top of the rock he scrawled a crude arrow pointing south. As he returned to the car he was adjusting his fly. Kist had no intention of risking a body search by the suspicious Erika when they reached their destination —and he had had no chance of attaching the device to the Mercedes. With an impatient snort, Erika drove on again.

Behind them the Venlo Team Scholten had stationed in Dordrecht had picked up the signal from the electronic device as soon as the Mercedes passed through the town. Keeping at least two kilometers behind the Mercedes, a plain van carrying six of the Dutch sharpshooters were now following the signal as Geiger proceeded south.

A short distance from where they had stopped to permit Kist to relieve himself Erika suddenly swung off the main highway along a track leading through a copse of trees to where an old barn stood well concealed from the road. Behind the barn stood the large gasoline truck that had been the transport used by the main Geiger Group to reach its destination. Installed with a special ventilation system—and with a concealed door cut in the rear of the vehicle—the terrorists had traveled inside the storage space until they arrived at the barn.

Geiger got straight out of the car and walked inside the barn. It was a strange scene. Neither the setting—the barn with its straw-strewn floor and stench of animal droppings—nor the six men clad in black ski masks, windcheaters, and ski pants really fitted in with the dapper Armenian.

"Everything is ready to blow up the Maas bridge?" he asked.

It was the leader of the action group, Jacek Wojna, who answered. "The bombs are ready. I was going to use timer devices but they could misfire—it will be done by electric detonation from a distance."

"And the guards on the bridge?" Geiger queried sharply.

"Only two." Wojna gripped the automatic weapon he was holding. "They will be easy meat. And the escape boat is ready."

"You must wait until the express is in the exact center of the bridge," Geiger insisted.

"That also is clearly understood," Wojna replied stolidly. "We shall be leaving here shortly in the truck."

He froze and a feeling of tension suddenly filled the barn. The men in ski masks gripped their automatic weapons tightly and looked to Wojna for guidance. In the distance, coming closer, sounding terribly loud in the hush that descended in the barn, was the sound of an approaching helicopter. Geiger turned to Erika. "We must leave immediately—to pick up our friend off the Atlantic Express."

A stream of reports continued to flow into Scholten's headquarters: reports of cars crossing the frontier into Holland illegally, which was so easy along the straggling border; reports from the torpedo command in the estuary of more powerboats heading for the *Maxim Gorky*. But one particular report attracted the security chief's attention.

"This message from a helicopter pilot, Sailer. It mentions seeing a gasoline truck and a Mercedes parked in the wilderness south of Dordrecht."

"Probably the driver just taking a rest, sir."

"The drivers, you mean—there are two vehicles. Taking a rest, you said? In this weather? In a benighted spot like that?"

"Does seem a bit peculiar. . . ."

"And it's close to the Maas," Scholten went on as he looked at the wall map. "More than that—it's close to where they have just found Joop Kist's abandoned electronic device." He stood up. "In any case, we have to leave for our rendezvous—and I think we've found the Geiger Group, thank God. When we get into the car, drive like hell."

"I have remembered where I saw Sharpinsky."

The Atlantic Express, well north of Brussels, had passed Roosendaal and was approaching the great Maas bridge when Elsa said the words. She had just returned to the original sketch and drawn a pair of horn-rimmed glasses on the image. Haller looked dubious but Wargrave reacted instantly.

"Where? When?"

"At breakfast at the end of the dining car. But earlier than that—in the middle of the night. He's in Compartment 19. The next car but one."

"We'll go there now," Wargrave snapped.

"Take a couple of Belgian security men with you," Haller warned.

Outside in the corridor Wargrave shook his head. "No Belgian security men. Just indicate the compartment to me—then we pick up a couple of other people first." Elsa followed Wargrave as Leroy let them out of the coach. Close behind him she grasped hold of the Smith and Wesson inside her handbag. As they passed Compartment 19 she pointed to the door and Wargrave nodded without slackening pace. Once he glanced at his watch, then looked out of the window where the landscape of Holland was flying past. They were within twenty kilometers of the Maas bridge.

Reaching Anna Markos' compartment, he gestured to her to follow him and then entered the next compartment where Nicos Leonides sat smoking his pipe. He introduced Elsa briefly. ". . . and this is Anna Markos, and Nicos Leonides—they're working with me."

"My pleasure." Leonides stood up and bowed. Anna Markos and Elsa stared at each other, one woman sizing up the other with a certain wariness. Then Elsa held out her hand and was startled by the Greek woman's firm grip. Impatiently, Wargrave went on speaking.

"Elsa has located Sharpinsky—we're going to get him now. And we have damn-all time to do the job."

Wargrave was still speaking when the express shuddered, gave a violent lurch, lost speed far too rapidly, and jerked to a sudden halt. They were thrown all over the compartment by the impact of the express braking so precipitately. Wargrave picked himself up as Leonides helped both Elsa and Anna to their feet. All through the express there was chaos as bags toppled from racks, as passengers were thrown bodily across compartments.

"A signal was supposed to stop us," Wargrave snapped.

"That was no signal," Elsa warned. "Somebody pulled the alarm—Sharpinsky . . ."

"He's getting off the train," Leonides guessed. "I saw a parked car on the highway flashing its lights a few seconds back—on the east side."

Wargrave led the way, running down the corridor, throwing open the car door on the east side, and dropping to the track. In the distance he saw the silhouette of a man running through leafless trees toward the nearby highway. "He's over there. . . ." They began running through a small wood toward the highway they couldn't see. As Wargrave burst out from the screen of trees a Mercedes flashed past, heading north. He was astonished to see a girl behind the wheel, a girl dressed in a chauffeuse's uniform. Two men in the back.

"Christ!" Leonides exploded behind him. "Two seconds earlier and I could have killed him."

Wargrave was standing in the road as a BMW traveling in the same direction came toward them at a more sedate speed. He flagged down the car. As the vehicle stopped he opened the door next to the driver, who was alone, a sober-looking man in a business suit. Waving a card at him, noting the French registration plates. Wargrave spoke to him in that language.

"Security . . . we have to borrow your car. There are terrorists in that car just ahead of you."

"I wait here—in the middle of nowhere?"

"For God's sake get out! There's a train just through those woods. Go to the rear Wagon-Lit and ask for a man called Haller. Tell him we're following the man we've been looking for."

Wargrave slipped behind the wheel as Leonides sat beside him while Anna and Elsa climbed into the rear seats. He was relieved to see the bewildered owner of the car plunging back through the wood toward the train as he moved off. The road ahead was deserted; he pressed his foot down. The driver of the Mercedes had made good use of her head start. From the back of the seat Elsa asked a question.

"You said something about a signal when the express pulled up."

"All arranged with General Scholten of Dutch security —to stop the train before we reached the Maas bridge."

"The Maas bridge?"

Leonides gestured toward the railroad track on their left, which they had moved closer to. "Is that your signal?" Above the line loomed a red signal facing the southern approach. Suddenly Wargrave began to lose speed. Ahead of them two vehicles were parked just off the highway: a Citroën car and a canvas-sided, military-looking truck. Standing beside the car in a heavy leather raincoat was the short, portly figure of General Max Scholten.

"No Mercedes has passed this way," Scholten said after Wargrave told him what had happened. "Obviously it must have turned down a track leading to the Maas—no doubt to some landing stage where a boat is waiting to pick up Sharpinsky and take him out to the *Gorky*. Everything is ready for you." He looked at Elsa and Anna Markos, who were still in the rear of the BMW. "Are they really the other two?" he inquired doubtfully.

"They're as good as men," Wargrave snapped. "In the past twelve hours one of them knifed to death a Communist agent."

"Point taken," Scholten replied. "And I know what the loyalty of women can be. Now we'd better get moving."

Behind the wheel of the BMW Wargrave drove off after the Dutchman, who was driving the Citroën. Behind them followed the canvas-covered truck. Wargrave could drive very fast but the pace set by Scholten was terrifying. Beside Wargrave in the BMW passenger seat Leonides blinked as Scholten drove like a madman, spinning around curves almost on two wheels, holding the road by luck as much as by skill. Then he swung off the highway to the right along a track twisting through trees and stopped in front of a barn. They all got out and six men with rifles met them.

"This is the Venlo Team," Scholten told Wargrave. "They have wiped out the Geiger Group." He turned to one of the men. "Jan, did you manage to save Joop Kist?"

"I am afraid not, sir." Jan led the way inside the barn and pointed to a figure lying on the ground. "It was the big bastard who killed him at the last moment. He must have guessed he was one of us."

"What happened to the bastard?"

"He's over there." Jan pointed to Wojna's crumpled form lying in a corner of the barn. "I gave him a full burst from my magazine."

"Good." Scholten walked over to where Joop Kist lay and gently spread a handkerchief over his face. The security chief could not keep a hint of emotion out of his voice as he looked down at Kist. "He was that old-fashioned animal, a patriot. Well, Joop, we will repay the debt one hundred times over." His voice stiffened as he looked around the barn where the bodies of six men clad in ski masks and ski pants lay dead, riddled with bullets from the automatic weapons of the Venlo Team. "You know what to do—we need four bodies put inside the truck I shall drive, Jan. And our friends"—he indicated Wargrave with a brief gesture—"will use the Citroën, which was, I regret to say, stolen from a garage in The Hague this morning."

"That leaves two bodies, including the giant," Jan pointed out.

"Throw them into the Maas," Scholten said brutally.

He turned to Wargrave as the Englishman moved close to him and spoke in a low voice. "Can you trust these men to keep quiet? And what about your minister? I don't want your head on the block, Max."

"The Venlo Team is devoted to me," Scholten replied. "You see, officially, they never left their base at Dordrecht today. As for the minister, he will swallow the story because it will suit him. Like cabinet ministers all over the world, his main concern is his career. Also, I have tipped off a news agency that the Geiger Group are planning something big in Holland. Now, Harry, we must move. . . ."

Aboard the Soviet freighter *Maxim Gorky* the radio operator had just run into Commissar Rykin's cabin in an agitated state. "That signal you asked me to send to Moscow—I can't send it."

"Why the hell not?" Rykin demanded. "It's vital we report the present situation."

"There is massive interference, Comrade. I can't send any signals at all."

On Scholten's orders radio-jamming devices along the Dutch coast were now operating full blast to neutralize the Soviet transmitters. The *Maxim Gorky* was now sealed off from all communication with the outside world.

The four figures clad in black ski masks, windcheaters, and ski pants moved cautiously down toward the landing stage below where the Dutch torpedo boat rode at anchor under the lee of a small headland on the Maas. The torpedo boat had been held in reserve by Commander De Vos at the suggestion of Scholten; quite why he didn't know, but he was a close personal friend of the Dutch security chief and had agreed without question. The two Dutchmen guarding it sat playing cards inside the cabin.

One tall figure slipped down alone through the reeds and slipped aboard with the practiced ease of a trained commando. Reaching the cabin door, he turned the handle carefully and then rushed inside. The first Dutchman had his back to the intruder as he coshed him not too hard— but hard enough to knock him out. The Dutchman opposite was half out of his seat when he, too, was struck with the truncheon and fell unconscious.

"Tie them up," Wargrave ordered from behind his ski mask as the other three figures followed him into the cabin, "and leave them in the landing-stage shed."

Elsa Lang and Anna Markos dealt with the prisoners while Wargrave led Leonides to the controls. "No problem here," he told the Greek, "I once drove one of these while I was in naval intelligence. British and French

ones, too. I just hope you can take the helm at th
critical moment—I shall be otherwise occupied. . . .

"I am a Greek," Leonides reminded him, "who onc
spent half his time at sea in the Aegean with motorize
caïques and other craft. Just show me. . . ."

Five minutes later the torpedo boat was moving ou
into the Maas with Leonides at the helm. He opened th
throttle to get the feel of the boat and then nodded t
Wargrave, who was watching him. The Greek was handlin
the craft as though he had driven it for years—with
certain panache as he felt the power building up, as th
bows cut through the heavy swell. Going out on deck
Wargrave found Anna Markos taking off the canva
cover from the swivel-mounted machine gun.

"Show me how it works," she demanded.

"This wasn't part of the plan."

"Show me how it works," she ordered him.

Shrugging, Wargrave quickly explained the mechanism
It was, after all, possible they might need to use it whe
he wouldn't be available to operate the weapon. Insid
the cabin Elsa Lang had picked up a pair of night glasse
from the chart table and was scanning the opposite ban
of the Maas. With shoulders hunched, elbows pressed har
against the ledge, she went on sweeping the glasses acros
the distant shore. When Wargrave reentered the cabi
there was excitement in her voice.

"A big powerboat is taking off from the far side. I'n
damned sure I saw Sharpinsky aboard—with anothe
smaller man. I focused full on them while they were o
deck."

"Are you sure?" Wargrave asked.

"Say that just once more and I'll hit you. . . ."

"Then they must have waited for the weather t
slacken."

And the weather was improving as the gale blew itsel
out. Already the heavy swell inside the sheltered Maa
was smoothing out as Wargrave watched the large power
boat gathering speed, heading out to sea, toward th
Maxim Gorky. "Do we try and head him off?" Els
suggested.

"Too late, but he could take us just where we want to go."

Wargrave went back to the helm, where Leonides was enjoying himself as he grew more familiar with the craft, as he built up even more power and exhilarated in the engine throb. They were now well out into the Maas, midway between the two banks with open sea ahead of them.

"Keep behind that powerboat," Wargrave ordered. "It will home us straight in on to the *Gorky*."

Inside the cab of the canvas-sided truck General Scholten himself was behind the wheel, with Major Sailer in the passenger seat, as he drove it down the twisting, lonely track leading to a point at the mouth of the Maas River. In the back of the truck lay their grisly cargo—the four bodies of the dead Geiger Group men still dressed in their hideous "uniform." On the cab seat between Scholten and Sailer lay a large signaling lamp.

As they drove on, it was more like night than day; overhead the sky was dense with low, dark, scudding clouds and Scholten was driving with sidelights only, not wishing to risk the glare of headlights, which might be spotted from a distance.

"You think we'll get away with it?" Sailer asked.

"We have a good chance. One thing I didn't tell you: by now my wife will have phoned a further anonymous tip to the news agency that it's rumored the Geiger Group have seized one of our torpedo boats. The whole outcome could be tremendously ironic."

"Ironic?" Sailer queried.

"The GRU control the Geiger Group—although we have never been able to prove it. Moscow is in for a very nasty surprise."

The powerboat carrying Colonel Igor Sharpinsky and Rolf Geiger toward the *Maxim Gorky* was moving at high speed as the storm died away, moving south toward the English Channel, throwing out a great wake as it bounced over the waves. Ahead, the twin-funneled

311

freighter with its masts laden with electronic gear was pouring out smoke as it prepared for its northern dash to the Kattegat, the Baltic, and Leningrad. It was only waiting for the powerboat's arrival before Captain Morov gave the order "Full steam ahead."

Behind the powerboat followed Wargrave's torpedo boat, moving at top speed with Leonides at the helm while Anna Markos, her ski outfit soaked with spray, crouched behind the machine gun, her powerful legs splayed to hold her balance. It was Elsa, with her glasses trained on the Soviet vessel, who first noticed the mounted machine gun on the *Gorky*'s deck, which Rykin had ordered to be divested of its canvas cover. At one point on the deck laden with cargo another canvas cover had come loose and was flapping in the wind.

"They have a gun on deck," she warned Wargrave, who stood beside her. "And I think I can see a tank. . . ."

"Probably an armored car."

"Goodies for the starving Africans," Elsa commented tartly.

Wargrave left her to direct Leonides to steer the torpedo boat into the required position. His glance fell on the two torpedo tubes, the ship's main armament, and he was trying to recall precisely the instructions a Dutch torpedo-boat commander had once given him during a dummy run. He would have only one chance to get it right. He looked at the two buttons, one for each torpedo. He was none too sure he was capable of pulling it off even in these calmer seas.

Through her glasses Elsa could now see the ladder leading down from the freighter's deck to a landing station below, a platform that was frequently submerged with water as the sea rolled over it. Above the ladder, men in oilskins were waiting to help Sharpinsky, Rolf Geiger and Erika Kern on board once the powerboat reached them. Estimating distances, Wargrave gave an order and Leonides swung the wheel over. At that moment Rykin's machine gun opened fire.

The range was still too great and a spatter of bullets

spurted tiny water spouts that danced across the sea—but the torpedo boat was moving closer into point-blank range every second. Behind her own machine gun Anna held her fire, her face frozen in a grim expression and showing not a trace of fear. Elsa was scared stiff—for Anna—and Wargrave was now staring fixedly through the target scanner with the fingers of his right hand close to the release buttons.

Sharpinsky's powerboat had now slowed down, was close to the platform, and through her glasses Elsa could see him clearly as he prepared to jump onto the heaving platform. Then Rykin's machine gun opened up again at much shorter range and a hail of bullets thudded across the deck of the torpedo boat. Tow of them struck Anna Markos in the shoulder and she slumped over her own gun. Elsa ran out on deck, hanging onto the rail until she reached Anna.

"Hold me up!" the Greek woman spat out. "I'm going to get the bastards. . . ."

Elsa hoisted her by the armpits, holding her own balance by hanging onto the wounded woman. Anna's gun began to chatter as she moved the weapon in a slow arc, and suddenly Rykin's machine gun stopped firing as the Soviet gunner collapsed. Geiger, lighter-footed and smaller, had jumped onto the platform and was running up the ladder when Anna swiveled her gun again, firing nonstop. A fusillade of bullets struck Geiger as he reached the top of the ladder and he seemed to leap backward from the ship and down into the sea. Below him, Sharpinsky and Erika Kern waited a moment on the platform, soaked to the thighs in sea.

Staring through the target scanner, Wargrave was hardly aware of any of this, of the fact that Elsa was now dragging Anna away from the gun toward the entrance to the cabin. His face tense with concentration, his cheekbones hard and prominent, Wargrave pressed one button, then the other.

"Number one gone. Number two . . ."

He had a brief glimpse of the two acoustic homing torpedoes hurtling into the sea—acoustic so they would

313

head for the nearest engine vibrations as the *Maxim Gorky* prepared to leave for Leningrad—and then they vanished Leonides spun the wheel, taking the torpedo boat in a wide semicircle before he straightened up and headed for the winking lamp on the shore where Scholten waited.

One torpedo struck the *Gorky* near the stern, ripping away a huge portion of the superstructure. The second struck as Sharpinsky reached the top of the ladder—but it was this torpedo that struck amidships and penetrated the main hold where two thousand tons of high explosive were stored. There was a massive roar. The center of the huge freighter lifted off—literally elevated into the sky— shattering the twin funnels, disintegrating into a thunderstorm of debris as a great mushroom of smoke rose to meet and mingle with the lowering clouds until it was impossible to distinguish one from the other. The bows of the freighter floated alone briefly, then upended and went down like the smashed fin of some misshapen shark. The echo of the boom was still in Leonides' ears as he reduced speed and beached the torpedo boat close to where the lamp continued to flash. There were no survivors from the *Maxim Gorky*.

It took General Scholten and Major Sailer—with the help of the others—only minutes to carry aboard the beached torpedo boat the four dead bodies of the Geiger Group men from inside the truck. They left them lying about inside the cabin. In the distance Scholten heard the engine of another torpedo boat approaching. "Get inside the back of the truck and keep quiet," he ordered Wargrave and his three companions. "And this may help the woman; we'll get her to a hospital as soon as we can." He handed a first-aid kit to Wargrave, who hurried inside the truck where Elsa and Leonides had carried Anna Markos.

The torpedo boat approaching appeared around a headland as Scholten and Sailer opened fire on the beached torpedo boat with automatic weapons, riddling the vessel from end to end, shattering every window. They had just emptied their magazines when the incoming torpedo boat stopped close in and Commander De Vos waded ashore in gumboots.

"They made a mistake," Scholten informed the tall, cynical-faced commander. "They came in too close and beached. . . . I think you'll find they're all dead."

"I'm sure I will," De Vos replied with a blank expression. He glanced toward the truck and then away again. "And I saw it all happen, so"—he smiled dryly—"if there is an inquiry I will be your best witness. Congratulations, General—the Geiger Group just made its last run. . . ."

26

Aftermath

One hour later a Boeing 707 took off from Schiphol Airport bound for Washington with General Sergei Marenkov, Julian Haller, and Matt Leroy aboard. Marenkov played a little joke on Haller, which the American, dog-tired from lack of sleep, did not fully appreciate. The Russian insisted on being shown that the altimeter registered thirty thousand feet before he consented to commence debriefing—to provide out of his phenomenal memory a list of all KGB agents in the Western Hemisphere.

One week later Harry Wargrave, Elsa Lang, and Nicos Leonides again visited Anna Markos in the Amsterdam hospital and found her sitting up in bed and being very rude to the doctor. "He keeps me here so he can stare at my figure," she complained in front of them.

"A very fine figure," the doctor commented. "So fine I regret to say I may feel compelled to discharge you as completely fit within a couple of weeks. . . ."

Anna's dark eyes flashed. "Meantime he will continue to fool around with his stethoscope, pretending he is being a doctor."

Outside in the corridor, when Nicos Leonides had gone, Wargrave took Elsa by the arm as they walked toward his parked car. "That's my last job," he told her. "I was keelhauled into it, anyway, by Julian Haller. So now why don't we go back to Canada, maybe British Columbia—I've always had a hankering to explore Puget Sound."

"We?" Elsa inquired. "Is that a proposition or a proposal?"

"Both."

"Then I shall enjoy the first and insist on the second."

On the tenth floor of the Baton Rouge Building in Montreal Julian Haller had called to say good-bye to William Riverton, the Canadian industrialist who had provided the funds and the accommodation for the Sparta Ring at the request of President Joseph Moynihan. And for the first time since the operation had started over a year before, Riverton stood inside the office suite they had used.

It was bare and empty now. All the equipment and furniture had been removed and their voices echoed hollowly as they spoke. "I see," Riverton remarked, staring straight ahead, "that Marshal Prachko has been removed from the Politburo along with his cohorts—that for a while, at any rate, the moderates are in control in the Kremlin. I read it in the newspaper this morning."

"Some kind of victory, I suppose," Haller replied.

"I'm going to miss you all," Riverton remarked, "but there it is. And as in the past—and as it will be in the future, the West will be saved by only a handful of men and women." His voice changed as he held out his hand. Even though no longer young, his tone was firm and decisive.

"In the end we'll beat the Soviets. . . ."